Swimming

Swimming

NICOLA KEEGAN

Alfred A. Knopf New York 2009

This Is a Borzoi Book
Published by Alfred A. Knopf

Copyright © 2009 by Nicola Keegan

All rights reserved. Published in the United States by Alfred A. Knopf,
a division of Random House, Inc., New York, and in Canada by
Random House of Canada Limited, Toronto.

www.aaknopf.com

Knopf, Borzoi Books, and the colophon are registered trademarks
of Random House, Inc.

Library of Congress Cataloging-in-Publication Data
Keegan, Nicola.
Swimming / Nicola Keegan.—1st ed.
p.   cm.
ISBN 978-0-307-26997-3
1. Swimmers—Fiction.   2. Teenage girls—Fiction.   I. Title.
PR6111.E344S95   2009   823'.92—dc22   2009014051

Manufactured in the United States of America
First Edition

For my mother, Kay Keegan,
and my fathers, Reuben George Keegan
and Joseph O'Mahoney

If this exceptional athlete wore all the Olympic gold medals she has won in her long career and jumped into a pool, she would sink.

Olympic Supercoach Ernest K. Mankovitz
Sports Illustrated,
June 1990

Swimming

❧

In Water I Float

I'm a problematic infant but everything seems okay to me. I'm sitting in Leonard's arms grabbing at his nose. I have no idea how prehistoric my face is, am smiling a gaping, openmouthed smile that pushes the fat up around my eyes, causing a momentary blackout. When the world turns black, I scream. I'm blessed with unusual eyebrow mobility; when I scream, they scream with me. Leonard pats my back, bouncing me gently up and down; his face is tired and drawn and as green as the lime green paint the nuns use for their windowsills. I recover quickly, push his big nose in with all my force, have no idea that a perfect replica is sitting in the middle of my own face just waiting to grow.

I have seven chins varying in size and volume; crevasses things get stuck in that my mother has to excavate carefully after each bath. We have ceremonies: Each morning she leans in toward me with a cotton ball dipped in baby oil, two purple sandbags of fatigue carefully holding down her eyes, and each morning I karate-kick the open bottle of baby oil out of her hand. Today she burst into tears as the bottle whizzed past her ear, shooting a trail of shiny oil across the room. I wailed with her in loving solidarity, the fat above my ankles flapping over my monstrous feet like loose tights.

I live simply; when something doesn't seem okay, I scream until it is again. I do not like closing my eyes to discover there is no music, lights, or people I know inside. I do not like being alone, being alone with Bron, finding myself in my bed alone, waking up in my car seat with no one in sight, the sound of silence. If I fall asleep listening to the beat of my mother's heart, pacing my breath in cadence with hers, and awake later to find myself lying on my back in a pastel-barred prison, I feel cheated and betrayed. I howl with my guts in a belly-shaking rage until someone comes and gets me, usually my mother, who is shocked and worried at how her second child could be so different from the sleepy, button-nosed first. Day and night mean nothing to me. Leonard is trying to think; can't.

We're at the Quaker Aquatic Center waiting for my first aqua baby class to begin. My mother's sitting at the edge of the pool, holding a shivering Bron, who's studying me quietly, an intent expression on her oval face. She won't get in and no one's making her. I grab Leonard's lips and pull; he taps my hand with one finger, whispers: *Stop.* I can't walk yet; he has to carry me everywhere and it's starting to hurt his lower back. He yelled at my mother yesterday. *What in the hell are you feeding her?* And she yelled back, hard. *The same damn formula we gave Bron.* I look over at my mother; Bron has moved behind her and is holding on to her neck with a hand that suggests possession. She's got one thumb in her mouth, eyes burning holes in my flabby face. I kick Leonard in the gut; he grunts. I jump a little bit, pointing toward Bron, gurgle, then speak. I'm trying to say: *She means me harm.*

Leonard says: *Shush now; the nice lady is talking.*

I don't know what the hell he's talking about so I kick him in the gut again, grab one of the long hairs that sprout from his eyebrows, pull.

There's a lady coming at me with a mermaid puppet on one hand. The mermaid is saying goo things, but Bron has destroyed the joy of puppets for me forever. I try to get away from it by weeping dramatically as I crawl up Leonard's shoulder and he scrambles to hold on. The lady is hailing me, but I don't know her face, so I won't look at it. She's wearing a swimsuit with a skirt attached and a necklace with a bright yellow plastic smiley face in the middle. Leonard bounces me up and down. I wipe puppet from mind, swallow sobs, lunge for the smiley face. Leonard almost loses me, says: *Whoooahhhh there,* a sharp satellite of pain pulsing in his lower back.

The lady says: *She's ready, all right.*

Leonard says: *You think?*

She says: *Oh yes.*

He says: *What should I do?*

She clasps her hands. *Let's put her in.*

He says: *I hope this works.*

She says: *Oh, this'll work. You'll see. It will change your life.*

He dips my feet into the warm water. I hop, squealing a high-pitched squeal that makes the lady jump. *Oh my. I see what you're talking about.*

I'm nine months old and the longest I've slept at one time is one hour and forty-three minutes. I think my name is Boo, but it's not. It's just one of the many things I'll be called: *Boo, Mena, Phil, Pip,* but the name on my birth certificate, *Philomena,* has four syllables and will be the first major disappointment in my life. No one will use it until I get to school and the nuns insist. I have various hobbies that consume me: kicking, screaming, pulling things down, kicking again, crying. Lately, I've been experimenting with howling like a wolf. I sit up in my crib three hours before dawn, grab the bars with both fists, and keen at the moon. I've started to pull myself around on the floor and, when no one is looking, roll myself up in electrical wire, get my fingers stuck in air-conditioning vents, and scream until someone yanks me out. Yesterday, I gnawed down half a candle, pooping it out this morning with horrible grunts as my mother wept: *I just turned my head for a second.*

Leonard's trying to write *Most Misunderstood Mammals,* which will be published at Roxanne's birth and will win him the largest grant to study bats ever awarded in the history of American academia. He will be pictured on the cover of the *Glenwood Morning Star* standing next to Rosy, a cuddly African fruit-faced bat with wide, dreamy eyes. He knows that his work is good, but at the moment he's just tired and poor, sleeping in his ratty old car with a pillow over his head when he can't take the screaming anymore. When he gets the grant, he will celebrate with his bat team, astronomer Gerald, Ahmet Noorani, and Dr. Bob, and then he'll fly all over the world studying bat behavior, coming back home with a burnt nose and a collection of exotic bowls things will get lost in. I will do things too. I will be ashamed of his job, pretend he's a regular doctor until the mini-Catholics turn into junior Catholics and find out he's the guy in the dumb suit that Channel 9 interviews every Halloween. They'll call me Batgirl, draw ears on my locker and all the school pictures I ever hand out until the day I win my first Olympic gold and they repent.

Leonard slides me in up to my belly; there are spaces in my diaper that let the warm water leak in. This makes me so happy, I squeal. I look over at my mother; she's clapping her hands and making goo sounds. She's pregnant again because I took so long coming that she and Leonard decided they'd better have the rest of their children quickly, *bam, bam, bam*. When Leonard said *bam, bam, bam*, he'd hit one open palm with the side of the other, a gesture I will soon come to dread. She'd agreed with him at the time, has changed her mind since, but doesn't know it because she's too tired to articulate thought. I look at Bron and my two eyebrows become one. She's been poking me through the bars of my crib with her Barbie. She's been pinching me hard with vicious claws. She pretends to be nice when they're around, but reveals her true face when they're not looking. She tries to scare me with it, and succeeds; I howl. At the howl, Mom and Leonard look at each other and frown as Bron smiles. I am one of those people who will never truly grasp the relationship between time and space. I tried to hit her from my high chair across the room as she played with her Barbies this morning, her hair lit in long golden shafts by the narrow winter light. I howled in frustration when my fist hit air and not her head as Mom and Leonard exchanged glances, unspoken worry darkening their eyes.

The lady with the face I don't know yet whispers: *Just let her go.*

Leonard gets nervous. *I don't think I can.*

The lady says: *Trust me. She's ready to go* and he lets me go.

I sink into warmth for a second, go into natural apnea. My eyes open wide with shock; this is new, but it's blue and not black so I stand it. I kick a little bit; it moves me. My diaper absorbs water, puffing out like one of those kinds of fish. It slides slowly down my thighs, eventually tangling itself between my knees. I kick again; my diaper falls off and I bob to the surface like a cork. Leonard says: *Wow! That was . . . should I put a diaper on her?*

The lady thinks for a moment, twiddling the puppet. *No, let's just watch her for a second. She seems . . .*

I look at him, and the sounds that come out of my mouth mean: *Hey! Where are we? What's going on here?* When he doesn't answer, I insist *Dah? Dah?* as I go under. He says: *She just called me Dad. Did you hear her? She just said Dad.* My mother claps; Bron squints. Leonard's happiness vibrates through the water; it helps speed me along.

All my life, I will kick things that find their way into my path: shoes, baskets, toilet paper rolls, money, rocks, tennis balls, rolled-up socks, gym bags, Roxanne once or twice, any kind of circular fruit. It will become an irresistible urge that serves me well. I kick; it moves me, and I feel joy. I have no idea that I'm floating in the center of Glenwood, that Glenwood is floating in the middle of Kansas, that Kansas is a simple state, a safe distance from the other, more complicated ones. I do not know that my mind is an ocean, collecting things that sift down through the sunlight, the twilight, the midnight, the abyssal zones to the pitch-black bottom, settling into the deep trenches nature dug below. I do not know that one day the winds will churn and that when the winds churn, the dust will rise, bringing everything up along with it. All I know is that when I kick, it moves me, so I kick again, liberated from my fleshy prison of gravity. I am as I was, churning in deep archaic memory, naked, filled with free-floating fatness, the world murmuring outside with sweet deafened sounds that lull. I pop up, open my eyes; I learn to glide.

I don't know Mom's pregnant, just think she's obese like me. We'll get bigger and bigger together until I wake up one morning and find that she's gone. I'll search the house, walking and wailing, as Bron paints with her fingers without saying a word. That knobby-faced babysitter will be there, pinching my chins and making goo sounds, will watch in horror as I kick dents in the refrigerator door until Leonard urgently reappears and takes us away. I'll look out the window at the trees whizzing by, deep in a sob until I find Mom in a strange bed holding a squirmy red-faced Roxanne. I'll throw myself on the ground and roll until she puts it down, then I'll punch her in the face with a sticky fist when she offers her cheek for a kiss. I won't remember the tall, full-skirted nun standing in the doorway holding a plate of cookies, assessing me with cool, professional eyes, but she'll remember me.

When a squirming blue-faced Dot shows up a year later, I've resigned myself to a life that will never cradle me in its center. I'll stand next to Mom's bed in the maternity ward, weeping hot streams, opening my palms in the universal sign of defeat, saying simply: *This one's blue.* This will come up over the dinner table until the day no one brings it up ever again.

I have never looked at myself in the mirror, will begin to suspect the grim truth when I finally hit puberty. I have no idea my feet are special, am simply impressed that they heed my call. I kick both legs at once, executing a perfect flip, as everyone, including Leonard, sucks their breath in. The Glenwood aqua aerobics class hears the commotion, stops in mid-twirl, and runs to the edge of the baby pool. I kick; it moves me. I do a perfect figure eight as the crowd gasps. I plunge, flashing a butt wrapped up carefully in layer upon layer of ivory lard; the crowd takes a step back, gasping again. My chins have piled upon each other like an accordion, squirting out water instead of notes. I have no idea what I am. That the world I will see will be experienced alone, from the inside out, but I suddenly remember I have arms, so I flap them. The lady with the face I'm starting to recognize doesn't know what to do. She's standing in the middle of the warm water, her rabbit teeth chewing on her lower lip, a limp puppet at her hip.

Mothers and fathers with their aqua babies squirming in their arms are watching, mouths agape. I speed by Leonard's pole legs, stop, turn, pushing off of them with heavily padded feet. I glide on my back, the world whizzing by. I recognize the lady as I pass, hail her with a gurgle, two worms of green snot inching out my nose. She wants to call Channel 9, but won't, will regret this until the day that she dies. I pop to the surface, both arms over my head; I squeal. The Glenwood aqua aerobics class and their instructor get a case of the shivers. I plunge again. I kick. It moves me. I skim Leonard's hairy legs and surface slowly like a submarine on its way home. I wind down in a soft whirlpool of energy that cradles me gently in tune with some clock. My eyes become heavy, the lids start to sink. Mom, under the influence of strong hormones, puts her head in both hands and weeps. Bron narrows her eyes, sitting back on her haunches for a big think. Leonard pulls me out and up, is holding me tight. I spit up warm water streaked with milk, pee on him, fall asleep for fourteen hours.

I don't wake when they put me in my light blue snowsuit with the thick thermal padding. I don't wake when they tie the dreaded scratchy hat under one of my chins, when they strap me into the car seat, when they pull me out and Leonard accidentally knocks my head on the door and my mother screams. I don't wake when they carry me up the stairs, put me in my pajamas, cover me in a soft blanket, turn out the light. I don't wake when Bron stands by my bed poking me with Cinderella's magic wand that lights her serious face with an eerie green glow. Leonard checks on me, Mom checks on me, they check on me together. It is an unspoken fact that they can finally love me now that I'm out cold. They bask in this love, as waves of breath ebb and flow, causing the dome of my stomach to sink in, then swell. The silence of the household has opened a space for hope. Leonard rubs Mom's belly, accidentally waking a sleeping Roxanne, who's hanging upside down in a mushy pre-birth stupor. She's listening when he whispers: *Look at that little bugger sleep.*

Life's Most Beautiful Day

Leonard's standing in the garage packing up the mist nets, talking to me about things I've never shown an interest in. He's wearing dark green pants, desert boots in beige suede, an old camouflage safari jacket with a gold bat pin stabbed into the lapel, a gift from the Bat Sanctuary.

They're expert fliers, Boo, perhaps the best in the world, swooping, clasping moths, bluebottles, mayflies between their teeth as they glide.

Sounds gross, I say, mind on other matters.

This morning, I cleaned out Baby Lenny's bowl, carefully putting him into a clear plastic bag, rinsing out his bowl, drying it by hand. I refilled the bowl with fresh water, not too hot, not too cold, put the conditioner tablets in, sprinkled his floor with the orange rocks, placed the small purple castle he likes to hide behind on the bottom, put the underwater sea guy in next to it holding his spear. I put him back, sprinkling the surface with a pinch of those flakes he likes that smell like poison. He swam around in looping circles, opened his mouth, sucked in some food. He stopped, cocking his head, floating still, the weird brainy lump thing on his forehead pulsing, his buggy black eyes vacant, his full cheeks fat, his small baubled mouth producing the occasional stray bubble, all his pretty wings swooshing to and fro. I studied him; his small face looked unusually sad and his pin eyes seemed to be screaming for help.

I thought a change of scenery would do him good, a glimpse of the outside world of weather and tree. I moved his bowl and Baby Lenny became perky, happy again, fascinated by the way the sunshine flashed off his golden gills. I watched him, happy again too, until I heard Mom screaming for me to clean my room and my feet followed her voice inside like well-trained pets. Fatal mistake.

I open my mouth to say something to Leonard, but the something gets caught in my throat like a bone.

He said no to the Destiny Dress, no to the flower petal tiara, no to the anklets with the embroidered studded cross, no to the white padded headband with the long-fingered ribbons and satin-edged bows. He sighed and said yes to the double chocolate cake with the communional frosting, yes to the fourteen-karat-gold First Holy Communion pendant, yes to the white patent leather ballet slippers with the golden heart-shaped buckles, but I have to wear Bron's old dress, the Cassandra, on my Special Most Holiest Day because it cost $80 three years ago and that's still too much.

Careful your face doesn't freeze that way, Leonard says, studying me, the exposed garage lightbulb flashing sharply off his glasses. *Grab that corner and pull until I say when. And it's not gross; it's a marvel of nature.*

My best friend, Lilly Cocoplat, is a Leo, born under the sign of extravagance, has two believers for parents, gets everything she wants. At swim practice, she describes her outfit in Cocoplat detail as I listen, chin on kickboard, legs churning whirlpools of irritation that foam and swirl behind me. She's wearing the floor-length Kerry Irish Shamrock organza dress, her veil cascading from a hair comb with five satin tails, scattered with a series of four-leaf clovers hand-embroidered white on white, edged in fine velvet piping. She will be carrying her Precious Moments Holy Communion Deluxe Purse Set, which includes a Precious Moments missalette, satin brocade purse edged in pale green lace, satin rosary case, blue-glass rosary beads with silver-plated links, golden angel wings bracelet. Her parents are hosting a party for over one hundred Cocoplats, both the vague and the highly defined. Strawberry shortcake and Mountain Dew will be served, along with cocktail sausages and other stuff.

Dot opens the garage door, squeaks: *Can I help?*

Leonard looks up. *Not tonight, twilight. Your sister's helping.*

Her face falls, her ponytail droops, her smile collapses; she shuts the door.

We're having what my mother calls an *intimate family brunch* at the Longbranch Family Diner. I hate the Longbranch Family Diner. There's a dancing bear with a mangy face who pretends to play a fake banjo, and everything in the entire restaurant is made of dry wood:

wood floors, wood benches, wood paneling, rickety wood-colored ceiling fans, wood toilet seats, wood-colored chocolate cake.

Leonard's a scientist, doesn't care about atmosphere or accessory. *If there is a God, would he really care about all this ballyhoo?*

I don't know what I am, but I like all the ballyhoo; it makes me feel holy. I want the tea-length satin skirt, the seed-pearl bodice, the sheer lace sleeves, the ruffled organza veil, a pearl earring in each lobe. I yearn for a party with a roaming band wearing colorful cummerbunds, center tables covered in white, a series of three-tiered cakes, a room devoted to gifts. At Lilly's house, I jump up and down on her single bed, yelling: *Wouldn't it be great if I got a golden piñata filled with golden collectibles?*

For Lent I gave up Sweet Bonny and all forms of chocolate except malted, went to bed without complaining, did not fidget openly in church, and I was really listening when Sister Seraphina explained that the wanting mixed with the can't have teaches us an important lesson about the lot of Man, and by Man, she meant everyone, even us; Lilly asked. But I figured that the giving up would counteract positively with the wanting, proving just how good I was, which would eventually end up in a get.

Wrong.

Leonard's got the mist nets folded and is now reading a checklist he's laminated in plastic.

Project name: BatBotswana.

Tranquillity bat detector. Check.

Head torch. Check.

Thermometer. Check.

Survey protocols. Check.

Recording sheet. Check.

Weather events list. Hmmm, need more of those.

Site map. Check.

Extra batteries. Check.

Clipboard. Check.

Extra pens. Check.

Bug spray. Check.

Eyedrops. Check.

Certs.

I don't want to go to the Longbranch Family Diner, I interrupt.

I thought you liked the Longbranch, he says, half listening.

I hate the Longbranch. I'd like to have an outdoor picnic or a garden party . . . The Cocoplats are renting a tent.

Renting a tent? He laughs, shakes his head. *A tent for an eight-year-old. I won't be back until the night before your Communion, grumpy face, and your mother can't organize all of that on her own.*

Almost nine, I say.

I stand corrected, he says, packing everything carefully back into the box, mind on other matters.

I edge toward the door, quietly escape. Bron and Roxanne finished cleaning ages ago, are playing Snap in the family room, Dot's sitting in the club chair watching them, half-asleep. I stick close to the shadows, becoming as invisible as a Shawnee scout, heart thumping in unison with my feet as I run up the stairs. I lie on my bed, wait for them to find the body, re-shivering the shock I felt when I saw him. I'm going to get it.

When Bron walks into our room, I'm pretending to read a book. She stares at me until I look up.

What? I say, heart speeding.

Oh, Boo. You've got to be kidding me.

What? I say, soul withering.

She's quiet. *So, that's how you're going to play it.*

What?

You're kidding, right? That's the best you can do?

What are you talking about? My eyes are shifting, stinging, squinting. I'm sweating. I need to go to the bathroom urgently. Number two.

She changes tactics. *Do you have any idea where Baby Lenny is?*

I take a deep breath, recite: *The last time I saw Baby Lenny he was on the mantel above the fireplace, perfectly fine.*

This annoys her. *That's funny,* she says, leaning on the door, *because one minute you were changing his water, the next, he's floating outside boiled to death in the hot sun. Would you like to see him?*

What? I say, pupils enlarging.

Outside in his bowl? I say, hands twitching.

How did he get there? I say, vision a scaly blur.

Very natural, she says, leaves the room.

I lie back down on the bed, stiff as a statue, holding a book in front of my face like a prop.

Roxanne sticks her head in the door, her face red with excitement, a sweaty ponytail lobbing off her head. *Baby Lenny's exploded!* she shouts and is gone.

I turn onto my stomach, put my face in my pillow, wait.

Dot knocks, sticks her face in the door, radiating sadness: *Bron says you killed Baby Lenny.*

Bron can shut her face, I say, and all is oddly quiet until I'm called for dinner.

The lie sits in the middle of the dining room like a crane with a car on it just waiting to drop.

Bron stabs a tomato with her fork. *Admit you murdered Baby Lenny.*

Murder is a strong word, Bronwyn, Leonard says.

I won't because I didn't, I say, voice three octaves higher than normal, soul sick with sin, hands twitching like leaves.

Roxanne has a laughing fit, chokes on her potatoes.

Admit you took him outside and left him there.

That's enough, you two, Leonard says. *I'm sure whoever left Baby Lenny outside—*

In the hot sun, interrupts Bron.

—didn't mean to. He's looking at me.

I have to go the bathroom again. Number two.

That night, she gives me an out. *Okay, let's say that you cleaned out Baby Lenny's bowl as planned. Things went well. Then you thought. . . . I can't imagine you meant for that to happen, the poor thing. Anyway, the right thing to do now is just admit it, and everything will be fine. Story finished. All forgiven.*

Relief is there in the darkness. I can reach out and touch it with my hand. She won't be able to see my face. I won't have to see hers. I stare into the night, black like black blanket, soft black spots, hard black edges, a thin strip of moon sliding in through a break in the curtain, cutting into the wall like a magical knife.

I didn't do it, Bron. Maybe it was Roxanne.

The day before life's most beautiful day, I have my first holy confession.

Do I use God's name in a loving way?

Do I say untrue things?

Do I obey my parents and other people who are trying to help me?

Do I forgive others?

Do I cheat?

Am I kind and helpful to everyone?

Do I pray regularly?

Do I lose my temper?

Do I make fun of other, less fortunate children?

I fold myself into the wooden stall. *Bless me, Father, for I have sinned.*

Father Tod is a cranky priest who likes cheese sandwiches. At picnics Lilly Cocoplat and I spy on him; he eats three cheese sandwiches, then heads for the pie.

He that covereth his sin shall not prosper.

I close my eyes, explaining the trail of lies that led to Baby Lenny's body; I lower my voice, explaining the train of thought that led to his demise. My soul de-withers, my heart soothes down. Father Tod is wheezing. I wonder if he's asleep, but he mumbles something, then blesses me. I should feel better, don't. Life is quiet and dusty and lonesome and I'm sick of it already. I leave the confessional to pay my dues to the tune of seven Hail Marys, but don't think it's fair that I have to believe and Leonard doesn't.

It dawns unnaturally hot on life's most beautiful day. Mom hits me on the head with the back of the hairbrush when I squirm, a couple of bobby pins clamped in her mouth. If I react, she hits again, harder, hissing: *Your father's been on a plane for two days; let him sleep.* The same sun that murdered Baby Lenny is bleeding through the window, burning.

My hair falls to my shoulders in studied ringlet and curl, the Cassandra hitting my knees in a crisp triangle. Sister Seraphina has been yelling at us for months, *Step and pause, step and pause,* her old body trembling with palsy. We're her last Holy Communion preparation class—in August she's retiring to the Avenue of the Saints; when she's not yelling at us, she's crying cool nun tears, the color of skin.

Lilly Cocoplat is visibly pleased, her veil falling dramatically to her ankles. She steps slowly, pauses, steps slowly, pauses, has replaced her normal face with a brand-new one she's modeled on Mary. She inclines her head, widens her eyes, lifts the corners of her mouth in a small smile. But I see under: She's deep in the throes of calculating gift. We form an arc under Jesus, sing "For Him, My Love." Father Tod mentions the devil more than once. The holy wafer balances precariously on my tongue before I stabilize the situation. *O luminous mystery. Thank you for letting me see that the world is more than a gigantic engine running out of fuel.*

I know that if I believe, I can send Baby Lenny somewhere better, not down the toilet, not flying through drainpipes, not stuck in the gray water-purification factory on the edge of Glenwood we pass on our way to the airport. The heat of my head connects with the heat of my palm, the patent leather of my shoes so hot they burst into holy flame. Lilly Cocoplat is sweating so heavily her satin armpits darken, veil drooping over French chignon like a windless sail. Henceforth all nuns glisten, parents and well-wishers sway with the heat, and Seraphina's reading glasses are struck with a light misting of fog. Father Tod puts both hands up in the universal indication of the end of confinement; we are released. The church exhales people in a whoosh, sweat dribbling down Leonard's tan face, the wind grabbing and tearing at the trees, thunder growling somewhere beyond the horizon, and my ringlets disappear instantly back into straight hair. Leonard winks a tired wink as a million Cocoplats swoon over Lilly in unison and Mom holds me so tight the seams in the Cassandra begin to strain.

The Longbranch Family Diner, as usual, is packed. I open my gifts: a coupon for Dilly Bars, a gold pendant—chalice shining, a thin envelope containing fresh green dollars. I order sweet ribs, eat them fervently. Leonard and Mother discuss their old tired things. Bron fixes the clasp of my necklace, whispering into my ear: *Just tell me what happened to Baby Lenny and I give you my solemn oath I won't mention it ever again.* She lowers her voice into creepy: *If not, it's war.*

The Cocoplats must be dancing under the tent by now, helium balloons rising from their trees like majestic pink and silver grapes. Lilly's dumped the veil, is wearing her favorite tiara. Leonard's explaining things to Roxanne as Dot listens intently. I look at my sweet ribs, no longer hungry. I don't know that death can waltz into life with a sharp pair of scissors, cutting someone out so neatly that all that's left is an empty space that should have been full. I think Bron will be with me for-ever, part of my landscape, and although I know war isn't good, any-thing's better than that look she gets on her face when she wins. I pull myself from her grip, giving her one of my mean looks with a sick feel-ing in my gut as the mangy bear jumps in front of our table, grabs its fake banjo, and begins to play.

I-da-ho Po-ta-toes
Arizona Cac——tus
The Dolphins Gonna Swim You
Just for Prac——tice

A northern wind is blowing across the plains, down into the Shawnee valley, whipping up snow against the side of our rented school bus, pushing it aside in gusts as we speed along Highway 5. We're eating candy on our way home from an out-of-town meet, muscles relaxing into box seats, hair drying under wool caps. We've drawn motivational images on the humidity of the windows. When we were younger, we drew happy fast dolphins, NUMBER 1! THE BEST! WINNER! Now it's our competition riddled in fat with tufts of body hair sticking out of their suits, slumped on the starting blocks like sick snails covered in inflammatory acne with Shawnee arrows running through their flabby asses. We can wipe it out if Coach Stan decides to walk back, but he sticks to the front, checking stats. We sing and stomp with both feet for maximum auditory impact: *Oommm chagga chagga chagga oommm chagga cha* as the bus coughs through tunnels of snow and the sky darkens around the edges before slipping completely into black.

There's a sword above my head just waiting to fall. Leonard let it be known that as soon as I reached junior high, education would take priority and my Dipping Dolphin Aquatic Club days would be reduced to summer hobby. This is my last full year of exciting Dolphin weekends and I'm pretending to know it.

Coach Stan clicks his penlight on and calls us up one by one for our evaluations.

He looks at me, sighs: *Sit down. Inconsistent. Apt to have an amazing set on Friday, then a perfectly lousy race. I was expecting something different from you today, thought maybe for once you'd break away . . . use some of that energy——*

I interrupt: *We won.*

Did we? he says.

My heart sinks; this is going to take a while.

Did you lower your time?

No.

Improve your technique?

I look out the window as the car passing below gets illuminated in a flash by a yellow highway light before disappearing back into empty road.

And how about the breathing . . .

I sigh. *I was breathing.*

He looks at me. I can't be trusted. Not until I face the truth.

I look back. *We won, Coach Stan. They went down.*

He clicks his pen on and off with his thumb, thinking. You can see the reddish tinge of his blood through the warmth of the light.

You're not hungry.

I am hungry, I say, the half-chewed Neapolitan caramel in my mouth clinging to my teeth.

That's not hungry. When you're hungry, you'll feel it, and when you feel it, I'll feel it.

In the locker room Lilly Cocoplat and I like to keep close track of Dolphin developments. Lilly uses her shampoo as a microphone. We're surprised if someone cries; it's just for fun. Lilly Cocoplat is older than her years and has always made me older than mine. When fellow Dolphins aren't laughing, they're hating us.

Listen up, Dolphins. Poor Kelly continues to house one bald vagina between surprisingly hairy legs. Lilly's talking into a bottle of Herbal Essences shampoo.

I jump up. *I agree with you there, Lill; it's quite a shocker and I'd have to say: Kelly Hill's naked vagina looks like an itty-bitty foot.*

A baby's foot.

And then we laugh so hard it's impossible to stop.

Coach Stan separates us as much as possible. If I'm in lane five, she's in lane one. If she's doing sit-ups, I'm treading water with weights on my ankles, but I still have laughing fits that almost get me killed. I say: *I can't help it. She just cracks me up* when Coach Stan pulls me choking out of the water with one strong arm. But we have too many things pulling us together for anything to pull us apart. We put the same Adam Ant song on our Walkmans at the same time, pushing PLAY at the count of three, then we sing and dance.

Don't drink don't smoke what do you do
Must be something la la

When I close my eyes, I'm saturated in a deep, peaceful, perfectly entitled, one hundred percent natural love of life and all life's things. I'm pulling myself through water at the end of a long swim, reaching for the endorphin torpor as the fatigue washes over me. Lilly Cocoplat makes me laugh so hard I choke on my own spit. It hurts to write with a pencil, to sit down on a chair, to pee, to take off my sweater, to run up the stairs, to answer the phone, to open a book, to get in a car, to get out of a car, to take off my shoes, to lie down on my bed. The ache is proof of an efficient swim; the more I ache, the faster I become. But when the sun cuts through the atrium and the steam rises up from the pool, the water takes on a bright, edgy haze and I lose myself. I watch my shadow crawl across the tiles below and don't feel the pain of doing as many as fifty sets although all the other Dolphins bitterly complain. All I feel is the sweet shuddering relief with each breath I draw and the relentless silence of my mind. I don't mention these bouts of timeless love of the infinite universe to anyone, not even Lilly.

Lilly started swimming when she was diagnosed with asthma, but I don't have anything specifically wrong with me yet. I just like swimming and all the things that happen around it. A cute collegiate swimmer comes out on deck to talk to one of the assistant coaches, some kids are making out in the parking lot and don't care who knows, a Dolphin brings a *Playgirl* hidden in her backpack and we take turns looking at sad guys with happy sausages looking out the windows of their unzipped jeans. And when there's a sleepover at a Dolphin's house, no one sleeps, but we wake up at six and swim for two hours anyway because the harder it is, the more we suffer, and the more we suffer, the closer we become.

Coach Stan stands next to the edge of the pool with a whistle in his teeth and a grim look in his eyes. I love training in the Olympic pool, watching the big shots work out, listening to their coaches scream *MOVE YOUR ASS; THIS AIN'T YESTERDAY.* We look at each other and laugh—*He just said ASS*—then we swim for an hour, an hour and a half, and dry off eating the healthy fig s'mores that Lilly Cocoplat's mother made. In the summer I'm a free agent, in the water so long my hair emerges from my head like strings of nylon.

At the annual banquet last year Coach Stan took Leonard aside and said: *I'd like to see what would happen if Philomena trained seriously for one second instead of partaking in these perpetual shenanigans with Lilly Cocoplat,* as Leonard half listened with polite disinterest.

Before a major meet, Stan slaps his clipboard onto one bent knee, lowers his voice, and speaks to us as though we were listening. *Young swimmers: The essence of potential. When this pool is combined with the best an individual has to offer . . . listen up, Lilly . . . with the best collective effort, anything is possible. It is an arena . . .* Lilly and I get bored, make vagina faces, yell: *Go, Coach Stan! Dippers Forever!* Coach Stan ignores us: *But you better make sure that you really integrate technique. I've seen world-class swimmers revert to faulty technique in times of stress, going back to their days in the pool with their first coach, and their swim falls apart just the way it did then.*

I make my eyes into big *Oh reallys* behind his back, flashing the peace sign, which is in fact V for *vagina,* as Lilly Cocoplat falls over herself. The idea that one day I will be standing next to the East German world-record holder Fredrinka Kurds as she spits chlorine out of the corner of her mouth and twenty zillion people scream does not cross my mind for one second. I don't even know where Moscow is exactly; I just know it is bad.

After practice we're in a hurry to go home; there's homework to finish and we're hungry again. Some Dolphins take the time to dry their hair, flipping their heads upside down then swooshing the hair up again so it frames their faces like nice fur. I don't; I stuff it under a knit cap and let it sit like that until it dries into funny shapes. This drives my mother nuts. *Dry your hair, for God's sake; it's twenty below.*

Leonard wants me to be a mini-Bron, but I won't. He wants me to be an intellectual success, skipping entire grades like rope, wants me to bring home prizes from French clubs, wants to display my medals, ribbons, shiny cups from tricky debates and interscholastic spelling bees. He wants me to look out at the world, curious and smart, then he would like to talk to me about it, over dinner. He's not the least bit interested in how fast I swim, barely listening when I explain how I lowered my personal best once again. He reminds me, on Sunday afternoons, during short trips to the grocery store. *You're eleven now.* He reminds me when he picks me up, when he drops me off, when we fly, his voice cutting through the static. *Well into the double digits.* He reminds me during commercials, when he's boiling water for tea. *Junior high is serious business.* But I am so overinformed that the end is coming, I don't believe it, just keep hoping that something miraculous will happen and I will be back, like Jesus. I am shocked, sickened, stunned, and amazed when I find myself standing by the pool on the last day of my last workout of the last season. I have no idea how right I am when I get dramatic: *Pieces of my heart are being ripped up and, and, and it's all downhill from here. I just know it. It's all downhill from here,* snot gushing out my nose as I weep myself into convulsions that get the Cocoplat and the few girls who can still stand me going. Coach Stan purses his lips, clicking his stopwatch on, then off.

Downhill

When Sister Nestor's face fills with displeasure, she looks uglier than she ought to.

Late. She's a mathematical nun with little patience for words outside the Holy Scripture.

I look up at the clock with the big round face and the steady black hands, the stubby one on the eight, the slender one getting ready to hit the fifty. Water is dripping down my ponytail onto the floor, making a puddle I try to swipe away with my shoes. I'm wearing a pair of navy blue Keds that match the stripes in my socks. I look down at my hand. I'm clutching my dripping backpack so hard my knuckles are green. I feel the palpable glare of teenage X-ray vision cutting through my flesh and finding all the weak spots. It lasers in, heating up my face, following the line of my wide shoulders, stopping to laugh at my flat, caved-in chest, swooping down my pole legs to gasp at the giganticness of my feet. I pull my backpack up over my shoulders, closing my navy blue sweater over my secrets with one cold hand.

Sorry, Sister, we say in unison minus one.

Late. Again. She's deciding what to do to us.

Bron's standing next to me. This is her fault, but I keep mum, avoid trouble. Nestor avoids trouble also, pointedly ignoring Bron and keeping her eyes on me because I'm now the tallest and they must have received instructions to steer clear of the evil one. Dot and Roxy are examining their shoes. We're standing in front of the school during morning assembly. Nestor stopped it to make a point. I hope Bron ignores her so intensely my heart moves into my mouth. *O Gloria in Excelsis Deo.*

I'm so sick and tired of this petty . . . crap, Bron says.

Her words snap across the gym like electricity. Nestor pulls both eyes slowly over to the direction the voice came from. So far I've been successful at not really looking at her, but now my head is being lured by a magnet of greater force. I suck my breath in.

Leonard told us Bron's just about cured, that the cause of a languishing fatigue that culminated in a bump on her neck the size of a fist has been located and that now it shall be eradicated. She doesn't look just about cured, and the only thing that's been eradicated is all her good moods. Her face is dark yellow, eyes billowing smoke, lips pressed together so hard her mouth looks gone. She's recently been threatening to tell the nuns *to put their money where their mouth is.* I study the wet laces of my shoes, cursing Leonard in my head. This was his doing; he insisted she finish her last year of high school even though I'd warned him: *You better not. She likes hair too much. You better wait until it grows back in again. When she hates things, you know what happens.* He'd said: *Hogwash,* and at that her fate was sealed and here we are.

Nestor weighs the situation, finally nodding our dismissal with her terrible chin. We join our homeroom classes in the bleachers and everyone starts to sing again. *This land is your land, this land is my land, from California, to the New York island.* I mouth the words, don't feel like making sound. Lilly Cocoplat is sitting behind me directing a false contralto toward my ear: *This land is your land, this land is my land, from Vagina to the Pussy Islands, from the clear brown poop balls to the spermy waters, this land was made for you to peeeeee.* I laugh a fake laugh, don't feel fine. Sister Augusta pulls me aside, says: *Don't think I'm not looking.*

Nuns never exercise, don't care about swimming or swimmers, don't believe in bodily exertion, don't think that sports are important, with the possible exception of softball. And just because they don't sin doesn't mean they aren't attracted to harmful things. I'm sure not all the donated cakes are presented at the cakewalk, that they prepare more caramel apples than they serve, that the cotton candy machine works overtime late into the night. At fairs, they meander, eating triple-scooped ice cream with small plastic spoons, their eyes hidden behind large glasses with butterfly frames that darken automatically in the sun.

After school I eat cake, and, although she loves cake as much as I do,

Bron does not. She is also not preparing an article for Holy Name's student paper, *Spotlights,* not standing in front of the mirror brushing her hair so that it falls from her head like a shiny blond curtain, not singing songs up the laundry chute because she thinks it makes her voice sound famous. She's not stuffed into the jam-packed cars with her best friends, who whiz by honking as I walk home alone. She holes up in our bedroom, lights off, door closed, not to be disturbed. I don't even hear any music. When I put my ear to the door, all I hear is nothing, as if she's not even there. Dot's sitting at the kitchen counter, perfecting herself through knowledge. Roxanne is in the basement figuring out how to build her own pot pipe with a toilet paper roll and duct tape, aluminum foil, and a toothpick. I don't know where my parents are; they're gone. When they're gone, June, a troubled parishioner's wayward daughter, takes care of us. She cleans the oven, folds clothes, talks on the phone, twitching with the genetic energy that keeps getting her entire family into trouble with both God and the Law. June swears when my parents aren't around, says: *I wonder where in the hell all that damn cake goes.* I shrug. She shrugs back. We have things in common. We like packaged foods, are never tired, can do many things at once, and she, like me, constantly walks into things, trips on stairs, or falls into space until one of her bony knobs hits something that leaves a mark. We compare bruises. She cleans the house in a spastic way, running the vacuum cleaner in looping disorganized lines that I follow like crazy trails. When she's finished, she sits on a bar stool twirling, reading magazines, watching TV.

Don't you get sick of swimming? She's watching me forage for food.

No. Three times a week is practically never. Most swimmers my age are swimming twice a day. I'm unwrapping the aluminum foil around a marbled Bundt cake with white creamy frosting.

I'd be sick of it already . . . She's picking at a frayed edge of her jeans. *What do you think about when you're swimming anyway?* She's fingering an earring.

Nothing. Swimming. I lie, pulling cream out of cake with my pinkie.

When Leonard shows up, he's incredibly busy; on the phone, buried in a book, intently staring at the wall with a posture that defies interruption. Whatever feelings he has are hidden, but his inside face is starting to show. The new one is stiffer, quieter, more alone. I interrupt, walking into his study and staring at him until he can't stand it anymore, has to look up.

Dad, can I start swimming with Coach Stan year-round again? The Sisters say that I've mostly stopped all the excessive flightiness. I'm almost thirteen . . . And I'm definitely not falling asleep in class. I have a feeling I'll never fall asleep in class again . . .

He stops me with one hand. *No.*

I find my mother in the living room tracing back time with her favorite friends, a pot of tea and a plate of old cookies from the tin canister above the microwave sitting untouched between them. I listen as she swirls back to her pregnancy searching for odd meals, strange yearnings, one cocktail with hard alcohol, secondhand smoke, synthetic clothing, bug repellent, moments of close proximity with the Glenwood power plant. I listen as she examines the history of her dead relatives. She stares at me with narrow eyes and a flat mouth when I break into a space she hasn't filled in yet with words, explaining earnestly with many hand movements the huge hole that not swimming for the Dolphins year-round has made in my now empty-feeling life. She stops me mid-sentence, says: *Be quiet* in a voice I've never heard before that must have hurt her throat to use.

Christ's Mass

Leonard's driving like a maniac, barely missing the cars that line the street. We're on our way to Christmas mass at Holy Name. Late. Nuns hate late. Late for Christmas equals late for Christ. I hold on to the strap of the door so I don't crush Roxanne, who's slumped next to me. If I crush Roxanne, she'll crush Dot, who'll crush Bron, then there'll be trouble; we'd gotten our orders the night before: *Leave her be.* I hang on to the strap of the door as we career and my mother sighs even though it's her fault; when we were supposed to be entering the church with other families, she was walking around the house in nothing but a chiffon blouse and black panty hose, her vaginal muff flattened underneath like a mongoose in the middle of a highway, her lips still chalkless. I didn't care where her skirt was but I wished she'd put it on. It was the same scene every year, snow falling in tufts, ground covered in ice, Mother half-dressed: in skirt but no top, in sturdy bra and jacket but no pants, wandering the house, hair done, face on, my father waiting in his study, stars glinting a million light-years away, other families already settling into the wooden pews, organ humming in the background, human breath mingling with Christmas perfume and incense.

When we arrive, we open the heavy door carefully and lurk, scanning the pews for space. The Schippers are usually later than us, but tonight I spot them sitting in the last pew with side parts so deep they reveal an entire ear. The pews behind the nuns are the only ones still open. Father Tod is mumbling at the pulpit, chalice in both hands. Jesus hasn't descended yet, is still up there, deciding. We're going to have to walk up the central aisle. Leonard sets his chin, whispers: *Come on.*

I've grown three inches, am now almost as tall as my father, and am having the first real lousy year of my life. My period won't come no matter what I do. I pray to it, earnestly, say: *I'm ready.* I check my underwear every chance I get. My heart sinks at the soft, perfectly white rectangle of little girl it reveals. The girls at school are bleeding together and everybody's talking about it. I don't know I've decided to sin until I pull my mother aside in the kitchen and sin: *I got it.* She goes into her bathroom and pulls out a maxi pad she hands to me with a short weep. Bron looks at me pointedly when I tell her; she knows something's not right, isn't in the mood to figure out what. When I tell Lilly Cocoplat, she looks at me and says: *Told you it sucks. I can't believe you were worried.* And I look at her and sin again: *It super sucks. It's like lousy.* I know it's just a question of time, carefully tape a maxi pad into my underwear.

I'm wearing one as I slide in next to Dot. It sits between my legs like a torpedo, absorbing the dry warmth of my body. I bow my head, pretending to pray for good universal things. When it's time for the sign of peace, the nuns turn, chins supported by dress cowls, clasp my hand with their warm hand bones, grant me peace. I've known them my entire life.

The granting of the peace always brings out the drama in my mother. This year she has decided that peace shall be welcomed with a thumping nervous breakdown. She's crying so hard she's wrestling with herself, and Leonard has to hold on to her so she won't fall into the nuns. Bron is not pleased; her face is tight and she's holding her back as hard and as straight as a board. Trouble. I grit my teeth, calculating escape; we'll sing soon, then the buffet with hot tea, cider, coffee, juice, and two hundred varieties of cake. I find Lilly Cocoplat lodged between her beanpole parents. She puts her middle finger up her nose and coughs twice. I have a hard time controlling myself; wimples rustle; my mother recovers enough to pinch me with nails she's filed into fangs. Life is delicately balanced.

At the buffet, Leonard is quickly surrounded by nun. Sister Atrocious is talking to him a mile a minute, a piece of half-eaten strudel sitting in her palm. Nestor is nodding vehemently here, then there, chewing on something I can't identify, but there's a field of pink crumbs lying on the ledge of her chest. I watch their mouths move, sure that serious information is being exchanged. I send the Cocoplat over to investigate; she comes back with a plate full of apple crumble, a slice of angel food cake, a handful of foil-wrapped chocolate, a glass of something red: *Nothing*.

What's that pink stuff Nestor's eating?

I looked for it. There's none left.

Bron's standing at the bay windows, half hidden by the sacred tree, every inch covered in tinfoiled angel. She's got one hand on the glass as the other waves my mother away.

Leonard and I have finally reached a compromise: I'm swimming on the Holy Name swim team and can practice with the Dolphins on Wednesday afternoons during the school year as long as my grades don't slide. Lilly jumps up and down when I tell her, but she's losing interest in the pool. I can tell.

The Holy Name swim team is coached by Holy Name's new addition, Father Timothy Heaver, tennis coach and Bjorn Borg fanatic. No one would notice if we didn't exist. Real high school swimmers treat our meets as a light practice, rarely bothering to cheer. Our first meet of the season, Father Tim sits us down and gives us a speech that mixes equal portions of the Holy Trinity and exciting things that happened to Bjorn Borg. Father Tim is a naturally sweaty person who does not fare well in chlorine atmospheres and is virtually impossible to talk to during practice because the tennis players swarm him like gnats. I try to explain some things to him through the privacy of the confessional, for example, how the progressive-overload principle proves that if you progressively overload someone just a little bit past what is bearable every day, they will become stronger. *It's a proven fact, Father. Coach Stan explained it to the Dolphins when we were six*. But Father Tim thinks one practice a day is fine enough, even though every other swimmer in the world my age is doubling up.

We won't get any faster, I whisper, finding his form through the dim gray mesh.

Of course we will, and *we'll have fun*. He's leaning on one elbow, his forehead resting in the middle of his palm.

I blast his profile with my eyes, raise my voice a notch. *Our muscles won't get any stronger; just ask Coach Stan. Call him up. He'll tell you; we need two hard practices a day. We will not improve.*

He whispers so softly, I can barely hear him. *Your muscles will get stronger. Why in the world wouldn't they?*

I whisper back, loudly. I don't care who hears. *Ask Coach Stan, Father Tim. And the speeches . . . I could give you . . .*

He breaks the Catholic confessional protocol of absolute anonymity and turns to peer at the hulking shadow I must be. *Is this why you're here?*

I cross my arms over my chest and look down. *Yes.*

He's still peering; I can feel his breath. *There's nothing else?*

My kneecaps are pushing down hard into wood. *No . . .*

Nothing you want to discuss . . . He waves one hand dripping with sleeve.

Everything's okay. Dad said, I whisper. He looks me straight in the face and blesses me with a sigh.

There are eleven other girls on the swim team, all of them recreational swimmers. Some of the recreational swimmers are tennis players in disguise; they talk about Chris Evert, wear socks with little balls attached that bounce when they walk.

I make him give me my own lane. I plant both feet into tile, make my face go as square as it can, say: *Give me my own lane, Father Tim.*

We lose every meet. Every single one. I swim badly, demoralized. I'm still growing taller and it hurts, a dull ache behind my knees, a strange feeling in my hip. I have existential bouts on the starting block, am prone to the extremities of moodiness. I say: *Boy, these cramps sure do ache* as the tennis players look over in suspicion.

My swim falls apart in the water like paper. Former Dolphin colleagues I have always easily beaten easily beat me. They're insincerely apologetic, give me a thumbs-up from afar, have high school coaches with mustaches and clipboards, fund-raisers and sleepovers, camping trips and morning workouts. I don't cheer but they do: *Holy Name is mighty lame.*

Father Tim says: *We did our best and I, for one, am proud* as the tennis players smile in unison and I sulk. Then he blesses us.

This annoys me. *Don't bless us for* real, *Father Tim. Bless us in your head.*

The only people worse than us in the entire state are the Arc City River Rangers. Arc City is home to deep-dish pizza and girls with celloshaped thighs and fat-encased torsos whose ripples you can count from the other side of the pool. I'm itching for one lonely win, but suffer from a terrible antsiness, diving in too quickly, disqualifying, stuck in the recall rope with my heart bursting to race. Father Tim says: *There'll always be a next time!* as an Arc City River Ranger flips me the bird, the underbelly of her arm wobbling to and fro. I call Coach Stan when I get home, a rubber ball of despair lodged in my throat. He sighs. *Con-cen-tra-tion. Next time up, belly-breathe like I taught.*

Next Time Up

Leonard's wearing a pair of mail-order beige slacks with the single neat pleat, a white turtleneck, his dark blue Windbreaker. He's bending over the small door cut into the immense door of the hangar. I feel detached and intent at the same time. It's very agreeable. I'm standing behind him, shining the flashlight on the lock, the sky behind us a pre-dawn sapphire blue. He opens the door; I shine the light in.

The first thing you notice about the fabulous Mooney M20K 305 Rocket is her wings, the jaunty splash of orange, the sliver of light blue that runs up the length of her fine nose. We fly often, on a rotational basis. Dr. Bob comes when he's not on call; sometimes Ahmet Noorani jumps on at the last minute. Mom occasionally braves her motion sickness with Wintermint gum, ginger drops, a bottle of water, and a plastic-lined paper bag, but only for the long cultural weekends when we stay overnight in small lodges, rent cars, go to fairs, fight.

When we got here this morning Shirley R. said: *Hi ya, bat man* when her eyes lit on Leonard. He smiled back, his thin face creasing. *Hello there, Shirley; weather's looking good today.* She didn't say hello to me, nodding coolly in my direction with both lips pressed together in a wide coral line. She'd caught the Cocoplat's rendition of her in the bathroom the last time we flew together; we'd forgotten to check the stall, a mistake we will not make again. I stifled the smile I was going to give her, wanting to say *I'm sorry* but not feeling up to the task. Some people give you one chance and after that you're dead to them forever.

This morning I'm flying alone with Leonard although it's not my turn. We didn't even draw straws—he'd said *Be ready by five* so I was ready by five. I laid my clothes out by the side of my bed so I could wake up and slide into them without waking Bron. She didn't wake. When I looked over at her as I was shutting the door, she was wrapped up, her long arms with the pointy elbows covering her face. She was in a good mood last night, sang "Cat's in the Cradle" until I got so sad I made her stop. Then she sang "Rikki, Don't Lose That Number," but I don't like that song so I crept into Leonard's office, stole some nun fudge, brought it back. I chewed a bunch; she nibbled some, said: *Don't you think it sounds like an English butler?*

I said: *What?*

And she said: *Hodgkin's disease. Don't you think Hodgkin's sounds like an English butler?*

And I swallowed my fudge and said: *Yeah, I guess it does.*

When we walk into the lounge, my heart twitters; there are a couple of Mooniacs sitting on the tweed couch, drinking tar from Styrofoam cups, open topographic maps lying between them. The Mooniacs are exactly like the swimming tennis players: they dress alike and have a hidden agenda involving the one subject that interests them: *Old Mooney, the new Mooney, the most powerful pistons in the sky*.

We luck out; today they are busy planning some treasure hunt that crosses the Southern states, stopping somewhere in Florida. They shake Leonard's hand and nod toward me as I slouch in to the Coke machine, which only takes quarters.

Good. I hate it when we're delayed, fling myself on the mangy couch with long sighs, staring at the centerfolds of flying magazines Shirley has tacked to the walls. Bron always brings a book, just in case, sitting sideways in the corduroy armchair, her legs dangling over its arms as Roxanne looks out the window gnawing on her nails. Dot goes up front and sits on Shirley's lap, welcoming fellow voyagers or drawing colorful planes diving into blue space. The odor of keen pilot coffee bites the warm air in the small room as people wander in and out with weekend bags slung over their shoulders and huge leather aviation briefcases containing things that hold zero percent interest for me.

We often make cultural excursions around the state, getting up at dawn to view the big well and meteorite in Greensburg, Monkey Island in Independence. We go to the Wizard of Oz complex in Liberal, feasting on towers of pancakes that come up to our chins. We go to Meade to check out the escape tunnel used by the Dalton Gang in 1929, a disappointing heap of dirt. We attend the annual black squirrel celebration in Wichita, where we buy figurines of squirrels whose frozen faces mirror the complexities of human joy. We examine the world's largest twine ball in Cawker City and the transparent woman with the illuminated genitalia at the Halstead Center for Health in Liberal. I study her glowing bits, her bright sunny ovaries, her hot pink tunnels of tube. I step in closer, wondering what vital womanly thing I'm missing until Bron grabs my arm and squeezes: *People are staring.* We fly into the fields surrounding local fairs, where we stack up on pots of apple butter the color of mole, pickles, fresh sweet corn we shuck, then freeze. We rent cars from airports sitting in the middle of lonesome fields like shacks and drive up into the Smoky Mountains, picnicking in front of a small lake with frigid green water we hold our breaths to dive into, flying home into a violet Kansas sun as Mother barfs loudly into one of her American Airlines necessity bags that Leonard collects on his commercial flights.

Sometimes we fly just to fly, nowhere, careening in wide, even circles, staring down at the world with hypnotized eyes and not saying one word until we land with a lurch, rubber on cement, sky shifting back into place. These are therapeutic flights that work on the principle that by removing ourselves from earth's grasp, we cool its sting. It works; little problems waltz across the world until the bigger ones give in and join them.

Dr. Ahmet Noorani, the Pakistani urologist, has the hangar next to ours. He flies a ratty Cessna he's named Ducky and is building his own plane. He's here every time we are, standing in the hangar in dirty white coveralls with a wrench in one hand and a bright yellow cigarette burning in the other. When he sees us, he puts down his tools and hugs us one by one, pulling us into his prickly face and kissing both cheeks with tight sound. He and Leonard are linked not only by their love of flight but because they both are the only men in a family of women. Ahmet has three of them, short, golden-haired, slightly fattish daughters who bear no resemblance whatsoever to him. We study each other from across the hangar, don't mingle, although Ahmet cries: *Talk, talk, girrlllls; what's the matter with you? They never stop at home* . . . If Dr. Ahmet gets to Leonard with one of his lilting questions, we're sure to spend an hour looking at the engine that's spread across the floor on a sheet of gray tarp. But today the hangar next to ours is dark, all tools packed neatly into a metal box, tarp folded sharply on top. Ducky is tied down, her eyes covered in silver isothermic material.

I say the same thing I always say when I see Ducky. *Hi, Ducky.*

Leonard looks up. *Don't mock. Ducky's a fine little plane.*

Planes are easier to move than go-carts. Leonard steers, door open, one beige desert boot poised on the outside step, his mind busy, humming with pre-flight happiness. I forget how strong I am, push too hard.

It's not made of lead . . . gentle, gentle now.

Our breath blows puffs of vapor into the air as we walk through the crunch of frozen green-smelling hay layered thinly on the ground. It's so still you can hear the rabbits scatter in fear. Leonard takes his time checking, double-checking. He puts his glasses on and flips switches up and down as I watch the sun tip the horizon with an arc of white light.

We taxi down the runway, Leonard murmuring stuff to control, control murmuring stuff back. He turns to me as if just remembering my presence, smiles, gives me a thumbs-up: *255 Oscar Papa Romeo, check.* The revving of engine echoes in plexus, speed pulling me back into my seat, until we are released from gravity, our internal organs floating slightly as we lift into air. I'm not comfortable sitting copilot because I don't ever want to die. I don't like the idea of dying alone with Leonard either. If we're going to die, we should do it as a family or else it's not fair. I don't mention this to Leonard because according to him we are much safer 24,000 feet in the air than driving our station wagon five miles down Thirty-fourth Street to Holy Name's annual Easter cakewalk. I know it's true, but it doesn't feel like it when the Rocket points her nose straight up in the air, breaking the pull of gravity as the earth falls away and I am pressed into my seatbones by forces I cannot see. It makes my stomach churn.

One of the nicer things about flying alone with Leonard is I get my own set of headphones, which keeps me connected to everything happening between control and the other planes hidden somewhere in the sky. I love to hear them, the pilots passing through Kansas, their swift observations, efficient requests for factual information, the rare jokester cutting through electricity, his voice vibrating off my inner ear, lulling me into a funk so deep and delicious I float in a semiconscious state as I dip my half-open eyes into cloud, into green wavy hill, watching the tin soldiers living out sweet meaningless lives below.

We cut through a colony of dense gray elephant clouds that Leonard says were designed for maximum gloom. The sky opens to a clear dazzling blue and there she is, the sun, patiently watching with one benevolent eye, and we are the lucky ones and life is a marvel.

Leonard's voice breaks through the static. *This is good, isn't it?*

I break back. *Yeah.*

He's quiet, speaking only to point out a strange natural formation in the midst of stalks of corn—broken gold hands reaching up from a blanket of white; the Missouri frozen to a standstill with a locked-in barge, gray and lonely, caught like a fat fly in a web of ice.

I keep myself busy calculating the space between land and sky. I plant my eyes on the ground and concentrate hard on the fall. Sometimes I have us catapult into the air before impact, landing on our backs, blackened, bruised, with smoking frizzy hair and oil-slicked faces; stunned but alive. We smile at each other in amazement, teeth a deep cartoon white. But mostly my mind is drawn to the crushing, our zest pierced by harder lifeless things, lives escaping our bodies in a mad hiss of steam, our noisy insides as blank as screens after someone has pulled the plug. Our simultaneous death moves me to delicious tears that I hide in the arm of my sweater as Leonard sweeps us forward through the sky, as confident of the machine that holds us in her metal belly as he is of anything in the world.

He clears his throat. *I need you to do something for me.*

This is new. I clear my throat. *Okay.*

When he doesn't say anything, I turn to look at him. We're flying steady over generous spoonfuls of white mousse. He feels me looking, doesn't turn, white clouds crossing his dark glasses like ghosts. He speaks quietly: *I need you to make things as easy as you can for Bron and your mother.*

I adopt his tone, whisper: *Okay.*

He's done, switches off the headphones; someone flying in from Kansas City is requesting permission to land.

Landing is tricky. Rushing sensations, bursts of adrenaline, sudden shudders, heaving sky, the descent toward gloom. Wheels touch concrete and out we step, gingerly, as though walking with new feet. I don't know exactly what flying does for Leonard but it always changes his face. We find Ahmet Noorani lounging in a lawn chair, his hairy ankles sticking out of the brightly colored socks he favors, *How to Build Your Own Plane* sitting open on his lap. He jumps up when he sees us, pulling me into his prickly chin and kissing me tightly on both cheeks.

I turn my back on them, walk out the door. The sky's full of planes zipping carefully amongst each other in a scary ballet. I watch them for a while, then start to run. I don't know where I'm going, but I know Leonard will probably find me. I run past trees, out into the open fields that lead to Glenwood. It doesn't feel bad, but I know that it is.

Six Feet High and Rising

It's family night across the state of Kansas. All the pizza parlors and bowling alleys are muggy with the steam of human breath, the streets full of family cars stuffed with square-headed family members eating freshly baked prune kolaches. Leonard passes them with a curse. I hang on to the strap of the door. Mom is doing something to her face she didn't have time to do at home. Roxanne is stoned, eyes lit from within, speaking when spoken to in monotones as though her tongue has been dipped in thick cream. No one else notices she's a big pothead except Bron, Dot, the nuns, June, all the kids at school, me. Father Tim's opting to believe her heart is having trouble hunting for her soul; sometimes I catch him blessing her twice. Leonard and Mom don't notice; they've got other things on their minds. Bron's looking out the window, absently braiding the fringe on the scarf that covers her head as though it were hair. Dot's staring straight ahead, knees pressed together to conserve space for those who need it more. We're on our way to the movies five minutes late. The trees bond with the wind, sending their leaves swirling into the gray sky before falling into slick puddles of rain that I ran through this afternoon with a heady satisfaction and the wrong shoes.

When I see Dr. Bob for my annual. I'm six feet tall. I take my socks off and slouch. Six feet tall. I remove my ponytail and slouch. Six feet tall. I turn dramatic: *This is just all I need right now, Dr. Bob.*

You'll stop growing soon.

You said that last year.

Well, it's true. You'll stop growing soon.

Leonard has to special-order his pants. I'll have to special-order my pants.

He ignores me. *How are your periods?*

My gut wrenches with lie-inspired terror. *Very good, great really.*
He looks at me over his bifocals. *No pain?*
Ohhh yes, pain. Some pain. But . . . not a lot. Of pain.
You can take an anti-inflammatory if it gets too bad.
Okay.
Are you on a twenty-eight or thirty-day cycle?
My gut re-wrenches with lie-inspired terror. *Thirty.*
Regular?
Oh yes.
He changes tones, grinds his voice down: *How's everyone holding up?*
I sigh, relief sifting out my pores. *Fine. Okay.*
But that's a lie. Most weekends Lilly Cocoplat and I go to Wool-
worth's with premeditated sin on our minds. We dress in layers; T-shirts
covered with bulky cardigan, thick-ribbed tights under our loosest jeans,
so when we stuff something down, it remains hidden. Lilly is curvy,
got her period when she was eleven in a dramatic to-do that lasted a
week, can get away with stuffing a couple of synthetic nightgowns
in shades of lemon and turquoise, rainbow socks with toes, T-shirts
with glued-on sparkles, but I have to stick to flat unobtrusive things:
sheer polyester underwear, powder compacts, thin flacons of synthetic
perfume.

Lilly has shoplifting theories she feels strongly about: know what
you want, steal as though you were buying, be quick, don't be greedy.
The apple-shaped guard stalks us, his brown eyeballs blaring out from
underneath his Groucho Marx eyebrows, standing at the end of the
feminine protection aisle as unobtrusively as an ape. We feign ignorance, grab a raspberry lip gloss, hold it up for all to see, and pay for it
with much flourishing of dollar, then go down to the cafeteria and have
our French fries and ice cream, our booty clanking in our jeans. He sits
behind us on break, frowning as he slices his Salisbury steak with his
fork before attacking the mounds of potatoes he's covered in muddy
gravy, ignoring us as we fall over ourselves laughing.

Leonard and Mom are in a double bad mood that doesn't heal with
the passage of time. They yell about nothing. Mom cries if I leave a wet
towel on the carpet, or slaps me hard on the arm, leaving a red hand that
takes time to go away.

The thought of telling Dr. Bob about the sinning to make amends for my lying heart crosses my mind, then disappears. There is something priesty to him without the God. He is president of an association for the protection of the Shawnees, wants them to get some of their land back, which makes him unpopular with the local yokels, whom he refers to, affectionately, as the local yokels.

Dr. Bob is probably the smartest person I'll ever know, but like all really smart people, with the exception of Roxanne, he is often boring. He whips out his pencil and draws in the lymphatic system on a neutral body with no detailed body parts, using lines and asterisks where Bron's been hit. I watch his papery skin, hairy knuckles, clean nails, and I nod, as solemn as he. Her body looks like it is sprouting flowers, but he leaves no space for commentary, so I keep quiet, nodding solemnly here, then there. I wonder if he is going to give me something; the paperweight with the scorpion in the middle, a rose rock from his vast collection, one of his narrow wooden men, but today nothing, not even M&M's. He grasps my shoulder with one of his dry doctorly hands, his light gray eyes shining with a kindness so simple it makes me squirm, says: *Take care. I'm here if you have any questions* and my heart twitters in terror. *Does he know?*

They've been checking her in and out of Glenwood Memorial. When she's home, it's hell. When she's not home, it's hell. Both hells have no gate. The hells are expanding like the universe—hot, boundless. When she's less sick, she threatens to hang herself with a leather belt, which gives Mother thumping nervous breakdowns that include nose-bleeds. I discover I have a vivid imagination. All I have to do is think *belt* and there's Bron's spooky hologram with one fist on her hip, Mother leaning her head back, holding a bloody Kleenex to her nose, June's sea green eyes meeting mine, Leonard's fist coming down hard on the table, his composure decomposing: *I said that's enough, all of you! That's enough.*

I take it upon myself to tell her to stop threatening to kill herself. I sit on the edge of her bed and speak to her back in reasonable tones as though now, due to extenuating circumstances, I am the senior. *You're freaking everyone out.*

She turns, hissing like a snake. *And if I do kill myself, asshole? What are you going to do about it? I can take this goddamn belt and hang myself from it if I want. Got it, Miss America? Look at me. Come on, both your eyes. That's a good girl. See this belt? People do it every day. So fuck off and don't try to tell me what I can and can't do. Got it?*

I fuck off. She scares me.

Leonard and Mom think that if they fight silently, we won't know. A mistake. They stopped using direct eye contact a couple of weeks ago, addressing each other with the voices they use when talking with various and sundry people who don't understand anything. Leonard looks at Mom's chair and says, as though to a waiter who's not doing his job: *Would you mind passing the turkey, please,* each word graver than the next. Then he turns to Dot, clasps her eyes in a warm visual hug, his voice exploding with fake happiness: *How's my bug-eyed flower face doing today?* as we all jump out of our skins.

The cure is taking longer than expected. They come home from appointments together as I sit on the kitchen counter eating doughnut holes. First Leonard then Bron then Mom, in a line like ducks. They come home from appointments together as Roxy, Dot, and I stand around the yard kicking up leaves and June smokes a minty cigarette behind the kitchen. Sometimes they get out of the car in the middle of a conversation our presence does not break. Sometimes they are quiet with a silence that momentary eye contact with them convinces us to maintain. June has taken over car-pool days, pulling up to the curb with a jerk, cranky.

The moon waxes, the moon wanes, Lake Shawnee's vivid green deepens into brown, green leaves kaleidoscope into color, and Bron needs help getting out of the car. She's pale and shaky. She's angry and her mouth's dry. What's left of her hair falls, her freckles recede, her arms turn into branches of new trees, her eyes turn into angry pellets, her cello-playing fingers stop itching for the chords, French club becomes secondary, and the debaters stop waiting and plan their strategies without her. I ride my bike fast, careening down hills, rushing through rushing puddles, coasting past sleeping houses, on my feet under slate bridges, all the way across Glenwood then back again.

I walk into our dark room; she says: *I taste like rust.*

I squeeze toothpaste onto her finger; she swishes it in her mouth and swallows.

I hear some kids at school say, *Her sister's contaminated.* I slam my locker, give them a look.

When she's sick, I have to leave the room or I'm sick. When her mouth is dry, my mouth gets dry. When she starts to cry and tells me to fuck off and get out, I fuck off and get out. Our bedroom turns into a damp cave; the walls fold in; it smells like moss. I don't like it and want it to be over. I sleep over at the Cocoplats anytime I can; we watch Adam Ant leap, fall to his knees, plead, both hands clasped under his chin. He's part swashbuckling pirate, part American Indian, part British soldier. He's wearing masculine boots, a fluffy jabot, three layers of mascara. When he sings, his hair vibrates. I'm so in love, I can't stand it. Lilly's in love too. But less. I'm the one who kisses the TV.

Roxanne goes out with friends, has sleepovers, disappears. If Mom and Leonard say no, she begs until they break down—signs of future trouble left ignored.

Dot excels in all matters: prudence, caring, quietude, studiousness, beauty, cleanliness, invisibility, and the absence of need—signs of future saintliness much admired.

Leonard plays chess with Bron until eleven at night, walks down the stairs like a tall kid with no self-confidence.

Mother says: *Eat, Leonard,* pushing the potato dishes he likes into his general vicinity. No direct contact.

He pushes them back. *I had something at the office.*

I'm giddy. *What did you have at the office, Dad, bat food?*

He's tired. *No, smarty winks. Kathy Stupek made some kind of health thing. I had the health thing.*

But he doesn't eat. And Mother starts lurking like a thief, walking in her stockinged feet on the boards that creak, slipping her head into the doorway of our bedroom when Bron comes home as we hold our breath and stop moving until she goes away.

Bron turns onto her back and stares at the ceiling. *She's starting to drive me nuts.*

I flip on my side and stare at the wall. *She's just worried.*

Bron turns onto her stomach and sighs into her pillow. *Like I need her worry.*

A couple of weeks ago, Mom stood by the window begging, bribing, pleading. Leonard was sitting on the edge of Bron's bed, his legs folded under him like the lawn chairs in the basement. He was using all his paternal power of persuasion in a discussion that started weeks ago and still isn't done. I was getting dressed for school, tucking my big shirt into the waistband of my big skirt.

Bron's voice was the same one she used in her triumphant argument against Uganda. *I'm not going to Southwestern College. I'll wait until I'm better, then I'll go to Columbia as planned.*

Leonard was being rational, but his fingers were jangling his keys. *Yes. But. It's. We're talking about your future here. You have a four point; let's not jeopardize your fu—*

I'm waiting until I can go where I planned to go, Dad. I'm not changing my plans now. She stared him down.

Mom adjusted the folds in the curtains. *You should be in school. What are you going to do all day long?*

Leonard stood up like a bent man. His eyes, when they glanced over and caught mine, had started their transformation into stone. I ran after him, standing next to the car panting as he rolled down the window. *I need to double up my practices, swim all year long, Dad. Stan thinks I can go places.*

He lifted up both his hands as if caught in the middle of a Western, sighed, and said: *Swim, then,* driving away until he was gone.

Swimming twice a day turns me into an extremely calm person. When Mom grabs my upper arm with her fangs and squeezes, leaving a series of raised welts, I don't say anything, just hold my arm and leave for school. When Bron wakes me up in the middle of the night, I listen to her, say: *I know what you mean,* then go back to sleep. When Father Tim asks me to try and make friends with the swimming tennis players, I say: *Okay, Father Tim.* I even tell a disappointed Lilly Cocoplat standing at the doorstep in a pair of jeans with a pair of red tights underneath: *This isn't a good day for me to be taking risks.*

The nuns are busy forging character; they pass me in the hall, their eyes straight ahead, their skirts slapping my legs in a heavy *swoosh* that I've seen knock some of the skinnier junior Catholics into their lockers, but I'm strong enough to hold steady. I prepare my face, remove my slouch, knock on the office door, and hand myself over to their metaphysical furnace to be molded. I'm as close to being a mini-nun as I'll ever be in my life. I work hard on weekly book reports that never get

anything higher than a B, sitting in a chair with a pen in my mouth trying to formulate strong enough thought in the kitchen while June peels
potatoes and distracts me with catchy humming. I am considered *flitty*, a
deep disappointment from Bron's intellectual stillness. That's what the
nuns say when I hand myself over to them.

They say: *What's wrong with you? Stop that infernal flitting.*

I clean out the attic using so much lemon polish the fumes make me
woozy. I volunteer for story time with the second graders without
changing any words in the book even when no one else is around. When
the snows hit hard, I help Leonard put the snow tires on. Roxanne and I
make a snowman who wears a hunting cap, looks cute from afar, but has
a hidden penis with two chestnut balls. We laugh hard at our master-
piece under a canopy of cold dwarf stars, our breath leaving our lungs
in wispy puffs that hang between us before disappearing.

We stare at the stars for a minute. She turns to me and says: *Wanna
get stoned?*

I don't do drugs. *Swimmers don't do drugs.*

She doesn't seem surprised. *So that's what you are . . .*

This makes me mad. *You got a problem with that?*

She sighs. *No . . . no.*

Pot's making you . . . weirder.

She says: *Take a look around, Phil . . . I'm not that bad.*

I don't look around; I look at her instead and I'm surprised—she's
not that bad.

Leonard pulls up to the curb with a lurch, sets his chin, and sighs, opening Mom's door and pulling her carefully from the front seat as though
she were a precious old lady. The theater is dark but empty—not many
Glenwoodians want to see *The Blue Lagoon,* Bron's film of choice. I
sink into the red velvet chair, stretch my legs into the row of seats in
front of me. I slump next to Leonard, who falls asleep the minute that
blond, fluffy-curled, girly-guy dives into the water, coming up seconds
later with a big fish in his little hands, and Bron gets in a bad mood that
lasts, more or less, until the day she dies.

A is for airway, make sure it is free
B is for breathing if life is to be,
C is for circulation to make your heart thump
D is for death to avoid like a chump

The first time I saw Manny, he was blind. He was crawling on top of his brothers as they fed, driven by a mixture of survival instinct, stupidity, and an innate ability to do the wrong thing. He stopped at the top of the pyramid, nestled in, began to suck on a tuft of his mother's fur with all his vital energy, as though if he were patient enough, he would eventually draw milk.

That one, I said.

Which one? asked Leonard.

The one on top, I said.

That one? Are you sure?

Yes, I said. *I'm sure.*

The dog lady's son pulled him off the fur and he mewled like a kitten. I held him in the palm of my hand and knew love. *This one,* I said.

Our yard is covered in the bushes that attract the fireflies Manny tries to catch in his mouth. I'm sitting outside, skin tanned taut, the muscles in my shoulders and legs aching with every breath, following him with my eyes. He jumps. Gets nothing. Jumps again. Gets nothing. He trips over a log, falls, rolls down the hill, gets stuck in some mud, yelps. He's six years old now and is, as Leonard says, as dumb as a turnip.

It's summer and I'm free. One of those anonymous balloons someone has let loose to meander across sky. The days start when I want them to—early, ending when I fling myself across my bed, eyes shutting of their own accord. Everyone is leaving me deliciously alone. *O Gloria in Excelsis Deo.* We don't go to mass every Sunday; sometimes weeks go by with the absence of nun, priest, long, achy minutes on our knees spent in the confessional, papery wafers stuck on the roof of our mouths until we make enough spit to pry them off with our tongues. After week upon week of scorching heat, five tornados tear through the state, killing twenty-two. All we get is an intense steamy silence, trees so still as to be frozen, a hysteric cacophony of nervous birds that make June crazy, followed by the absence of bird, which disturbs her. New storms follow; massive black thunderclouds moving in slowly like zombies, needles of rain falling down hard, arrows of lightning springing up from nowhere. Roxanne and I stand under it getting pelted until June opens a window yelling: *Electrocution, you idiots.* Now a cooler, farther-away form of the sun is back in a flat blue sky and all is well. I love these atmospheric conditions; it is the only time of the year the air is cooler than the water in the outdoor pool at the Quaker Aquatic Center, or the Quack as I now call it, my home away from home. I put my face into Manny's burry neck. He stinks like socks.

I'm learning CPR with Coach Stan and the members of the Glenwood Fire Department. We have a mannequin named Doug with wiry brown hair and a long, dead-looking face. When the firefighters turn their heads, Lilly Cocoplat French-kisses him, making sure spit splatters everywhere with rabid use of her tongue. She gets more daring with each day that goes by. We're split in two, laughing in a roar, as Stan and various firefighters look up from their Styrofoam cups of steaming black tar and shake their heads, unaware of how awful we are.

Most members of the team have been growing into something I have not. They're slowing down, don't care, one eye on the cute boys plunging through the lanes next to ours. When Stan blows his whistle, they sigh, plopping back into the water like well-fed sea lions. We have casual meets against country clubs and some rural summer clubs, beating them easily and getting home late. I learn the Heimlich maneuver, cardiac massage, pupil-reading techniques, exploding-vein indicators, how to tell when a person is finally dead.

The Cocoplat and I bathe in the joy-tinged disrespect of referring to our parents by their first names when they're not around. Lilly slips a turquoise eyeliner under her bra in the Woolworth's beauty aisle and whispers: *Roger would definitely not be pleased with my outrageous behavior.* Later, I contemplate a pair of $70 sneakers. *I'll have to ask old Mother Mary what she thinks about these.* We Dolphins will become licensed lifeguards, will spend two weeks as trainees under a real lifeguard at one of the Glenwood outdoor pools. We draw straws; I get the uptight Glenwood Country Club, Lilly gets the fun Beaver Park. My shoulders are a wide brown triangle.

I can almost save people now, I announce over dinner.

Bron looks at me, holding a wing of bronzed chicken between her fingers, and says: *My guess is you'd freak.*

That's the first thing they teach us: Don't freak.

Leonard is impressed. *I'd like to sign us all up for that.*

Roxanne kicks me under the table, mouthing *MFPF,* which means *motherfucking prissy fuck.*

Bron's eating again and holding it down—not a lot, but she chews and swallows. The droning vibrations of cello sound up from the basement; the telephone rings with her voice singing *I've got it.* She lets her friends come back. They push me out of the bedroom with both hands, lock the door, speak in whispers with the music on high so I can't hear a thing. When they come into the kitchen to get something to eat, they laugh hysterically at my flat ponytail, my pole chest, my pole legs, and I fear my secret's been discovered. I cover my tracks by loudly asking Bron for a maxi pad. She says: *What's wrong with you? They're in the bathroom under the sink.* But I catch her studying me later with a question mark in both eyes and my heart starts to twitter.

Mom sleeps, wakes up in the morning, does things to her hair, buys new chalk for her lips, marinates vegetables in ceramic bowls. Dot has stopped the incessant praying; the bruises on her knees lift back into skin. Roxanne takes advantage of the relaxed atmosphere in the house, crouching under the willow tree in the garden with a one-hitter and a lump of hash.

Leonard's flying regularly again but mostly with Dr. Bob and Ahmet Noorani. He talks Mom into going away for a weekend. June orders deep-dish pizza two nights in a row and we sit watching TV until we can't stand it anymore. When Leonard and Mom return, they're back to normal, holding hands in the car. Colleagues are invited over for annual BBQs. They drink German beer with sliced lemons, standing next to ribs Leonard has rubbed with a disgusting red paste. All things are exclamation worthy. Astronomer Gerald overindulges. His voice gets louder when he's drunk, wobbling up the air into our open window. *And that is why, dear friends, the moon keeps missing the earth. The simplicity is genius.* Bron says: *He's wasted.* I make no comment, eavesdropping until their voices tune together and warble like birds, singing in my ears until I fall asleep. In the morning, Leonard tries to coerce me out of practice. *Come on, Boo . . . let's go for a fly.* I pay him back for all the trouble he's caused with a steady boycott I deliver with a shrug and an apologetic smile that does not reach my eyes.

Usually we spend a couple of weeks soaking in black rubber tires on the green waters of Lake Shawnee, but this year they've planned a trip to France, the proud home of my mother's ancestors' ancestors. We've been taking French lessons with Sister Belly since we were five because there are Bouviers buried deep in the foliage of Mom's family tree. A worn dictionary comes out at the dinner table. Corn is *maïs.* Hot dog is *'ot dog.* Rice is *riz.* Water is *oh.*

I'm okay. But sometimes I laugh so hard I feel weird and have to lie down.

Mom and Leonard clasp their hands together and make their eyes wide when they speak to us, as if somehow we've lost the capacity to understand the normal speech patterns, the usual eye language. Everything starts with a *let's: Let's swim at the QAC. Let's have melon for dessert! Let's take the top off the car!!!*

This annoys Bron. *Quit talking to us like we're retarded.*

Leonard's temper surges at the strangest times. He gets up, slaps both hands down hard on the table, opens his mouth, closes it, looks at her, looks out the window, pounds his hands down hard on the table again, leaves. Mother refrains from both eye contact and speech.

Bron looks at me. *What?*

I look at her. *What, what?*

She makes her eyes unusually round: *What what what what what what.*

She's very unpleasant, but I won't take the bait. I stand up, grab my jacket, lace up my sneakers, and go. I walk down to Indian Creek. There's a small stream there with frogs that blend into the grass so well you don't even know they're there until they croak.

Paris Is as Paris Does

We're on our way to Paris to uncover our inner Bouvier. Bron's sitting next to me writing in her dream book, long fingers forming long words, wrists as slim as pencils. She covers up the page with her hand, says: *Do you mind.* Jets start reverberating in my innards, decibels rising as the hostesses strap themselves in, their orange faces set underneath their triangular caps. Leonard looks at me, nods. *They're revving the jets.*

The guidebooks he's checked out are lying on his lap, and although he can stretch his legs out in the aisle, he doesn't; he's sitting straight up in his seat, exactly where they put him, thinking we'll confuse his outward calm with a certain form of inner serenity. We don't. We make looks over his head. Roxanne says: *Don't you find Dad unusually boring?* She's wearing a striped shirt, a striped skirt, black-and-white bowling shoes, fingerless gloves, a red beret.

I hold my legs in a bent-kneed, open-armed, slope-shouldered surf stance so I can ride out any unexpected turbulence. I stand in the aisle looking down at them and say: *Look at what gravity has done to my face.*

Bron says: *What are you doing? You look like a . . . Sit down and shut up.*

Roxanne says: *Your face looks like modeling clay.*

I say: *Like I don't know it, twerp.*

We look like a game show family flying to Paris with tokens in our pockets—except for Dot, who sits between Mom and Leonard sketching animals in peaceful positions. Mom's motion sickness miraculously disappears upon contact with jet. She's dressed in a pair of white jeans with a colorful smock, lips chalked peach. She looks up from her magazine and waves at me as though I were far away.

I find Paris stinky, unusual, exciting. It doesn't seem part of real life but like a funny parallel life where I don't exist, thus nothing real can happen, good or bad, happy or sad. I take a break from caring about my absent womanhood, pick my nose in public because I don't know anyone, thus don't care. I travel well, like a sophisticated thoroughbred, but Bron is too tired. Too tired to eat breakfast. Too tired to take the steps down into the metro, too tired to walk back up. Leonard changes the subject by offering $20 to the first person who spots a Dalí mustache in the flesh. The competitor in me awakes and I concentrate on the hunt, looking through a swamp of naked faces, searching for the waxed tendrils under some unknown nose. My eyes start to roam museums, skim the city, hunting.

We are staying in a snazzy hotel off the Champs de Mars. One-third of the Eiffel Tower shines through our window before the Eiffel Tower tenders flip the switch and turn it off. We sleep heavily at the wrong times, lightly when it's dark. Bron's restless. She moves her feet around, is prone to violent flips, her thin appendages knocking into me like cruel hammers. She is one of those sleepers who emit heat and wake up sweaty. I'm a cool sleeper who drools. I can't stand it.

I push her: *I'm going to sleep on the couch.*

She pushes back: *Like I care.*

I pull a sheet over myself and sleep until bells sound from some distant church, dawn lifts the gray out of the black, and the edges of the Eiffel Tower turn into bronze iron flint.

It is not a good trip, although technically I love it. There is no real reason for this love other than the freedom of not existing, the brief suspension of real time, and being able to tug at my underwear right inside my jeans in the metro at high noon without having to worry about a dry maxi pad popping out and exposing me for the liar I am.

Parisian girls are growing up faster than us; they wear their hair in ratty chignons, blow thin streams of gray smoke out their trim nostrils. They turn their bored llama eyes on us, giving Bron's scarf, our flat shoes, our ringless fingers, our naked faces the once-over. A look that dismisses in one rapid glance. I don't care about them, my eyes screening crowds for mustache, absently say: *What bitches,* but Bron's face hardens into her hard face and Mother and Leonard make like they don't see. They hold out their maps with wide-open arms while people stare at Leonard's gigantic height and funny pants. Bron's French-club French doesn't sound French even though she's gotten straight A's since the beginning of time. A red rash appears on her neck when she has to say something twice, victim of her own perfection. She quits. *I'm too tired to talk anymore—you talk.* I don't care, speak in whole paragraphs, point with my finger or my chin, pulling people where I want them without asking their permission first. I can tell by the look on their faces that they are amazed.

We spend two days in the Louvre. A short Japanese guy moves in right in front of me as I'm staring at the *Mona Lisa,* breaking the spell I'm supposed to be under. I find the *Mona Lisa* small, oblong, slightly yellowish, relatively humdrum. The Japanese man has zero manners, a long torso, two short legs tucked into a pair of baggy American pants. I laser two holes into the back of his head with my opaque glare: *The Japanese Have Zero Manners.*

Just look at the detail on this ceiling, shouts Leonard, and up our eyes flip to gilded naked angels riddled in fat and God pointing One Finger down below.

That's my next trip, Bron says, laughing so hard she has to sit down on a wooden bench, and we have to stand around waiting until she recovers.

Flashy synthetic clothes covering people who don't matter to me move in front of the backdrop of the glues and the inks, the plasters, marbles, precious metals, and woods, while God up in His World looks down upon ours—newer, faster, hotter, keener, with a furrow in the middle of his gold face. Still no mustache anywhere. My eyes cut through crowds of people roaming, feverish with hunt. Dalí is luck. Luck bring me Dalí.

At the Rodin museum, I stand on the second floor looking down on Bron and Leonard, who sit under a tree drinking water from a small bottle. Bron leans her head back, exposing her throat to the sky. Mother has a quick nervous breakdown next to the bust of a child's perfect head— she says *oh oh oh oh* while the museum guard pretends her flashlight is interesting and I slip out as quiet as a Shawnee, calling: *Come to me, mustache, come to me now.*

It starts to rain. We order crêpes and eat them standing up.

Bron made a list of things she wanted to taste before we left: a real crêpe suzette, a real café crème, a real croissant, a real baguette, a real glass of wine, cassis sorbet. But now that we're here, nothing appeals to her. We wait as she stares silently at miles of pastry in pastry cases and the pastry woman's daughter twists her eyebrows into question marks and Parisians start to shuffle and sniff, their way of signaling dissent, until finally she says *Rien* and the pastry woman's daughter says *Pardon?* and her neck flushes red and she says *Rien* again.

She sits in restaurants in front of plates of delicately seasoned fish with open gills like angels caught mid-flight, says: *I can't do this.*

At one restaurant, the waiter who seated us without a word and took our order with a sigh removes her untouched plate, bringing back a soft-boiled egg without being asked. It sits in a small silver cup next to a folded linen napkin and six strips of perfectly grilled baguette. She eats the egg slowly with a silver teaspoon. Pleased.

Roxanne spots the Dalí mustache on the Boulevard Beaumarchais. It's on a tight-bellied biker with an old-fashioned face and funny James Dean hair. I see him first, but Roxanne says: *Isn't that weird little guy over there wearing a Dalí mustache?*

Leonard opens his wallet with a *Bravo; some said it couldn't be done, but here we have our Dalí mustache winner.*

At the end of a quest, a trip loses flavor.

We take the boats weaving through the center of the city, the sky so low it touches water, city birds flapping by with city-bird faces. Roxanne falls asleep with her head on my shoulder. I jab her hard with an elbow. *I saw it first.*

Mom starts counting down, pushing the present into the past with the future. No sooner here than gone. Over breakfast she says: *Just think, tomorrow we'll be home,* and home looms colorful and wise, simple and good. On the plane, Bron says: *Well, that sucked* and all loud voices are discontinued until further notice. I look out the porthole at the darkness swirling below. Sometimes a lone spark of light appears, here, then there.

Thee Thou Thine

Dot and Roxanne are playing Ping-Pong; Dot's losing because she keeps stopping to pull up her jeans. The sky's shining a flat, even light over the yard, the wind blowing invisibly into the trees. I like this weather; sitting under the sun when the wind stops, I get as hot as I do in the summer. I'm reclining in a lawn chair, holding a red and white plastic bag of malted milk balls, eating them one by one. Bron's reclining next to me, quietly watching Dot let herself lose. She's cold, is wearing her orange parka, a heavy wool cap, a scarf, and a blanket.

Wanna malted? I hold the open bag out to her without turning. Roxanne is playing viciously, slicing her paddle down hard at an angle, the white ball reacting in a spastic, impossible flight you'd have to be inhuman to follow.

She pushes it away. *Dead people don't eat malted milk balls.*

I don't want to, but I look anyway. She's looking at me already.

What?

Dead people don't eat malted milk balls.

This is new. I have to be careful. *You're not dead.*

Actually, darling . . .

There is no medical doctor in the world who would agree with you, I say carefully.

Like I give a shit who agrees with me.

Bron is expert at saying things no one can respond to; it's part of the debate technique that won her many matches across the state of Kansas. I think hard, but my brain lets me down; all I feel inside is a white electric blank and, stuck in my gob, sliding slowly down my throat like a hunk of clay, a malted milk ball. My lousy year is lengthening into two, school's just started again, the Cocoplat has a boyfriend who leans his body into hers when the nuns have their backs turned. Her world is spiraling away from mine at warp speed, and my body is still refusing to accept the natural curse that unites all women, even nuns. I check every day, am still girl. Worry gnaws at my innards.

Well . . . no one would agree to . . . that, I say, trying to swallow the sugary lump of cement, fail, hacking up shards that scratch my throat on their way up and out.

Look at them, she says, pointing to Dot and Roxy with a hand composed of toothpicks and glue. Dot's face is sweating flame with effort. Roxanne's lips are a cool blue, her eyes filled with a relentless killer instinct she will one day turn on herself. *That's alive. Now look at me.*

I won't.

Look at me.

I won't.

I'm going to pull you by your hair, Philomena Grace. I swear to fucking God. Look at me.

I hate it when she uses my full name, but obey anyway. Her sweater is swallowing her neck, her scarf is swallowing her head, her pants are swallowing her legs, her shoes are wondrously normal.

Good-bye table good-bye mush good-bye old lady who says hush, she says.

She's been seeing southeastern Glenwood's most popular psychologist, Benny Chap, who has an office above Fanny Farmer. *You should explain this stuff to Benny Chap,* I say, hacking up some more malted milk shards.

Benny Chap would freak, she says, shading her eyes from a shaft of sun.

He would not, I say carefully.

She gives me a look. *You don't know him. I do know him. I dream I'm as thin as a sheet of paper.*

She *is* as thin as a sheet of paper, but I don't mention it. *Tell Benny Chap. He should definitely know about this paper . . . situation.*

I want to . . . but his head is so big compared to the rest of him . . . She sighs, stretches two broomsticks out in front of her, crossing them at the ankle.

What's his head . . . tell *Benny Chap about the paper thing, Bron. I'm no good to talk to; you've said so a million times yourself.*

Have you taken a good look at his skin? She picks up a dry leaf and crushes it.

What? I watch it fall through her fingers and onto the ground.

Have you or have you not taken a good look at his skin? She picks up another dry leaf and crushes it.

No. I have not. I watch it fall through her fingers and join the other one lying on the ground.

She rolls her eyes, flipping them back toward mine, leans in close. *Adolescent inflammatory acne . . . He's scarred for life and it's iffy waters for me, sis. Hit or miss. Sixty-forty. Come or go. Win or lose. Sad. That kind of thing. Mother sits in the waiting room reading* Woman's World *. . . Oh how did it go, baby, she says, like I've been to the dentist. Yesterday I said: Fuck off, bay-bee, that's how it went. And she didn't say one word. And do you know why, Philomena dear? Other than the obvious reasons, of course.* The tonal component of her debater's voice is starting to shift, her face moving in too close. I start looking around for June. I indicate with my eyes that I do not know why Mom is suddenly accepting the F word. Then I sigh. Then I shrug. Then I concentrate all my energy into pulling June from wherever she is to here, where she isn't.

Because she knows I'm dead, stupid. *Who gives a flying fart about a dead man's vocabulary? A dead man can say whatever he wants to whomever he wants. Carte blanche, if you will. But it's a sad, useless freedom.*

She looks at me, the debater in her singing in triumph.

My mind is having difficulty churning out some sentences that don't have a *dead* in them.

She says: *Duhhhh* and laughs, suddenly light, putting one of her birdy fingers into the bag and pulling out a malted milk ball.

Dr. Bob's calculating my life exactly like he calculates how much fuel it will take to get to Florida. Old Chapologist knows. I saw him know it just like he knows no more hair will grow no matter how nice he is to his head . . . And, Dad, the poor dear . . . I'm not so sure about you, though. Does she or doesn't she? Suspense, suspense. She slips the malted milk ball into her mouth. *These taste like Styrofoam covered in wax.*

She has no eyelashes, which makes her eyes seem eggy.

I try to pull Dot and Roxy over with my stare; there's a little me inside each eyeball, jumping and waving like people at the scene of a bad accident. But their game is turning ugly. Dot's pants have fallen to reveal a skinny ass sitting in a pair of skinny underwear; Roxanne's hair is dripping with mean sweat. My mind turns to song under duress: *You've got to accentuate the positive, eliminate the negative. . . .* Song takes over, blending in with parts of Coach Stan's speeches. I'm the worst debater in the family next to Dot, who's erasing herself with goodness.

Malted milk balls are good, I say. *Just suck off the chocolate, then let that center thing melt.*

Look at me, she says.

I try.

Both your goddamn eyes, fucker. Look at what I've become. I listen to people talk about life and I have nothing to say. Looking at me makes people sick. Their eyes play Ping-Pong with everything in the room except me. Ping ping ping ping PONG ping ping ping PONG. You know what's making them so uncomfortable? My eventual demise, darling. They feel bad about it, but the snow must continue to fall. My sun went out and they felt it. And it is rather sad as I haven't done anything yet. Do you understand? Practically nothing.

June has recently shown her how to tie a scarf so that it falls flat and smooth around her head. The one today is pale blue with big tan roses.

Don't you ever wonder if your brain's making this all up? I say, defying direct orders.

Making what all up? Making what all up? She's so mad she's spitting. *You? This wonderful chair? These ugly shoes? Malted fucking milk balls? That stupid cloud? Just what am I making up?*

All that stuff you're so sure's going to happen, I say carefully. *Like why should your brain know more than anyone else's brain? I don't think it works that way,* I say carefully. *And the future is . . . the future is a . . . vast . . .*

My brain, wonder woman, knows what it knows. She's not mad anymore, just annoyed. *And I know what I know, asshole, and I'm fucking sick to death of people pretending they don't know it too. You can lie to yourself, but don't lie to me.*

I get red in the face. It's genetic; Leonard gets red in the face too. Every time I visualize Bron getting well, the same image drifts to the surface of my mind: her in a box in a sparkly sweater with gray makeup on her face. Super dead.

Don't sweat it, wampum woman, she says and laughs.

I find June sitting in a field of white tube socks in front of the TV. She's matching them with one eye while the other scans the screen. I interrupt. *Bron thinks she's dead.*

She looks up. *Did she use the word dead?*

Like a thousand times. . . . She said that everyone knew it, but that no one would say.

Leonard calls an emergency meeting while June whisks Bron to the library. Mom is standing behind her chair, leaning on it with both elbows. Leonard says: *Sit.* She says: *Thank you, no.* He sighs, tapping the table with a rolled-up newspaper, *tap tap tap tap.* Dot has changed into a dress, brushed her teeth, and wound her hair into two strict braids that sprout from her ears. I smell mint as she breathes my way. Roxanne is slouchy. I am slouchy with her.

This is going to be the difficult part of the healing process. Dr. Bob says she'll get worse before she'll get better. We mustn't be worried. And we certainly mustn't be worried in front of her. She's very sensitive . . . He looks at us, changes his mind, looks down at the table. *As you know.*

Mom says: *It's poison, it's poison, it's poison . . . they're pumping my baby full of more and more poison.* She leaves the room, has a thumping nervous breakdown up the stairs. Leonard continues to tap the table with the newspaper. He looks at us, *tap tap tap,* speaks softly: *That is exactly what I'd like to avoid.*

Without Gravity

Stan works his whistle. I follow sound, enjoying the ancient technique of destroying all human thought, plugging my ears with water, the pressure creating a pleasant vibratory hum. But sometimes Bron defies the ancient technique of destroying all human thought, walks across my darkened lids, and starts making noise. I stretch one arm up from its socket, stretch one arm out into air, slicing as deep as I can, pulling with all my force. Stan's voice is chanting now: *Moooovvvve it moooovvvve it moooovvvve it.* I follow the thin black line until it stops in a cross that indicates imminent wall. But sometimes the ancient technique of destroying all human thought relaxes me into nothingness and I forget about the imminent wall until I hit it.

Hey. She's standing over my bed wearing my striped knit cap and an Irish sweater. *I'm not responding. That's the news. I'm steadfast in my resistance. Can you believe it? Another minuscule mystery in a vast sea of . . . are you listening to me?*

It's between very early in the morning and horribly late at night. The moon is low, spilling a yellow-gray light through a vertical shaft of open curtain. She'd been lying in bed all day thinking with her eyes shut. Now she's awake, standing like a ghost in the middle of the room.

I'm half-asleep. *Yes, yeah, I am, and quit always asking me that; my ears work.*

She's energized by the moon. *Well, quit always not looking at me when I'm talking to you. It aggravates me when I can't tell what you're thinking.*

My eyes are adjusting to her form. *Like you can tell what I'm thinking.*

She's whacking a leather belt against a skinny thigh. *I can even tell what you're not thinking.*

I look at the belt. *What am I not thinking now then?*

She throws the belt on the floor, turns back to her bed, lies down on her side with her face to the wall, not bothering to reply.

There are pictures of her winning state debater three years in a row. She's standing in front of the Gold Cup; first in braids and triple-striped pants, then in a high ponytail with a red ribbon, smiling with big lips and no visible teeth, then in her navy suit, her long blond hair pulled up into a knot and stabbed with two chopsticks. Her Uganda triumph. She must have been talking when they snapped the last picture; you can see her molars, followed by a dark tunnel of throat.

When is all this going to stop? I ask my mother the next day.

She's writing out checks with a frown on her face. *Soon.*

I watch her hand slash out signature. *You said that before.*

She looks up. *Soon; I said soon. Go do something.*

I run water, brush my teeth, fill up the sink, stick my face in with both eyes open. Afterward, my eyes are cooler, my breath is minty, my hair unattractive, my vision impaired.

Manny moves his bed from the armchair in the kitchen to the foot of Bron's bed. When she's home, he follows her. When she's at her appointments, he lies waiting for her, head on the ground, ears alert. When she becomes difficult to approach, he lies down with her and doesn't make a sound, sometimes for hours. We watch him walk into the kitchen, eat, stretch, lap up some water, look up at us, smile, shake his head, nod, then go back to lie with Bronwyn, who's thinking with her eyes shut.

June says: *That dog is the truest dog I'll ever know.*

When I ask Bron what she did all day, she says: *I was thinking with my eyes shut.* Every day the same thing: *You can talk to me; I'm not asleep. I'm just thinking with my eyes shut.* But sometimes she is asleep and I'm talking to Manny, who looks back without blinking, his pond eyes shining from the inside out.

Manny has difficulty finding solutions to practical problems and does not recognize people he knows by heart if they have something on their heads. I tried to cure him by putting a hat on in front of him, but the minute it was on my head he no longer recognized me and started barking and snarling and backing away, foaming in fear even as I dog-talked in my familiar dog-talking voice: *It's me, my man; it's just me, me, me.* His fear can be measured in degrees; he runs away from anyone in a fedora, cowboy hat, baseball cap, straw hat, helmet. He barks and snarls at berets, wool caps, large sunglasses. He will accept scarves and, later, Leonard's scary beard, but we have to lock him in the basement for Halloween.

I walk into the room and Manny reacts, stirring Bron. *He's just protecting me; he knows. Death is animal,* she says without opening her eyes. I hate it when she does things like this, leaving me with nothing to say back, nothing that won't sit in the air like a piece-of-shit lie. I just stand in the doorway, my backpack on my shoulder, my hair melting onto my face, hungry, my wool cap in my hands.

I have the dreaded Atrocious—a pesky traditional nun—for homeroom, which means I have to make sure my socks are even, my shirt tucked in, my tie flat, my ears clean, my hair neat, my prayers said, my homework complete. This morning I watched her remove eyeliner from Tanya Slaughter's eyelids with her own spit. But spring is coming, so I think of summer. I make a list: *fins, Carmex, maxi pads, Mountain Dew, sports bra, flip-flops.* I bury my face in Manny's neck. He stinks like shrimp.

I create a simple routine I follow like a map. I ride my bike to school, then listen without saying much for six hours. Kids animate the halls with urgent discussion between classes; drama reaches its peak during lunch. I observe, do not partake. Bron's ex-friends' little sisters and brothers avoid me. Their faces deflate if I catch them smiling. After school, June picks me up, throws me a sack with two apples, a chocolate crunch protein bar, a slice of corn bread dripping with honey, and says: *Eat.* I get to the Quack, jumping out of the car fast with a *Thanks* she doesn't wait around to hear. The air is good; college kids are walking around with backpacks on. I put my backpack on too, blending in, making my way to the locker room, which smells like bleach, rubber-soled shoe, talc, shampoo, burning hair, dried blood, bananas. Stan is standing on deck, a baseball hat on his head, a sheen of sweat lighting his face. He's all business, grinds his voice down, shouting: *Come on come on come on come on let's go let's go let's go let's go.* I swim myself into a trance, make fun of anyone more than five pounds overweight in the locker room, then Lilly and I wait for Mrs. Cocoplat, whom she refers to as *Aleta.*

When Bron's in the hospital, Mrs. Cocoplat drops me off at Glenwood Memorial on her way home. I drink a Gatorade and talk about school. When Lilly and I were organizing vaginal areas into subgroups, she placed Aleta's in Category Four: *Rip Van Winkle.* Mrs. Cocoplat lets me out in front of the automatic doors. The hospital reception lady looks up from her magazine and waves. The elevator is as large as a horse's stall. Nurses nod. I nod back. They've sedated her. Mom is somewhere else demanding answers. There is a chair next to the bed. I sit on it and stare at things. Her slippers, pink velour with Vichy checkered bows, brand-new with plastic grip bottoms. I'd been jealous of them, wanted the same, now do not. Her cello is lying in its case in the corner, her music stand folded up beside it. Her backpack remains zipped. I unzip it, rummage, find *Seventeen: The Beauty Issue,* *Time* magazine for debate, a lifetime reading list the Superior Sister Fergus handed out at the end of World Ethics.

Her eyes open for a second, focus. *I know exactly what you're doing,* she says. Her eyes close, but now she's smiling like a creepy cat. My heart sinks. It's dark already, the darkness humming with the sound of clinking needles on metal trays, water running, people complaining in murmurs and bursts. Someone's TV says: *I can name that tune in four notes, Bob.*

The nuns say that church bells are the voice of man calling for the voice of God. God is called *thoing thoing thoing thoing.* The voice of God is occupied, but the occasional ambulance answers with a shriek. I stand by the window, watching what's left of the sun sink in the sky. I try to swallow out hospital taste, my tongue sitting in the middle of my mouth, dry and useless, as Bron dozes. I jump every time I hear a siren.

Something freak you out at the pool? I've woken her up.

No, no, I'm good, I lie.

You look like crap, she says, acknowledging the lie.

Thanks. I'd cut some bangs to look different and am living to regret it.

I'm just saying . . . Mom says you're racing like crazy now. Eyes close.

Yeah, yeah. I wish Mom would shut up.

She drifts in and out, jerking awake again if I make big noise.

Quit fucking jumping around! I command myself internally. I concentrate hard on the eventual siren, imagine it tearing through the air, but the harder I try to remain calm, the more intense the startle. This is an early warning sign of a weak constitution, but I don't know anything about early warning signs or weak constitutions; all I know is I can't get my heart to stop thumping, which makes me so antsy I have to leave the room. I breathe better wandering the corridors, slipping past the nurses chatting behind their oval domes, candy stripers pushing half-full carts. I lose track of time; an hour gets confused with fifteen minutes and sometimes, when I get back, she's wide awake with a dinner tray she doesn't pay attention to sitting in front of her and it's already time to go.

Where in the hell have you been? Mom's been looking for you everywhere. She's too tired to enjoy the drama.

Just looking around. You want something for tomorrow?

Bring the checker set, will you? Maybe Battleship . . . we haven't played that in a while.

When Mom appears, she won't look at me. We ride the elevator down four floors in a crackling, electric silence. She lets it out when we're in the car. I'm not exactly frightened, but I'm not comfortable, hanging on tight to the strap above the door as she pushes down hard on the gas.

You'd think that you'd spend some time with your poor sister who . . . who . . . who's just waiting to have a little taste of the world outside and what do you do? Wander the halls *for over an hour.*

People are starting to honk. *She was asleep.*

She looks at me with narrow red eyes. *She slips in and out.*

I am bitten by the pointy teeth of shame. *Her eyes were closed. Okay? It got . . . I got antsy.*

Her face collapses and she starts clutching at the wheel, speeding an inch away from parked cars. *Tough titty for you. Antsy. Antsy. Antsy. Antsy. Antsy. Antsy. She gets antsy. She got antsy. Tough titty. Do you hear me?* She leans over, fangs my arm, and the car jerks to the side. When I pull my arm away, she slaps the side of my head and the car jerks to the side again.

They join forces. Leonard points to a chair and has me sit down, his arm around Mom's sad waist, listing hospital rules that involve consistent sitting, homework completing, magazine reviewing, water from the bathroom getting. He raises his voice, grows stern, chopping the palm of one open hand with the other: *No out the door going. No hall lurking. No disappearing.*

I sit in her room consistently. I go into her bathroom and look at myself in the mirror to see if the hospital has done something to my face. Nothing major, but my lips look blue. I sit on the toilet and stare at the gray and black diamonds that repeat themselves on the floor—*gray, black, gray, black, gray, black*—until Tanya Slaughter appears in my mind. She's sitting on her ten-speed staring me down with narrow navy eyes. Kelly Hill and her probably no longer bald vagina are standing behind her, smiling a small smile that does not reach her eyes. The Cocoplat is standing behind me, hands on her hips, but she's shaking inside; like all mostly nonviolent people, she is hating the idea of being hit. I try to make peace by being universal.

I spread my arms, encompassing their bikes, Holy Name, the sky, the world. *Listen, Tanya, there's no reason . . . for . . . you to get so upset over . . . these little . . .*

Tanya Slaughter looks at me with *I don't give a shit* eyes, gets off her bike. *I heard,* she says.

I'm stumped. I can't think of anything we've done to Tanya recently except for the PIZZA FACE we'd written on her locker when she'd had that bad breakout. But that was months ago.

I take a quick look at the Cocoplat; she's puzzled too but playing it cool. *What's up, Tanya?*

Tanya isn't going for it. *You know what . . .*

She's a short, burly Catholic with bandy legs and a lovely, sour face. I don't know what's going on but we're probably going to get punched. This must be the Cocoplat's doing, but I can't look at her in case I laugh. Slaughter pushes me out of the way, grabs the Cocoplat by the throat and squeezes, giving her time to turn red and squirm. She rips Lilly's white blouse in half with one of her meathook hands, revealing a thick white bra with extra-sturdy straps.

I know what's what and who's who, cunt chip, she says, spitting in rage. Kelly Hill flips me the bird, two hairsprayed wings sprouting from either side of her head, and I watch them ride away into two specks of metal that disappear into the sun.

Lilly is holding her neck, where four welts are forming, her eyes welling. She tucks what's left of her shirt back into her skirt, buttoning up her sweater. She's always been good at controlling her voice. *What in the hell was that about?*

The list of possibilities remains vague. *Maybe the pizza face . . . I don't know. You might have been set up. That Kelly Hill hates your guts.*

She rubs her neck, clears her throat. *Where'd she get the cunt chip?*

I'm still surprised at the turn events have taken. *I don't know.*

It's good. Her red lids are almost spilling.

I try to make her feel better by averting my eyes. *Are you kidding? It's better than good; it's great.*

What are you doing in there? Bron's awake and shouting.

I jump. *Nothing.*

Come here.

She's quiet for a minute, studying me, then she changes her mind and looks out the window. I watch her struggle, watch the words escape. *Do people ask about me?*

I look out the window with her. *Like everyone.*

She looks at me. *Like who?*

I still look out the window. *Ummmm, Emmett, that cello guy. And Mandy asked about you yesterday and Troy wanted to know when you were coming back. Joy asked if you wanted some more music and Augusta said she was going to stop by tomorrow. Lauren said tell your sister I said Hi and that Joeanna chick with the big mouth said Hi and Mazie said Hi and Maxwell Grant said Where's your hot sister?*

She's still looking at me. *Hot.*

The window holds a square of glass in each eye. *You don't look so bad.*

She doesn't care about the window, but looks anyway. *Depends on how you define bad.*

The window darkens. *Don't start debater stuff.*

She's looking at me again. *Then we'd get nowhere.*

The window sits still, boring a hole in the flat sky. *Why are you so mean to me all the time?*

She's looking at me harder. *Why do you think? I'd be interested in hearing your theory. Go on.*

There's a jet up there. I can't see it, but it leaves a big trail. *Shut up.*

She's looking at me harder. *You shut up.*

The trail is dissipating into blue. The window watches poker-faced. *I will.*

She's decided to examine her hand. *You never say anything anyway . . . I don't think I've ever heard you say one real thing.*

I look at her. *Shut up.*

She's looking through her hand as though it were transparent. *It squeaks.*

Come on, Bron . . . please. Things are gurgling inside.

She's looking through her hand as if it were diamond. *Not one real thing. In all these years.*

I can't take it anymore. *I never had my period.*

She drops her hand. *What?*

I never had my period, I repeat, exploding.

What? She's so quiet now, I can barely hear her voice.

I lied. Okay? I lied. I'm not . . . I'm still . . . I lied. I'm not . . . There's something seriously wrong . . . My convulsions are serious and steady, rhythmic and pure.

She grabs my hand and pulls me toward her. *You poor retard; it's okay, it's okay. Listen to me . . . Listen . . . Stop crying and listen. There's nothing wrong with you. Some people don't get it until later. Stop crying, Boo, Jesus . . . listen, listen. Don't worry, you've been . . . you've been . . . you poor little . . .* Then she detonates. I feel her heart beating against her rib cage like a slim-hinged bird flapping at a closed window, her body a sack of burning sticks. Our breath mingles out into whimpers that quiet as the window lets go of the sun and watches it fall. Then we both calm down and play checkers without cheating.

She knows things. *Some people don't get it until they're eighteen. It's rare, but it definitely happens.*

Once, when I get there Sister Fergus is with her, standing by her bed, leaning in close. Bron nods *yes,* shakes her head *no,* nods *yes* again. Fergus stands up, puts a hand on her forehead, blesses her: *In the name of the Father, the Son, the Holy Ghost.*

This makes me suspicious. I interrogate my mother later while she's standing at her sink.

What was Fergus doing in Bron's room?

She's wiping a cotton ball carefully around one eye. *Visiting.*

Her eye becomes naked, smaller. *Fergus doesn't visit . . .*

She puts lotion on another cotton ball and starts attacking the other eye. *I'm sure Sister Fergus wanted to talk to your sister about her education.*

Now she has two small eyes surrounded with rings of real-colored skin. *Bron said she doesn't want to think about school.*

Sister Fergus has convinced her to start. She's massaging cream into her face, is becoming uglier by the second.

She blessed her, I say.

Her fingers stop swirling. *Sister Fergus did not bless her.*

I look at myself in her mirror, wondering if I look as bad as she does. I don't, but I'm so tall I'm sloping sideways like a huge mountain. I'm not going to back down. *I know what I saw.*

Hark How the Bells

The wind was high last night, pulling flakes of snow into crazy patterns as they fell. I stared at them from my pillow a long time before I fell asleep because I know. I woke up early this morning anyway because I know. Outside the sun's burning off the white snow because it doesn't. I stand in the kitchen squeezing half of a grapefruit hard over an empty glass, watching a car snake its way down the driveway, but I ignore it because I know perfectly well what's sitting inside. Mom and Leonard walk into the kitchen. Leonard is holding himself still like a drunk who doesn't want to be discovered. Someone let the air out of Mom's face.

I don't say: *I know.* Instead I shout: *I couldn't find the plastic juicer thing.*

Mom puts a bag I won't look at down on the table and says: *She's gone,* then has a new type of nervous breakdown that involves long moments spent catching her breath. I look at my father, who takes the option of not looking back. He's standing at the sink looking at all the snow that has accumulated in the bird feeder overnight.

The only other dead person I know is Kent the dead sledder. He'd run his sled out into the street on a busy Saturday. He had red hair and sloping teeth, chased us on our way home from school, vaguely threatening with a budding pre-masculine violence that was erased from the universal mind once he was dead. At first he was *poor eleven-year-old Kent,* then he was *Kent the dead boy,* then he was *Kent the dead sledder,* then he was *the dead sledding kid,* then his parents moved and he was *the boy who didn't listen* until they built a fence that protected the hills from the highway and he disappeared into the air forever like a shiny bubble that had been popped.

Leonard turns toward me, says: *Let your sisters get some sleep while they can,* then disappears as Mom falls up the stairs. My feet carry me around the house from one room to the next, my brain conjuring things. It's darkly unpleasant everywhere I go, but I keep going back, hoping. I feel the immense power of the dead, as if someone's flipped a switch and now I can see what's been making the shadows. I can hear Bron saying things to me in a high-tech debater voice and I can smell her hair conditioner and that lemon stuff she sprayed herself with when she wanted to make an impression. I don't know what to do; my insides feel thick and dark and muddy like hollows.

Bron says: *I'm dead now, can you believe it? Look at my bed; it looks dead too, don't you think? Like it died too, can you believe it? I knew I was never going to go to Columbia and I was right.*

I say: *No, no. I can't believe it. I thought I did, but that wasn't real.*

And she says: *Me too! Exactly! You don't believe it until it happens. The rest is just projected thought.*

I leave, walk around the house passing rooms I do not enter, until I find a spot on the floor behind the piano. Manny walks into the room, looks around, heads for me. He puts his face in my face, shiny eyes pooling. He puts a dirty paw on my lap, shiny mouth drooling. I rub the tangled fur and claws, caress the gnarly patches he's ground in with use. He starts breathing deeply, becomes quiet and calm.

I hear them getting up, but stay where I am. I hear them wandering into the kitchen, but stay where I am. I hear cries and whimpers as Manny pricks up his ears and is gone. I am aware of the horribleness of my person.

The nuns show up, the station wagon with five of them in it, one of them for one of us. I always get Aloysius. Leonard is in and out all day long, walking round and round as though everything were *extremely urgent* and it would be greatly upsetting should he be stopped. We stay away. Aloysius wears tortoiseshell glasses that take up half her face. She has a twitch; her left eyebrow trembles up, pulling one of her ears and one side of her glasses up while the other half of her face falls. I get irritated until she pulls out a package of salted caramels from her pockets and we eat them. I suck on mine; she chews on hers.

We lie on our beds for three days, bolted down by invisible bolts. Dot and Roxanne visit me. Then I visit them. We look out the window at the zillion flakes of individual snow heading slowly toward the ground as casseroles arrive from all four corners of Glenwood and Leonard moves so fast all we see is a blur. On the third morning, Leonard knocks on the door, walks in, nods at us, says: *Good morning, girls,* opens her closet, pulls out a pair of good jeans, her nicest sweater, makes to leave, pauses, looks at me, requests a pair of socks. I won't open her drawer, so I open mine, give him a pair of the light blue anklets Lilly stole at Woolworth's, and he thanks me and leaves.

The drive to the church passes in silence. Mom is sheathed in black, bent in two, her chin to her chest, her elbows to her knees, her body curling over Bron's winter coat. Father Tim meets us at the door, his white face covered in the pink dots of the closely shaved. Fergus and Augusta appear, speaking in the warm, rhythmic tones of waves rolling in ocean, pry Mom's fingers from Bron's coat, draping it gently over the pew. They escort Leonard and Mom to the secret room behind the pulpit, and all is quiet. I sit in the front pew next to Roxanne and Dot. We wait. People file in, then settle, breathing softly in and out, in and out, in cadence, their souls smothered in skin. I won't look at the candles, the flowers, the pulpit, the box. I want to amass everyone and everything, the entire church, gather it together, knead it with both hands.

Bron's still talking. *And my coat, my coat looks dead too. When I was looking at it this morning it was like someone smothered it. I can't believe I never noticed that damn coat.*

I answer her in my head, telepathically, get the coat twirling around with no one inside, which means: *I agree with you. That coat looked okay before, but look at it now.*

Both Fathers officiate. Father Tim mentions the cello playing, the French club, the promising future.

Father Tod speaks about peace, lambs, golden rays, abundance, the pure of heart, dust, dirt, earth, mud, sun, God, angels, war, tragedy, sorrow, Christmas, faith, hope, and the endless foreverness of time that exists for the most superior pure kind of beings who confess their sins, know true atonement. Then he sits down and looks stern.

Father Tim lights candles, drinks wine, chanting Latin, his Adam's apple sinking down then lifting up, swooping his robes around the place with a *whoosh,* a sincere marbly owl. He is one of those priests who are never bored. He concentrates hard and wakes people up with a modulating voice, unlike Father Tod, who mumbles, frowns, sighs when he loses his place.

I make my eyes into two fat O's and aim them at Roxanne, who looks back. *What?*

My brows answer back, puzzled. *Can't you see?*

The Glenwood Junior cello players are present; sitting behind cellos with their knees splayed, dressed up in different shades of dark, aligned like the smudge of a hand on a window. The cello tune they choose turns out to be brain-blastingly hollow. Bron usually sat next to the oily boy with the short pants. She called him *oily boy* but I know his name is James.

Mother pinches my arm hard with her fangs and I put my face forward. I am wearing my dressy dress from the year before, but it's too tight and my neck is sticking out of it like a giraffe's, my movements physically restricted by cloth, so when people hug me, I jolt like Frankenstein. I explain: *My dress is too tight* and they look at me as though I were speaking Chinese, so I stop.

Sister Joy plays the organ. The sound reverberates along my spine. Hopeful angels glide up toward God's pearly feet. Up and up and up they go, zooming like gliders in an air without glitch. Clouds thin into wisps, disappear into nothing. Time ticks metallic ticks, chalice clinks on marble, nail from flesh cuts through wood, cello string taut under padded thumb.

Bron's class is back for Christmas vacation, weeping friends and enemies alike, sitting together with their heads bowed, their parents behind them in Christmas scarves, ties, earrings, and shawls. Leonard's team is here; the bearded doctoral candidates I've always seen in jeans and flannel, dressed up in corduroy and tweed. They clear their throats and do things with their eyes that involve shifting, rolling, squinting, the long unnatural blink. Astronomer Gerald pinches the bridge of his nose with his thumb and index finger, squeezing both of his eyes shut. I watch him until my mother's fangs bite into my arm like a dog.

Dr. Bob is sitting behind us with a dry-eyed Linda, the nice nurse, and the uncontrollably weeping Sheila, the awful one.

Leonard looks like someone folded him up and seated him with strict orders: *Don't move.* Dot follows the ceremony by heart with her lips. She feels me looking. Her face seizes; her look is tender and damaged, suffering and sad. My dress is crushing my rib cage, pulling tight at my armpits, cutting off the circulation that leads to my brain. *Quit looking at me with those goddamn cow eyes,* I clench, and she turns her face away.

Roxanne disappears into Roxanne. I close my eyes and she surges out of the darkness swinging one fist. She has a fixed steady stare that waters readily into blank, says: *You can't make me go up there* to no one in particular. One of Leonard's hands tells her to do as she likes.

My legs straighten; my feet start to move. Bron's face has been emptied like a puppet without hand. I genuflect, make a sign of the cross and, for the first time in my life, a good poem: *O empty God You Vast Wastrel O warty moon O fritter.* The French say *vide* like *weed* with a v. Her turtleneck gleams with a million silver sparkles. I look at her face and something snaps into place and clarifies; it's factual, hideous, mathematic, luminous.

The Dolphins are five pews behind with Coach Stan and his wife, Emily. They try to catch me urgently with their eyes, but I am uncatchable and will remain that way until I get caught.

The incense holder swings from Father Tim's skinny hands, puffing clouds of frankincense and cinnabar. My eyes wizen into squint. My throat constricts. I want out.

Mom has a series of nervous breakdowns, one right after the other. They make her eyes fade into her head and her hand veins stand out. She wears an unfortunate hat I've never seen before with a veil she pulls down, which turns the face I know into the face I don't.

We are seated under the Stations of the Cross. I'm sitting under . . . *and Jesus fell hard for the third time that day.* He's struggling on the ground, wounded and gentle, but determined and strong, his face as white as milk.

Everyone thinks the funeral lovely. They shake Leonard's hand and peer through Mom's veil a moment before looking away. I stand behind them like a lurking tin hulk, breathing shallowly in my tight dress.

The ride to the cemetery is silent. Some guy is pulling his dog on a walk. It begins to snow, the invisible wet kind you can't see. Father

Timothy's cheeks turn pink; his fine hair stratifies. He looks like a kid dressed up as a priest. Faces stall like old cars. It's cold. I look at the tip of Leonard's shoes, black with black stitching. I study the middle of Leonard's shoes, black with black shoelace. I study the back of Leonard's shoes, black with black heel. I find an edge of sock, black. Pants, black. Jacket, black; shirt cuffs a bright, blinding white. My feet follow his blackness, thus I am absorbed when we leave her there in the cold dirt, stiff hands folded up the way dead people are supposed to sleep.

Eventually everyone freezes up; freezes in different ways, at different times, for different reasons. Some people live through war, then freeze in a checkout lane that lasts one minute too long; some people freeze when they see themselves for the first time and thaw only when they're dying; some people freeze and don't know it, wonder what's wrong; some people freeze, thaw out, freeze again; some people freeze once and remain frozen forever. Being human is awful.

Only the nuns with the lowest voices can sing the O Loneliness song. *O*—low—*Lone*—low—*li*—lower—*ness*—lowest. It starts in the lower abdomen and travels up along the spine. It is a song whose strength reposes in repetition and simplicity—two words, four notes—nuns in dress black, wimpled and cowled, a cappella.

We Fall Because That's What We Do

I do not like having Leonard out of my sight. I sit next to him as he pretends to read. We do not speak. Sometimes we play checkers. Dot does not like having Leonard out of her sight either. She sits next to him as he pretends to read. We have mini-wars as to who will find him first. Problems arise over the checkerboard, but we have to be extremely careful; Leonard will send us away if it gets out of hand, or worse, say: *You two play* and leave.

Mother is making us go to mass every Sunday. She pinches our arms with slow, strong claws if we aren't ready on time. I have auditory hallucinations, hear moans and groans, *ohhh*s and *ahhhh*s, creepy humming. I confess, am absolved, confess again. I keep a stash of mint whips deep in the pockets of my coat just in case. I no longer care which priest I get in the confessional, don't bother checking the shoes before opening the small wooden door, folding myself in. Father Tod's wintery frog breath suffocates the dusty grill. I'm aggressive, confessing to his bunched-up black and gray shadow that I hate school, that I don't care, that I am a liar. He sternly ordains me to pray to Mary twenty times in one sitting. I won't, kneel into the pew, bow my head, think about random selfish things.

Before, Leonard would go to church to be a good sport or for special occasions, but those days are over. We come home from church to find him in the yard with a mucky shovel or in the garage banging things. We find him on the roof cleaning gutters, fixing light switches with pliers, pruning trees—an activity he particularly dislikes. Sometimes I can't find him in the regular places so I walk around calling *Dad . . . Dad . . . we're home*, crossing Dot, who's calling *Dad, Dad, we're home.*

Once, I find him standing at the bottom of the garden touching a tree as though it were covered in braille, but sometimes when we get home he's gone and there's a note on the counter: *I've gone for a fly.*

He seems all right, busy, his reading light casting sinister shadows down the hall deep into the night. But then the tears come. He cries when we say hello, cries standing in the bathroom door watching us brush our teeth, cries when we model our new jeans, cries at the dinner table. June and I try to figure out what dishes make him sad, but the tears go off indiscriminately no matter what she serves. When he cries, the food on our plates looks obscene, our chewing jaws animal. At first, he clutches us to his chest and weeps into our hair as we hold our breath, freezing into statue. Later, he becomes pragmatic about the tears, so that when they start, he ignores them, continues doing what he was doing— speaking, eating, shaving, looking out the window, watching a particularly difficult tennis match—with wet streaks down his face that leave trails he doesn't bother to wipe away with his sleeve.

My new thing is to eat dinner like breakfast, in a bowl with a spoon. No one cares. He cries in the car, cries watching TV commercials that aren't sad, cries when he listens to music designed for teenage tears, cries when it rains, cries looking out the window at the spiraling snow, cries at the rushing streams it leaves when the weather warms and the world thaws. He cries at the first sign of flower, sitting in his corduroy chair, the world folded up and left unread by his side, his head in one hand.

Besides the tears, his voice thickens and he grows a scraggly beard that winds its way around his mouth like a fence. Manny doesn't like it, makes a slight rumbling sound in his chest until Leonard kneels down, scratches that place behind his ears.

When Leonard cries, Mother gets up and goes. She walks around the house punched in at the solar plexus, grabbing on to things as though the world were lurching. She no longer comes down when Leonard comes home; her sad chair sits on its sad legs as I eat a bowl of white rice and beans with a large wooden spoon normally used for stirring. I follow him in spite of the tears, Dot trailing behind like a living shadow. I find him watching Johnny Carson talk to an old comic who is not funny. He's holding up a rubber fish with round holes in it screaming: *Holy mackerel* as no one in general America laughs except Leonard, who also happens to be crying. I try to think of something good to say. Nothing good comes. He turns, says: *Holy mackerel,* shaking his head. I walk upstairs to my room, where Bron's tightly made bed stares at me until I close my eyes.

We become schedule-oriented people. I awake at dawn, creep out of bed, down the stairs, into the kitchen, where I turn on the TV set and listen to it chatter. Leonard awakes at dawn, creeps out of bed, down the stairs, into the kitchen, to the window, where he studies the creepy sky. I look up from my bowl of cereal and there he is, a tall black smudge lit from within like a well-worn candle. Mother awakes at dawn, lies in bed waiting for the anesthesia to take hold. Roxanne awakes at eleven, lies in bed with her eyes closed until she can't take it anymore. Dot gets up at seven and kneels, praying for Bron's everlasting life, a healing love for our parents, the abolition of war, free school lunches for all—especially those kids in Africa—and, on a personal note, a good pair of boobs. Through the Infinite Mystery of Life, she will hit puberty a full year before I do, use one of my maxi pads without saying a word.

Wondrous and Wonderful, Amazing

Leonard is standing next to the toaster waiting for two pieces of Texas toast to pop. When they pop, he covers them with an inch of mole-colored apple butter, then slides one over to me. I watch his hands, thin-fingered and knobby.

Thanks. I'll wake up when my body hits the water.

He studies me, breathing dust. *I don't think the sparkles in that thin sweater will keep you warm on a day like today, chickpea.* I'm wearing a green sweater with multicolored sequins scattered throughout the yarn.

Not cold. My voice has acquired a sulky timbre.

He shrugs, puts three heaping tablespoons of sugar into his coffee, standing in front of the window stirring as the bird feeder he's just filled sways in the wind and behind it a few grayish streaks light the edges of sky.

We leave the house together. I ride my bike through the tight gray dawn that holds all of Glenwood in, following his car until he turns, watching as he puts one hand up to wave, and is gone. My bike knows the way; I pump hard with my legs and it carries me straight to the pool. I plunge, grasping water hand over hand, kicking the shit out of it with two of the most powerful feet, avoiding all Dolphin contact by keeping my eyes on the thin dark line that defines my lane, my purpose, my world. If a Dolphin gets in my way, I pass her, churning. It annoys me to have to breathe, so I don't. The locker room is subdued, wintry.

On the way home my muscles are so tired, to move them is to suffer. I coast downhill standing on pedals, clutching the handlebars with fingers that whiten, then ache. I ride up to our house. Satan has taken it in his red leather hand and it's tilting off-kilter. I stop. If you move an atom, somewhere else an atom stops and starts twisting in the opposite direction. Something like that has happened; things are exactly the same but twisting. This is the opposite of joy.

Things go slow-mo after a hard workout. Thoughts appear in single syllable images with dramatic punctuation.

I spot the dusty yellow Buick that says *nun* and I think *Fat!*

Dr. Bob's silver Suburban is sitting in the drive next to it, but the lights in Leonard's study are off. *Odd!*

The front door is emitting a sonorous brass echo, is now the color of worn brass bell. *Dark!*

I open it. The only sounds I hear are the old radiators sighing. I stop, watching the windows darken as the sun slumps slowly down.

I take the stairs one step at a time. Left or right. *Right!*

Fergus is sitting at the piano in the living room in casual Saturday gray. I'm drawn to her so my feet keep moving. Everything is in place—the glass table, the Greek urn, the green plants, those copper angels with the wide expansive wings—but twisting. I look at her. Neither one of us speaks.

Death sits on the couch in a dark velvet suit with deep purple plumage.

Fergus takes a deep breath, her low voice scratchy and comfortable: *Come here, Philomena.*

I take a hollow breath: *Why should I?* The sound that comes out of my mouth is unused and croaky.

She says: *Come over here and sit down next to me.*

I say: *I don't think so. Where's Mom?*

She says: *Your mother's fine.*

I say: *Where's Roxy?*

She says: *She's with June.*

I put my hand on my hips, my voice aggressive. *Where's Dot?*

With Sister Ruthie.

Where's Manny? I ask. *I'm quite surprised he let you in.*

He didn't, she says. *He's locked in the basement.*

He doesn't like headgear.

I gathered, she says, waiting.

Is Mom . . .

She's fine. Dr. Bob's with her. Sit down for a minute.

I do not want to sit down for a minute. *I don't think so,* I say, shifting from one foot to the other.

Take your coat off then, she says.

I want to see my father. I know.

There's been an accident. She stands, is one of the taller nuns.

I look out the window. It's still September. Trees are locking up their color for winter. A coldness slips under the door, a clear stillness that comes from those atmospheres where falling waters crystallize into flakes of pure snow. It creeps into the room as transparent as mist, sinking slowly into my bones. The coldness does not touch Fergus, but as the stillness gathers force, she stops watching me for a moment to lift her eyes heavenward. She puts one of her dry hands on my shoulder, says: *Would you like to sit down?* She's tired. I can see it in the set of her lids, the way the edges of her mouth fall down.

Thank you, no. I'll stand. And I brace myself, for I am strong.

Bye Now

And they come, a continuous, nutritious stream of nuns, whole families, both priests, various doctors, dentists, colleagues, neighbors, acquaintances, a couple of deans and their wives. They politely sip the coffee, tea, or apple juice that June supplies from the kitchen, cafeteria style. They mill, look at pictures, talk quietly about current events, mill again, asking neutral questions before disappearing into eternity. Sad good-byes fill the air along with the odor of perfume and cake. I lean into the piano feeling one hundred percent nothing. Occasionally a slash of feeling, a stab that slices through internal tissue, then nothing again. The nothing feels fine, neutral. My mind's humming: *That's it then, that's it then, that's it then, that's it then, that's it then.*

I don't feel unwell, but I don't sleep at night. I don't know what I do exactly, but it's definitely not sleep. My face is as blank as cardboard. *Funny.*

I wonder why Leonard doesn't say anything. I press my hands to my temple.

Nothing.

Bron says: *I can't find him. Isn't that strange? He's not here.*

I speak telepathically, using a form of echolocation that spells out words. *Something must have happened. Keep looking.*

Bron won't speak telepathically, preferring to roll her eyes and stick her face up toward a sun she just materialized out of thin air because she can.

We have a ceremony for him in the same room the bat symposiums were held. Dr. Bob reads from a piece of paper he holds in his hands, speaking so softly my ears strain, and I whisper: *Come on* out loud by accident. The paper shakes. The more it shakes, the more it shakes. I keep my eyes busy following patterns in wood. Mom's on a drug that makes her lean heavily into people, places, and things. Roxanne says: *I'm going to be sick,* goes outside, stands behind a soggy tree under a soggy sky until she gets drenched. Dot weeps and prays; it sucks the humidity from her skin and shows us what she would look like should she make it to eighty.

Ahmet Noorani cries, big oily tears that make his brown face shiny and soft and beautiful. He's leaning heavily on the heavy shoulders of his wife. *I can't get over it. I just can't believe it. It can't be true. Ohhh girls ohhh girls ohhhhhh.*

June sits next to me folding a program into tight little squares.

A production belt of still people in uncomfortable clothes rotates by, all of them saying the first thing that comes into their heads.

He was a very great man.

Such a nice guy.

A tragedy.

How can I help?

Ohhhhhhh girls.

How is your mother holding up?

You have to be strong.

You can be strong.

No one mentions God or any God-like associations, neither nuns nor priests, nor deans nor colleagues—not anyone. Some people take a deep breath, say *Well . . .* Get stuck. Back off. Other people open their arms, palms up, shake their head, let their eyes water then sprout, hugging us tightly, squeezing our shoulders hard, sighing, before disappearing forever.

When the interviewer from the FAA comes, a nice dandruffy guy, we, due to a common accord we never openly discuss, don't mention Leonard's tears. We explain that he'd been understandably sad, that we were all understandably sad, that life was splattered with understandably sad events. We say *sad* one hundred thousand million times because it starts to sound in the air and I try to think up another word but no other word comes to mind except *dandruff.*

Dot counteracts *sad* with *love,* says that we could feel his love for us, that how much he loved us was palpable. That he wouldn't let himself go because he loved us, would continue with diligence and honor because he loved us and loved the world, loved Rosy, his favorite bat, that Rosy herself was now sad, wouldn't eat her mayflies, her dragonflies, her stone flies, but that Rosy would recover one day because Leonard has great lab technicians and assistants whom he loved and trained well, that Leonard also loved Dr. Bob and chess; he loved chess. When she stops talking the air is dripping with love and eye contact has been smashed to smithereens.

I make my face seem perfectly normal, speak slowly in a semi-shout. *He had Plans.*

This sets Dot off. She has spots on her cheeks like a country clown. *That's right! He did! He did. He wanted to fly cross-country to some islands. The Bahamas or next to the Bahamas or past the Bahamas but not Cuba; isn't that so, Mena?*

I look at her spots. *No. Another place. But close to the Bahamas. The Indies, I think.*

The Indies. That's it, exactly it! She's hopping up and down in her chair. *He did, he did, he did have plans.*

Roxanne's in Beaver Park hidden behind the petting zoo bathing in the joys of hash from a bong.

We are waiting for Mother to come down. Last time I checked she was lying on her bed fully dressed with shoes.

Air is technically fluid. That Saturday while Leonard was flying through sky, I was flying through water. I glided for one moment, breaking the surface without sound, moving my arms, my legs like living propellers as he flew from Glenwood over the Smoky Hills following the Solomon River until it reached Mount Sunflower. He then veered off and headed home in a perfect figure eight. This is where we flew when we were going nowhere. I try to imagine what he was thinking behind the dark prescription glasses he reserved for flight, the gold ones that made him look mean. I see the clouds weave their way across the lenses, the sun in the middle, set, unmovable. Each second he remains gone, the more mysterious he becomes. From time to time he even seems a bit sinister—like a man with heavy secrets, impossible to know, a spy.

Everyone refers to it as the *horrible tragic accident* except Dr. Bob, who never says.

I'd followed Ahmet Noorani's progress. I saw the creation of an engine step-by-step—its metal gadgets, sockets, pistons. I'd watched as he hit things with the butt of a heavy wrench, *thump thump, That should do,* a droopy yellow cigarette dangling from his mouth.

I'm never going up with him and you can bet the farm on that, I'd said.

Shhhhhush, Leonard said.

Minds disconnect when they're doing familiar things. Maybe Leonard didn't see the ground coming until it was there.

He underlined things and circled words, had a small notebook the size of a deck of cards in his left pocket with the pen his father had given him when he got his doctorate. He never misplaced that pen; it went from one shirt to the next or sat on the ledge above his window waiting while he dressed. I never once saw him try to infiltrate a particularly long line or get something for nothing. People do that. He didn't.

The FAA found nothing wrong with what was left of the engines; the black box had been recuperated but held no clues; there was no weather-related phenomenon reported in the area. In his final report, Brian, the nice investigator, said there was a ninety-three percent chance of human error: The pilot was simply coming in too fast, got lost in a dive.

The house takes on shadows that hold. June moves in for a while, stays two years. Dot prays, standard memorized prayers, on her knees, like one of the porcelain figurines the nuns give especially good kids for Christmas. I watch, my eyes boring two holes in the back of her head. She prays by the book with ferocious repetition, but Manny is her true comfort; she holds him in her arms, using his fur as a living rosary.

Manny and I understand each other as only he and I can. I avoid him and he avoids me. But the atmosphere in the house weighs heavily on his soul and one day he jumps up for his bowl and dislocates his hip.

I tell the vet: *I can't fucking believe this.*

His eyes say: *Language, young lady.*

My eyes say: *Fuck off, vet man.*

I have to physically restrain Dot while they reset Manny's hip. She moans and weeps as the vet purses his lips, and his assistant grinds her teeth.

Roxanne starts hanging out with the hard-eyed Tanya. Gets rows and rows of C's. Sister Fergus calls Mother in for an important Catholic conference. Mother dresses up in a violet potato sack with a belt. I see her from homeroom. She takes baby steps, shielding her eyes from the blinding sun that exists in her mind. Atrocious yells: *Posture!* into my ear and it takes my heart a full five minutes to rev down.

Mother is preparing for a life in detention. June and I try to feed her things—soup from can, rice from blue box, omelet from egg—but her cheekbones still look like sledgehammers, and I can count the bones in the hands that grip tightly on to mine.

The important Catholic conference changes nothing. Old days curve into new days like hills without valleys. I ride home from school and make noise: doors slap, plates crack, shoes thump, the refrigerator trembles.

June hisses: *Be quiet for Christsakes, Mena, your mother's just fallen asleep. It's been a bad day.*

I'm in a bad mood too. *I didn't do anything.*

She's yelling like a lunatic, wild-eyed. *Quit yelling. Shut your trap.*

I'm not yelling, you're yelling, you ugly little freak. I was normal and without rage only moments before and now I'm filled with a burning horrible fury that takes all suppressed things and puts them smack in the center of my eyes: *Ugly bad teeth doom poor stuck forever fucker.*

Don't you look at me like that, Missy. I won't have it. She's holding on to my arms with nails she's chewed into weapons.

I don't want to be human anymore. I don't know what I want to be. Not this. I'd like to be something quieter, wider, harder surfaced, something that doesn't know. I close my eyes and the world goes blank. When I open them, she's out by the tree smoking one of those cigarettes that crystallize in your lungs when they kill you, her back to the house.

Dark Angel Laugh and Dance

I'm a sloppy-shouldered, small-breasted, strong-jawed, tall girl sitting next to an undistinguishable lump in the bed and studying my feet. My slippers are the fur-lined suede ones I got for Christmas one hundred thousand years ago. They're too small and have splotches on them from spilled things, but I don't care. I'm guarding Mom. I can't leave her alone under the creepy canopy of Dot's praying eyes. I'm afraid they'll drive her to the dramatic end. I've stopped swimming cold turkey, am watching Mom sleep, moving in close to make sure she's still breathing. When I'm not guarding her, I lie on a couch and watch the TV shows that make me laugh. I catch myself wondering how the TV people are when the television is dark, although I do realize they don't exist. Sometimes I watch the TV shows twice and laugh just as loudly twice. I'm universally unpopular; highly subtle avoidance techniques have been put into operation. I often find myself on my own.

I pop corn and chew as I look out the window at the swinging bird feeder no one bothers to refill. I'd have to take the ladder out of the garage and lean it against the house, climb up with a small sack of grain. My mind sends out urgent messages: *You should refill the feeder; go get the ladder!* which I ignore while making stacks of unusual pancakes I take the time to arrange in attractive shapes. When my mind isn't yelling, it busies itself with disinterested commentary.

The Cocoplat is uncomfortable being herself around me. When I strongly suggest she be normal again, she lies: *I am normal* with a sad smile pulling down hard on her face. Roxanne says we're under death quarantine, that people are afraid they'll die if they spend time with us, and although I know Roxanne is a crazy pothead, it seems true: death pulls everything down with it; we are the obvious proof. Father Tim looks at me insistently on Sunday mornings but says nothing. Coach Stan calls and tells me to come back to the Dolphins when I'm ready. Mother creaks around the house as I listen to the TV speak quietly to itself in a corner.

We lose all notion of time and are often late for school. I blame the slashing rain, the howling wind, the thin layers of sleet, and later, when the storms abate, I blame the sudden disturbing lack of weather; the flat skies, the flat sun, the flat air that contains a stillness that causes us all to sleep and sleep and sleep. Sister Trout, the office nun, listens, holding her mouth in a wide flat line, until we start always being late, standing vaguely in her doorway like thugs.

I do not explain that Mom does not care about school, sunshine, vocabulary, general nutrition, tight schedules, winter clothing, personal hygiene, poor grades, curfews, bedtime, the quality of air, scientific discovery, international politics, the famine in Africa, discussions about mental health. I do not explain that Roxanne needs to smoke a doobie the size of a spear before going to bed, that Dot's yelping in her sleep like an animal, that June's dating a guy who's up to no good.

Roxanne decides that according to her calculations, Mom is now three-fourths agoraphobic.

I'm watching some groom drop his bride on the ground as the TV cracks up. *She goes to the grocery store, the church, the library,* I say without moving my eyes from the TV set.

She opens the refrigerator and looks inside. *See? Nowhere else. Like ever.*

I don't look over. *She picked me up from school the other day.*

She doesn't look up. *Did she get out of the car?*

I look over. *No.*

She opens a cupboard as the TV laughs loudly. *See?*

Roxanne plants the seeds of worry in Dot's fertile garden. Dot runs upstairs shouting: *Mom, Mom, can you take me to get a haircut?*

Mom doesn't budge. *Have June do it.*

The need causes Dot's voice to rise. I turn up the volume. *June can't.*

Mom doesn't budge. *I can't either; I'm not feeling well.*

They devise scenarios to get her out of the house and shake things up, putting their heads together and knocking new ideas around. But Mom is always one step ahead.

Roxanne brings up the fact that I don't do anything.

I bring up the fact that doing something accomplishes nothing.

Dot says: *That's not the point, Philomena, and you know it.*

I only appreciate drama when it happens to fake people. Roxanne doesn't like drama unless she's creating it. Dot accepts drama as the weight she has to carry as naturally as her bones, but drama opens a third eye in my mother, who now sees the drama in all things. She hyperventilates in front of the open refrigerator with both hands clutching her throat; she hyperventilates on the highway, slowing the car down to five miles an hour on the part with rocks, blue-knuckled; she hyperventilates at night in a bed surrounded by books, spines open about her, anti-hyperventilation medication on standby.

The Encouraging Catholics stop by in twos and threes. They make their own tea and sit on the couch, knees together, legs pressed to the side. Mother gives herself illnesses through the power of suggestion: bronchitis, flu, sinusitis, insomnia, mysterious intestinal disorders, pulsing headaches. These things are discussed in loud whispers punctuated by frequent nervous breakdowns that require breathing into a brown paper bag.

The Encouraging Catholics leave. One of them stops by the door, opens her purse with a soft click, pulling out a mint she hands to me with an encouraging smile. June rinses their teacups and dries them by hand. I put the mint in my pocket, eat leftover cake. The TV keeps talking quietly to itself, sometimes it chuckles, sometimes it weeps. The brown paper bags are for my sandwiches.

The Suffering Catholics come in droves: widows, divorcées, mothers of the morons of Glenwood, the sick ones, the old maids, those who have memorized the schedule for the visiting days at the state prison. They converge in the living room, spilling out into the kitchen, lurk in the hallway, scanning the photos on the wall. They make pots of coffee, arrange cinnamon rolls in dripping layers that would make a nun sigh, settle in, sip their coffee, stretch their legs, and suffer, because nothing is as keen as the joy of suffering together when one has felt the emptiness of suffering alone. I watch them, first amazed, then bored. Mom tries to keep up, crashing quickly, bitten by a deep inertia, worse than before. I walk her up the stairs, taking the steps one by one, waiting for her to catch her breath on the landing. Dr. Bob stops by, has talks with her, has talks with us about her, then changes his mind in the middle and has talks with us about us.

I say: *It's okay, Dr. Bob. We're okay.*

Dot says: *We're okay.*

Roxanne doesn't say.

I don't like the Suffering Catholics, but they keep coming back. I frown at them when they ring the doorbell, step outside, putting my body in front of the door like a linebacker, say: *She's still asleep* in an aggressive tone while tapping my foot, my eyeballs staring pointedly at their cars. I smile encouragingly at the Encouraging Catholics on Sundays, but they seem to feel as though their job is done.

The Suffering Catholics soon tire of Mom's lack of participation and their visits trickle down. I fling myself on the couch in front of the TV set, relieved. I have no idea that I am experiencing the unnatural calm that heralds the arrival of the Dark Catholics.

They've lost husbands to alcohol and sons to speeding cars, overcome teenage pregnancies and adoption scenarios. They've been tried and tested and denied like Job, and like Job they are not going down. They easily push past me carrying sponge cakes, packages of herbal tea, essential oils, small figurines with creepy eyes said to represent the lesser-known saints. They go straight upstairs to my mother's door, rapping with tender knuckles, softly slipping in. When she's resting, they stand sentinel beside the windows, silently observing the naked trees outside. Sometimes they go into Leonard's office, touch one of his books, ask: *This was his?*

This annoys me. I have Roxanne flush the toilet with the clanky pipes just to watch them flutter and jump.

They take over, hovering in the kitchen with an arsenal of recipes to serve a person who won't eat. I supervise them. They ignore me.

It has to have no taste.

Preferably liquid.

Put some protein in it. We can crush some C.

That's a good idea. And oat. Oat has no flavor.

Here's some vanilla.

She won't eat that, I say. I'm just giving them the facts.

She can sip it through a straw.

Just make this for her and put it next to her bed.

She won't drink it, I say, just letting them know.

She will. You'll see. We'll make up a couple of batches and freeze them until June gets the hang of it.

She sips. Her hair becomes shiny, her nails take on a rosy hue, her eyeballs whiten; she gets a toasty look as if she spent the weekend in Florida. I call it grimlock.

June has a strange effect on the Dark Catholics. When she walks into the kitchen, her thin arms full of groceries, a pack of menthols hanging out of the back of her jeans, her hair a gorgeous, frizzy mess, they scatter, and my heart lurches with joy. When they show up, I have her paged at Wal-Mart, begging her to come home. She says *I'll be there in a minute, honey,* and sometimes she is. June relieves my mind. She understands my need for atmosphere, leaving the radio on all day, a small light in every room. She opens all windows, sometimes all doors, as the cool air sweeps through the house in streams, and all the curtains billow, lilting up into the air like kites. She understands my need for the cereals with dancing rabbits and 452 types of sugar, knows I like the zest and the color and the milk that turns pink. I sit in front of the TV watching Diana become Princess as June smokes a cigarette out by the tree. I wave. She holds her cigarette between her teeth and waves back, her face lost in a veil of minty smoke. I rip open a package of pie, one of those half-moon crescent things filled with shiny red stuff and pieces of exploded cherry skin but no cherry.

Dot appears in the doorway with an apple in her hand. *You can't eat that.*

I don't look up. *I beg to differ.*

She takes a bite, admonishing me. *You'll be sick; eat some vegetables or an egg or something.*

I sigh. *Where's Roxanne?*

She sighs back. *I don't know. Out, I guess.*

Days sink. When I open my eyes, a new one with the same face rises. Weeks roll into months punctuated by rain and heavy thunder until spring arrives and Mom wakes up before dawn one morning to find the mystic holograph of Mary the Bless'd Virgin and Mother of God floating at the foot of her bed. The general Dark Catholic consensus is that She was most likely messengered in to make Mom feel better about her awful, shitty life.

She was standing at the end of the bed not saying anything for the longest time. Then shook her head very slowly and looked sad and sweet . . . then after a while she motioned to me with her hands: Come, come, come. Mom's lying in bed in an ugly light blue housecoat with silver frog buttons, a gift from the Dark Catholic with the underbite. She's just washed her hair and it's starting to dry. The mystic holograph of Mary has made her both calm and deeply excited.

I'm standing by the window, sucking on a watermelon pop, my arms crossed over my chest. *Where do you . . .*

A flock of Dark Catholics turns toward me, murmurs: *Shhhhhhh . . .*

. . . I don't know. But I said no, no, no, no, not now of course; I have three children left. I can't just . . . says Mom, pausing to find the right word, *. . . vanish.*

I look at a herd of clouds trotting across the sky, pull the pop out of my mouth, say: *Was she floating?*

A flock of Dark Catholics turns toward me and mutters: *Shhhhh!*

No. She wasn't, says Mom, rubbing a silver frog's head with one finger.

I look at the bird feeder swaying in the wind, pull the pop out of my mouth, say: *Did she have a Middle Eastern accent?*

A flock of darkened Catholics turns toward me and hisses: *Shhhhh!*

No. She sounded normal, says Mom, taking a sip of chamomile tea.

I turn, keep the watermelon pop in my mouth, stare down the frog buttons. *You mean like us.*

Yes.

I look at the Dark Catholics, pull out my watermelon pop, say: *Well, then it wasn't the real one.*

They roll their hands into fists, fighting the natural human penchant for spiritual bloodshed, hissing *Shhhhhhhh!*

Of course it was, says Mom, looking around uneasily.

The Dark Catholic with the putty face grits her teeth, says: Real *angels don't sit in the* heavens *watching* real *people suffer in* hell and I realize with a pang of excitement that she hates my guts.

The one with the flabby neck tries to get rid of me. *Why don't you go downstairs and wait for Father Tim?*

I stare at her neck, take the easy way out. *Why don't* you *go wait downstairs for Father Tim?*

She cares more; I go. I take the stairs down two by two until I reach the bottom.

Climb Ev'ry Mountain

I'm staring out the window watching a storm brew during algebra class as Sister Nestor makes complicated mathematical phrases with letters and numbers, her chalk hitting the board like an angry woodpecker. She stops; the Trout's standing next to her, whispering into her ear. She hands her a dreaded yellow slip, then both of them look over at me. I feel a keen bite of dread as Nestor brings it to my desk and says: *Gather your books.*

Fergus is standing in front of the window in her office looking out at a sky that storm has divided perfectly in two. She looks like the Mother Superior in *The Sound of Music* but her wimple is short and dark blue and her skirt is knee length and not long like a nightgown and we aren't in Austria and I'm not funny like Maria with a hat and a guitar and an ugly dress although my skirt is very saggy and droopy and the pleats are not lying flat like they should because either the high sugar consumption is making me skinnier or I've grown taller again but don't know how much because I haven't been in to see Dr. Bob for my annual and no one is making me go.

Good memory requires she not ask me to sit, so she doesn't. Good memory also requires she not look me in the eye, so she doesn't. We watch one half of the sky try to take over the other.

Father Tim tells me you've stopped the swimming, she says, watching a branch of lightning shock a dark spot with yellow veins of energy.

Yes, I say, as the trees shiver in response.

Does that feel right? she asks, as a couple of birds swoop for shelter.

Nothing feels right, I say, turning toward her.

Yes. It wouldn't. She sighs. *You've had trouble. Difficulty. Eventually we all do. No one is spared. But you've had it now. You're young enough to let it fester. Festering begets sores. Sores beget misery and misery begets more of the same. You're going to need to hold on to something. Reading is good. Studies in general . . . Swimming. Why not? Choose something and hold on to it, young lady. If you continue wavering with lassitude, you risk stagnation, waking up one day, perhaps decades from now, filled with regret, remorse . . . Who knows? All that misplaced energy.* She sighs again. *I've seen it happen more than I've seen it not happen. Thou . . . No one other than you can give you what you need. Such is our lot.*

God obviously doesn't exist, I say with my eyes. *I feel better when I'm in the pool,* I say with my mouth.

Then swim. She smiles, and the sky cracks open like a black and purple egg.

Human people don't like facing the sad facts and nuns are just human people, I say with my eyes. *Yes, Sister,* I say with my mouth.

She studies me and I let her because I want her to see. She isn't wearing a wedding band. Some do.

Things can go either way; up or in, down or out. I am close to popping endless bowls of popcorn in a pair of ratty pajamas, observing pats of yellow butter as they melt into transparency over sufficient heat. I am close to lying on the couch and watching the sky birds fly by remembering when they used to land, close to watching the empty feeder sway in the wind, my heart pretending that life is this way for reasons I am too temporary to understand. I walk past windows revealing various wimple in phases of explanation, past maps of the round world flattened into two dimensions, past kid's stretched-out feet crossed at the ankle, past kid's leaning on single elbow, past kid's hair hanging over kid's face, past kid's eye glazed and shiny, listening and not, all in the midst of becoming. I look down at my gigantic feet—gray of lace, loose of sock, limber of ankle. My knees are moving rhythmically, my heart bleating in my chest like a simple toy. I kick the ground, squeaky rubber on cement breaking the hush of the empty corridor. *Swim.* Why not? At least I love it.

Father Tim is standing on deck in a V-neck cotton sweater sweating with a whistle around his neck that he's blowing so weakly I keep on going until he swooshes his hand in front of my face to make me stop. I'm out of shape, easily winded, breathing hard after an easy drill. My lower body drops into the water at an angle that is heavy to pull. A couple of tennis players glide past me with triumphant feet. I curse into water.

Father Tim is confident. *Well done, well, well done. That's good for today.*

He buys books—*Swimming Faster, Coaching Girls, True Speed*—reads about splits, yardage, form, technique. He has discussions with Coach Stan. *If you really want to double up, you can train with Coach Stan in the morning. I spoke with him and we can work it out.*

My strokes become tighter, my body begins to glide. I swim myself into serious hypnotic swim states, swirling into a vortex of internal calm. Swim joy. Swim Trinity. Serious hypnotic swim states are so good that once you start to experience them, they become necessary.

Coach Stan isn't sure what to do. He checks my stats, scratches his chin, warns: *You're coming in too fast; you could break a finger that way.*

The snows come and Mom occasionally braves the outside world to take me to practice. She looks at me as she drives, checking her bag for almost forgotten things, noticing new paint jobs on front doors, reading garage sale signs as if she cared, waving an *I'm still sad but have to continue for the children's sake* wave to people on the streets as our car veers across the center line before she lurches it back with a lurch that makes the tires squeal. I have to remind her. *The road, Mom; you're driving.* She never knows whose turn it is at stop signs, takes her foot off the gas, then jams it down again as other drivers raise their fists and swear. When there's ice, she skids sideways into things, and some of the more energetic witnesses call the police. The presence of the police sets off some secret bomb inside of her; her eyes sprout, her body shakes, her horrible story pouring out into the air while I silently observe the windshield, my face as smooth as stone.

The plains are filled with neighborly people who grow visibly quieter and steadier when confronted with someone of obviously vacillating character. The person under the police uniform is eventually disarmed, even the nastier ones with the neutral glares end up towing us out of the ditch, all of us: the lost husband, the lost daughter, in the dead winter, streetlights flickering on at five p.m., illuminating vast mounds of sullied snow into glittery shards of diamond.

Treating undiagnosed semi-agoraphobics in denial is a tricky business. She goes to church, driving with skewered, graveyard eyes. She makes it to the grocery store, where she buys the essentials, sometimes sweating, sometimes not. She comes home out of breath, leaving the bags on the countertop even if there's ice cream inside, gets into bed, giving the rest of her orders quietly from there. We are well provided for; there is no sense of the widowed urgency some of the darker Catholics have. June whips up spuds from a box; I drink Mountain Dew, chew pink gum with soft liquidy centers that explode in my mouth, watch TV.

Dot, Roxy, and I see Benny Chap on Wednesdays, thirty minutes apiece. He wants me to keep a dream journal, which accidentally brings out the liar in me.

I sit in my orange bucket chair and fabricate: *Nothing to report, Dr. Chap. I don't dream.*

He sits in his orange bucket chair and says: *What makes you say that?*

Just that morning Leonard flew across my mind held up by the seat of his pants by a flock of quarrelsome brown bats, his face dark and cavernous, long legs dangling.

There is nothing in my head when I wake up. I did what you told me; I lay there breathing and not moving for a long time. Nothing comes.

You're probably trying too hard, Philomena. It will come on its own. He's smiling his wide-open psychologist's smile, his poor skin covered with deep pallid craters. I smile back, the sad smile of a liar, but I enjoy basic smooth sailing and swim-fed exhaustion until Manny dies.

I wake up one morning to find him lying outside the front door as hard as a rock. I touch his fur and his fur is rock. I touch his nose and his nose is pebble. I drop onto the ground beside him to think, my insides swirling as I touch his poor fur. June didn't come home last night. I am alone. We need a man to bury the dog so I call Father Tim, waking Father Tod, who puts the receiver down so hard I jump. When Tim gets on the phone, I explain the situation and suggest aggressively that he bury the dog. When everyone wakes up they are surprised to find me sitting in the kitchen waiting patiently, both hands at my sides. I explain what has happened in the hushed voice of an in-church nun, and my calmness overtakes them too; they stare back at me patiently, both hands at their sides. At the burial out by the tree, I maintain the quiet until the quiet stops, and I find myself rolling around in some soggy leaves. My mother kneels beside me and I can tell by her kneecaps and the freckles sitting on the kneecaps that she does not know what to do. She has sad little hairs growing out of her kneecaps and kneecap wrinkles like the rings on trees, which carries me into a deeper nervous breakdown. She does something to my hair with her cold hands. This enrages me. I speak quietly: *Get your fangs off me,* in a possessed-by-the-devil voice. She immediately removes them and steps aside.

Dot gets down on her knees, eyes leaking, tries to explain some Dark Catholic/Buddhist emergency procedure. I don't listen, prefer watching Roxanne smoke openly in front of a tired Father Tim, who is leaning on a shovel with one green rubber boot on the metal part, ignoring her. I grab on to the tree, pull myself up, wipe thawed mud on my pants, say: *Give me that cigarette,* smoking it so hard I almost barf and eventually someone calls Dr. Bob, who comes over dressed in a brand-new gray sweat suit with a great gray hood. By the time he arrives, I'm on the ground again, calling for June, my face to the sky, watching the underside of the tree weaving above me like a living umbrella. Dr. Bob kneels down in the mud next to me, says things I do not listen to, giving me a shot I do not feel.

June arrives in her brown polyester uniform, her face zooming in so close to mine it floods my vision. *Poor little Manny,* I say. She clasps my big hands in her little bony ones, squeezes hard, and is strong. I look at her hands, small and worn, look at her face, folded in worn creases, her name floating in plastic on her pocket. *Poor, poor Manny.* She's murmuring things to me, her nails bitten down to nothing, surrounded by broken skin, jagged cuticles, edges stinging red with dried blood. I don't listen, just clasp her hands, feeling their heat radiate out into mine. When I think of Manny's fur, my mind recoils. When I think of Bron's voice warbling up the laundry chute, my mind cringes. When I think of Leonard's charred broken body, my mind bursts into flame. There is a whole new section of my self burning with magnetic repellent. I look June deep in the eyes; they're green with greener swirls, a shiny black center watching steadily from the middle: *What should I do?* I ask. She squeezes harder, does not reply. I remember reading something somewhere that spoke of the flashes of lucidity in life. How they come. How they illuminate. How lucidity emerges then, plain cold lucidity, born old like a crystal baby and then you know, and once you know, parts of you are over.

Sedation rolls into my body in a warm wave. I lean back into the scratchy bark of the tree, let June push the hair out of my eyes, and it slowly dawns on me in a yellow-gold way that the present is just a portal leading to a future where things will be better; all I have to do is make it there.

Press On

I dive into the pool with three swimsuits and my sneakers on and drag myself across like some guy in a muddy trench who doesn't want to die. The first wins are small. I ride them like little waves that disappear neatly into sand. One tidy win followed by another. Certain swimmers congratulate me while others sulk. I make a goal, beat the goal. I make another goal, beat the goal. The inside of my head gets big ideas; the outside remains the same. Almost everyone doesn't care. The world is sleepy and peaceful.

I think she broke a state record.

You think so?

Two hundred free.

When?

Two weeks ago. Then again yesterday.

Coach talk. I stand in third person and listen with both ears while keeping my eyes parked elsewhere.

Coach Stan is consulting Coach Coates of the Southeastern Clippers, leaders this year in a highly competitive second division. Everyone knows he was on Omaha Beach on D-day, where the waves were red with froth and his swimming and apnea skills saved him. He has one of those mouths with the thin hard lips like Sister Trout. He turns toward me; I straighten up.

All right, he says. *Warm up—I'll tell you when to swim full-on. When I say full-on I mean give it everything you've got. Got it?*

He coaches me on his own time Wednesday afternoons, is tough, expects rapid execution, secretly wishes I were a guy. The state meet is coming up and I easily qualify, but interest in female athletics has dwindled to a solid zero. Lilly Cocoplat has chemically straightened her curls and is hanging out at the track laughing at things she doesn't really find funny. Girls are wearing subtle brown eyeliner the nuns have difficulty detecting. Some ugly people stop being ugly and become cute people; some of the cute ones retire from cuteness forever.

Kids pair off; unusual kinships are formed. The halls fill with tension and drama as the nuns sigh and frown, smaller in their skirts and crosses, fully aware that the older we get, the more their power diminishes. We stop needing the nicknames, use their full titles both publicly and privately with a hint of compassion. *Poor old girls, poor dear sweet ones, poor fatty nuns.* Puberty eludes me; other than my size, nothing changes. Boys treat me exactly the way they've treated me my whole life: ignoring me and my gigantic height with masculine suspicion. I am flat, lanky, pimple free, have the type of light brown hair that does not inspire romance, am still a hidden girl.

National Velvet

My life is freer now that I'm sixteen and have a driver's license. Mom takes advantage of my newfound freedom and I've ended up doing the parts of her job she doesn't like, throwing gallons of bleach into shopping carts next to family-size boxes of cereals, mounds of apples, doughnut holes, bananas, ginger ale, milk, eggs, sliced turkey, powdered potatoes in a big red box. I make a big scene about going, but grocery stores relax me. I push my shopping cart in slow circles, idling up and down the aisles, hypnotized by creative packaging. Shopping carts with mothers attached pass mine with friendly feminine utterings. But they wish they hadn't seen me. And I wish I hadn't seen them wish they hadn't seen me. I wave *toodle dooo,* grabbing two giant pink boxes of maxi pads and throwing them in, shifting my eyes onward as if I'm in a hurry. As soon as they're out of sight, I slow down, pushing my shopping cart in slow circles, idling up and down the aisles.

Leonard's gone. Bron's got both arms crossed over her chest. Mom's in solitary confinement, doesn't wash her hair as often as she should, wears pajamas all day long. June's been transferred from electronics to the photo lab at Wal-Mart. She comes home with a selection of creepy pictures we laugh at. I discover with dismay that not only has Dot got her period but she's been hiding two huge boobs under unsightly sweaters. I hide my dismay with indifference. When I say something to June about it, June says: *Let it go,* so I do. Roxanne cuts her hair; it looks awful, but she thinks it's New Wave. I lift weights every day although it is not recommended, hang out with Stan after I've finished my sets, sit in the bleachers, watching divers hover, then drop. These are excuses not to go home. The Cocoplat is living on planet Boy Crazy, gets in big trouble for illicit note passing, her cheeks blooming with drama. The nuns are exasperated. I have no friends.

Father Tim's office looks like the inside of a dusty walnut. He's sitting behind one of those ancient desks with fancy legs, drinking an endless cup of the tea the nuns supply. Depressed leather books line the wall, their pages collecting moisture. Father Tim ignores them, wants Mother in Kansas City for the state meet. I can't believe it. There has been much discussion about how to break her out of her bed-church-library pattern and now he's found the carrot.

I'm firm, cross my arms, stare at the books. *I can't believe this. She'll throw me off.*

Ahhh, she won't now. He's doodling holy doodles with a pencil.

She'll have one of her episodes. I don't budge.

She won't. I'm telling you. He means business.

Something else will happen. I'll be distracted. I hesitate.

Nothing else will happen, he says, putting the pencil in an empty mug embossed with an artfully stabbed heart. *You've trained hard; you'll swim well. Your mother is just going to watch.*

She makes me nervous. I'm starting to plead.

It's the perfect occasion for her to leave the house. She's so happy for you. He's a reasonable priest.

Happy! She . . . she doesn't care about swimming. I know more about this than he does.

But she does love you. Priests see the big picture.

She's not ready. I'm with her every day; I know it won't work. She'll have one of her . . . things. It's too soon. I'm serious about this.

But nothing can shake his conviction that priests are ordained to drive families together because life is designed to pry them apart. *We'll give her a chance, won't we? Let's give her a chance!* And with that he defeats me.

Pilots treat highways like runways, drive fast as though for imminent takeoff, observing their own set of rules because they are used to having nothing around them but air and cloud. Leonard was a rapid weaver, weaving in and out of traffic as though we were in a video game and not on a highway. Fellow Kansans grew testy, would honk and scream. Father Tim takes zero chances on the way to Kansas City, is prone to indecision at inopportune moments, a thermos of watery coffee and a red and black plaid blanket by his side. He makes frequent rabid eye contact with rearview mirrors, lets cars pass, flicking his lights to give them the okay, slowing down to a crawl when in the proximity of truck. It takes us five hours to get there. With Leonard we whizzed in at four.

I make him pull over to put his magic fragrance tree into the trunk. *It's making me sick.*

Mother turns. *Calm down. Everything will work out just fine.* Her eyebrows bunched together in the middle of her face like one of those stuffed animals that the troubled of Glenwood sew out of socks.

I am calm. Father Tim gives me a look in the rearview mirror and I slide my eyes out the window before he catches them again.

Dot and Roxy suffer from a terrible form of moodiness whose only known antidote is absolute silence. We look out the window at cars speeding by, watching the billboards that lead to a happy Jesus, the billboards that lead to stacks of steaming pancakes, the billboards that lead to a happy Jesus again. We look out the window, lulled by the dark arms of trees stretching up into sky, wisps of lower cloud, high trenches of snow, Dot hiding her boobs under a fuzzy blue turtleneck, her head dropping off to the side in a half-awake sleep.

We stay in a motel not far from the natatorium. It's filled with swimmers at the pinnacle of their form. They're laughing and shrieking, getting sodas from the machine, throwing ice cubes at each other, playing loud music, dancing. We see them that evening in the restaurant still laughing and shrieking, complicating their ponytails with glitter, standing behind their chairs and twirling as sparkles rise up around them before settling on the floor. Our table is quiet. Father Tim closes his eyes and mumbles a short prayer. Mother pushes things around on her plate. She's wearing a gray sack with a rope in the middle and her hair looks bad, dark and damp at the roots. Dot and Roxy have turned into two clams with long hair and four staring clam eyes that never blink.

I stare them down. *Quit staring, you guys. You look like—*

Roxanne's black mood reveals itself. *Shut up. You've been staring since we got here.*

Dot seconds her. *She's right.*

I laser them with both eyes. *Have not.*

Calm down, Philomena . . . everything's fine, my mother says, her face folded tightly like an envelope with a letter in it no one wants to send.

Quit saying that. My moods are swinging like the Glenwood Brass Boogie Band. Father Tim sighs and blesses me in his head.

Dot sleeps next to me, doesn't move a muscle, just lies down and closes her eyes like Snow White. Roxanne puts her headphones on, turns her back. Mom sits up reading, the light shining down on her face. I wake up intermittently, sometimes to her dozing face, sometimes to her reading face. I watch her for a while, then close my eyes, but her face remains pasted on the inside of my lids and my mind becomes so involved in senseless, animated chattering, it won't let me sleep.

The sight of people chewing at the breakfast buffet, their eyes morning-vague, trays filled with boxes of cereal and anything else that fits, makes me lose my appetite. Swimmers are quiet, exuberance transformed into anxiety. I try to chew, but my jaw locks. I try to drink, but I cannot swallow.

My mother looks at me with destroyed eyes. *Eat something, Mena . . . everything will be all right.*

I've had enough. *Quit it! I don't want to hear that everything will be all right coming from someone who doesn't think everything will be all right. Okay? So just stop.*

Philomena. Father Tim is sugaring his coffee carefully with a leveled teaspoon. *Your mother's right; eat something, take a walk, stretch, clear your mind.*

I send him a message with my eyes. *You know nothing about the world, God man.*

I run in looping circles to loosen up, yet do not loosen up. We get to the natatorium early, standing by our car watching waves of out-of-town swimmers flowing toward the building in groups, filing out of buses en masse covered in contrasting colors, drenched in complementary colors—the blacks and yellows, the yellows and reds, the blue and whites, holding stuffed animals, hanging on to lucky charms, listening to Walkmans, following people carrying victory balloons on strings, wearing backpacks covered in pins that say NUMBER 1!, that say

WINNER!, that say SWIM!, their parents hanging on to big sponge hands they are already starting to wave.

An uncomfortable internal buzz starts whirring inside me.

Father Tim goes ahead to check in and verify heats. *I'll be back in just one minute.* Mother leaps upon the occasion to be normal for one last nanosecond, then stops, making an *oh* as though someone invisible were punching her in the solar plexus. She doubles over, falling to her knees on the snow. I look down at her sweaty, crumpled hair and see a vista of sadnesses as one sees Glenwood in its entirety from the top of University Hill when one stops one's bike and looks down, prolonging the time between pool and house.

Not here, Mom, come on, Mom, get up. Please. The begging in my voice sounds hollow in my own head, as if my ears have been carefully folded over and taped shut. A blackness takes over my features like frozen dirt. I've gotten good at talking her down. But that's at home.

Roxanne is twisting her hair into twists, aching for a doobie. Dot is standing, both hands dangling, her smooth high forehead and empathetic eyes making her look too pretty to think straight. Both of them have their eyes glued to Mother's folded form on the sidewalk. I know what they are doing; they're willing her to *rise, rise like the sun!* with all the telekinetic power they do not possess. We've recently seen a TV show with a guy in a turban who moved a spoon and some pencils using only the energy behind his brown cow eyes.

I harden my face. *Your heart won't stop beating. Do you hear me, Mom? It won't.*

She's still shaking. *It's the stress, a consequence . . . you wouldn't understand.*

I harden my face harder. *A heart won't stop just like that. It's designed not to. You have to stab it or fire bullets into it to make it stop and even then it's fixable. There's this monk in Tibet who doesn't breathe anymore, but he's not dead. . . . Ask Sister Augusta, she knows all about . . . Mom, Mom, I have to go now. I have to go in there and swim. This is important. Like right now.*

Father Tim jogs toward us, kneels down next to her, putting one hand on her shoulder in the international sign of priestly concern. *Are you all right?*

My heart's acting up again. I'm just going to stay out here for a minute and then I'll be up. She's breathing in gulps like a runner.

Why don't you take a nice quiet walk around the grounds and I'll take the girls inside. Don't you worry about a thing now. He's using the tone he adopts for the dying.

Yes. Yes. I'll do that. Listen, Mena, don't mind me. I am fine. Really. I'm not going to . . . This is an unfortunate setback in a . . .

One of the Dark Catholics convinced her that children choose their parents from their perch in the heavens, whizzing down to earth like ticks with a vision. This makes her feel good. Occasionally she tells us that we need her to be the way she is so we can become the way we need to be and we laugh.

I look at Father Tim and my eyes say: *Told you so, little priest man.*

His eyes don't change. *We had to give it a try.*

I run into the immense locker room, bumping hard into a thin blonde with white eyelashes who's peeling a tangerine over the garbage bin. The locker I find has LIZA SUCKS ANYONE WHO ASKS written in red Magic Marker, a bad sign that makes my heart slump. I take my socks off, revealing transparent feet, violet toenails, veiny soles. I struggle getting my swimsuit on; it's new, pale blue with two burgundy stripes down the side, two sizes too small, for maximum speed. A couple of swimmers look me over in a mean competitive way. I'd made my ponytail too tight, so when I take it down my head tingles in pain. The pain feels delicious. I sit bent over the wooden bench with my back curving over my knees in a deep stretch, listening to the growling storm of noise lots of people make when they're in a high-ceilinged room together, and I think *Life fucking sucks life fucking sucks* in that deep-mind voice a couple of octaves lower than my own.

I plunge into the warm-up pool, pull myself through. I pray not to shake and vomit. *Please, God, Our Holy Father, no fucking shaking and no fucking vomit.*

Mothers in bright T-shirts lean over the stands mouthing *You'll be great* to their children with trails of mascara dripping into the corners of their smiles. There's an old package of smoked almonds in the pocket of my sweats. I rip it open, suddenly ravenous. I watch swimmers preparing, coaches consulting, timers flirting, people in the stands drinking soda pop, kids in and out of the thirty-three stages of boredom experienced at a giant swim meet, old people getting older by the second, sitting patiently on their seatbones. I keep two almonds in my mouth, suck off the salt, rub them together, swish them around my tongue. They make clicking sounds as I knock them against my teeth, staring blankly at the pool.

Coach Stan had a talk with me before I left. He slapped his clipboard on his knee, stuck his jaw out so that it looked like a box someone had sliced in half, and said: *Keep your head. Just*—he paused. *Don't*—he paused. —*You swim the intelligently paced swim and it's in your pocket.*

Coach Coates looked out over the water and sighed, slowly chopping the air into neat slices with one hand: *Take them out one by one. They won't know what hit them.*

I grasp the edge of the platform with my sturdy toes and watch them whiten. There are fifteen levels of muffled sound punctuated by bursts of sound, murmuring sound, last words between swimmers and their coaches, the best swimmers giving each other the *I'm going to win* leer. Champions walk around with Kansas champion swaggers, making a big to-do with their goggles, whipping their arms through the air like irregular propellers, shaking out their thighs in one smooth block of muscle. They don't look at me. I have a stupid name and came with a guy in a collar, two clammy kids, and a gray, sweaty heart convict trembling somewhere outside.

Father Tim is standing on the other side of the pool, fidgeting with the program, looking down at his twisting nervous feet, which fills me with a biting pity and under that a roaring, volcanic rage: *Next time listen to me, God slave.* He doesn't need a collar to look professional. Everything about him says priest: soft skin, gentle chin, the side part that stretches his springy hair across his unlined forehead, the white hands and the way he moves them as though he were wearing something with impressive sleeves.

At the first long whistle, I step onto the starting block. I crouch. My knees smell strongly of lime shaving cream. At the horn, I squeeze every single one of my muscles and spring into air. *Now.* My swim is tight, aggressive, strong, relentless. I touch in two whole body lengths ahead of the best swimmers in the state and I'm not even winded. It's as if I no longer need air. I pull myself up and out, barely panting.

Timers get together in a huddle, whispering. I feel the glare of hundreds of sets of eyes studying me. I pop two almonds into my mouth, stretch all ten toes, lulled by the insular silence that exists when people realize that something's just happened but they aren't sure what. When it is announced I've broken the state record that Hanna Kia registered in the late seventies, that this time rivals national levels recorded earlier this year, my heart thoinks in my chest.

I hear people talking about cannonballs, flukes, one-shot wonders. I pay no heed.

I break a second state record in the 200 free.

Dot and Roxanne sit on their hands in the stands, jaws set. My eyes find theirs and hold. Blank looks with no obvious message inside. They think they are moving me with their thoughts, are afraid to break the spell.

Coaches who are not my coaches touch my shoulder blades and speak words of encouragement. Mediocre swimmers I've never met before give me a thumbs-up, the good ones carefully averting their eyes so as not to be damned. Everyone else moves out of my way, leaving a small circle of empty space around me. Father Tim blesses me in his head *one, two, three, four.* I ignore him, swooshing the almonds in my mouth, clicking the almonds against my teeth.

When I set a national high school record in the 100 butterfly, people start talking about the *Olympic trials* because next year is an *Olympic year* and maybe I could be an *Olympic hopeful, an Olympic KANSAN. Look at those numbers!* Coaches look at Father Tim with envy, one of the original sins. He tells me later it was one of the most exciting moments in his priestly existence, which he'd already explained to me was filled with the erratic bursts of pure joy that loving One God can give.

My mother is sitting in a Denny's three blocks away reading easily solvable murder mysteries. Later, we find her in the car with her head leaning against the window, staring at the sky. *I prayed,* she says, when we tell her. *I prayed and I prayed and I prayed and I prayed and my prayers were answered.*

I should be happy, but I'm not. My happiness is dancing with something in a dark suit I don't want to identify. They're turning fast—bright, black, bright, black, my mind turning with them. I do not know what kind of creature I am. The deep fatigue of continuously being girl combined with the great width of an open future, the narrowness of individual fate, the shittiness of death, and the infinite immeasurableness of the human mind is making me shaky and bewildered and tired to the marrow of my bones.

Super Superior There Is But One

We're sitting in the sitting room with the most celebrated Olympic Supercoach of all time: Ernest K. Mankovitz. I'm strongly wishing I couldn't see his socks and the ginger-colored leg hairs curling out of the tops of them, but my mother has already informed me she's noticed with significant use of her eyes. When he got here, he stood in the middle of the doorway, tan, with a white baseball cap on his head he immediately took off, leaving a crescent moon of deep dents on both sides of his ginger hair. He is short for a masculine man and tremendously fit; the hand that clasped mine squeezed so hard something creaked. I said *Hi* and waved, his excessive significance transforming me into an idiot.

I don't look directly into his face, keep my eyes on the dent in his hair or one of his feet. Dot and I'd pulled Mom out of bed earlier, dressed her up in an attractive beige sack, tightening a dark brown leather belt in the middle as tight as we could, so it wouldn't slide off and scare him away. We doubled the ration of vitamin C, supervising as she sipped an entire jug of frothy grimlock through a straw, and although she is sweating into the roots of her hair, she now has enough energy to pretend she has a collection of soft blouses in a highly ventilated walk-in closet with plush carpeting, because she instantly hadn't liked him, the Mankovitz: his confident handshake, his steady gaze, the way he sat down on the couch and crossed his furry ankles, the way he requested a plain glass of water, ignoring the silver pot of lukewarm coffee sitting next to the hard cookies placed artistically in the middle of a polished tray.

I'm sitting next to her on the blue couch poor old Manny had been forbidden to sleep on when he roamed this mortal earth. I'm dying of fright.

Swimming families? Mom's voice is driving slowly up a high road in a sleek, classy car.

Yes. Families that recognize the swimming potential in one of their children and do the best that they can to help them maximize that potential. He's a friendly neutral.

If it's meant to be, it's meant to be, Mr. Mankositz. Mom's voice is settling into a philosopher's leather-booked study.

You won't get any gold medals with that attitude, Mrs. Ash. He's a friendly neutral.

Life isn't a big game with fireworks at the end, as I hope you know by now, Mr. Manopitz. The philosopher has opened her favorite book and is reading.

He looks at her without speaking for a minute, king of the pregnant pause although this does not detract from his natural authoritative manliness. *I agree with you; life's probably not a game,* he finally says, his voice still relatively neutral, *and swimming is just a sport, but it's a sport your daughter has a phenomenal talent for. I don't think in all my years as . . . With some of the right training, she can go to the Olympics. We'll talk about other opportunities such as a full scholarship to Stanford University later. But just think of the Olympics for a minute. She may be one of the best swimmers we've got and she's had no real, formal training. Who's to say what results concentrated work might bring?* He's opening up his palms now, the universal sign of supplication.

She's sixteen years old. A flibbertigibbet, a will-o'-the-wisp, a clown.

It's time. He's laced his fingers together, an indicator of imminent decision whether one likes it or not.

Time? Time? Just what do we know about time, Mr. Manolist? How much time is there? Her car is bouncing down the peaks and valleys of an uneven hill. She's losing him; I can tell by the way his heels dig into the carpet. I grow nervous, know what this can lead to, but she steadies herself through the power of pride. She swivels toward me so suddenly I jump. *Is this what you want?*

I was born to race, Mom, I say, shouting and whimpering at the same time.

She looks at me, thinking. I look at her looking at me, thinking—she's wondering what kind of creature I am. This goes on for a while because my eyes get stingy and I notice that one of her earrings is pulling down hard on one of her lobes.

It's time to stop talking now. I tell her with my eyes.

I'll stop talking when I'm through talking. She responds with hers.

Yes. But it really is time to stop talking now. He's normal; he won't understand. I insist with two brows and a quiet sigh.

I'm the boss now and don't you forget it, she says, pressing her mouth into a gravel road. She swivels his way. *Okay, we'll see how it goes this spring. If she makes it to the Olympics later, good enough, but* I want her home next year. *She can train just fine with the coaches we have here until she goes off to university, I'm not losing anyone else in my life, Mr. Manlo . . . snitz. Do we understand each other?*

He nods, stands up, his pants falling back down over his hairy red ankles, and it's done. The nuns are informed that at the beginning of spring, when Lake Shawnee is preparing to flood the trailer courts and certain parishioners will lose their homes, I shall be flying to Colorado Springs to train for four months. I'll be moving in with the Peggys.

Mother says: *That little Mankyvitz has a Napoleon complex—I've seen his type. Don't let him bully you; that's how they get their power.*

I don't care. *He flew here . . . to Kansas . . . to Glenwood, I mean.*

She looks up at me from the vista of her bed. *I know how he got here. Just promise me you won't follow blindly; I have a feeling about this.*

I still don't care. *Okay, whatever.*

At the Glenwood International Airport, Roxanne says: *The deserter deserts.*

Dot says: *Have fun.* And I leave them standing with Father Tim in the gray terminal with the gray spatula seats. Mother doesn't come to see me off; 1983 is the year she feels gravity is playing strange games with her; she suddenly loses balance while standing still. Father Tim puts up one hand, blesses me, then waves. Dot and Roxanne put up some fingers and toodle them. I don't have any tears stuck anywhere. I'm perfectly fine.

The Peggys

Mrs. Peggy is standing in arrivals holding in a thin brown hand a card that says PHILOMENA in tight black letters. She's styled her hair into a pesky red shrub and shined her lips with a pearl gloss, has hound dog eyes that tip down at the edges but are not sad. She smiles, giving me a thorough toe-to-temple scan in under a second, is difficult to impress.

The house is divided in two—a woolly rustic shag corduroy cabin and a brassy glass prison where everything you touch leaves incriminating prints. The kitchen is neutral, the refrigerator plastered with motivational literature and dietary fact. There are baskets suspended above the kitchen table filled with dried wildflowers, ceramic renditions of breads from all over the world, and a green plant that drops white buds into the air. I watch them spiral down into the food and eventually learn not to pick them out—one of the things I do to integrate my presence at the Peggys'.

I know that Peggy's father is an orthodontist and her mother an orthodontist's wife, know that Peggy is eighteen, one of the best backstrokers in the country, that she swims year-round with the Colorado Springs Aquatic Club. *Swimming* did a feature on her in their Spring issue. She talked about her dog, Dave; hiking; wanting to meet Ric Ocasek; her daily mileage; favorite sets, all under a barely hidden Olympic innuendo. There was a close-up of her at the FINA meet in Berlin. She is pretty in an even-featured lipless way, but she makes herself seem more so. She wears halters that tie around her neck under her sweats and says: *Look at my shoulders; they've gotten so big,* even though they haven't changed.

I wasn't for.

This is the first full sentence that Peggy directs my way. Later, she makes light of it. *No, I said: You're a fat whore. No, no, I said: What a skanky bore! Wait a minute . . . I remember now; I said: You stink to the core.*

Mrs. Peggy opens one door after another, now revealing perfectly made bed, now revealing neat toilet, now revealing perfectly made bed again. *And this is Peggy's room and* this is Peggy*! You're back.*

Peggy is lying on her bed with both legs up on the wall listening to music I don't recognize.

She doesn't change position, her wet auburn hair hanging off the edge of her bed, a gray toy poodle with a proud poodle face lounging on a velvet pillow by her side. *Looks that way.*

Mrs. Peggy's voice remains *a visitor is listening* bright. *How'd it go?*

The set of Peggy's upside-down head doesn't give a shit about listening visitors. *Fine.*

Mrs. Peggy opens one arm and says in a serious tone. *Philomena, this is my daughter Peggy.*

This is Peggy's last chance to flip around and greet me like a good human and she knows it. She flips, her face flushed with the unusual amounts of blood it has just ingested, says *Hi* in a Colorado monotone.

Hi. Kansas can be monotone too if it wants.

Mrs. Peggy sees an out, gets all sparkly. *I'll leave you two girls alone to get acquainted,* and disappears.

Philohhhmenaahhh, says Peggy. She sits up and scans me. *I wasn't for. First of all, you leave my room alone. Second of all, during practice you're like the other rookies—I don't know you. Third of all, no talking about my family to anyone, not one word. And my friends are my friends not your friends, so don't count on doing things together.*

I've had dealings before. *Okay.*

You can go now.

Okay.

But the desire to master the intrigue gets the better of her, as it so often will in her loud Peggy life. *Wait a minute . . . how tall are you?*

Six-two.

She lets out a whistly stream of air. *Mannishly impressive. What's your personal best on the 200 fly?*

Two-thirteen.

Eemmmm. You're from Kansas?

Yeah.

That sucks . . . You can go now, Philohhhmeenahhh. She gets in a fight with curiosity, loses. *Hey . . . Mom said your coach was a nun.*

It is not the first time I get the feeling I will wear nun like an invisible coat. *No . . . a priest, but I have a real coach . . . and a stroke master too.*

A priest? She snorts.

And a real coach and a stroke master too. We stare each other down. She has pictures of magazine people stuck onto a cork wall between pictures of real ones. I make a point of looking at the magazine people with Bron's French-club face, then I leave.

My room has a window that looks out over a lawn that sinks down into a small wood that has footpaths that lead to a tall black fence. There's a fragrance pine tree hanging in my closet. I open the window and throw it out. The air is different, tight and clean, but my bed has been sprinkled with a dose of synthetic lavender. I find a towel that smells like towel, put it over my lavender pillow, and sleep like a worn and tired worm. The first practice is at five-thirty the next morning.

Mrs. Peggy tries to wake me for dinner. She stands at the door and yodels. *Wake up now, it's not ni-i-ght.* She comes in, leans over the bed: *Dinner, dinner, come now, dinner,* trying not to sound irritated when I shut my eyes harder. The world feels hostile. It's their turn to take in a swimmer; Peggy isn't for.

So what? Don't love them.

Serious training is so shocking, it pulls the old me out and puts a new one in. The new one laughs less, sleeps in the wrong places, nods *yes.* I'm totally surrounded by a cushion of professionalism directed by the hand of science and the amazingly effective Ernest K. Mankovitz. I work with a team of assistant coaches; every time I turn around, a different one is standing in front of me with my name, my stats, and orders I must obey. Earnestness, dedication, perseverance, seriousness, and swimming passion fill the air with purpose. I breathe purpose into my body as I sit at the edge of the pool at five-thirty in the morning, the new me thinking *Yes.*

When E. Mankovitz speaks, a hush skims the surface of the pool. He clears his throat and divides the world up into swimmers, and it gets so quiet the only sound I hear is the steady cadence of my own heart and the faraway purr of pool filters. It is during this period that the name *Fredrinka Kurds* makes its first auditory appearance in my life, followed by a picture of a big girl in a big face with a tiny nose planted in the center. It turns up on senior assistant Kyd's desk with a bio that says she's been training tough in the darkly celebrated Leipzig Institute since she was six years old and that her closest rival in the world is teammate Dagmar Bitten (no picture available). Supercoach E. Mankovitz squints and says: *You'll have to prepare yourself for what's out there* and my Kansas-based brain explodes.

I work my way up through the rank of senior assistants, listen to them harder than I ever listened to nun, so hard my brain gets stuck in their syllables and I momentarily stop understanding English so they have to say it again.

I'm Ron; let's look at your kick. Ron parts his hair like a priest, yells like Coach Coates, wants to coach a Division 1 team, preferably masculine.

He has me race from a dead start in the middle of the pool, swim full on for as long as I can. He has me tread water as the other rookies try to pull me under. I fight; *if there is room for only one, let it be me.* I drag myself across the water with shoes on, swim on my back with both arms limp at my side, put my chin on a kickboard and kick with both legs until I can no longer feel them for burning. He stands at the edge of the pool, says: *Again,* then passes me off to another one.

I'm Kyd. I want one hundred one hundreds. A tall freckled blonde, former world record butterfly holder, lone female in a landscape of men. She watches me carefully, a whistle clamped between her teeth, designs my workouts based on her belief that one day women will swim faster than men. She's careful to raise her voice in volume but never in tone. She studies me, yells, *Where's Arch? We've got a thrasher.*

Mr. Arch Naylor aka the stroke doctor. He's from the old school, coached Spitz, has a foxy mustache sitting under the gnarly spud he calls a nose. He uses eccentric breathing methods, is known to experiment freely with proven technique, can end a career with a quick shake of his head.

He appears before me, tall, with the slightly bent stance of a man used to ducking. He makes me stand in front of him, then slowly turn. He touches my neck with one finger, spends a long time studying my great feet. *They say you're a thrasher,* he finally says in the swarthy voice of a renegade cowboy.

I'm squirmy with fright. *I don't know.*

Well . . . let's see about that, he says, visibly at ease in the company of squirm.

I nod *yes.*

Suddenly he's impatient, clapping his hands hard enough to make me jump. *Well . . . get in the water, why don't you? What are we waiting for?*

I stop, suddenly stupid. *What do you want me to do?*

He shakes his head and my heart twitters. He sighs and says: *Swim. I would like you to swim.*

What do I swim? I ask, dumb with fright.

He shakes his head again. *Your best.*

I swim slowly at first, groping for perfect technique: *fingers, wrist, shoulders, head, torso, streamline, teardrop, kneeballs, noseballs, earballs, windfalls,* then I decide to sprint like a nutcase. *Fuck him.*

When I finish, he isn't on deck anymore, is speaking with the Mankovitz in the Mankovitz glass prison suspended above pool. I can see their dark smudges pressed against the window, both of them looking down.

Kyd stares at my feet as she sips her morning tar. Ron yells less, takes the time to explain what he is about to make me do before he makes me do it. Naylor appears at the edge of the water after one of my sets, explaining how the angle of my left shoulder creates unnecessary drag. The Mankovitz looks at his clipboard, squints, looks at me, then calls a meeting and asks me to come.

Naylor's leaning against the window, long arms crossed over skinny chest. Kyd's seated, strong legs crossed at knee. Ken is tapping his clipboard energetically with a pen until Naylor bids him *halt!* and he stops. The Mankovitz is sitting behind a desk buried under mounds and mounds of paper he presses down absently as he speaks.

He's formal. *Thank you for coming. Arch, why don't you begin?*

Water is your element—you don't need to fight. There's too much movement, not enough glide. A strong voice doesn't need to shout. You need to feel your swim. You don't feel your swim. He pronounces *feel* like *eeeeel*, moves his hands like two sea turtles without breaking eye contact, as if he suspects that because I am young I am retarded.

Then . . . there's the breathing situation, he continues.

This makes Kyd jump. *How bad?*

Bad enough, Arch says.

How are you breathing? She's looking at me, her head cocked to the side.

I've learned to be careful about my responses to their simple questions. I pretend to think about it a minute, playing with my goggles. *Let me seeeeeee . . . I breeeeeeathe when . . . I neeeeeeed to.*

This shocks them. They suck lean muscle into lean cheek.

You need to breathe before *you need to in case you won't be able to breathe* when *you need to. Do you understand?* Kyd shrieks.

Swimming mechanics need to be revised so thoroughly they become reflex, Arch drawls, ignoring Kyd's feminine outburst. *And I'd like to take a closer look at winning the inner game.*

Mankovitz looks at me. *Do you understand?* I nod *yes, yes.* A lie.

I swim from wall to wall to wall to wall, wearing weight belts, holding on to tubes with one immobile arm, pulling myself across the pool. I feel the pain, nod *yes;* pain is progress. I grow new shoulders, grunting like a wrestler as hard little tears slip out, mixing with water as they slide down my face. I come home at night with just enough energy to play with Peggy's dog, Dave, until Peggy notices and calls Dave away. He's a crafty toy poodle, prancy and intelligent, recognizes me in my baseball caps, licks my face, is genuinely kind.

I think about breath, count breath, swallow breath, time breath, holding oxygen in until my heart thumps in anger, but every time I race, I yuck it up.

This annoys Arch. His caterpillar eyebrows join in a deep **V**. *You didn't breathe until the last five meters when you did not need to breathe.*

At the sight of the **V**, my heart sinks. I swirl the truth around my forked tongue, lie a lame lie. *I'm getting it down.*

His caterpillars dive sharply, turning his forehead into an **X**. *You stopped breathing until the last five meters. We were looking at you. If you would like to see yourself breathe as you touch in, that race was filmed.*

You stopped breathing, then you ran into the lane divider with your left shoulder. You lost.

My heart deepens its descent into depth. I lie lamer. *I skimmed the lane . . .*

He makes me work with him on breathing exercises he's designed to resemble death so when I near the portals of nothingness, I won't freak.

I slip under water, sculling it slowly with my hands, and wait, watching pale faraway bodies pull themselves up and down the lanes. I close my eyes and Bron appears sitting on a coffin with wheels, a serious expression on her serious face. I feel a wildness surge, a deep pressing that opens my eyes. I wait, sculling the water with my palms, my body thumping violently until I can't stand it anymore, break the surface of liquid to join that of air.

Naylor's unimpressed, says: *Now do it again.*

Sometimes they have me observe. I watch world record breaststroker Babe Alberts glide for meters and beat everyone before breaking the surface, hands moving in some slow ballet, streamlined into a silver shadow, mysterious and shiny. I worry: *Where is she? She has to come up now; she'll lose.* Next to her, other swimmers look like they are trying to do an anxious and impossible thing.

I study Peggy; she makes up for her lack of natural talent and her smallish feet with an admirable intensity and by swimming recklessly like a guy. She's true to her word, does not acknowledge me. She turns out to be a verbally gifted individual known for her edgy humor, team spirit, leadership qualities, witty word associations, operatic voice. *Ernie Crampovitz. Sir Wormy Mankybliss. Lordy Mankovitz. Little Poopy Pantsovitz.* People like her; she's popular.

She hits me on the head with a kickboard one morning during warm-up. Like that. The coaches are on deck in a huddle discussing drills. I see her coming at me with the board held high over her head and her teeth bared and am too dumbed by the sight to react. She hits me so hard my ears sing.

Consider yourself part of the team, she says and laughs.

I use new motivational skills, say: *You are not going to let that monkey ruin your day, are you? Bluff her out. Stay cool as a CUCUMBER, do you hear me A CUCUMBER. She's all wind.*

One of the rookies detaches itself from the exhausted group on the bench, the tall and starey-eyed Sunny Lewis, all-American backstroker, possessor of one large Armenian nose and not one but two sets of hammertoes that she tries to hide with a towel. Peggy gave her a nickname the first week: *Hammernose*. She comes up to me while I'm putting on my sweats, says: *She's just fighting her own insecurity by being loud* and we become friends.

That night I knock on Peggy's door as cool and as green as a cool green cucumber, my legendary non-confrontational palms rubbing their sweat on my jeans.

She's painting her nails a weird shade of blue, doesn't bother to look up. *What?*

I'm going to beat you and I thought you should know. Look at me, Piggly . . . as soon as the breathing works out and I stop doing that . . . thing with my shoulder, I will beat you. I'm almost as good as a good debater.

Ooooh, I'm scared. Not. *We don't even swim the same strokes.* But she licks her lips.

Not now, maybe, but Kyd's been talking potential. She says I'm highly versatile. Don't hit me ever again. I saw your face; you looked like some sort of . . . bug. I feel my face turn colors. *Don't do it again.*

She smiles at my flushed face. I've lost. *Bug? Now what? Hail Mary full of face, light a candle with some mace.* She's blowing cool Peggy air onto ugly Peggy toes.

I'm mad. *I will beat you, Piglet. I saw you.* This toe-blowing thing is the last straw.

As if. Just try, Philippino ringlet rug spot rotgut. And call me Piglet again; you'll regret it. There is a touch of the monkey to her features, something about the nose to upper-lip ratio.

Most swimmers start to swim because they have some kind of a problem. At least half of them are serious asthmatics or suffering from dryland weakness with atrophied arms and deeply rooted genetic neediness. They suffer from attention deficit disorders, dyslexia, chronic dryland awkwardness, a minimum dishonorable number of friends. They suffer from bad divorces, monoparental abandonment issues, the sudden death of a gregarious twin. Piggly is an astigmatic, asthmatic only child. Something happened to her when she was born; something that required oxygen tents and special care; something that prevented the

Peggys from making another one. There is a picture of her, seven, standing next to a diving board in a bright pink swimsuit with two white planky appendages holding up her flat torso like an easel. Her bedroom is covered with medals and pictures of her snowboarding, hiking, windsurfing with a sweat-free Dr. Peggy.

Dr. Peggy is as mild and as steady as a boat in a bath. He has a special hair spray for men he uses that has FOR MEN! written on it in masculine letters the color of blood. Hair spray is the first thing I smell in the morning. Hair spray is the last thing I smell at night. The Peggys do not like the scent of naked Colorado air; they like to enhance it. There's cedar perfume emitted by the things someone plugged into the walls that I remove surreptitiously and bury deep under garbage in order to survive. I have slight burns on thumb and forefinger from snuffing scented candles out by hand, but I don't miss home for one second. Colorado is good for me; its landscapes offer texture and relief and things my eyes can dig into. I feel safe surrounded by people in shorts holding stopwatches, blowing whistles, checking clipboards, wearing flip-flops with special poolside grip. I feel safe surrounded by densely packed wooded areas filled with trees with sweet-smelling needles, by large rock formations that cup the sky and hold cloud in. And no one knows anything about me; I walk around as plain and as blank as the faraway sun.

I'm not a weight-room person, dread my sessions with the dreaded Ken, who trains my muscles like monkeys and is content only when I'm a trembling, silent mess. I walk into the weight room the way I always walk into the weight room, as quiet and as invisible as a Shawnee. Peggy is finishing up, lying on a mat stretching with Babe. Her little eyes shift over to my direction, catch.

Je-sus she's huge—have you grown again, Phil? she says. *Perhaps there wasn't enough time to glue your dick on . . . You weren't premature or anything, were you, Full—Oh—Men—Ya!* They laugh until Peggy says: *I've got it . . . let's call her Pip!!!!!!!!!!!! Pip is perfect!!!!!*

PIP!!!!!! everyone screams.

It follows me like a vigilant nun. I watch in horror as its usage grows exponentially with each passing day. I accidentally look up when I hear it, find myself reacting when it's called, but I whine: *Come on, you guys. That's not my name.*

Peggy loves it. *Don't get your PIP in a knot.*

I'm not a Pip. I'm sulky.

Peggy loves it even more. *Look, everyone . . . PIP's being a POOP.*

I'm the opposite of a Pip. I'm sad.

When I'm not imagining the Olympics in a golden haze of red white and blue, I have serious daydreams where she swims so badly that people leave the stands. She's taken away the only chance I ever had to name myself. I'm not going to get over it anytime soon. I hammer my pillow with my fists at night, call her Piglet in the company of everyone, but she makes sure it never catches on.

Change the H to a P and You Have Porny

Peggy's stretching her Achilles by standing backward down a curb. She puts both arms over her head, sticks her chest out, sticks her butt out, and stretches, letting her hair flip with an invisible wind. When she can't stand it anymore, she breaks her vow of silence.

Is he looking at me? she whispers.

No. I'm glad.

What's he looking at? She's got her head between her knees.

I don't know, something on the ground . . . I don't know . . . maybe he's just . . . He's a tall blond swimmer with solid gold possibilities who swims through girls like a speedboat with sharp propellers.

Shit. She takes off her jacket, putting it around her shoulder like a cape, touching her toes with sexy-me fingers. *Is he looking now?*

He's drinking a Gatorade. *No. Wait! He just looked over.*

Don't fucking wave. She's standing up, her hands on her hips.

He saw me looking. I'm leaning on a stop sign.

Don't fucking let him see you fucking looking at him, Kansas girl. My God. Is he looking now? She flips her hair, smiling a big smile that isn't meant for me.

How in the hell would I know, asthma face? I'm sick of this.

Just look. She's playing nice.

Screw you, Piglet. You look. He's your guy. I'm sick of this. I put my Walkman on, tune her out.

We're standing in the parking lot waiting for Mrs. Peggy because Peggy's little red car is getting serviced. Delayed-reaction puberty is hitting me hard and I'm unusually mopey. I've grown two kiwis and a mini-shrub, and am secretly having hot, dramatic dreams, but I don't trust anything my age with a sausage. I spend my time clamming up in front of the loud, hairy, obviously horny ones, a fact that Peggy finds infinitely amusing, not missing a chance to point out loudly when my face has changed color. *Look! Pip's face has popped.* I'm still girl, and even though I've spent my entire life in a swimsuit, the thought of actually exposing my secrets to anyone fills me with a deep and terrible dread, one of the many symptoms of all those years spent in the company of nun.

Horny swimmers beget trouble. They leave pain in their wake, destroy careers, don't care. There are stories. Legend has Chrissy Hughs, world butterfly record holder and Olympic champ, quitting when she falls in love with Leif Benson, world butterfly record holder and Olympic champ. Mutual passion gets her pregnant by accident and they have a baby boy they name Little Leif. Later, bored and chubby, her tired red eyes brimming with remorse, she tries to relaunch her swimming career, but never reaches the same level, no matter how hard she trains. Being pregnant changed her center of gravity, the baby sucked too much of the x-factor out of her, and her name had become too long to sound right on the podium: *Chrissy Hughs-Benson.* Legend has Arch Naylor taking one look at her and shaking his silver head.

She shouldn't have taken on his name, I say in the locker room after practice.

Babe's drying her hair. *What in the world does that have to do with it?*

I look at her and shout, *What doesn't that have to do with it?*

She shakes her head, turns off her dryer. *That's the same question, only backwards.*

I know what I'm talking about. *Chrissy Hughs-Benson doesn't work.*

Peggy chimes in. *If Babe would have been born a Rhoda . . .*

It's the first time we agree. *. . . And Rhodas don't swim.*

She finishes my sentence. *Chrissy Hughs-Bensons don't win golds.*

I'm basking in harmony. *You got it.*

She goes in for the kill. *If you follow that kind of logic, then Philomena of course would be . . .*

Harmony is fragile, but I know what I'm talking about. *A four-syllable anomaly. An exception to the rule.*

She's putting lip gloss on with a wand. *Convenient.*

Peggy is attracted to the horny masculine swimmers, the ones who whip towels into weapons and leave welts for fun. She likes the ones who refer to their colleagues as rookie balls, prick, dickhead, and rover, the squinty handsome ones who drape an arm casually over her shoulders, looking up when someone interesting walks into the room. She brings them home when the Peggys are out; they make out in the living room as I hide out with Dave in my bedroom, Adam Ant blaring in my ears. My lonesomeness fights long, weighted battles with fatigue, but fatigue always wins and I eventually close my eyes to a dark velvet dreamworld inhabited by the soaring silence of a flock of nectar-eating mega bats until I open them up to a fresh new day.

Supercoach E. Mankovitz stays out of our private life, but it's obvious by the way he tugs at his mustache, slowly shakes his head, clicks his tongue, and sighs that he does not encourage swimming love because everyone knows that in swimming love it's always the girl who sacrifices her future for the sake of great passion and not the horny swimmer, who keeps on winning medals, eventually stepping down to get a great job in marketing, communications, finance, sports psychology, or pediatrics. I have due reason to avoid boys with balls, a real excuse for turning mute and red and clammy, for standing back, slightly bending my shoulders forward to hide puberty's kiwis.

But I like the kind ones who hold the locker room door and don't say anything gross when I walk through. The sweet ones who say *Good set,* who ask me what I'm listening to on my Walkman because they really want to know, who won't make fun of Adam Ant even if they want to. When I spot a certain nice swimmer with a shy smile standing on the other side of the pool, I squirm, thinking *naked* as he looks back and waves, the muscles in his lean arms undulating like water. Yearnings wrestle inside of me like ferocious animals, sending feelings into parts of my body that up until now have been sleeping.

But avoiding horniness is like avoiding life. The continuous stream of hot thought mixes with keen curiosity, eventually wearing me down, girl or no, and I find myself on a couch at a Friday night swimming party, his tongue in my mouth, and my old world empties, the new one filling up with sexy stuff: He turns his head, breathing slowly into my ear, causing both my ear cords and my vagina to whir.

My vagina has done many things in her short life. She's jumped down hard on new bike; ridden the occasional, misbehaving pony; sat quietly in class listening to nun. She's plunged off a high dive the wrong way, vibrated along with a vibrating plane, idled sweetly with an idling bus, spent many summer hours soaking up heat from a faraway sun, but up until this moment, she'd never whirred.

He stops kissing me, whispering: *You okay?*

I say *I think so*, and Holy Name shoots up toward the heavens, small and smaller the faster it goes, exploding in a shower of burning black stars that disappear as they fall.

We make out in the parking lot, at the Peggys' behind their wall of trees. We make out in the shady parts of the street, we make out lying down on the floor in the empty weight room, we make out by the bluish light of an empty pool. He's never pushy. I no longer worry about the breadth of my shoulders, the muscular boobs that flex when I move; I'm basking in the discovery that kindhearted, cute but not handsome swimmers love everything about me, not suspecting for one second that I'm still girl.

Peggy doesn't understand. *Are you really going out with him? He's so . . .* She looks for a word she doesn't have the patience to find. *I can give you one of my old ones if you want.*

Keep the squints over on your court, Piglet, I say, accidentally piquing her curiosity.

Mom calls every other day.

How is it?

Good.

You always say that.

Yeah, well . . . my times are down.

So . . . you're happy . . .

Yeah, Mom. I'm happy. . . . Roxanne okay?

The same.

Hmmmm. Dot?

Top of the class.

Mini-nun.

What?

All that goodness and prayer. He's going to call her.

I doubt it . . . She's got a boyfriend.
What?
Paul Sloan.
You're kidding me.
Why do you say that?
No reason. Just surprised. That's all.

Paul Sloan. One hundred percent squint; one of those skinny guys who walks around with his shirt off anytime he can. He says *yo* and does *yo* things with his fingers. The nuns have him pegged as a future divorced person. He is the first of Dot's sympathetic salvation loves that causes great grief in her life, thus ours.

My body starts doing things that incite reaction in the assistants: the milliseconds start coming off millisecond by millisecond. Kyd informs me that E. Mankovitz is pleased. She grabs my elbow, draws me in, whispers: *Ernie seems pleased.*

I meet some of the greatest people in my life in Colorado Springs, girls I'll spend the next ten years swimming for or against depending on the meet. The entire silver medal squad from Seoul is there. One day we will be in our twenties, hopping mad, writhing in rage, making fists with our hands and punching the air. But Seoul is five years away. It's 1983 and I'm seventeen. We're tall kids who do kid things when we're not swimming. We eat ice cream sitting on curbs, talk our way through movies, make tapes we put on our Walkmans to fire up, hitting each other's shoulders and screaming *FIRE UP,* pretending not to think about the Olympic trials nine months away, but anytime we have a chance, we bring them up, imagining all sorts of crazy scenarios, letting our words trail off to the encouragement that follows. We sit in the dining hall plying our plates with thirty percent carbohydrate, fifty percent protein, and twenty percent fat, dreams tightening our minds, holding them in. I keep the embarrassing ones to myself, especially the one where I'm lifted up by an enormous hand that plunges to earth from the sky while Supercoach E. Mankovitz weeps like a baby. *I just knew it. I just knew it and knew it and knew it. The first time I saw her, I knew.*

"O Lo and Behold" Sang the Angels, Rising from Their Mucky Torpor with Clay-Covered Wings

I'm not feeling well and hiding it. When we walk out on deck and Kyd calls to me with weights in her hands, I want to slap her, have to hold one hand down with the other so I don't. I flip Peggy the bird behind her back, not noticing Babe sitting quietly on the bench in front of her locker, rubbing a smelly oil onto her feet. She says: *What'd you do that for?* I don't know, shrug, fighting the desire to hit her shiny blond head with one of my shoes. Ken yells at me about maintaining technique for over five minutes and my chin starts to tremble like a washing machine before I can stop it. My head hurts, my eyebrows hurt, my teeth hurt, my gums hurt, my shoulders hurt, my pelvic cavity hurts, my ass hurts, my thighs hurt, my ankles hurt, breathing hurts, chewing hurts, sleeping hurts, sitting still hurts, and it's starting to get on my nerves. Last night, when I watched the white buds spiral their way down into my pasta, I rebelled, picking them out one by one, sighing loudly as the three Peggys stopped chewing and watched.

And Leonard keeps showing up. Today he's on the bottom of the pool, sitting in a stupid three-legged chair staring into space with dirty brown caveman hair that reaches down to his feet and eyebrows as dense and as flowing as a windy field of dry bamboo. When I see him, I get irritated, clamping my teeth down so hard my jaw hurts. Arch Naylor materializes from his dark den in a flash of silver, says: *Just who were you trying to thrash out there?* as I stand heaving, begging my fingers not to flip him the bird. I've discovered the joy of being mean to my nice boyfriend; I can't help it. He grabs my gym bag before I can, opens doors like a gentleman, massaging the small of my back with his warm hands, and I think *Slow, slow, now retarded.* My eyeballs laser right through him and I don't say a word, but when he tries to kiss me with soft minty lips, I push him away.

After dinner, Mrs. Peggy knocks on my door, waits a respectful four seconds, comes in, and sits on the edge of my bed.

Are we a bit homesick, honey? she asks, about one hundred thousand freckles I've never noticed before scattered randomly throughout her face.

I laugh a mean *no.*

Is Peggy being . . . she's got quite a character; don't think I don't know. I know my daughter. She's shaking her head, twisting a perfect diamond on a thin brown finger.

I stop laughing the mean *no,* say: *It's not her. But she's no piece of cake.*

What, then? Are you not feeling well? She touches me on the forehead with a freezing-cold hand. *We're all just two or three degrees away from a fever.*

Sometimes when I get back from the pool early, she's singing in the living room with a yoga woman whose voice vibrates up the staircase like a sad cello. One sings, then the other sings, then they sing together as the windows quiver and poor Dave the poodle gets so upset he shakes.

I'm in a bad mood, I say. *I'm . . . I don't know why.*

She studies me for a second, says hopefully: *Is it your time of the month . . .*

I look at her and my gut wrenches out of solidarity with my past. I cover it up by laughing a mean *no.*

Are you sure? Sometimes the stress of training throws your body out of whack. You're probably just getting your period, early . . . or late as the case may be. Then she looks at me, waiting for an answer.

I don't know, I say, braiding the fringe of my blanket. *I don't know why.*

The next morning I meet dawn with a pounding head, a pounding gut, pounding eyeballs. I sit at the breakfast table stirring my oatmeal until it turns to crumbled brick. I sit in Peggy's car watching pine trees with snow in their needles greet the vast day with an ache inside an ache inside an ache like an evil Russian doll. When I open the door, the locker room blasts me with humid, chattering life. I say nothing, sitting on the edge of a bench, the gray lockers clanking, vapors from the pool attacking my dry, stingy eyes. I slide my white hundred percent cotton underwear down to my ankles and discover I'm bleeding like a pig.

I'm so surprised, I say it out loud. *I'm bleeding.*

Peggy turns. *What?*

I recover, lock my knees together, hanging on tight to my underwear. *I'm bleeding; there's blood. I have my period.*

She forages in her locker. *Do you want a Tampax?*

A Tampax? My heart twitters its way down a lifeline of lie.

She laughs. *Well, you're not going to swim in a maxi pad, are you, Kansas girl? Or is that what the nuns taught you?*

Everyone finds this immensely funny as I sit on the bench folded over myself as mute and immobile as a statue until the room clears out. I open my palm and study it, a miniature toilet paper roll with a fine cotton tail. I creep into the bathroom bent in two like a woman selling matchsticks, sit on the toilet, pray. *Please God our Holy Father make this work.* It's so simple, it's complicated. I close my eyes, sliding it up down there until it seems okay, but when I stand, it falls to the floor, and I freeze. *What do I do now?* People are looking for me. I can hear rumblings, an occasional yell. I put my feet up on the door and stop breathing, my body aching in hell.

I'm stuffing a wad of toilet paper down my pants, planning a quick escape when Kyd walks in and says: *What are you doing?*

I can't take it anymore, explode into nervous breakdown, throwing both hands up in the air, toilet paper flowing behind me like tattered wings. *The blood. There's a lot. More than I expected. I feel sick. I'm bleeding. A lot. And lately I've been so . . . so . . . so . . . mad all the time, like worse than normal.*

She looks at me. *What?*

I have a bigger nervous breakdown, with flapping feet and trembling teeth and whapping arm movements she has to deflect. *I'm bleeding. I've got the, the, periods. I'm menstruating, Kyd, and it's awful, worse than I ever expected . . . Lilly was right, but I lied to her . . . I lied and Dot, that bitch, she could have told . . . but Bron said . . . she said . . . she told me I was relatively . . . normal.*

She looks at me, whispers: *What?*

I have an enormous nervous breakdown, with rivers of snot and red splotches, bleeding into a foot of toilet paper, a makeshift towel diaper wrapped around my thighs, my pants falling at my great feet, an ache pounding in my groin. *The blood,* I say, *the blood is so awful. What's the . . . how . . . do people do this, do you know, Kyd? Do you? So this makes me normal? The fuckers.*

She studies me without speaking, apparently confused, then her face lightens, she takes her voice down a notch, practically whispering: *Were you afraid you were pregnant, honey?*

My nervous breakdown is so surprised, it eats itself up like a monster, stops dead in its tracks. *What?*

She breathes a sweet sigh of relief. *Would you like a Tylenol?*

And I say: *What?*

And she says: *For the pain.*

Yes please, I say in an electronic voice. *Pain is no good, and I'd like a box of Tampax or a Tampax, but with the box please.*

She looks concerned, but says: *Okay.*

Life is all about gliding straight things into angles, being human, but not so much that people can tell. Life is all about curving around corners without falling and removing any bodily leaks as fast as you can. I sit on the toilet and read the instructions; simple words flow into simple words like enigmatic poem. I stand up, try to figure out the angle, my mind filled with grim urgency. It takes seven to get it right. When I finally crawl out of the bathroom stall, bent in half like a dying opera woman, Kyd's standing at the sink with a bottle of Tylenol in her hand. *All better now?*

I reach for the Tylenol, avoid any contact with her curiosity, sitting down and staring at the floor until she gets the hint, and I'm finally alone to study my new face. My face is a sheer pale green, my hair wild as though I've been wrestling with the devil, my eyes morphed into two hollow plums. I grab my cap, stuff hair up underneath it, look myself in the hollows, say: *Me as woman* in my new robot voice, then go out and get into the pool.

O Misery O Philosophy O Jargon

When I get back to Glenwood, summer's over, and I'm a highly charged, brand-new, international senior woman. Dot, Roxanne, and Father Tim are standing in the exact same spot I last left them like a painting in a museum, except they've changed clothes. Father Tim is a vision of tennis-playing health in beige slacks and a light blue polo, his transparent skin bronzed the color of oatmeal. Dot's now taller than Roxanne, whose eyes are ringed raccoon to match her black tights, black dress, black bangles, natty piece of lace holding up her hair. Roxanne is wearing funny makeup. Dot is wearing funny makeup. They're makeup-wearing miserable people. I look over at Roxanne, who looks back at me and says: *What?* I say: *What, what?* and she looks at Dot and says: *She's back.*

Priests often say the wrong thing. Father Tim looks up, says: *What did they feed you in Colorado? You've grown!*

When I get home, Mom is fully dressed in bed, propped up on an arsenal of pillows, waiting for me. Her bedside table is packed with life's necessities: a telephone, a smorgasbord of pills in clear brown plastic with the child-protection tops screwed on sideways, a thermos of something, a half-eaten family-size pack of M&M's, three detective novels, a jar of cream, a toothbrush with dried-on paste, an empty plate void of crumb, a roll of toilet paper, a blunt knife, some speckled bananas. She hugs me and says: *You've grown even bigger than I ever, more than I ever, you're just like . . .* then has a tired nervous breakdown with gentle seismic trembles and a couple of clear blue tears that light up her eyes but do not fall. I watch her carefully: she's lost all muscular tonicity and her skin has turned the color of paste.

Have you been feeding her the grimlock? I accuse Dot in the kitchen later.

She takes offense. *No! Not for months. She's eating food again.*

What's she been eating? I open the fridge and look in. Raw potatoes, cooked potatoes, milk, butter, cheese, new potatoes, a frothy pitcher of grimlock with an oily green sheen on the top, mashed potatoes.

She likes potatoes, says Dot, getting nervous.

Potatoes! There's like hundreds, I say, throwing my hands up in the air . . . *I can't believe this.*

June puts things in them—broccoli and cheddar. She's speaking fast. *Bacon and cauliflower. I chopped up some chicken and mixed it with butter, then I baked it again with mozzarella . . . She liked that one.*

I shut the door. *So what's the deal with the M&M's?*

She shifts her eyes in the international dance of all bad liars. *They're for visitors.*

I speak slowly, reeling her in. *Are you sure?*

She shifts her eyes to the ceiling, her face an unholy hue. *Yes, I'm sure.*

I go in for the kill. *She has two chins. When I left, she only had one . . . She was better off on the grimlock.*

She looks at me, her sad eyes ringed in blue: *She's turned . . . that color . . . because she doesn't go outside and you can't live on grimlock.*

I sigh. *Better grimlock than potatoes and M&M's.*

She gets both defensive and shifty. *I told you: those are for the visitors. And it's not just potato. We add healthy ingredients.*

I look at the shifting landscape of her face. *You can lie to yourself, but don't lie to me.*

I go through an unfortunate big-shot phase, pretending that Colorado obliterated all that I've been, thus changing me forever. I make it known to one and all that I've won a full scholarship to *Stanford University* in *California,* where I will swim under the guidance of the immensely amazing *Supercoach E. Mankovitz,* the most successful coach since the beginning of time. I subliminally advertise the fact that Kansas has finally been revealed to me for what it really is: a river of flatness and snot, a sad mixture of tornadoes, crushed mobile homes, pizza parlors, stores that sell items no one really wants, people whose small stories no one wants to hear. Most junior Catholics spent the summer lazily floating around Lake Shawnee on tires, experimenting with pot, getting their cherries popped. They have brownish arms and noses that fade faster than you can say *snap*. The real me is a serious person with serious desires, way too serious to be contained by Kansas. I am already half out and want fellow Glenwoodians to know it so that I can know it even more.

At first, the sisters deal with me and my slouchy classroom ways the way they always have: *Straighten up, missy, or the only pool you'll be swimming in today is one of your own sorrow.* But I'm zooming up into the stratosphere, breathing ozone, dreaming of the world championships in Moscow, where I will most excellently skim water and beat the rest of the world. I fling myself down on one of the Cocoplat's twin beds and think about winning as she calmly explains her deep endless pure heart-wrenching gut-disturbing love with this idiot guy who used to be so skinny we put glue on his chair in sixth grade to see if he'd stick. I have perfected the art of half listening from Dr. Leonard Ash, am swimming so fast in my head, no one in the world comes close, as Lilly Cocoplat speaks of the joys of disguising hickeys with a cream made with zinc.

But I feel sorry for everyone stuck forever in their small local lives. In gym class, I stare at poor old Augusta standing at the top of Mount Mercy in her red parka miming and pointing at her sad nun knees. I run, her speck becoming larger and larger until I see the poor broken veins in the corner of her poor Polish nose. There's Ugly Helena, the history nun, reading sad passages from history books she'll never grace. All Sister Belly has to look forward to is tossing up a disk of pizza dough and catching it behind her back. Poor Sister Fergus whooshes by on her way to deal with human disaster, emitting a perfume of ham and clover, her cross glowing in the sun like the light saber of a Jedi before a good smite. I give her a sad little wave and she gives me a normal wave back.

But after a while, things switch. Kansas becomes real again and Colorado fades away; mountains turn to clay, Kyd's hair becomes haystack and her teeth turn to marble, Arch Naylor's mustache turns into parts of that old red broom the nuns use for the sidewalk. The nurses who drew the blood out of my arms turn into bored dental hygienists. Mrs. Peggy has a plate face with spaghetti hair and two halves of a tomato for lips. She's got olive earrings and ham skirts and cheese sticks for feet. Dr.

Peggy has one of those cork heads that grow wheat out the top. Peggy jumps up and down gnashing sharp gorilla teeth. Only the superior E. Mankovitz remains steady in his flesh and blood. He takes off his cap, scratches the dent in his hair, says: *That'll do.*

Coach Stan is overexcited with thrill, a deep, borderline hyper. I sit in his office as he describes everything he thinks it will take to cover me one day in the near future in six grams of pure Olympic gold. He says *Okay* at the beginning of every sentence, opening both his palms. *Okay, by the end of this year, this is what you'll be swimming the 200 m free,* he says, sliding a piece of paper across his desk and clasping his hands as I unfold it: *1:58,* faster than the fastest time yet recorded by a human woman. I look at him and he looks at me, his face twitching with edgy athletic energy, his hands tapping the table, his feet tapping the floor and we sit, all serious until it starts to get embarrassing and he says: *You could be faster than the fastest swimmer in the world.* Then he says: *Okay, this is what you'll be swimming in the 200 IM* and he slides another piece of paper across his desk: *2:12.* His face is twitching again, his hands and feet still at it, until he can't contain himself anymore and says: *This is what you'll be swimming in the 100 butterfly.* I unfold the square: *1:00.* I look out over the empty pool. Even those crazy East German Berliners don't have these times. I tape the pieces of paper above my bed. They are the last thing I see at night, the first thing I see in the morning. When I'm in the mood, I kneel down and say crazy stuff, nothing prayer-like but crazy still. When I'm in another mood, I dance around in my underwear and swear. *Fuck you, fuck you, fuck you. You're going down.* Sometimes Dot and Roxy join me and we dance, and when we dance, we flip off the East German Berliners, our walls, the window, the world.

I say things like: *I'm going to beat those East German Berliners* because the words *East German* and *Berliner* make me feel bigger and darker and more mysteriously heroic. Someone writes EAST GERMAN BUTT LINERS on my locker and Lysol and bleach won't remove it.

Lilly Cocoplat takes me aside and tells me to knock it off. She's wearing barely detectable brown eyeliner and clear Vaseline on her lips. *Knock it off with the East German Colorado thing.*

What? I'm sitting on the curb waiting for June.

You know what. She's added a heart charm to her cross.

It's exciting! I mean, can you believe it? It's me. I wish she were swimming; we could be champions together.

Yeah, but like quit talking about it all the time. She is over the swimming, has been hanging out with people who are not me, thus fun. *Every second you're like Ohhhhh the East German Berliners and Olympic Supercoach Ernest Manvinch is so super . . .*

Man-ko-vitz. And I don't talk about it like every second. Now I'm surly. I put my *I feel sorry for you, Lilly,* face on and she sucks in a breath, pivots, and walks away.

I swim with Coach Stan five days a week before school and all afternoons except Sunday. Mother makes the commitment to drive in the morning and Coach Stan takes me home at night. I have specific rules I have to follow: No attempting to roller-skate backward, the wearing of seat belt at all times, even in the backseat, fifty grams of protein at each meal including breakfast, whole grains, whole pastas, whole meals, whole pajamas, whole muffins, whole doughnut holes, whole hats, whole scarves covering whole head. No skating, no sledding, no biking, no running, no sliding, no tripping, no hammering, no dancing, no falling, no hurting, no breaking. I take mixtures of vitamins and minerals and essential acids at different times of the day, drink a gallon of water, sleep the sleep of the genuinely tired for ten hours straight, rolling out of bed and into my sweats, making it to the pool in twenty minutes flat. I have a weight trainer from the U, the cute Chip, all to myself. I eat a stack of pancakes that comes up to my chin, four scrambled eggs, two English muffins, a banana, and am still hungry.

Fredrinka Kurds is getting faster. *She's superhuman,* I say to Stan the day we learn she broke a minute in the 100 fly.

Stan's sitting at his desk, tapping the floor with his sneakers. *Well . . . it almost seems impossible.*

You said anything was possible, I say, biting into a disgusting sandwich June made, but hunger keeps me chewing.

Yes, yes, I know I did.

Fredrinka Kurds swirls around in my head, then swirls around in the pool moving so fast the water remains still. She's practicing as hard as I am, or—and here my heart sinks, revolves a little bit, twitters, sinks again—*harder.* People I don't know want to talk to me about it. There's a write-up in the Sunday supplement of the *Kansas City Star* with a photo spread. I wear ugly shoes and striped pants that don't fit right. The Dark Catholic with the putty face volunteers to do my hair and I accept, only to discover she thinks ugly hair looks good. As an extra bonus, she paints my face orange and uses a brown pencil to accentuate what she calls my *strong brows*. In one photo my orange face is looking at my white hands as if it's thinking about what color to paint them. The caption next to it says: *I'm really concentrating on beating the East German Berliners. I think it's time they know what a real American from Kansas can accomplish*. In the pool shots, I look as anonymous as any other swimmer from any other place on the planet: big-shouldered, cruel, determined. Roxanne points out that with the eyebrows and the orange face, I look like that guy who lives fearlessly with bears.

I don't care. I'm going to wear dress sweats, meet Team USA in the terminal of Chicago International Airport, where we shall fly to the backward part of the world like tall venting angels, and when we get there we're going to show them a thing or two. I hop around to the beat of a different drummer in my bedroom, put violet glitter on my eyelids, am never tired but often possessed by a wave of scary Peggy-like horniness. Puberty has decided to hit me hard; my small breasts throb when I lie flat on my stomach, and my genital shrub is thickening into category three: woolly and wild. I examine it and consider taking measures. I learned in Colorado that a real swimmer's hairy bits are rarely wider than a stick of gum.

Faced with the perplexity and internationalness of the situation, the nuns steer clear. I wonder out loud if I am going to stay in a type of *Moscow Marriott* not so far from *Siberia*. I wonder out loud what would happen if the *KGB* steals us and sends us to a *gulag in Siberia* with other dissidents. Jealous locals don't want to have lunch with me anymore so I have lunch with kids who pretend to like me more than I pretend to like them. Coach Stan concentrates on my taper, worries to excess, calls the superior E. Mankovitz on the phone, says: *I'd like to speak with Mr. Mankovitz, please* until it's time for me to depart.

This is what the world looks like out the porthole: a swirling pit, an ocean of blue and green undulating beans until we hit the blob of moss that is Greenland, water again, this time slate-colored all the way to the tip of Europe, which reveals splotches of sunny green when uncovered by cloud. I can't tell what time it is anymore when we descend into the black and gray quarry pit that is Moscow.

You think that your regular things will do something unusual when they are in an unusual place, but I am amazed that my body remains integrally Kansan even when it's in Russia. My sneakers squeak across the marble in the hotel lobby exactly the same way they squeak down the halls of Holy Name, but my brain excavates drama. It says: *Steady on, now; steady on. We're in enemy territory.* This makes Moscow very zesty and exciting even though Radmilla, our guide, is so shy she uses only half of her mouth when she smiles. She looks at a spot above our heads. *To your left is the Cathedral of Christ Our Savior; to your right is the Kremlin.*

Peggy is deeply affected by the abundance of male beauty. *I'd have sex with nine out of ten of them . . . I think I'd even have sex with an old one . . .* E. Mankovitz accidentally hears, becomes very frowny, disappointed, and stern but says nothing.

Moscow snows fall heavier and harder than Kansas snows, have a bitter, stinging edge to their flakes, but I'm burning with happiness, thus do not care. I explode from the starting block faster than a hammer of a gun, but I can't keep up with the East German Berliners, headed by Fredrinka Kurds, one of the greatest swimmers in the history of the world, beard or no. I swim behind her like a guppy in the wake of a speedboat, watching her feet churn as fast and as ruthlessly as steel blades. She is so amazing, I forget to breathe.

I know zip about psychological warfare, openly study her from the streaks of her frosted hair sprouting rooster-style from her small head, to the harrowing shoulders wedging out of her neck like craggy mountain rock, to the sturdy thighs with visible veins, down to her knobby ankles and the longest, widest feet I've ever seen on a human being outside of a museum. Fredrinka has decided to deal with Team USA by rendering us invisible, but teammate Dagmar has a different theory, standing behind her, arms crossed over barrel chest, squinting at me with two raisins for eyes. The rest of the team chant and stomp, have dark sideburns, long nose hairs, red spots, really thick necks. The East German Berliner chant is sufficiently potent that it resonates down to my feet as I'm blessing them in my head.

Peggy stares them down from her perch in the bleachers. She's wearing a white baseball cap with a big blue star in the middle of it, is chewing down hard on some pink bubblegum.

Look at that redhead—she's definitely packing one; there's a bulge, she whispers. *What do you think?*

Concentration is the key to mental preparation, I say, watching Dagmar stretch her rubbery neck in seven creepy directions.

Peggy ignores me. *I'd beat them if they were still girls—even steven.*

They sweep us cleanly, tightly, perfectly, pulling themselves through water at speeds Mankovitz hasn't dared yet mention. Afterward, Dagmar shakes my hand, looks me straight in the forehead, says: *Gut schwimmen!* Fredrinka slumps up behind her, both shoulders curved in as though to disappear, shakes my hand, looks me deep in the eyes, and quietly whispers: *Gut schwimmen!*

Peggy says: *They have guy voices, did you hear them? Like lower than my dad's.*

On the plane home, Supercoach E. Mankovitz maintains his usual high optimism and enthusiasm: *Our time will come.* He calls me over to the empty seat next to him and we discuss the intelligent swim. I'd gone out too fast, lost milliseconds in senseless breathing, but my technique was tight and I'd lowered my times. E. Mankovitz seems pleased, thus I seem pleased. If Supercoach E. Mankovitz is spending time with you, things are good in a burning bush in the middle of the desert kind of way. If he believes in you, it is because you are.

Up the Downhill

I ride up hills, tires cutting through fallen leaves. I ride down hills, tires cutting through rushing gutter. Seniors are participating in lighthearted thieving, open irreverence, lots of highly effective lie. Lilly tries to coerce me into breaking the Catholic bylaws one by one with all the other fun seniors who smoke secret cigarettes, filling up plastic cup after plastic cup of beer at hidden kegs that sprout around bonfires when night falls. I look at her and say: *I can't, Lilly. I'm really busy.*

And I *am* really busy. I travel from bed to pool from pool to school from school to pool to bed again like a human train; Mom's starting not to feel well up in her bed, until now her secret haven, and June's having a tough, lonesome year that's driving her to the ledge and showing her the bottom.

When I get home from practice on Friday, shoulders aching in pain, June's brandishing one of Leonard's Japanese knives from his special elite barbecue set, its blade so sharp it could cut an entire newspaper in half with one swipe. She's adding ingredients into a large pot filled with smoking oil; hacked-up potatoes, unpeeled carrots, spoonfuls of chutney, chunks of onion, pieces of still-frozen shrimp. She holds the knife up behind her ear, then brings it down hard on the chopping block and a whole chicken collapses like a house of cards. I take a step back. *What's going on?*

Something's wrong; her eyes have been invaded by a mean animal who doesn't recognize me as an old friend.

What's it look like? She says, and something in her voice makes me shy.

I don't know. I'm using the careful voice I usually reserve for the company of nun.

You don't know? She takes a wooden spoon and starts stirring it up.

No. I look for an out.

What's this look like? Her knobby face is perched at the edge of the steaming pot.

I look down at a bunch of vegetables sizzling in pain. *I don't know.*

You don't know. The insides of her eyes are different—rheumy, dull. *Gumbo. Look what you've done to yourself . . . You've swum the girl right out.* Then she laughs like someone who's pretending to laugh and doesn't care who knows it. A nuclear mushroom of fear heats up, then blossoms in my chest.

Dot grabs my arm. *We should put her to bed or something.*

This makes June jumpy. She grabs the knife, starts swinging it around like a samurai. *I'm not going to bed. No way. I'm cooking up a gumbo.*

I swam one hundred million sets, all of them hard and fast. Leonard appeared at the very last wall bathed in cement like Abraham Lincoln, but with wide-alive eyes.

I'm not hungry, I say, starving.

She's got the tip of the knife under my chin. *You're not hungry?*

I barely move my lips. *No.*

She looks at the knife, surprised it's in her hand, takes a step back, lowers it. *You, you are not hungry.*

I barely move my lips. *No.*

This isn't good enough for you? Green Giant. Does everything you eat have to come out of a box? She laughs, forgetting about the knife again, swooping it through the air as though it were a chopstick. *Go. Get out. Go. Scoot. Scoot now. Get out. Pronto.*

I escape into my bedroom. It's March outside, night falling with a thud, like a heavy object off a wall. Dot comes in. *Can I stay with you for a while?* I say *okay* and we watch March trees sweep their budding arms against the window until we fall asleep.

The next day June sits on the couch avoiding all eye contact like a lady in court. *I don't know what happened yesterday . . . nothing I said was . . . it wasn't the way . . . just promise me one thing: Don't drink like I drink. If there is anything I want you to understand from me: Alcohol is shit, worse than shit, double worse. You can tell who you want what you want.* She looks down at all the nails she's bitten off her poor worn hand. *I'm not going to be denying anything. What I did was . . . after what you've been . . . I don't know what happened.*

She's taken a shower but nothing's washed off. Her hands are trembling and her face is crumpled and her eyes are trembling and crumpled. I feel scared again. I look around. The bird feeder is full, the house has been cleaned from top to bottom, the windows are clear, the sunshine is tangible, but fear blooms hot like a red flower.

Just promise me you won't drink like I drink, she says again.

I won't. This from Dot, who means it.

I won't. This from Roxanne, who's mastering the effective lie.

I am a swimmer, I say, stressing the syllables to jiggle a memory, pave apology's way.

She looks at me with no-color eyes, face no-colored, teeth a translucent greenish gray. *You ain't gonna be a swimmer forever, babe.*

Trials and Tribulations

It's hot; the air's holding so much liquid, it's difficult to breathe. Coach Stan is standing behind me anguishing, his eyes ringed in brown like an owl's. This is it, the hardest race in the world. This is it, harder than Worlds. Legend says it's harder than the Olympics themselves. This is it, the Olympic trials. One and two qualify in each race. The rest: Out.

Earlier on, Supercoach Ernest Mankovitz made a joke: *It will be one of the only occasions in your life where second is as good as first* as hundreds of swimmers pretended to laugh. This is his favorite part, the watching, the waiting, the weeding, assessing the culmination of thousands of hours spent chasing one's shadow across the floor of one's pool. But third isn't funny. Third is purgatory, the real one that flares from the tip of hell where you look up at the angels gliding by in a vision of blue and you're not yet burning yet you're not entirely dead.

Coach Stan is speed-talking into my ear. *Keep it steady and smart and strong.* He's folded his forehead into his eyebrows, his ears stretching his mouth into a nervy line. *I'm talking speed and pace the whole way through, got it? And don't think about the breathing; just don't forget to breathe. Okay?*

Smart and in-pace and in-telligent with my head on straight as I continue to breathe before I can in case I can't. I echo, but inside: *Fuck that. Swim like an asshole.*

Before I leave, Father Tim blesses me. *I'll pray for you.*

Mother says: *Did you pack shoes? Remember your shoes.*

Dot grabs my hands and crushes them. *You can do this. I know you can do this.*

Roxanne says: *I wish I were going somewhere.*

June says: *Take it as far as you can.*

Lilly Cocoplat is still dating Skinny Pants, who plans on being a lawyer as soon as he possibly can. She's excited; forgetting our diverging paths, she hugs me hard, says: *You'll* so *win.*

This is it. I put two almonds in my mouth and click them against my teeth, looking outside of myself as quietly as a well-behaved pet in the back of an expensive car. Everyone is moving; swimmers stretching next to me, their legs twisting; swimmers pulling themselves into sprint, then slowing down to rhythmic crawl; swimmers drinking strawberry-flavored protein drinks; swimmers listening to music, some eyes shiny, some eyes vague; swimmers in a state of trance, hoods covering heads, goggles woven through fingers; swimmers rubbing long, flexible feet; swimmers twisting long, flexible toes. Fellow Americans have now officially become competition; if I make eye contact with someone swimming in one of my heats, I look away.

I click the almonds, flex every muscle in my back, hop, put my cap on, check my goggles, rotate my arm propellers, count every rib in my rib cage one by one. There are more than I thought. I click the almonds on my teeth, chew them into pulp, wait.

When my name is announced, I salute with one strong arm, which Peggy kindly points out later seems slightly Nazi of me. I jump, shake, wrench my fingers, twist my wrists, get on my mark, freeze until the beep sounds and I explode.

I make it to the finals in six events. Coach Stan chews his blue lips white. He's standing next to me indenting cement with the heels of his sneakers.

It's down to Babe and me for the 200 butterfly. She looks at me, nods, makes the sign of the cross, breaks her own world record. I touch one hundredth of a second behind, another personal best.

Journalists ask: *Disappointed by the second place, Pip?*

I frown at the *Pip. Don't you know second is as good as first?*

Theoretically. But she beat you.

I warm down like a drowning person in a long dress as my name is etched into the wall of Olympians and Coach Stan gets two mottled patches on his neck that take a week to go away.

I find a dark space in the locker room, discreetly throw up in a garbage can, brush my teeth twice, put my sweats on, stand under the dryers I put on full blast so I can warm up. The heat invades the surface of my skin, turning my face burgundy, the mind behind exploding in deep attachment to life and all of life's things, the source of all suffering. My brain speeds up as fast as the Whirly Wizard on Shawnee Days and I start to shake. Leonard's gone, the tiles underneath my feet are white squares caulked in blue, Bron's cello is lying on its back in the closet with the coats (it drifts into my mind, its cords moaning), my mother is sitting in front of the TV she's set up at the foot of her bed, her face the color of green M&M. Someone who isn't going to the Olympics is lying on a bench crying as her coach massages her temples, whispering urgent things into her ear. I cut my nails too close to the skin; Coach Stan has broken some blood vessels in his eyes through the mystery of what a big shout can do in the chain of bodily events. The world is deepening like blood in a state of permanent coagulation. I don't like it. I walk into a stall, sit on a toilet, put my head between my knees, panting like a warhorse.

Pip, Pip, Pip . . . has anyone seen Pip? Peggy's calling.

I hold my breath.

She stands in front of my stall, voice yodeling.

I say nothing.

She stands in front of my stall. *I see your feet.*

I remain invisible through the magic of silence.

Everyone's looking for you . . . Her tall voice cuts easily through the short door.

I speak. *I'm sick.*

Why? Now? . . . How sick? She's confused.

I'm shaking . . . I don't think I can walk and I . . . can't . . . unclench . . . my jawbones.

Want me to get Kyd? Now she's concerned.

No! I shriek. *Not Kyd. I'll be okay in a minute.*

Herr Professor Spankypants wants to give a speech, she says, trying to make me laugh.

I'll be better in a minute. I just need to warm up. I feel better.

Want some Chiclets? She knows I like Chiclets.

No. I don't care about Chiclets.

They might help, she says, then sits outside the door, guarding it. Her silence is punctuated by the sharp crack of popping gum.

Every once in a while, she checks. *How is it now?*

Better.

People waft in and out. I breathe slowly, putting all bad thoughts into canoes and sending them rushing down the river to the trenches of oblivion.

Coach Stan is calling.

Peggy yells back: *She's in the bathroom; she'll be out in a minute.*

Did you have to say bathroom? I'm better.

Who cares about bathroom? Everyone goes to the bathroom. She knows I'm better, is back to herself.

It takes fifteen minutes for my attachment to worldly things to subside. I open the door slowly with a horrible-looking face Peggy does not mention. We find E. Mankovitz, who solemnly shakes my hand, gives me a quick hug, says things with his lips. I shake his hand, accept the hug, feel pockets of air with sound inside leave my mouth. Babe and Sunny and the rest of Team USA find us and we jump up and down. We look into each other's eyes and a deep love is born; a love of six-year-old bodies thrashing through pool, a love of white toes clutching the edge of a scratchy starting block, a love of a prom dress pulled over linebacker shoulders, a love of the lonesomeness of the lane, a love of the lonesomeness of the empty pool, a love of the lonesomeness of spent energy and hot pain, a love of all the things we had to do to get here, right where we are, now. Love picks us up, then puts us down again. We love each other at the top, then we love each other at the bottom. We hop and we hop and as we hop, I feel the love and the tears that carry love to the surface for all to see. My mind whirls, hunting and gathering. I will know this moment again and again; it will become one of the measures I use for my life. I whoop a crazy gut whoop and deep love makes them whoop with me as life advances forward and our whoops catch and mingle together in the thick chlorine air.

Cold War II
XXIII Olympiad
Los Angeles, 1984

The press people are constantly surprising me. I wait for them to ask me questions about the dramatic Eastern bloc boycott, my new fantastic breathing technique, the hours spent torched by the legendary Arch Naylor, the unusual dryland stretching sessions, how many seconds I dream of cutting off my personal best, but they pretend to consult their fake notes, then respectfully inquire if I have a boyfriend back home in Glendale, and how long does it take, exactly, to ride my bike across town, and wherever do I go during those highly destructive tornadoes.

This annoys me. *It's Glenwood. Twenty minutes if I pedal fast. And we go to the basement with a flashlight and a radio like everyone else.*

They lean in close. California *must seem like an entirely new* planet *for you, Pip.*

This doubly annoys me. *No, California seems normal . . . just fine . . . and my name is not Pip.*

Peggy bullshits with them, hooting and joking, rolling her eyes, flipping her hair, emphasizing her best profile, but I can tell they unnerve her because she's talking a mile a minute, tapping the legs of the table with one of her ugly red shoes. She's having a difficult time hiding the fact that she's thrilled not to be swimming against someone she refers to as the daughter of Thor. She screws her face into fake, says: *We'll really miss them.* Babe had gotten the shaft for the Olympic boycott in Moscow in '80 when she was fourteen and already one of the fastest middle-distance swimmers in the world. She smiles calmly, murmuring assent, and speaks about the result of hard work, dedication, devotion, and a world-class coach. But she's as pissed as she'll let herself be, was dying to race the best in the world and beat them fair and square. She's clicking her nails together under the table like a Kansas cricket before a storm.

When we're alone, Peggy drops the bullshit. *Can you believe all this boycott bullshit?*

The breaststroking chick from Arizona I will gladly trounce until the day she retires says: *They're probably chicken.*

Babe says: *Don't forget; we did it to them first.*

Peggy says: *Yeah, but they deserved it.*

I say: *Maybe we deserve it back, then. What if something's happened to them? Like what if poor old Fredrinka . . .*

Peggy says: *Whose side are you on all of a sudden?*

I get annoyed. *I'm on our side. But without . . .*

Arizona starts hopping. *It's all bullshit. They're afraid.*

I'd learned to scoff from Peggy. *Afraid?* I scoff. *Look what they did to us at the Worlds.*

Peggy stares at me. *Seriously. Whose side are you on?*

Ours, *you idiot, but remember the Worlds.*

Babe sighs. *The Worlds are over.*

But without Buffalo Kurds competing, I have a chance at gold; many chances, even. I eat my protein-enriched oatmeal visualizing gold, swim vast, easy lengths visualizing myself swimming vast, easy lengths visualizing gold. My mind is synchronizing, the future has caught up with the present, the past has slipped away, everything is perfect, and I am saturated in a high-energy peace that does good things to my face.

Supercoach E. Mankovitz says: *Babe, I know how deeply disappointed you are, but you go out there and swim your best against the clock. Back home in East Berlin you-know-who is probably watching; let's send her a message she won't want to read.*

Peggy won't let it go. *We would have kicked their butts for sure.*

Leonard thought of the world in terms of an interesting interconnectedness; if someone left the door open too long in Siberia, he and Dr. Bob would eventually feel the draft in Glenwood. I think about the world in a more personal way. I'm interested in it in terms of myself and all things connected to myself. If I am not directly involved, I don't really think about it until someone else makes me. I look at myself in the mirror in my dorm room in the Olympic village when no one is around, praying with my palms together like a realistic figurine, trying to remain focused, because being an Olympian is like striding around an important cakewalk naked while everyone else is in their Sunday best.

When the Superior E. Mankovitz catches my eye, he nods. I'm not sure what the nod means, but I nod back as though I am. Mankovitz is more relaxed than I've ever seen him, except he's chewing a tight wad of gum so hard the muscles in his jaw contract the muscles in his face and he looks stern. He chews it economically but hard; you can see his neck cords move, but the sound that comes out of his mouth when he speaks is smooth and modulated as though he were discussing cake with a nun on a yellow and blue Sunday afternoon. He's very quiet, unemotional, and calm. *Everything we've done until this moment has led us to this moment. Not one second of it has been wasted. Think of all the years you've spent in the pool in order to reach this point. There is only one thing to do now and all of you know what that is.* His words resonate in bright holographic splendor: *One. Thing. To. Do.*

Olympic drama is starting to excavate sleeping Catholic ceremonial practices planted in my mind long before I could think, and I now have to fight the urge to bow or genuflect when the Mankovitz speaks. He looks at me and nods and I have to restrain myself in order not to genuflect or cross myself in response. He schedules a private conference with each of us. I sit on my hands, compose my face, listen. He knows everything. He clasps his hands together, evokes the lonesomeness of a life understood by only the very few who understand the terms of a dedicated train. He leans on his elbows and reveals what I am living now, what swimmers all over the world are living now; baby swimmers, adolescent swimmers, swimmers who gave up a long time ago, master swimmers who almost made the team, how they are watching, waiting, searching for inspiration to continue. He takes a sip of coffee, sits back in his chair, and tells me who I am, what I am, what I am capable of.

Now, he says, opening his palms.

Here, he says, closing them.

I want to fling myself on the ground and slobber with relief. I want to unleash the wave of water that is pressing hard against my eyes, put my head down on his desk and sleep fourteen hours. But I am aware this might cause concern, so I stand up and thank him.

Thanks, Coach.

No, Philomena. Thank you.

I face each new day filled with universal excitement and happiness. The Buddha in me has awakened Jesus, God, all the angels and saints, renewing the possibility of a secular heaven. The pool at the Olympic Aquatic Center at USC is a sheet of glass floating in a gravity-free zone, and I accidentally become semi-famous for eleven days for having a nervous breakdown on the podium.

I stand next to a smallish West German Berliner, a Dutch chick, a Swedish chick, two Aussies, and a French chick who keeps pulling out her bottom lip while making a sucking sound through her teeth like a precious locked-up monkey. The West German Berliner whips a fist at the air and says: *I'm going to smash up everyone,* bobbing up and down like an emergency light. I hide some almonds in my cheek, use reverse psychology, speaking slowly so she'll understand: *Yes, I believe you will,* and she gets so confused she shuts up. I know what I am, who I am, where I am, why I am and so does Ernest K. Mankovitz. That makes two.

I take my mark.

I wait for the beep.

I plunge.

I am ferocious animal, my brain engaged in physical behavior that ceaseless repetition has made deeper than urge. The pool is hard and so fast I feel like I'm gliding on ice. When I look at my races later on film, all I see is one arm floating out of the water and one arm following, very quiet, almost sedate, half a body length ahead of the flailing arms behind me as I move toward the now.

I discover the joy of the international relay. We stand in a huddle holding each other's shoulders. Babe says: *Let's get the world on this one.* Peggy nods. *The world is ours.* When I feel their eyes light on me, I try to think of something great to say that doesn't include swear words, nun-generated Latin phrases, lyrics from songs I can't put my finger on. I roll my hand into a fist, bend down low on one knee, close my eyes, and pump the air *go go go go go go go go go go.*

Peggy hops. *She's yucking right; let's go.*

Babe gets businesslike when she's nervous. *Save it for the pool.*

We put our palms together, six sweaty, two dry.

The crowd creates a disturbing rhythmic African sound: thick, melodious, and so intense it causes my skin to contract. I don't feel the starting block beneath my feet, don't see the watery sheet of glass as it opens before me, don't feel my own body cutting through air, the pressing buoyancy of lungs, the ropes of water twisting with convecting energy as I let them pull me through. The only tangible sensation is felt at the wall and that's when I touch it.

The Mankovitz catches my eye and nods and I know exactly what the nod means; the nod means *now*. I take my first Olympic gold. The Mankovitz remains calm, squeezes my shoulder softly. I pull my hood up over my head, close my eyes, click the almonds, wait. I open my eyes when someone taps my knees and there, dancing across my line of vision, is Peggy, huge and hopping, her eyes frantic with exhaustion and a deep inner excitement. I nod, pull the hood back over my head, take another gold: 200 free.

I do not cry. Tears sit behind my eyes, lodge in my throat, swell up my neck, get stuck, cause other bodily things to happen. Sometimes when I want to cry my head tingles, my throat swells, my swallowing reflex goes into overdrive, my chest constricts, my gastric juices clutch, but no tears. During one of Mom's nervous breakdowns, she sat at the edge of my bed, grabbing at my shoulders with her fangs, weeping *Cry, cry, cry,* water firing out from her eyes in all directions like bullets from a machine gun in the hands of a child.

I hop up on the central podium as I hop up on all central podiums, proudly. On my left, the bronze, that psycho Aussie with the moon-pie eyes. On my right, the silver, the white-haired Petra with the strange feet that flop loosely from her ankles like empty socks. I hop, raising one arm high above my head. I bow my head, wait for the lady in the blue suit with the red white and blue bow to anoint me in gold. The noise of the crowd explodes in my mind, the world rolling into a sea of face. The national anthem starts to wail, creating a dreaded musical pressure in my chest as the flag slowly rises in a celebrating-the-dead kind of way. Something churns and my mind says: *Wow! This is exactly like a giant funeral!*

That nasty photographer from *Time* zooms in, capturing the red eye-balls, the heaving shoulders, the grinchy grimace, the rivers of snot. I split in two, now horrified and ashamed, now crazy and disgusting. I wipe my dripping nose with my Team USA jacket, try to tuck my head back into my shoulders, fail. I don't think about the fact that I'm being attentively televised until I watch two guys in navy blue suits and red silk ties talking about me later on national TV as I lie like a zombie on my Olympic bed.

There I am hopping up. There I am grimacing. *I don't think I've ever seen an athlete react quite like this one, Sherm.* There the flag rises gently as I wrestle with myself, lose.

There was Hanna Markindovia at the world wrestling championships in Bucharest, says Sherm in the low conversational tones that made him famous.

My snot is flowing; they've superimposed a translucent weaving flag across my red scrunched-up face.

I don't remember that, Sherm. . . . Cut to Petra, who's staring at me, her face filled with a mixture of pleasure and pity.

After the brutal headlock when she relinquished her four-year winning streak to Anke Tarnowski . . . Sherm's leaving space for Mark to consult his inner database of useless knowledge.

That's right! That's right! Her teammates had to carry her off the mat. . . . *Come to think of it* . . . *remember Lippy Sultz at the five-hundred-meter mark of the '76 marathon?* I'm thumping and trembling now. They cut to the Mankovitz, who's staring calmly at the flag, his hat over his heart.

They were worried she'd lost her sight . . . *that was terrible* . . . *terrible, Sherm, grueling* . . . *but here in L.A. at the sunny, hugely successful twenty-third Olympiad we have the seventeen-year-old Flipma Ash, who seems to be suffering from some sort of emotional exhaustion on the podium.* I'm wiping rivers of snot away with the back of my sleeve.

I'd have to side with you on that one, Mark. . . . *There's definitely a lot of emotion today here at the Olympic Aquatic Center, which took five billion dollars and fourteen tons of cement to create. Newcomer Philipma Ash has broken one world record and just this morning won her third gold; that puts her up there with* . . .

I'm told even Mankovitz wasn't expecting this one, Mark interrupts, as images of me wobbling like a Weeble flash across the screen. It's almost over.

Ohhh, I doubt that, Sherm; Mankovitz knows exactly what he's . . . Ooops, it's Philomena, *Sherm,* Philomena Ash, *who hails from the sweet state of Kansas . . . Hey! It says here that her teammates call her Pip.*

Well, Mark, that's quite a funny name for such a tall girl, says Sherm, looking straight into the camera with his famous eyebrow raise.

She's six-two, weighing in at a healthy 145 and I'm with you on that one, Sherm; she certainly doesn't seem like a Pip, but I have to say she's a kid who's got one heck of a career ahead of her. They cut to me levitating out of water as I beat the world.

That's right, Mark, says Sherm. *She's got a full scholarship with Mankovitz this fall at Stanford University, so we'll definitely be hearing from Pip in the future . . .*

Nervous breakdowns pique people's curiosity; they want to know why, even if they don't care. Calls are made to the center of Kansas. *Glenwood Morning Star* archives are consulted. Later, at the press conference, the short, barrel-chested Milt from *Newsweek* gets a sad-but-professional look on his face and says: *What would your father have said . . . Your sister? Do you think they would have been . . . proud?* And I do accidentally dive over the table and push him and his chair over, and we do roll on the ground for a millisecond, and I do bruise my left elbow pretty badly, calling him the worst names I can think of, and it is photographed by that one bearded guy, but I win and Milt loses because I become America's Saddest Sweetheart.

There are close-ups and, later, psychological commentary from a respected sports psychologist who explains the impact of drama combined with a never-lived youth. They have stills of me looking sad and sorry, pull out the photo of me with the orange face. People look at me, their faces dripping in pity. Peggy puts her arm around my shoulders, lowers her voice. *You could have said something. Now I feel like an ass.*

Well, that's good, I say, *because you* are *an ass.*

Supercoach E. Mankovitz puts a hairy red hand on my shoulder, squeezing. *Go get some rest now. We'll meet up at the Farm.*

I nod and smile. The nod and smile mean Stanford University, the Farm, the future.

Later at a photo op, Mary Lou Retton gives me a bouncy hug that knocks the wind out of me, starting a pulsing ache between two ribs that I can still feel during times of physical duress. In the photo my eyes look like pasta shells glued onto a grizzly cub face, but I understand, finally, why my mother has so many nervous breakdowns; they empty your mind of every thought it ever had.

California Catholics
Wear Dark Shades

❧

The Complicated Coast

There were things I did not know about Sunny Lewis when we decided to room together at Stanford. I did not know she was going to be a psych major, that she played sad songs on a sad steel-string acoustic guitar, that she hummed along as she strummed her sad guitar with wrinkly swimmer fingers, that she hummed and strummed other objects that were not a guitar when her guitar wasn't around to calm herself down from all of the human behavior classes she was taking that were secretly making her crazy. I already knew that she liked to give free psychological counseling, but I didn't know that I would be her guinea pig for the human emotional experience, that I would look up from my position on my recliner when the sad strumming suddenly stopped and she would be staring at me, analyzing.

Swimmers fall into two camps: those who want a balanced life and those who don't care. Sunny cares. I don't. I fall asleep every time I sit in a chair. I fall asleep in the middle of lunch. I fall asleep in the car with my key in the ignition. I fall asleep reclining in my recliner as Sunny strums a tale about what kind of horse a good cowboy rides in heaven. I fall asleep on the phone in the middle of a boring conversation with my mom twice in a row and she calls Napoleon Mankovitz the next day demanding action. They take my blood and analyze it for horrible things, but the verdict is plain and simple: *Just tired*.

I call my mother back and tell her to quit it, that swimming is an anchor, that it holds me steady, that I have to give it everything, then let it give back, that I have to do this or lose.

Full scholarship, Mom. It's my life.

It is not a life, she says.

It is a life, I say.

It is not a life, she says.

Shall we have discussions about life? I say.

Your fath—

I'm hanging up now.

Did you just hang up on your mother? asks Sunny, staring.

No, I say, reaching for the family-size pack of malted milk balls that I stash in the cubbyhole behind the phone.

Stanford University is easier than Holy Name. Nowhere, not under the cafeteria tables, not lurking in the wide corridors, not directing classes with long wooden rods that they point and jab, are there any stone eyes boring into my secrets, pulling every sin I have yet to commit to the surface and punishing me for it just in case they are not around when it happens. Neutral professors stand, clear their throats, and talk to those who listen. To those who listen not, they take no notice. Nun-inspired stenography skills turn out to be essential. I almost weep with pleasure as my hand slides across the page, every word down verbatim as other kids struggle, stuck in the middle of an unfinished thought.

My academic adviser is the handsomest man on campus and has the unfortunate name of Robert Boggs. Bob finds me *academically difficult to pin down,* tells me that my answers to his simple questions *create more questions.* Eventually it becomes clear that I am one of those people who should march toward a non-specific future, so I opt for an English major with a French option.

English is better than perfect. I sit around listening to real people talk about fake ones. Some students are animated, while others are tired observers, old beyond their years. Clever students who need their cleverness authenticated become quickly intolerant of other clever students, shouting and raising fists as TA's scream *Keep it down* or lean their chairs back on two legs and watch, visibly pleased. The drama stimulates me, keeping me awake. Every day is almost exactly like the day before, bright orange and purple skied. I awake when it's still night, eating breakfast and commenting on the new shapes Sunny has slept into her face as she ignores me through the power of radio, then we go to practice. Later, I sit through Comedy and Tragedy, Greek and Latin for

Vocabulary Building, Chaucer's Women, Astronomy, Basic Translation, then I practice again, going over the vast pockets of new knowledge in my mind.

O to talk to ye of little knownst yonder porridge.

O ye of yonder porridge know thee of over yonder.

OOOO ye weeping tears of leaking porridge yonder yonder yonder.

We have a team dietician named Mona who wears skirts made out of plant. She explains the energy ratio output nutrition factor and has us keep food logs. Peggy says *I totally love your skirt,* totally lying, and Mona is pleased. *Thanks! It's made from the yarn of a yucca!* I pack my food log with lie, halve the number of candy bars, turn cherry turnovers into fresh cherries, transform mint whips into protein bars. The only thing I don't lie about is the banana and peanut butter sandwiches made on Texas toast, the vats of popcorn I smother in butter, then salt, the three bowls of optimistic breakfast cereal I cover in sugar and consume every morning.

Mona wants me to meet her in her office for a private discussion. She puts her face close to mine and tightly mouths the words: *Private discussion.* We meet after practice the next week. I put my big yellow watch on just in case I need to look at it pointedly; Mona is someone who enjoys a good talk so much she forgets to check how everyone else in the conversation is doing. She also takes too many vitamins and has no vices, which gives her excessive amounts of energy. She's wearing an organic hemp sack with thin purple tights, offers me a cup of African tea she keeps warm in a silver thermos.

Bush people drink it when there's no food.

It's the color of weak blood. I take a sip anyway, say: *Wow, hits the spot.* An obvious lie.

They walk through the Kalahari by night. Miles and miles. It's really quite . . . well . . .

I look at my watch pointedly and she swipes the tea chat from her face. There are *urgent* things she wants me to know, that are *imperative* I do know. She fumbles, pulling out papers and graphs, articles highlighted in purple and yellow. She unrolls them, talking. She wants me to know that my body is an oracle or an edifice or a large library containing a memory of every thing I have ever consumed. *Do I know this?*

Nod *yes.*

Would I throw garbage into a temple? Would I put rotten things on an altar? Would I offer poison to a loved one? She stops, staring at me like an irritated Father Tod when he asks an obvious question about the devil.

I shake my head. *No* to garbage. *No* to rotten things. *No* to poison.

You are what you eat, she says, using her hands like an Italian although I know she's from Boston.

. . . Yes O verily, I say.

This is important, she says.

I'm sorry, I say.

Sugar does things. Unspeakable things. It takes your body hostage and your body *adapts* . . . like Patty Hearst. Am I familiar with Patty Hearst?

Nod *yes. I know who she is, Mona.*

Mona has a map of the human body standing skinless next to colorful posters of dancing señors and señoritas from Barcelona, her last, best vacation. The important organs are dissected into neat slices of pie; eyeballs are plucked, floating out like planets above the dry sockets of the human skull, the almighty brain rotating above like a beige Hormel ham. She swivels her chair, lowers her voice, solemnly says: *This is the human body . . . and* this *is sugar.* Teeth chew, sugar dissolves, teeth rot, falling. Planetary eyeball orbits contract, sugar laughs, igniting a fiery red trail that fuses straight to the heart, giving it a false sense of energy so that it ups its thumps. Sugar laughs harder, driving a truck straight into the human spleen. It jumps out, dances a jig, and the spleen dances with it for a while before collapsing from exhaustion. The pituitary, the epicenter of the human hormonal universe, goes haywire, trembles, barfing up some insulin, which sucks all the leftover energy from the human body, causing the human swim to collapse.

She turns, clasps her hands, weaving finger through finger. *Eventually sugar is . . . Do you hear me, Philomena? . . . There is no way on earth you can maintain a world-class time if you eat breakfast cereal from a box soaked in sugar for breakfast, and when I say no way, I mean it's lucky you're not pre-diabetic.*

She takes a deep breath. *You're an addict.*

This makes me laugh. I'd copied stuff out of Babe's perfect food journals. Under "snack" she'd written: *12 almonds, 1 pear.*

Sugar kills, Mona whispers.

Sweetly, I say, not mentioning the fried dough pockets stuffed with synthetic fruit and rolled in white refined poison powder that I buy from a baker so fat she has rolls on her wrists and sweats with the exertion of standing.

Mona taps my food journal with her knuckles. *I'm not kidding,* she says, and I notice that her dark brown eyes are the exact shade of Manny's. I compose myself; Mona is making me feel ashamed.

Have you ever read Bud Lancer? she asks, changing tactics.

No. I'm an English major, not a . . . you know, the great classics. Chaucer, Shakespeare, etc. . . .

That's fine. Personally, I think Bud Lancer should be required under-graduate reading, but anyway. I want you to think about the original man . . . or woman, in their original environment. Think about our bodies, their bodies; what they were designed to do since the beginning of time; how nature hasn't changed, how little we have . . . The nutrients that were needed to maintain a constant body temperature, help the body survive in extreme conditions. Do you think they would have survived for ten minutes if they consumed high amounts of sugar? Our bodies can't handle it, and our brains, our brains . . . Let me tell you about br— We know nothing about brains, actually, but we will, and when we do, we'll understand what all the excess sugar has done to us. Look around . . . Not in here. Out there. Look around. What do you see?

I look. *I see a light blue and orange sky that is stretching as far as the eye can see. The windowpane has a small hairline fracture . . .*

She's getting irritated. *The people . . . how are they?*

Often irritated.

She closes her eyes. *Okay. And . . .*

Squinty . . .

Okay. And.

Snooty . . .

And fat, no? They are fat, aren't they? She's throwing her hands in the air like an Italian again. *You're from Kansas, aren't you? They're fat there, aren't they? Fat?*

Well . . . it's hard to say, I lie.

Oh, ho . . . ho . . . hold on a minute here. There's a lot of fat in Kansas. She takes a sip from her African death tea to steady herself. *Let's just say this: Sugar-based societies create sugar-based peoples, and sugar-based peoples are characterized by intense unclassifiable yearnings, cravings that will never be assuaged. . . . Opening your dinner and heating it up . . . it's nutritional nothingness, a large nutritional abyss filled—Are you listening to me— filled with hidden sugars and bad fats. . . . Some scientists say it's slow suicide but it's homicide if you ask me, and who do you think they're killing? Not the smart advertising people and the wealthy manufacturers, noooooo. They wouldn't feed those things to their dogs . . . and I mean it. My brother's in advertising and you wouldn't believe the things he says. His wife has an organic garden and they order all their proteins privately from farms where they know the names of all the animals; I'm not kidding, one hundred percent organic . . . Anyway . . . he helps sell . . . he used to be so . . . when we were . . . You just wouldn't believe it.* She looks away, but not before I see her Manny eyes go shiny.

Now that she is so upset, I accidentally become so upset also. The air in her office hovers with the heavy chill of the air-conditioned disappointment that exists in everything once you think about it. The African tea that sat steaming with health in my cup a second before has a rusty tinge to it like water in an old toilet. The fluorescent lighting has heightened a notch; her posters of Spain have taken on a sinister air. She opens a drawer and takes out some essential oils that she drips into a white ceramic dish before she decides to attack the subject of cells—original cells, dying cells, fresh cells—as I sit slumped in the chair, a complicated series of simple cells casting long, obvious looks at my yellow watch, whose face is as large as a plate.

I look at the body on the wall; it's red and white and blue and yellow and green and brown and beige—exposed, veiny, dead. I interrupt. *Okay, okay, so I'm like a sugar addict.* She smiles with relief, then tortures me with nutrition and dietary fact until her face breaks into a million wobbly pieces, all of them with mouth. She slides a three-ring notebook filled with her inky blue swirls across her desk and says: *You'll be needing this,* then, as an afterthought, hands me her favorite Bud Lancer book: *Destination Destiny.*

On my way home, images of Roxanne squirming her way around Glenwood with buds of marijuana tied up in a pair of gym socks and hooded groovy eyes ride through my mind. June opens a family-size can of beans, dumps them in a pot, throws in mound after mound of sticky brown sugar, a few squirts of ketchup, and stirs it up, her eyes as distant as new moons. Mom lies in a bed of book, her face folded in half, a two-pound bag of peanut M&M's by her side. Dot's laughing with Sister Augusta over fresh sponge cake. Nuns are roaming the malls on Saturday afternoons, pockets bulging with caramels, eyes hardened into stone. Leonard had a jar of Thin Mints in his desk drawer, ordered seven boxes of Holy Name Nun Fudge every fall, liked his golden almond solitaires with the Sunday paper, Life Savers and butterscotch drops in yellow cellophane for road trips. He flies through my mind with an open package of pink and white coconut delights in his hand, absently throwing them into the air one by one, watching them float upward unhindered by gravity, and I am as close to crazy as to be overtaken with fright.

I fill the refrigerator with organic eggs from cage-free hens and local-grown organic vegetables, packages of flattened organic turkey, packages of flattened organic soy, packages of grains and seeds that resemble bird feeder food. I take boxes of cereal down from the top of the fridge and crush them with my feet while Sunny looks on. I grab my Kit Kats, my turnovers, my doughnut holes, my bite-size Worldwide International Variety Grab Bag, my Cheetos, my yogurt-covered pretzels, and put them in a bag I take outside and bury in the garbage bin. I finish the last package of malted milk balls in my bedroom later, in silence, slowly sucking off the milk chocolate, letting the Styrofoam middle melt into my tongue, vowing not to buy another pack until the season is over as the moon spills in through the window in gentle streams of yellow and Sunny sings about how in Nashville love is just another day.

But avoiding sugar is like avoiding life; it is everywhere in everything, and I become more complex than the only sugars I can now consume. The new things sit around waiting for the new me to come cook them and the new me sits around waiting to want to. I awake each morning, crawl slowly on all fours through the dark sugarless tunnel that is life, sweating with an individual headache hammering behind each eye, and I'm afraid I'll feel this for the rest of my life—a yearning for a sweetness that will not harm me; a yearning for a sweetness that does not exist. But Sunny stares at me, says: *You're just changing, and changing's uncomfortable. That's why people don't.*

It is a known communal team feeling that with my serious diet designed to remove the giddy inconsistency that characterized my swims of yore, I'm going to swim faster. Mankovitz is starting to apply the secret form of Mankovitz pressure that transforms people into fish. *I want you to swim it ten times under sixty this time, concentrating on the placement of your head. Hold it in a comfortable position, no straining, but I want you to be conscious of the waterline at all times.*

I grit my teeth, turning to grimlock as a last resort, try to remember the Dark Catholic recipe: *whey, curds, protein powder, vitamin C, kiwi, flaxseed oil, crushed walnut, holy premonition, dash of doom.*

I call Mona, desperate. *I don't feel well. I think I'm one of those people who can't live without . . .*

If you feel like something sweet, have a yam, she snaps.

Sunny finds recipes for yam-based soups, hosts Friday night yam bakes, flips Sunday morning yam waffles over the griddle until I pretend my crisis has passed so everyone leaves me alone. But without sugar fueling it, my regular personality grows old and tired and shaky. I fall asleep during fiery Chaucer discussions, jolting awake when someone slams a book in an excess of passion. I try to explain to a Chaucer person over coffee that striving to be the fastest person in the world isn't any weirder than looking for love in all the wrong places, dreaming of a big car, watching television for three hours a day, sitting down punching things you don't care about into a computer, helping two out-of-love people separate equitably, sewing up a cut from a bad wound, or stacking bananas so they don't fall when people take a bunch.

Peggy looks me over in the locker room one day and says: *I do believe that what Glucogirl here needs is some good sex.*

My virginity becomes global locker room discussion, of interest to one and all, even the lady who cleans out the stalls.

There are stories. Peggy says she knew a girl who had sex with a carrot and had to go to the hospital because she got some kind of vegetable disease. Peggy says the first time she had sex it was in the back of her boyfriend's car. She pretended she liked it by saying things like *ohhh* and *ahhh,* but she cried when she got home and the ever-alert Mrs. Peggy heard her and brought her a Tylenol and a bowl of lime Jell-O with green grapes suspended in the middle. Babe says the first time she had sex she was in her boyfriend's newly dead grandmother's apartment, that she too pretended to like it, but it was awful and she cried herself to sleep and woke up with swollen eyes and her mother made her stay home for two days, suspecting a hibernating fever. The lady who cleans out the stalls lost her virginity to a distant cousin. *We didn't know until it was too late.* Sunny won't talk about the first time she had sex. She closes her face like a door. *That's highly personal.* Lilly Cocoplat says that the first time she had sex with the lawyer it was pure, squishy, orgasmic heaven. Peggy says: *Your dear friend's lying.* But that breaststroker from Auburn says that the first time she had sex, her body trembled like a washing machine and she wanted to do it again but her boyfriend couldn't. That chick from Arizona says the first time she had sex, she got mono and couldn't swim for a year and didn't have sex again until she was nineteen, but there was a girl from her high school who'd lost her virginity to her favorite dog. The first time Tanya Slaughter had sex turned into Glenwood legend: nine months later, she was weeping with triplets. Kyd says the first time she had sex, she knew for sure she was a lesbian. Peggy says: *Bet she knew before that.*

Roxanne says the first time she had sex, she was so drunk she couldn't for the life of her remember who it was with. She looked deeply into her own forehead and said it could have been this one guy, or that one guy, or maybe the guy with that cool earring. Dot thinks that sex is no laughing matter, that the first time she had sex she hadn't planned on it. It was up against the golf shed at the Glenwood Country Club; she'd lost control of the situation and it had happened like that, fast and furious. She said she'd felt so bad she thought seriously about leaving her tattered life on the shores of the murky Lake Shawnee, but in God's Book that was worse than having sex.

The idea of having sex fills me with a cool, specific dread. I'm afraid it will be embarrassing, that I will die of embarrassment—not literally, of course, but in an English major way. I'm too tall, too strong, too gangly. I laugh at the wrong moments, have breakdowns at the wrong times, am always the last at everything except a good race. But Peggy says there are important milestones to be crossed, that I should quit avoiding them and cross already to the non-virgin side of the road like the rest of the team (except the lesbians).

Sunny says: *Do what you want, Pip. Take your time.*

I start looking around for candidates, make out with some nice swimmers here, then there. Strategies are discussed.

Don't tell him you're a virgin; you'll freak him out, says Peggy.

Don't mention your problem with yams right away, unless you really like him, says Sunny.

Don't laugh, even if it's funny, says Lilly Cocoplat, from her dorm room in Wichita.

And don't cry either . . . That'll make him feel bad, says Peggy.

She should cry if she feels like it, Peggy, Sunny says.

Don't cry, Pip. I know, says Peggy.

Cry if you need to, Pip. Just let it out, says Sunny.

I have the facts. There will be pain, but just for a second. Peggy says it's like ripping off a Band-Aid on an almost healed sore. Peggy says: *Don't be afraid; a girl in Mexico lost her virginity to a can of refried beans.* Babe says: *Don't tell her things like that.* Peggy says: *It happens to be true.*

I wear a tube top and tight jeans to a major barbecue. I make a nice ponytail, gloss my lips in a sparkly way, try seducing a swimmer with a boomerang-shaped scar above his left eye and a barely perceptible stutter but end up scaring him with my advances and he runs away.

I change tactics, blow-dry my hair and part it on the side, holding it in place with a sexy black barrette. Sunny carefully lines my eyelids in an Egyptian way. I buy a black dress with two thin gold chains holding it up and a pair of strappy sandals that emphasize my toes. I go to another major barbecue, lean into a palm tree, ignoring everyone with America's saddest sweetheart face. I have a package of purple condoms in the first handbag I've ever owned, black with little gold chains that match my dress. I drink two frozen margaritas so fast my hot heart cools down. *There will be blood, but less than a period.* I make eyes at swimmers who bore me because you can't die if you don't care.

It is Tom who rescues me under the tree dripping with fake sadness, a frozen margarita thumping in my chest. He's wearing his glasses with the black metal rims that make him look plain yet interesting. He didn't brush his hair when he got out of the pool and it's dried into shapes I find comforting. Some guy is singing about diving for pearls and I take it for a sign and say: *Hey, that guy sounds like a sad Adam Ant* and Tom looks at me and laughs. *That's Elvis Costello.*

I assess him out of the corner of my eyes. Like most swimmers he has a beautiful body, wide shoulders, narrow hips, long legs. We have another frozen margarita and I'm now officially drunk enough to make out under the palm tree, then in his car. We make out in the driveway, then on my couch. I've memorized the phases of sex like the moon: (1) mental stimulation, (2) manual lubrication, (3) gentle penetration, so when things get too hot, I solemnly take his hand and pull him to bed.

He can't see without his glasses, so I take them off and hide them under some sweaters. His hands are rough and sweet, following the length of my body like a road on a map. And I am pleased to note that I am soon (1) mentally stimulated, (2) physically lubricated, and (2+) squishy, and that everything should go according to plan—but that is before I drive my hands gently down the length of his body and discover a pulsing, extra-gigantic, yam-slash-genetically-enhanced-cucumber-slash-living-softball-bat-slash-spicy-sausage and I almost have a nervous breakdown, but talk myself down.

Life is a series of complicated errors. Life is all about gliding through angles with curves. And I have real proof, once again, that my mind cannot prepare my body for anything outside a pool, so I close my eyes and swim into sex in a ghostlike glide, knowing that with time this will be funny, that one day in the vast and glorious future, I shall be sitting on a beach outside of the Sydney harbor with Peggy. We'll be tan, exhausted, exhilarated, watching tight, energetic waves dance deep into sand, horizon blend into water, water lap into sky, and Time will wave her magic green wand and we'll laugh so hard we'll end up crying. *His thick glasses, that hair . . . those socks, his white teeth, that baby skin, his creased jeans, those hiccups, that huge, horrible penis.*

And Lo We Offered Our Thanks to the Savage Shawnees Before Stabbing Them Repeatedly in the Heart

I like asking E. Mankovitz non-swimming questions just to see what he'll say.

Don't the years tick by like seconds?

He thinks about it absently, says: *Yes, I believe that they do.*

Don't you think the notion of God is ridiculous? I ask.

Not so sure about that, he says.

Do you ever lie?

No, not usually. He sighs.

So you really think anything is possible.

Yes.

Anything?

Within reason.

So that rules out God.

I didn't say that.

I swim nine miles a day, hold seven U.S. records and twelve U.S. national titles, set my first world record in Madrid. We're NCAA champs two years in a row; Peggy sticks her naked butt out the car window and spends an hour in jail, gets an $80 ticket and a serious, embarrassing warning before they let her go. Sunny learns forty-three new folk songs that explore the subtle variations of human misery. Technique is tightened. To strengthen myself I experience pain; pain is accepted because it means speed. I stand in front of the mirror studying my strong naked body. Dot secretly marries a major squint. They meet in Costa Rica on a humanitarian semester abroad and it's sick love at first sight. There is something wrong with him in a Damien kind of way, but she's so worried something's wrong with her she doesn't notice. She's wearing a peach backless dress and no underwear, confusing the sadness of sex with the sadness of love. Stan takes a job coaching women's swimming at the University of Iowa; his wife, Emily, has a baby boy. Roxanne goes to university. Quits university. Goes to university. Quits university. Mom has difficulty locating her.

Mom says: *Come home.*

I say: *I will.*

Mom says: *Come home.*

I say: *I will.*

But I don't.

Another year passes. I spend Christmas with the Peggys, spring break training in Colorado, summer break training in California.

Mom puts her foot down, locates Roxanne, says: *Come home.*

I say: *I will.*

Sister Fergus takes her glasses off, makes the sign of the cross, fingers her rosary, prays for good health, new admissions, a state-of-the-art water heater, the end of famine, the destruction of ignorance, universal peace. She wipes her forehead with a cotton handkerchief she embroidered in bluebirds when she was a novice, joins God in His Kingdom quietly before dawn. A mystery town in southern Florida absorbs June, no one knows where.

Father Tim is called upon. Guilt is evoked through a short speech whose underlying theme is the brevity of life.

He wins.

It's November 23, 1987, and I have three days of pure non-swimming freedom marked in on my calendar with a red X: Glenwood one, Glenwood two, Glenwood three.

Mom takes a blue pill; pulls herself down the stairs; opens a freezer the size of a small pickup truck; roots around for a while, clutching the edge of the door to keep her balance; finally pulls out a roasting bird she bought on sale in July. She drags it upstairs to the kitchen, dumping it into a basting pan. She takes another blue pill, puts her arm up into the bird, rips the gizzards out, setting them aside for Manny until she remembers he's decomposing outside along with everything else. She has a nervous breakdown up the stairs, dials 911 from the phone near the bed, convinced this time it's Her Time. The ambulance rushes to the house with its lights off. Technicians take her pulse and blood pressure, shine a flashlight into her eyes, give her a shot of a powerful tranquilizer, holding her hand until she calms down and falls into a dreamless sleep.

She calls me late that night to double-check on my arrival, mentioning only that she'd had a slight spell, but Lilly Cocoplat has moved back to Glenwood with her lawyer, has her finger on the pulse of Glenwood, and has already called to give me a detailed everything.

Mom gets up the next day, grits her teeth, takes half a blue pill, pulls herself down the stairs, washes her hands up to her elbows, and relentlessly stuffs the bird with enough mixture of crumb, cranberry, walnut, and butter to clog the arteries of a dinosaur.

We sit at a full table with red candles burning sinister orange streaks across our thankless faces. Roxanne brings a glass of wine to her lips and takes a slow draw, her red eyes shining out over the rim. Mom can't stop talking about Thanksgiving fatigue. *Whew, this is exhausting. Whew, I'm exhausted. Whew, Thanksgiving is a lot of exhausting work that does me in. Whew, I wish I were in bed with a good book.*

Roxanne nods like a puppet, says: *What a drag, Moooooommmmm* really slowly as though she were an estranged whale swimming in the depths of her own private sea.

Been dabbling in ye old bong juice again? I say to Roxanne when Mom leaves the table.

Roxanne is a great liar, but like all great liars, she often makes me think she is lying when she is telling the truth. When she lies, she is perfect, sincere, spontaneous: *New York is full of opportunity.* She holds my eyes in her eyes and the words slide out of her mouth as if they haven't spent any time at all twisting around in her mind. When she tells the truth—*I need more money for food*—she looks up, as though the words were floating like a hummingbird somewhere above her head. We fight when she's telling the truth, but I accept more than half of the sneaky, horrible, ulterior-motive-driven lies she's told me.

She looks at me, laughs, stops, laughs again, stops. *Bong juice. Like . . . you . . . are always . . . Bong juice . . . why do you . . . I do not.*

Living with a nutcase and doing good things for the unfortunate of Costa Rica have given Dot a hard voice. *Finish your sentence, Roxanne,* she says, snappy.

Roxanne takes a swig of wine like a pirate, rubbing her mouth with the back of her sleeve. *Okay . . . like if it's going to be one of these crappy bong juice Thanksgiving piece of finish-your-sentence dinners . . . I'm outta here and I don't care what Mooommmm . . .*

I'm watching Dot. Something has happened to her, but I can't tell what. She's lost a lot of weight and it's taken most of her boobs and parts of her personality with it.

She looks at me and starts to mock. *And yams are nature's answer to sugar addiction . . . Look how white my teeth are now that I've worn my plastic thing . . . Francesca Keds has buffalo shoulders . . . Have you seen my new watch that can plunge 250 meters into the depths of the deep dark sea.*

I am surprised. *Kurds, Fredrinka Kurds. Why are you talking like a . . . like that, Dot?*

Just trying to help you listen to yourself go on and on about bullshit, she says, tucking hair behind an ear. *Anyway, I just want everyone to understand that it ends here and now. I am no more Dot of all, no more Dot'll do it . . . that Dot is gone. Does everyone understand? It's over. The cycle ends here. I've had enough . . . enough . . . playing mommy.*

No one understands. This is something only hindsight will reveal, but I put an understanding look on my face anyway. Roxanne keeps the *like I give a fuck* face that works well with her New York haircut. Mom sits down hard, putting both elbows on either side of her plate. She's rolled up the sleeves of her sweater into the crux of her elbows like a pastry-making woman. Her face looks the same as it did before the new Dot started talking to it. Not bad exactly. But not good either. She's gotten so used to her solitary library Dark Catholic life that she wants us to leave. I could tell the minute we found ourselves in the same room together, all of us, looking at each other as weary as old hogs before slaughter, then shifting the attention toward her, the mother, lasering her up and down with our daughterly eyes, measuring, recording. She's as round as a hen, wants her house back so she can skim the walls the way she likes to, slipping away upstairs into her room as quiet as a Shawnee. She will lie on her bed, read about someone who doesn't exist until she doesn't exist. It's written all over her newly minted moon face as clearly as ink; she was dying for us to come, and now that she's seen us, she's dying for us to go.

Dot has always been Mother's number one champion daughter,

daughterly in the best of all ways, deeply attentive to Mother's changing humors, encouraging, listening to her woes, concerned, a fat frown between her big eyes. She is classically show-champion daughterish— shiny of hair, pink of gum. The nuns love her, the non-nuns love her; she greets friend and foe alike with bright eyes and some kind of physical sign of affection that illustrates without excess the brotherhood of brother, the sisterhood of sister, the universality of all human humanity, one for all, etc. How many times did I see Mom grazing words in a bed of book with her glasses on as Dot handed her a hot cup of tea she'd taken the time to sweeten? How many times did I see her in the kitchen measuring and stirring to get it just right?

Sunny told me that this is a case of classic mother/daughter role reversal, that Dot was not acting the role of a perfect daughter, she was acting the role of a perfect mother, without having given birth, which turned her into a minor modern Mary.

She'll crack one of these days, she'd said, looking up from Lancer's *Dictionary of the Ancient World.*

Dot? No way. She won't, I'd said, clipping my nails.

Well, I hope she does for her sake, she'd said, looking back down into Lancer's *Dictionary of the Ancient World.*

If you really want to die, Roxanne, it's easy enough, Dot is saying in a calm creepy voice. *We're in Kansas; they'll sell guns to any idiot here, even the ones with ridiculous hair. People do it every day. You don't need to go to New York to do it, unless, of course, you want the* company. Her mean face is becoming meaner by the second. *But . . . you'd rather torture us, wouldn't you? How could we, insensitive fuckfaces that we are, possibly understand it, your grand-ass suffering? How could we imagine how much you fucking feel? Go out and get a gun, risky woman; live your life like a wild fucking animal for all I care. I have other things to think about.*

I try to change the subject. *Grand ass?*

Perhaps it's time you stop that. She swivels so violently the table trembles.

What? I say, yam purée stuck in my throat.

What. That little smile thing, that's what. She's knifing a poor avocado.

Ridiculous hair? I have ridiculous hair? says Roxanne, lost in her time warp.

It is true that Dot was always fine and always-fine people eventually become semi-invisible holographs that float around the complaining ones. She is better off mean; it puts people on edge, forces them to look at her, and I rather like the new Dot, although she does, at times, frighten me, but it appears to be a very difficult task reversing a classic mother/daughter role reversal without any casualties.

Mom grabs me in the kitchen. *Why is Dot being such a . . . There are* seeds *on those salads and* special water chestnuts *and* avocados. *I had to go to the* store *and you know I don't . . . I had to put them in* brown paper bags *to ripen them . . . you'd think she'd have . . . What's wrong with* her? *What?*

Her claws are ripping into my skin, churning up bad memory. *You don't leave the house, Mom . . . and that medication stuff you're on makes you . . . You call us acting like you're normal when we know perfectly well you're not. It's insulting. You can't keep treating us the same way. Things are different. Sunny says you've got a major . . .*

She lets go of my arm. *What are you talking about?*

I rub the welts. *You know what I'm talking about. You don't leave the house. Admit it. And you take pills. To live.*

I can go out if I feel like going out, she says, lying to herself and thus lying to me. *I just don't feel like going out. And I know what* this *is. Girls turn against their mothers. This is*—she looks into her forehead—*classic. After everything I . . . I . . . we . . . I didn't think it would happen to me. I really didn't. After everything I've had to live through.* She gets mean. *I let* you *do whatever you wanted, getting up at the crack of dawn preparing all those sandwiches . . . You had a great life. Just you wait. Just you wait . . .* she says, backing out of the kitchen and pulling herself up the stairs as quickly as she can without having a heart attack. When I get back to the table, Roxanne is gone and Dot has locked herself in her room.

You're the leader of the family now. I'm not putting up with this anymore, Mom says to me the next morning, lying greenish on her perfectly made bed. She's put lipstick on her lips to give a good, normal effect, but the lipstick's so old it's cracking.

I sit down on one of the heavy dining room chairs that a lazy Dark Catholic brought up during the months of heavy surveillance. *Listen, Mom, next year is an Olympic year. I can't be the leader of the family.*

She turns her face to the window. *No one listens to me. No one knows what I'm going through. And frankly I don't think anyone cares.*

I do care, but don't feel like telling her anymore. *And it was* June. *Poor old June made my sandwiches,* I say, leaving the room.

Downstairs, Dot's face is still and hard.

I try walking the path of good-natured forgetfulness. *What's up, Buttercup?*

She is tired of walking the path of good-natured forgetfulness. *Shut up for once, will you?*

I change the subject. *Mom says I'm supposed to be the leader of the family now . . .*

Her eyes are tired. *Sick to the end,* she says, and I wonder again what's happened to her.

But she can't resist becoming the moral leader of the family, calling me up and demanding things in a strict *rat-a-tat* voice.

How could you have given Roxanne cash?

What did you say to Mom?

What were you thinking?

How can you tell? How do you know? That is unacceptable as an answer.

Are you still dating that boring guy you don't even like?

No one wants to go to church, so Mother goes alone, coming home with a closed face before hitting bed. I have dinner with the Cocoplat, who insists on bringing the lawyer. He's gained weight but only in the head area; his legs are still pegs. He squints at me across the table, making heavy eyes at his watch as Lilly looks on helplessly.

There are things I know I should do but don't.

Go to the cemetery.

Visit the nuns.

Find out where June is.

Say hi to Dr. Bob.

I lie on my bed staring out the window until I can't stand it anymore. Then I visit Father Tim, have talks with new Dolphins and the Holy Name swim team, who manage to maintain their healthy twenty-year losing streak. They weep, tell me how much they love me. I feel a weep in my throat, but stuff it down, telling them how much I love them with a froggy voice. And it's true, I do.

Secret Message Shush

She'd called me a year before with the orders: (1) I will stuff my shoulders into a lilac dress with an asymmetric ruffle. (2) I will walk down the aisle with the best man, standing directly to the left of Father Tim. (3) I will be perfectly calm. (4) I will hold a bouquet of calla lilies or long-stemmed white roses or maybe something with color. (5) I will not become antsy, will barely move except to wipe away the occasional stray tear. (6) If I do weep, there will be no convulsions. (7) All notion of laughter will be permanently suppressed. (8) If I do feel a laugh rumbling, I will do anything it takes to stop it, even if I have to think about horrible shit.

I stuff my shoulders into a lilac dress, am not pleased with the asymmetric ruffle. I walk down the aisle with the best man, step and pause, step and pause, standing directly to the left of Father Tim, who winks. When Father Tim winks, I remain perfectly calm, but when he talks about unions and duties and eternity, I become antsy. I stare at the back of Lilly's veil until I am absorbed by sheet upon sheet of sheer ivory net that falls behind her to the floor. I blink, lasering the lawyer's profile: forehead *ledge,* nose *potato,* chin *bucket.*

Lilly's diamond engagement ring flashes for a second. I look at it and think *flashy.* She's got a new name now, but I will never use it.

I accidentally date swimmers who equate love with saying yes all the time. There are no fights, no scenes in public places, no biting jealousies that make me sit in a chair with my face in my hands, tears sprouting through my fingers as the people who don't like me watch with pleasure and the people who do squirm with shame. My boyfriends and I agree with everything I say and sex is sweet, like riding a speedboat on a fresh green lake, nothing like the heaving sweaty stuff Peggy describes. Peggy seethes with passion, her heart constantly smashed into a million smithereens before it regenerates in a process that Sunny calculates to take between eleven and twenty-three days. Even Babe creates havoc when she dumps her boyfriend from forever for a newer, faster one who waits for her every evening after practice. He sits outside by the doors patiently reading medical textbooks ten times thicker than the Glenwood Yellow Pages. We call him Dr. Babe. And Sunny, who irons everything so carefully it never wrinkles, is now dating a guy who makes her late for practice. She's been late *more than once,* has been singing "Misery Means Business" in a sweet, whispery voice, keeping her cards close to her chest.

I plunge into the pool and concentrate on form, lengthening my extension, prolonging a powerful glide, the white doves of Seoul flying through my mind, their beaks filled with gold. I'm twenty-two years old. That's eleven twice.

We're at training camp on the island of Kauai. We train, talk about love and love's cousin, sex, and sex's cousin, betrayal, and betrayal's cousin, boredom, and boredom's cousin, blind infatuation, until I can't take it anymore and leave the room. When I get back everyone is lounging on the porch talking about love again. Babe lies in a hammock and talks about her and Dr. Babe's plans to work on Indian reservations for free. She gets choked up, and everyone becomes quiet, lost in their own love and their own love's future plans to do great things together in a sexy fun way. I listen to the rhythm of the faraway waves, feel the energy of the green weaving palms, the ease of warm sand under my feet, the vibratory underbuzzing of the overfed bee clash with the continual threat of lava, not missing my boyfriend the way everyone else misses theirs. I'm dating a swimming architect. He has floppy hair and deep green eyes, soft hands, a pale, muscular body. He sits at his drawing board creating impossible buildings the wind will pull down as I recline in my recliner in a post-practice slump. He's so kind that to balance him out I have to be an asshole. He says: *What can I do to help take some of the pressure off, sweetheart?* And I look at him and say: *Shut up, that's what,* as I stab a pair of golden yam balls sitting on a plate of bitter greens.

Here in the land of the powerful wave, all I do is sigh when I think of him, that and stare at the huge clouds lit by a sun so white my eyes sting.

Mother informs me that she's been changing cognitively, miraculously making it out of bed with a spiral notebook in her hand noting (a) her feelings and (b) the validity of her feelings and (c) possible other feelings and (d) ratings on the basis for rational reasonableness on a scale of 1 to 10, 1 being stupid. There she is, dating a dancing golfer—3! She buys brown and white leather brogues that grip the earth, is following the white ball with light blue eyes she's hidden behind a pair of sunglasses that take up half of her face—7. She's pretending to enjoy but is watching other participants enjoy and wondering why she cannot—1. She has decided to be secretive about this—0. She's cut her hair short like Peter Pan; it gives her nose a depth and dignity it did not have before—9! There she is, running out the door to a big dance with the dancing golfer. He's short, so she's not wearing pumps, but ballerina-type slippers she's chosen for their festive shade of gold—7. They're twirling around the floor under a canopy of stars as select pieces of beef roast in a special sauce containing one pound of brown sugar—2.

The Superior E. Mankovitz has me in the Mankovitz observation tank at the moment, sensing that my mind is floating on another plane. He puts his lips together for a moment before squinting. *The more success you have, the harder you work. Nature wrote the book; read it, and you will see that it applies to everyone and everything.* It's part of a new coaching phase he's going through that involves saying things out loud to annoy me and infuse what he calls my current *lackadaisical swim* with zest. I flip him off in my head and work so hard that days turn into blurry resemblances of light, as if someone's holding a camera out a car window and all it captures is ribbons of color.

But I almost hate swimming and I'm afraid it's going to slow me down. My fellow team members are starting to grate; their voices scratch the inside of my ears like chalk. They put their faces too close to mine and yell, laughing at something I hadn't heard because I was not listening on purpose. And certain teammates are taking the low road, choosing to hate me so they can get mad enough to win. They think I won't notice, stuff their ferocious animosity behind friendly seeming eyes, easily finding fault in my simple gestures, looking at each other knowingly when I slam a locker, spend too much time putting gloss on my lips, dump yet another kindhearted swimmer. They do not like it when I partake in lengthy arguments with the coveted E. Mankovitz. They feel the time I spend with him takes away from their time, that they are lesser swimmers because of it. They do not like it when Arch Naylor smiles a rare smile at me, revealing a set of creaky white teeth. I feel their glare when I turn my back, but the time it takes for me to turn around has them looking heavenward with vacant, dreamy smiles.

One of the younger, vacillating nuns stops believing in God and becomes a legal secretary instead, eventually stealing Mom's dancing golfer from right under her feet. A terrible relapse occurs somewhere in the scaffolding of Mom's mental structure: she burns her notebooks in the fireplace—o, pretending she prefers life inside her own walls—o. Now the minute she tries to leave the house, her heart flutters and she has to take a pill—o. It's autumn in Glenwood, the wind cool and clean, the trees so orange, so yellow, when she draws the curtains, her light eyes smart with the sunshine. She sighs and holds her own hand for a second.

Dot is secretly struggling with the psychological traps the husband we will never meet is arranging in her path, but she's convinced he's the only rubber raft she'll ever have on this ratty ocean. Out in the world, her face remains resolutely rational, her hair right, but when she's home, her personality wavers this way and that. When he's nice, she evaporates in a fizz, like bubbles in a crystal glass; when he bangs the door a certain way, she liquefies, spilling under the floorboards, stilled into invisible; when he watches her quietly, his face an unreadable mask, she freezes into a block of opaque ice unless he smiles, and her body melts into itself with relief. Her coworkers roll their eyes when she turns her back, mouthing *B.I.T.C.H.* while she complains bitterly about the coffee mugs with the permanent stains even as she tries to remove them.

Roxanne's been missing for months. When I talk to Mom, I get the updates: Roxanne sightings, old Roxanne letters, things that happened to Roxanne when she was a child, Roxanne's harsh reaction to hardship, her attraction to the bad man. One by one, Roxanne's wild moments are taken out and scrutinized, the first of her wild trends examined. The creation of a possible toll-free Roxanne hotline is discussed.

Just let her be, Mom . . . We're on the speakerphone. I'm lying on my bed, my feet on the headboard. *She's always been reactive and she's been addicted to drugs for a long time now.* . . .

She feels things more. . . . *She always has since the very beginning. She used to cry all night long. Leonard put her in the basement* . . .

The downstairs bathroom, and that was me, I say.

That wasn't you, she says.

That was me. *He'd read that article on total extinction.*

No, no, you were a bit on the hyperactive side and you hated your playpen, but a bottle of warm chocolate milk would make you happy every time. . . . *Roxanne, she was my feeling child. And she was always antsy. She almost got electrocuted* . . .

That was me, Mom. *I was antsy. And I'm the one who bit through those wires. That's why you took me to the pool. It was me, the antsy one. The nuns wrote it on their reports, remember? Flitty* . . . *giddy* . . . *antsy. Roxanne was* sneaky. *She was the* Sneaky One.

I was the one up all night with her. Maybe when they interview you, you could say something like "Roxanne, call home," or "Roxanne, we urgently need to talk" or "I'm having a bit of a problem with my sister Roxanne." Just explain the situation . . . *People understand these family things* . . .

Are you kidding me? Tell me you're kidding.

I have a Roxanne theory that Sunny qualifies as a series of stupid thoughts.

I think: *Let her sink to the bottom. There she would open her eyes, feel the pressure of not breathing and either push herself up toward the oxygen or lie there and drown, and since no one would overtly choose to be dead she would hit the point of no return and return.* But Roxanne is unpredictable. She sinks to the bottom, feels the pressure of not breathing, the lack of oxygen, says: *Fuck the point of no return; I'm not returning* until someone vigilant notices her shadow on the bottom of the pool and dives in to pull her out. She is one of those people who slap and weep after mouth-to-mouth resuscitation.

But underneath my series of stupid thoughts I am worried, and when I am worried I usually break down and call Dot, who says: *I'm living my own life for once. Does this pose a problem for you?* I ignore her, think about something else, have a feeling that fast swimmers are getting faster and will soon make themselves known. They're out there, somewhere. Fredrinka Kurds's times have started to falter and I think that whatever they've been doing over there is starting not to work or maybe she's in the middle of a burnout. Burnouts are fierce and inexplicable; sixteen-year-olds who beat the world, then disappear as suddenly as unhappy men.

Olympic years are different from normal years; they bring out the worst before bringing out the best—the cadence of training peaks, then ebbs—and I seem to be having trouble trying to hide the fact that even the Mankovitz has turned into one of those books I don't have enough patience to read through to the end. I watch him speak like I watch a foreign film, guessing, because I'm too lazy to read the subtitles. I climb into stinging water and sink into it like a lead pellet and the last thing I want to do is pull myself through. And it's cold. If I don't slurp enough grimlock for breakfast, my legs turn blue.

There is no room for complacency in any sport. Just ask the champions, says the Mankovitz one morning at the breakfast buffet.

Quit saying things, I say, holding down the bird I cannot flip.

I'm giving you the facts, he says, leveling his eyes on three palm trees dancing on the horizon.

E. Mankovitz likes to stress that just because I feel as though *I* am swimming through moist cement does not mean that teammates or competitors feel as though *they* are swimming through moist cement, that the twenty-fourth Olympiad is only a matter of months away, which means weeks, which means days, which means hours. He caught a cold on the plane over, is a baby about it, sucking on some kind of noxious mint I can smell in waves. *Never underestimate anyone or anything. Nothing must be deemed too insignificant for your esteem.* I get back in the pool and Bron drives a navy blue convertible along the bottom, a bullhorn to her mouth. She turns it on and yells: *You better listen to him; when he's gone, there won't be another one.*

Along with outdoor practice, body surfing, stretching, hiking along the Kalalau trail, we sit in the glassed-in atrium of our hotel listening to a most famous eight-foot-tall life coach motivate us. He has a long, cordy neck with a little chin stuck in the middle and J. Caesar hair. He bounds onto the stage, bounding off again when he wants to make a point, and even though he hops like a little girl when he gets excited, I can tell Peggy wants to sleep with him. She sits next to me, her long legs stretched out under the seat in front of her, listening.

I lean over. *Look at him . . . He's hopping like a gymnast; someone should tell him. Maybe one of his motivating buddies or his mother . . .*

She won't tear her eyes away. *Shhhh . . . He's cute.*

His hands are sprouting from his ape arms like a pair of ivory gloves. *He has short bangs, Peggy, and I don't know if you've noticed them, but . . .*

He's been through a lot . . . He counsels presidents, she says, not moving her eyes.

You just want to sleep with him, I say.

Not really, she says.

Not really means not right now, I say.

Shut up, she says. *Spankovitz is glaring.*

J. Caesar is sitting down on his haunches with his hands clasped in front of him. He's decided to take it down a notch.

He's acting like he's giving us some Big Secret Message or something, I whisper.

Shut up, Peggy whispers back.

I will if he will.

I'm not sitting next to you tomorrow.

Just answer me one question, one.

If you'll shut up.

How many gold medals has he won? I ask in Bron's debater voice.

This surprises her. *He counsels* presidents, *Pip. We swim.*

J. Caesar summons us before daylight to experience the mystery of dawn in front of some of the biggest waves in the world. We're shoeless, our toes digging into particles of cool black lava. Big waves curl up like a living wall, then collapse in a roar. My hands and feet are freezing. Mankovitz is staring at the water looking like a statue of a hobbit. Babe's thrown herself into one of the deep hypnotic trances she's thrown herself into since her third year of med school. Big waves curl up like a living wall, then collapse in a roar. Peggy gets dramatic with fake tears; she's wearing a see-through tank top and her littlest shorts. I look over at Caesar; he's looking at me. I shift my eyes to the heart of a big wave as it curls up into a living wall, then collapses in a roar.

He clears his throat, speaks softly. *Ladies, I'm going to tell you something that most of you here already know but that perhaps some of you need to remember. If your mind can think it up, your body can find a way to do it.*

I'm supposed to get goose bumps, don't. *He called us ladies,* I whisper.

That's because he's a gentleman, Peggy whispers back, shivering.

He has bangs, Peggy, I say.

We have a lively dinner banquet with a fresh seafood buffet, seven flabby dancers, and a couple of guys jumping around hitting each other with burning sticks. I squint over my pineapple frappé. J. Caesar squints back.

I wait until dessert. *What if your brain thinks up a ton of awful, sick things and they feel real?*

His mango has been artfully carved into a pinecone. *You choose where you put your energy.*

I hate this kind of response. *That's the easy way out.*

It happens to be true. He holds both hands out, palms open, an international indication of a fake Gandhi. *You put your energy where you want it to go. It's your choice.*

I get the results I want, I say.

For how long? he says, carefully slicing.

Are you trying to psych me out? I say so loudly the Mankovitz looks up sniffing from his hot lemon tea spiked with a generous amount of cloves.

I'm trying to help you, he says quietly, his J. Caesar eyes burning with Brutus.

Who helped you? I ask.

Gandhi helped me. The hands again. *Jesus helped me,* but no thorns. *Buddha helped me,* I'm breathing. *Nelson Mandela helped me,* I've had troubled times. *Bud Lancer helped me,* I am an intellect. *Joseph Campbell helped me,* Zeus, Herod, that guy with the horse body. *Certain parts of the Bible helped me,* Thee, Thou, Thine. *Martin Luther King helped me,* I know no color. *Malcom X helped me,* I can pounce. *Mother Teresa helped me,* the poor will suffer. *Jung helped me,* I dreamt I was my mother and she dreamt she was me. *Einstein helped me,* time is the sum of all light speeding through the portals of one vast mind covered with extra-short hair.

Who helped them? I ask, and Peggy kicks me under the table so I kick her back and at that the fatty dancers reappear with burning spears and we all clap and whoop in unison.

On the plane home, I sit next to a burnt-nosed E. Mankovitz. *That Caesar guy takes the easy way out.*

He looks up from his reading. *I don't think so. You should pay attention; he's accomplished a lot.*

Still. He did go on and on about all that whiskey stuff, I say.

He looks down at his reading. *He got over the whiskey stuff.*

I stretch my legs. *And that dead father thing . . .*

He looks up. *What dead father thing?*

That thing about the dead dad.

I don't remember anything about a dead father. But I liked that story about Churchill.

I don't remember anything about Churchill. *What story about Churchill?*

He looks back down. *You weren't listening, were you?*

I was, I lie.

He closes his magazine and his eyes at the same time. There's a picture of a GI with a receding chin on his way to a stupid war. I look out the porthole at the mass of atmosphere simmering below.

Life has already offered up many of its very best milestones: girlhood, womanhood, virginityhood, Olympic goldhood, world recordhood, full scholarshiphood, new Jeepdom, nice boyfriendsinsuccessionship. But nothing big enough outside has happened to make anything inside seem different. I'm still the same: tall, annoyed, loveless, and lonesome in a way I can't explain, not like I try.

Hey Sister, Seoul Sister

Peggy shakes the water out of her ears, pushing her head to the side at a stupid angle and shaking it like a dog as though there were something inside rattling around. She complains about her muscles, her hair, her teeth, her hair follicles, her gums, her perfect parents, her not-in-love-enough boyfriends. She looks at a freshman swimmer and says, loud enough for her to hear: *When did we start accepting fat girls on the team?*

Every time I get faster, she gets faster, like jogging with a pet.

Why does it take me getting faster to get you getting faster? I ask her over sushi.

A gorgeous awful swimmer recently left her for someone Peggy refers to as a bottled bitch. She is often in bad moods she punctuates with leaps into a sick-seeming joy. Today is not a good day. *Fuck you,* she says without looking up.

I'm just trying to help. It's your inner game. You can get faster before I get faster. You don't need me to do it for you. I know it.

You're so deep. She sighs.

I don't want to ask, but do. *What's wrong?*

She looks at me and her eyes say: *I'm sick of all this Olympic shit,* but her mouth says: *Nothing; I'm just tired.*

This is the wonderful atmosphere that leads us to Seoul.

God's Holy Olympic Fire starts in the temple of Hera to rhythmic drumbeating, braided priestesses humming and swaying, dancing and twirling, old prayers directed to Zeus, old prayers directed to Apollo, old prayers directed to Zeus again, the Olympic flame bursting forth, glowing with hope. It's carried through woodlands, over hills, past

Greek villages set in stone, relayed through the sweating hands of politicians, well-regarded clergymen, handicapped kids with photogenic smiles, really old people with good motor skills, Miss Universe, mayors from the four corners of the earth. It travels on foot, on horseback, aboard ship, in car, by airplane before arriving in South Korea, the land of the morning calm.

This is how calm Seoul is: Ladies in white gowns twirl like magic teacups with dark pretty heads, big-eyebrowed warriors bare long swords, long-gowned yellow girls, long-gowned red girls twirl parasol-size fans, *peaceful loving welcome, universe loving welcome, welcome.* Karate-chopping guys hop, creepy guys with triangle hats chop, white-faced, white-shoed, white-panted, white-tuniced, red-sashed, blood-lipped. Balloons float, firecrackers explode, white pigeons fly, white pigeon shit falls, happy aircraft survey, twenty-one guns salute, *Welcome world, Welcome universe, Welcome.* There are outdoor guides, indoor guides, lounge guides, seating guides, kitchen guides, identification guides. There are entry controllers, exit controllers, inside controllers, enormous Olympic buffets with Western food controllers supervised by the buffet overlords. Communists, Democrats, left-wing neutrals, right-wing neutrals, neutral-neutrals stand patiently in line for the breakfast buffet. Huge Russian wrestlers, necks as thick as living trees, ply trays with Western-inspired food; tiny gymnasts, asses as hard as living rock, ply trays with Western-inspired food. A whole pack of volleyball lesbians from Romania pass, trays swaying with pancake. Peggy tweaks my arm, says: *Get a load of that.*

All human beings go through a period where they are assholes, except for the fake ones who are assholes full-time. I'm a big asshole but don't know it because being an asshole deadens self-censorship, universal empathy, the ability to recognize when one is lying to oneself. I pretend not to know the people I do know, pretend not to need the things I do need, pretend I possess rare things I do not possess, pretend I am different than I have always been. The only surprise at the Olympic trials this year was an older swimmer, twenty-four, who came out of nowhere, setting a world record in the 800-meter free. She was still crying when I congratulated her, said: *I was swimming so fast, I thought I'd die.* I was nice, said: *But you didn't.*

I called my mother after qualifying for five events. She was going through a box of Roxanne's report cards.

I'm so worried. So worried. I have this feeling she's dead, she said. *Here, Sister Helena says: "Trouble concentrating."*

If she were dead, I'd know it by now.

But how? Has she contacted you?

No! Are you crazy? I would have told you.

Then how do you know she's still alive?

I can't explain. I just do, okay? I know. Trust me.

The asshole in me has tiny flags manicured onto my nails, an American flag dyed into my hair, a waterproof eye shadow in mermaid green. For the first time in my life I make big to-dos on the starting block, flopping, hopping, flexing, snowflake smiling, big thumbs-up, number one, V for the universally peaceful international vagina, shoulder propellers, lengthy goggle adjustment, water as a holy element adornment ceremony.

There is a chilly menace from the shrouded communists in the north. We are told to keep our heads up, accept no packages, are escorted by small Koreans who smile like realistic toys. They are a slight, white-faced, shy-voiced people, a foot shorter than I. Everything different is becoming similar and the things that remain different seem irrevocably so. We are all wearing the same shoes, hats, T-shirts, listening to the same music, desiring the same food, but we don't speak the same language.

Thus the outside world fades, is suspended, becomes ethereal like dust caught in a tight strip of sunshine.

Thus I lie on my single bed, watch the ceiling fan turn, wait.

At the breakfast buffet we sit near a table with the fastest person in the world and six synchronized swimmers in full makeup who hold themselves with the pointy inward stance of ballerinas. Everyone is almost exactly the same but oddly different, like sisters with the same hair. Fredrinka Kurds is lying low; I perceive her gliding giganticness at the juice bar, concentrate hard on keeping my gaze away, my heart thrumming like a giant Korean drum.

Thus energy is gathered, hunger restored.

I've turned professional, have an agent, Hank, and a family of sponsors who have chosen me because I am positive. I smile an awful smile, make crazy impossible predictions. *Cutting three seconds off my world record! Winning eight golds! I don't even need a mustache!*

Supercoach E. Mankovitz is concerned. *Don't lose focus. We've trained too hard.*

I won't look at him. *I'm on it.*

This is how I see it: Fredrinka Kurds is burnt out; her muscles have grown large and rubbery, creating drag. She's so slow the world says *whew*. I, on the other hand, am someone with hunger. I can feel it eating at me. I beat her, badly. So badly I'm kind. When I shake her hand and say: *Gut schwimmen*, I will mean it.

I wait.

I swim.

I wait.

I swim.

The East German Berliners pulverize record after record.

E. Mankovitz bites down hard on his gum, scratches his head.

I wait.

I swim.

I wait.

I swim.

The East German Berliners pulverize record after record.

Kyd lets out a heartfelt sigh.

Peggy gives up.

Babe holds her mouth in a straight line, clicking her nails as she stares at the pool.

I get annoyed.

Fredrinka Kurds looks me in the corner of one of my eyes with the corner of one of her eyes. I keep my face still and hard, slide my gaze away, both eyeballs dipping left, feigning a concentration I do not feel. *You're going down, East German butt liner.*

She bends over the pool, takes a sip of chlorine, rinses her mouth out with it, then spits: *pah*. This *pah* sticks in my mind all the way to the starting block: *pah pah pah pah*.

Assholes exist because they know something about them isn't quite right—it is a suit of armor that few feel the energy to crack. I chew on my almonds, but they have no taste. I swoosh them against my teeth, but they make no sound.

I won't let it go, hold one arm up, jump up and down. I'm giddy. *I'm going to* BREAK ZERO; *it will be* OVER *before it starts.* Journalists smile those smiles that say: *They are going to demolish you and you know it, Pip.*

It is when you lose that you know how your mettle is forged. My mettle is placebo mettle. To counteract the placebo effect, I cover it in bug repellent. My mettle is weak, crackled as easily as iced mirror. My mettle is a chocolate-coated suit of armor in a piece of shit life with a puddly pig laughing at the end and I swim in Fredrinka's wake like a gravity-stricken lead robot with hand-painted $120 toenails.

I'm barely silver.

I'm barely silver.

I'm bronze.

I'm bronze.

Babe gets trounced upon twice by Brigitta Hoffmann. She looks bewildered, says: *Who ever heard of Brigitta Hoffmann?* I'll never forget the look on her face; tired but deeply, as though an old woman had moved into her body. *I guess that's it for me,* she says as she rubs her silver medal and I say: *Don't be stupid* as I rub mine.

My final final, the sun is sluicing sideways through the blue glass window above the ready room and falling at our feet in a translucent blue square. I maneuver one of my feet into the blue square and it becomes blue. I relax using the ancient technique of positive self-evaluation, but am so annoyed my toes are curling. The crowds in the natatorium are chanting converging hollow sounds that mushroom out into the heavy, wet air. Fredrinka Kurds is standing in front of me, her eyes fixed on the ground, her shoulders sloped in like those of a person with no self-confidence, perhaps a tactic, perhaps not. She hasn't put her cap on yet, and her frosted hair sprouts from her head in the form of one big hand as though she slept hanging upside down from the rafters like a solitary bat.

The West German swimmer with the anger-management issues is loudly hocking up a loogie and spitting it into the small drains that lead from the pool to the showers. She makes rough metallic sounds out of her throat. Everyone ignores her at a high personal cost. The Australian chick, whom I personally have no trouble beating, looks over at me, rolls her eyes, and smiles. Assholes ignore random kindnesses; I keep my face facing forward. We all look the same: height encased in muscle encased in Lycra, holding goggles loosely in one veiny hand. The new-comer, a fourteen-year-old from Rotterdam with yellow streaks in her hair and a naked sailor tattooed on her left shoulder, is so nervous she has to bend herself in two to breathe. The Polish chick with the funny lips snarls and barks, shadowboxing the air in front of her. *Polish people know what they want.*

Fredrinka looks over, then away.

We walk out on deck and the roar that ensues is so intense I get goose bumps on hair follicles shaved so cleanly they sting. I jump up and wave a new wave—a U.S. Marine salute with a queen of England twist. Fredrinka stands up glumly in her ho-hum way, putting one hand up tentatively as if to ask a heavy question. I hop up on the starting block, my toes curling white with rage, my muscles curling white with rage, the strain in my mind curling white with rage, Leonard sitting in his chair, still cobwebbed with a Mesolithic hungry hunter face and lean hungry feet. I hear the beep. *Now.*

I sense her nearness even though I'm swimming like a subatomic asshole, breaking the golden swimming rules one by one: *In pace: fuck it. Breathe: fuck it. Turn: tight.* I know that once you start to lose, it's almost impossible to stop, don't give a shit if I have to crawl out of the pool on all fours, I'm going to get at least one gold. I lunge hard, breaking two fingers in a snap like table crackers and the twenty-fourth Olympiad is now over for me. I rip the goggles off my face, but the roar is so dense, I can't focus on anything, just my breathing and the scoreboard. Then I see it, *Lane 4 USA WR.* Joy rises from my gut up into my head in one strong wave and I hit the water with both fists. I feel no pain, although logically, there must have been some.

Gut schwimmen. She shakes my hand with a hand the size and consistency of a baseball glove.

Thanks. Good swim. I shake her hand, my fingers screeching in pain.

Mankovitz laughs. *That'll get them.*

I get my fingers set in a splint, find Peggy back at the village sitting in front of a stuffed suitcase, her hair slicked back with a purple glittery hair mousse.

Let's party, she says.

Okay, I say. *Pass me some of that mousse.* I stand in the mirror and mousse the flag up around my face with my left hand, creating a jagged, interesting effect.

Peggy looks in the mirror. *How do I look?*

I look at her, lie. *Very good.* Then we run.

Fredrinka Kurds never swims again. I ask every German I ever meet if they know where she is, what happened to her, but they never do. Oral-Turinabol. That's what it's called. Anabolic steroid. When the wall falls, I will scan the dancing Berliners for a glimpse of someone Fredrinka-like, but it's hard to recognize a swimmer outside of the pool and all I see are sturdy, rubber-nosed Germans exalting, their cheeks flushed with the high color of joy. Oral-Turinabol. *Chlorodehydromethyltestosterone.* It travels directly to the base of the brain, where it whispers: *You are no longer Fraülein,* setting off a chain of bodily events that will last an entire lifetime. Guy stuff installs: dark wiry hair, voice boxes grind into low gear, budding oranges swallowed up by booming pecs, ovaries frozen mid-twirl, vaginas quiet, wondering *What the hell,* and a flush of adolescent acne that covers the face, the torso, the butt, as if the girl inside were chanting *nein nein nein nein.* They gave it to girls, not yet women, just to see what would happen before testing it on men. Blue vitamins in a large glass jar. When the wall crumbles, I will watch the world change, brick by brick, hundreds of thousands of East German Berliners becoming whole Berliners once again, the world Fredrinka-less.

Seek the cold of the moon and you shall find the heat of the sun.

Seek the cold of the moon and you shall find the heat of the sun.

A nun said that. I forget which one.

Swimming in America

I'm giving my first official interview as a professional swimmer to NBC Sports. The journalist is second-string, hired to interview the losers, tired, harassed, couldn't care less about swimming, looks at me over the rims of his round gold glasses with unfiltered eyes. I'm sitting on a tall stool in my dress sweats and flip-flops. Someone painted my face a jolly shade of orange. I pretend to be in a good mood until I realize he's going to ignore me until we go on air and I get annoyed. I barely got a *hi* when I walked up. He's a traditional squint with a traditional squint name he threw at me when I sat down. *John.*

Three to five hours a day? he asks, consulting fake notes.

Uh-huh, yes, John . . . Sometimes. I smile into his forehead.

In the water? he asks, consulting fake notes.

No, not all training happens in the water . . . but I am a swimmer and swimmers—

Yes, yes, I know, he interrupts with a cough, smiles a fake smile.

We all start out swimming, you know; it's not that unique or weird, I continue, burying myself with an invisible shovel.

Excuse me? This interests him. He thinks I may say something universally foolish.

Well, if you really think about it, John, we all start out as sperm, every one of us, even you . . . and sperm swim, I say, smiling a fake smile. *It's true.*

Yes, they do . . . You're right; they do indeed. He's starting to enjoy himself.

So we all start out swimming. It's a natural, urgent human sort of state. I'm getting a bit lost, but I have a hangover, so my brain says *Oh never mind.*

What's urgent in it for you, Pip? He leans in. *I mean, there's no ovum on the edge of the pool, is there? A sperm isn't a . . .*

No, no, no, of course not. I'm trying to scramble backward. *I'm just saying . . . it's a theory. Nothing's urgent for me.*

Nothing? He sits back and smirks.

Well . . . no, sometimes I have urgent things and appointments and things I . . . stuff like that.

But no egg to find, no essence of something you are searching for that will make you complete, that will transform you into something more human . . . He pretends to consult his fake notes.

I am *human! Swimmers are really, really human. You should know that, John. American swimmers are even . . . It's an* image. *It's* nature. *I meant that people are always talking about how unnatural it is to spend so much time in water . . . swimming . . . people think that baseball is somewhat more . . . that football is normal or . . . because there are* balls—*Have you thought about it* Balls—*that chasing a ball makes it more . . . that capturing a ball . . . you know, makes it more . . . but it's all part of the same thing if you think about it. And we are all swimmers from the very beginning, well, sperm . . . swimming even before we were . . .*

Embryos? he says, raising a brow. *Interesting, but water polo has balls in it.*

Yes, yes. I'm just saying . . . I don't want to talk about this anymore.

There are no balls in track and field, gymnastics, fencing, boxing, poker . . .

Poker . . . why are you talking about . . . He's trying to throw me off. I get mad again. *There's a shot put in track and field; there's poles and hurdles and stuff, those rhythmic gymnasts have balls and ribbons. That's a lot of accessories, John. A swimmer is practically naked, just the swimmer, the water, desire . . .*

A shot put's not a ball and they're not chasing it; they're throwing it, he says, the voice of reason.

But runners . . . you can see them. Seeing changes everything . . .

Underwater cameras. He used to be a debater.

It's not the same thing. I sigh. Debaters drive me nuts.

Okay. Why?

We're below the surface.

Yes. Yes, that's true. Soooo . . . He decides we'd better get back to business, consults his fake notes. *Let's get back to . . . What did you think of Fredrinka Kurds?*

Oh, I don't look, I say, relieved. *You can't look. If you look you're as good as . . .*

Dead? He's got that look on his face again.

No, no. No, I meant . . .

Her times, then? What did you think about her times? They exploded out there, those East Germans, didn't they? You must have been shocked when she demolished you, he says, aiming low.

Swimmers don't demolish; they beat the clock, John. Now I'm an ice sculpture. *Fredrinka Kurds beat the clock and I lowered my personal best. I broke three American records and no one cares about anything except the gold . . . but anyway, she . . . it was almost . . . her times . . . her times were . . . super fast. She's an amazing swimmer. I was amazed.*

And the allegations? He's getting political.

If there were any infractions, we'd have heard about them by now. This makes me nervous; I'm careful. *She does have . . . some women do have hair issues, but I think it's bad form to follow up on the she-man theory without any proof. All I know is her feet . . . I've never seen feet like that.*

Feet. He's doing it again, but my agent, Hank, says I gave him the ammunition.

I don't know how to describe them without sounding . . . I mean a foot, when you think about it, is just ten toes, solid heels, and those ankle rotators . . . but on Fredrinka . . . amazing.

Well, he says, consulting fake notes again. *Thank you very much, Pip, for the inside glimpse into the world of swimming.*

Philomena, actually, or Mena if you like. Pip's a . . . Pip's not my real name. It's . . . Thank you.

Babe Takes a Bow

On the way back to the United States, I sit next to Babe, who can't sleep. She has special socks she wears on the plane to keep her feet warm, pale pink ones she pulls out of a cream-colored leather traveling bag her father bought for her as a gift. She's just finished explaining to me how her mother is a single-handed saint while her father remains amicably invisible.

I say: *Men do that,* although I know not one thing about men.

She looks down at her hands. *That depends.*

Her fingernails are naturally oval, dull pink, white-tipped, always the same perfect length as if they never grow. She has two flossy currents of blond hair that swing to the tip of her chin, also unchanged by the variations of growth. Her lips are natural with a light sheen from a vitamin cream her mother makes herself from beeswax and organic essential oils. She makes a big batch every year and sends it to the team, a pot for each of us with labels written in by hand, then painted. Babe's schedule is taped to the inside of her locker, colored in sections for the activities concerned, a dense rainbow: pool, upper-division science courses, Pilates, pharmacolgy, anatomy, clinical rotations, pool, dryland training, evenings spent studying with Dr. Babe, every second accounted for. I like watching her when I have nothing else to do. She brushes one tooth at a time from gum to crown, rinses her toothbrush, puts it in a glass she keeps next to the sink. She does it with economy of motion, not losing one ounce of energy to excess. She flicks the tap on, flicks water on the brush, flicks the tap off, brushing in silence, the hardest-working swimmer I will ever know. She has a 3.963 cumulative grade point average, was elected *Swimming*'s Swimmer of the Year two years in a row, started breaking world records when she was fourteen years old. When E. Mankovitz talks to her, his voice is easy. She combs her hair with a wide-toothed comb, organizes her impressive eyebrows with a dab of gel, rubs lotion onto her legs with uncommon grace. I spit white foam onto the mirror I have to swipe away later with my sleeve and I can't really remember learning anything. I go to class, come back, go to class again. *Dost thou not remembreth to forgetteth me and mine? O fie!*

Peggy makes her laugh; she says: *Peggy stop stop stop someone make her stop.* She doesn't like it when I swear, says: *Can't you think of another word?* I try to explain that it is a Catholic thing, but she looks at me as though I were nuts. When she showers, she carries a mesh bag filled with small replicas of her favorite organic biodegradable products that cause no harm to anything anywhere. I use products so enriched in what is not natural that I can cover my entire body in a gluey foam that remains intact until I stuff it down the drain with my big toe. When she gets a headache she says *I must be dehydrated* and drinks a glass of water. She has two tiny squares of black chocolate she keeps wrapped up in foil in her backpack *just in case.* I ask: *How can you eat just two?* And she looks at me with a pleasant *What are you talking about?* smile. She plans on doing her residency in Maricopa County Hospital in Phoenix with Dr. Babe, then they're going to work for less than free on Indian reservations in New Mexico. You cannot not love Babe, although there are times I avoid her because she makes me feel bad.

Every time Mona sees her she says: *Hi, Babe! How is everything?* And Babe says: *Great, Mona! Love that scarf.* When Mona sees me, her voice grinds into a lower gear and she says: *How's it going, Phil—oh— mean—ahhhh,* pronouncing my name like an embarrasing disease. *And stay away from those carrots; they're packed with powerful secret sugars.*

We fly through the night, the sky outside seventeen shades of black, schools of transparent cloud swimming by like lost spirits. Babe looks out the porthole, letting a single river of tears slip out of the corner of her eyes she wipes with a finger wrapped loosely in Kleenex.

What's wrong? I ask, squirming.

She has the kind of voice that gets lost in jet drone. I have to lean in. *I don't think I can keep doing this much longer,* she says, tears gliding, *I really don't. I'm practically a doctor. I need to move on.*

I feel a jab in my gut. *Quit?*

She looks up, annoyed. *No . . . retire.*

I look out the porthole. There's nothing for my eyes to hang on to. *Retire?*

She's curious now. *Don't you ever think about it?*

Of course I think about it, I say, lying. *I just didn't think you thought about it.*

She closes her eyes. I stare out the window at the rough earth rotating motionlessly below. Retirement. I close my eyes and feel the twirling black pit which is the universe, the droning of jet and the reverberation of energy and the cold dry air blowing onto my face, throwing me into a sick, dreamy stupor. That is when a fat purple pig with purple breath floats into my mind. It's lying on its stomach naked, with visible udders and a curly tail. It says: *Retirement is credible once you know you're edible,* which is so freaky I refuse to close my eyes again until we hit LAX.

Sperm Girl

I'm back. The residual fatigue of flight lodged in body, the brackish sadness of Babe's retirement lying on tongue. There are a thousand messages on my answering machine and my apartment smells like blocked air. The phone rings.

Philomena! Hank here!

Hank! My agent. I forgot about him. I'm standing in front of a mirror. I look like shit; my skin's the color of paper.

Hank attended the University of the Pleasantly Neutral with the Superior E. Mankovitz. *Speedo just contacted me about some sperm interview you gave NBC,* he says.

It wasn't exactly a sperm interview, Hank. I don't want to talk about the interview.

Well . . . He thinks for a minute, leaving white space on the phone. *It appears that you mentioned sperm a number of times.*

They did a sperm count? I don't want to talk about the interview.

That's funny. He sighs. Hank works sixty hours a week.

I said sperm . . . well, I was talking about . . . Hank, that interviewer guy was making it seem as though swimming was easy or . . . the sperm thing came into my mind. Do you know what he said to me after the interview? He said, "By the way, sperm come from balls *when you think about it, really, really, really, really think about it,"* and he and his fat camera buddy were laughing like it was the funniest thing they ever heard. Even that horrible makeup chick got into it.

Well, you did leave the door open to—

I had to say something, I interrupt, indignant.

I agree with you, he says, pleasantly neutral. *One hundred percent. But*

Speedo didn't like it. You were wearing their T-shirt and their hat and it was just a very good opportunity to talk about nationals or your forthcoming trip to Perth, a world record in the making. The sperm thing caught them off guard and they don't want people to think Sperm! when they see Speedo.

Hank! Why would . . .

You have no idea, darling. He sighs again, New York rumbling up behind him. *None. You could be sperm girl faster than . . . well, I hope not, but in theory . . .*

Hank, I'm not, I say, looking at my stuffed suitcase lying on my bed.

I agree with you; you're not. But then again in that interview you were. Weren't you?

What in the hell are you talking about?

Sperm girl, he says.

I'm not sperm girl, I say, looking in the mirror. I do kind of look like a sperm girl with my stupid hair, that stuff Peggy gave me for my eyes.

You're going to have to prove it, he says.

They do swim, though, I say in a jet-lag daze. *It is natural. Why can't we talk about natural things in a natural way? The whole world's a crazy nun.*

The world's hardly a . . . nun. General Americans just don't really . . . At the moment anyway, the trend is more toward the contained. Natural things are best reserved for private life and your general American population, if they think, even for a second, be it subconsciously, swimming-Speedo-sperm, well, that's not what Speedo had in mind when they hired you. They're a bit worried. He's pleasantly neutral.

About general America? I say, looking in the mirror, trying to remember what that hairdressing chick said about washing out the flag.

About you.

Me? I say. *Worried about me? Just tell them I'm not a sperm girl, Hank. It was just a theory. Do you want me to call?*

No, no. He thinks again for a minute. I can hear his mind churn behind his breath. *They think you're a bit green.*

I am not green . . . way less green than before. I'm tired, lean my forehead into the mirror. My fingers hurt.

They've suggested a coach. He's pleasantly neutral.

I have *a coach.*

A speech *coach.*

A speech coach? I'm speechless.

They're going to teach you not to take everything to heart; keeping the head cool, as they say. Not getting so worked up. They've been working with champions for over sixty years now; they understand the pressure you're under, all that expectation right down the drain. They know how it goes. They'll teach you how to take control of your sentences, how to—

I have perfect control of my sentences and I lowered my times, Hank, I say. *Peggy says I'd need a dick to swim faster.*

I wouldn't mention that either, he says. *And in the future, if there's a question between adding a sperm or subtracting a sperm . . . give yourself the time to make a judicious choice. Swimming's going to be big in America. It's going to explode. And you're going to help keep it cool by keeping cool.*

I'm cool. I'm starting to see the asshole.

I know, he says. *Speedo knows. But . . .*

If we were in Australia . . .

You beat Australia. He's firm.

Yeah, but in Australia, they love their swimmers no matter what, I say, looking at the asshole emerge and take her place in the mirror. *They even love me and I'm not their swimmer.*

I spend twenty minutes under a hot shower trying to wash the flag out of my hair, collapse on my bed, listen to my answering machine: seventeen frantic messages from my nice boyfriend, the rest from my mother. Roxanne's back. Glenwood's Chubbiest Sheriff found her on the national sheriff general alert network; she crashed a stolen car into the side of a cherry tree in Haight-Ashbury, has been living exactly forty minutes from me for over a year.

Roxanne

At first she looks like an old grainy person with a shiny wrinkled face, then she looks like an incompetent Roxanne impersonator, then she looks like parts of a Roxanne puzzle someone has given up on and left scattered on the bed.

Her eyes focus on me for a second, then they close. *Your hair . . . why . . . a flag . . . what's . . .* , she whispers.

A nurse sticks her head in the door and shouts: *The doctor will be with you in just one minute.*

This startles her. She jumps, looks at me, whispers *I can't take this*, then gives me a shoulder, some oily roots, and an ear to talk to, so I speak to them.

So . . . It's been a while.

. . .

Almost a year . . .

. . .

. . .

She turns. *I can't talk right now.* Her face trembles, crumpling, her arm branches attached to pipes, her pipes attached to bags holding liquids she needs to recover. She covers her dry lips with a transparent hand.

I'm not prepared. *No one's mad at you. Not one person in the . . . Not even . . . Mom's going to try to . . . She's being helped by some sheriff guy . . . and some version of Dot will be here in a couple of days.*

Okay, okay, she says, swatting me away. *Quit yelling.*

I'm not yelling, I say, pretty sure I wasn't yelling.

Please stop . . . fucking . . . shouting, she says, hands over ears.

Okay, okay, I'll just sit here then . . . and sit, I whisper.

I watch the side of her head pretend her face is sleeping, but the set of her shoulders tells me this is a lie. I swing my feet, grab my arms, twist them into the new millennium yoga moves I've just been taught, but am still invaded by antsiness. I knot the corner of her blanket into knots, belly-breathing the hospital energy out of my mind. Another nurse sticks her head in the door. *They're coming! The doctors are coming,* she says, which causes me to run to the door faster than a tornado drill.

I watch them walk down the hall. One major doctor surrounded by three minor ones, clopping like horses. The major one skids to a halt in front of me and starts to speak, giving me a long list of probables starting with adrenal exhaustion and finishing with the hepatitis and AIDS tests that haven't come in yet. He says: *Please, take a seat* even though there isn't one, realizes there isn't one, rubs his eyes, sighs, then speaks about addictions to drugs from a family of drugs that ends with *-ine.*

He says: *Your sister's had quite the time of it; we almost lost her.*

I hate hospitals, but like the way some doctors talk, the ones with the measured words and the discreet pauses they leave between them so you can ingest the information before they continue with more, even awfuller stuff. He's one of those. The minor doctors next to him squint with squinty med-school faces. I swipe them with Olympic vision.

My mother's trying to come, I say. *If she makes it, you'll have to be careful with her; she'll be nervous.*

I'll keep that in mind, he says. *As you know, the police are involved. There'll be a hearing, rehab. It's routine. You'll also have to stop by administration before you leave and take care of the paperwork.*

I take an elevator full of depressed people down. We stand sinking in unison in groups of four. I end up in administration in front of a woman with a head full of tight curls holding up a no-nonsense face. She's filed her nails into salmon pink fangs she uses as pointers. *Sign here . . . and here . . . and here.*

I take an elevator full of depressed people up, watching the doors slide open to reveal white halls, white walls, white tiles, white ceilings, beige chairs, pale people in colorful shoes, professional people in white smocks.

Heroin is as death-inducing as a well-planned suicide. You'd end up in the dirt turning black with all other decomposing peoples in the decomposing universe. Taking heroin is like standing on a ledge of a skyscraper when it is windy, naked, on the edge of your toes, a murderer in a bad mood with nothing to lose standing behind you. I walk into her room and stare at Roxanne's sleeping face, not understanding. I sit beside her bed and stare at her sleeping face, wondering why. I am the national spokesperson for the Living Well, Living Safely program sponsored by the Red Cross. I wear a seat belt every time I get into a car. I have breathing techniques, nerve-taming behaviors. I study self-hypnosis with a clinical psychologist who's trained some of the best athletic minds in the history of the universe. I take power yoga, Spinning classes, Pilates. I stand at the front of the class, stretch myself into infinity. My feet are so flexible I can touch the back of my calves with my big toes, something henceforth humanly impossible. I typed my B-average term papers *Oooo ye of yonder pudding* sitting on an exercise ball to work on dryland balance. Every night I sink into the black-velvet sleep of the physically exhausted, wake up naturally before the sun. My mind is bionic; if I visualize something long and hard enough, it comes to pass.

When Roxanne awakens, she doesn't speak, gives me a birdy shoulder and some sad roots to look at. Then they give her a truth serum medication that makes her very nice. She hugs me, smiles, tells me everything. Her quest for the perfect bong. *Pot, herb, weed, grass, ganga, hash, spleef!* The first time she went shrooming to school *the nuns looked like shadows yearning to fly!* The money she stole from Mom *right there in her room while she was reading!*

LSD was cool, but not good, she says. *Remember the Thanksgiving I never showed up? John and I took a hit of acid. We watched bricks move.*

Acid? I say, thinking *burn. Bricks in a building?* I say, thinking *crazy.*

Yeah. It was incredible. She sighs for all lost memories ruefully earned.

How did the building stay up, then? I'm rational.

It was like a contained set of dominoes, she says carefully, as though she is explaining a sick science project. *But then I got scared that if the bricks were moving and I didn't normally notice, what else was I not normally noticing? Things in the air, things in my eyes, things sinking into my skin. I freaked out. My first bad trip.*

I can't stand the burning, the acid, nun shadows, her eyes. *I'm sorry, Rox; I'm a bit tired today.*

Roxanne's rehab psychologist calls a meeting. She sits behind a clear plastic desk with a dull gold Buddha glowing internally upon it. She explains that Roxanne is suffering from an acute form of human loneliness that being smart doesn't make any easier because she has a good argument for almost everything, especially bad behavior and near-fatal experience.

She has trouble accepting life's limitations as a sober person, she says.

I look at the Buddha. *Yes, that may be true, but running stolen cars into trees makes it worse.*

She has trouble envisioning a world in which she has a powerful role.

I look at the Buddha again. *Yeah, but now she's sick and itchy.*

Mom calls, weepingly worried. *Tell her I love her. Tell her she'll be fine.* But they change her truth serum medication to one that makes her nervous and mean without informing me and she starts telling me to fuck off when I walk into the room, a new way of saying hello. Her eyes travel slowly from sneaker to ponytail. I am also informed that I am *an absent selfish sick fucking bitch. And the worst fucking nonexistent full of shit swimming asshole.* I almost call it quits, but her psychologist says that Roxanne needs me; that *fuck you* means *help.*

Roxanne's new medication enjoys keeping me waiting in the hall, one of those wide institutional corridors bathed in fluorescence. I sit in an uncomfortable chair and study the ground. Everything is designed to repel—stainless steel, high-glazed plaster, cold concrete. Nothing here will stay, no memory, no taste, no thought. It will be wiped clean, the night terrors, the daymares, the people without the capacity to cope, the pitted silence of those who watch.

I feel like something two-dimensional, ready-made, commonplace, with icy bits that resist life's heat. The upper echelon of the ward—doctors, nurses, psychiatrists, psychologists—are cool customers, as busy as bugs. They look at me and smile with a quick nod. If they know anything about swimming, they hide it. I watch the janitors clank down the halls; they have the hard looks, the large pores, the thick uniforms that don't breathe. I watch the orderlies clink down the halls after them; they are younger, look like they could use a dose of rehab themselves, are often cute.

Roxanne makes friends with Cat, Susi, and the dying Manfred, who looks at me and says: *Save it, darling; I'm as good as dead.* It's impossible to put an age on them, as though they'd drunk an elixir or were under some magic spell. I see them from afar, read their body language, think they are kids, until they get closer and the kid faces dry up into sunken walnut, hair into brittle wire, teeth into bruised banana.

They collapse in each other's arms, weep long hard tears. They lock eyes and laugh at mean barbs directed at the other rehabbers. Their judgments are based on hard socio-physical criteria; they make fun of the ugly, the uneducated, the poor. *She's a piece of crap,* they say about a hideous girl with acne marks pitting every inch of her face.

I smile at said hideous girl while waiting for Roxanne's mean medication to wear off, include a casual Olympic wave.

Fuck off, ass wipe, she says without removing her gaze from the horrible face in the mirror, and it seems obvious that the world says a lot of things, and if you listen without choosing, you become the one you hear the most.

When I pick Dot up at the airport, she's secretly divorced, unbearably bossy, and I have to defend myself against her wild accusations of my appalling management of delicate familial situations.

Let's take a look at erasing yourself with goodness, I say finally. We're driving directly to the hospital to see Roxanne.

She says: *Let's take a look at changing the subject.*

I say: *Okay . . . let's take a look at erasing yourself by fixing everyone else.*

She says: *Do you have to get nasty? Every time.*

That's the pot calling the kettle nasty, I think. *You could have opened an office with Benny Chap and charged us a fee,* I say.

Massive doses of therapy have made her intolerant of anyone else's inner life. *So, that's your answer,* she says. *One of your special Benny Chap commentaries.*

There is no goddamn answer, I say, *and quit bugging me about everything. Quit telling me that every little goddamn thing we lived through mattered. Some things didn't.*

Like what for instance? She's toying with me.

Like . . . let me . . . like Mom wanting chickens. You always go on and on and on about it. *The fucking veiny fucking chickens. I like chicken. It smells great when it's roasted and I like the sauce they put on those potatoes, although potatoes should* . . .

When Dot explodes, her voice gets hollow. *I was* a vegetarian. *There was nothing for me to eat. Those fucking potatoes were swimming in chicken grease. She didn't nourish me. I was like a* . . . *like her fucking slave girl. She never wondered about me. She never thought about me. Do you remember my sixteenth birthday?*

I try to calm her down, take one hand off the wheel in the international sign of universal peace, say: *Let's not get into this.*

We're into it. Do you remember? She's using the voice of no return.

Yes. No. I say.

Which is it? she says.

No.

She made hamburgers *and* chocolate peanut butter pie, she says, exploding again.

The significance escapes me. I say nothing.

I was a vegetarian and I have hated peanut butter since the day I was born, she says, sobbing out words. *I always fucking hated peanut butter. Bron was the one who loved peanut butter, remember? She'd eat it with a spoon. Sister Augusta used to make me an angel food cake with strawberries* . . . *Remember Augusta's angel food cake?*

This is exactly what I want to avoid. *No. Yes. Fuck. Don't cry.* . . . *This always happens, every time. Rehashing all this.*

They were good to me, those nuns. They were. I tell people, but they don't believe me. She is sad now with lost nun eyes.

You were almost one of them, I say, turning into a parking lot filled with anxious dusty cars.

I was just a sweet kid. Dad . . . *he* . . . *he* . . . *he* . . . *Dad when Bron* . . . *Jesus, Bron. Fuck. I can't take this. I can't take this.*

I change the subject, try to stick to present fact. *Look, Dot, things are okay now. I think Mom likes that chubby sheriff guy* . . . *who, lo and behold, is one of Glenwood's most eligible bachelors. Roxanne's new medication seems to be bringing her around to her old self and, you, you seem* . . . *annoyed* . . . *but* . . .

You know what Augusta used to say? She's tired, her face empty.

What?

She'd say, *"You just flute what anyone else thinks; take your life and run with it."*

That was the softball coach talking, I say, pulling into an empty space next to an enormous white truck with a big rusty door hanging from warped hinges.

You never knew her. She was so funny; she made me laugh, she says, wiping her bleeding mascara with the corner of a scrunched-up paper towel. When Roxanne was still talking to me, she told me that she thinks Dot has been so secretive about her life because she dreads coming off as human.

We go to court and Roxanne's life is read out loud like troubled news. A tall judge with a brown leather face tells her that she has to continue regaining her health in rehab and then she shall pay her debt to society through community service. The judge also tells Roxanne that if he catches her driving under the influence of a controlled substance again, she will do hard time.

Mother weeps into the phone, begging me to thank the lawyers, the judge, the stenographer, and other untitled court patrons, and we waltz her back to rehab to do her time.

All the windows in rehab are covered in bars so desperate people won't fall out by accident or design. I stand in the rec room watching rectangular slashes of sky through the bars. *Just get me a joint, Mena. It's better for me than alcohol or drugs. You don't even have to think of it as a drug because it's natural, like lavender.*

I cross my arms. *No way.*

She leans in, wheedling. *Come on. A little joint. A couple of hits in a one-hitter. No one will suspect you. We'll walk outside, la-di-da, one little puff puff. None the wiser.*

I lean in, not wheedling. *You heard the judge, didn't you? Did you hear the judge? Are you out of your mind? Read my lips: no way.*

She changes tactics. *Fuck you, shithead.*

I'm not a shithead because I won't bring you drugs in rehab, Roxanne. Maybe I should have a chat with the chubby sheriff—see what he says about it.

She flings herself into a ratty tweed armchair, starts talking like Scarlett O'Hara when she's the belle of the ball. *Oh, June! Is that mashed potatoes and beans? Oh, please tell me that it issssss.*

I almost whack her. Some poor skinny kid is making a piñata, engrossed in soaking strips of newspaper in a small bowl filled with liquidy glue and smoothing them out with both hands. He's too skinny to be real, his veins bright blue and raised. I look closer; he's fifty. I look closer again; he's in his eighties. I don't feel well; the cigarettes, wax, medication, and glue are waltzing with the chlorine in my head, no one's inner faces match their outer, June keeps being disappeared and I keep never searching for her, this poor old guy is stuck living with a little-kid vibe, and the will to whack Roxanne remains strong, so strong I almost do.

My eyes tell her that she is a scarecrow, that she is straw-colored, mismatched, and heartless, that her funny makeup is designed to frighten birds.

Drugs have immunized her to anything my stare can do; she just looks back, mashing the sugar out of a thin strip of green gum like the documentaries you see of GIs during combat. *Fucking cog in fucking wheel.*

I brace myself: *Don't start, Roxanne.*

What's not cog about you, Phenomena darling? You're a fucking ruler, with little straight lines, a straight-edged cog, a metal compass; you're a calculator, plus, minus, plus, minus. And P. fucking S., boo hoo, no more spuds and beans for you, my dear. No more June. Disappeared. Into thin air. Where oh where could she be? . . . You're so fucked up.

I'm *fucked up?* I say, pointing to the bars.

Yeah. She ignores the bars.

The addict in rehab begging for pot . . . I point to the bars again.

I'm not the only human being in the world who needs a crutch, she says, hunting around in her jeans for a smoke.

You barely made it, Roxanne. That tree almost got you.

She lights a cigarette, blowing smoke in my face. *My psychologist says everyone in our family is fucked up, even the ones who think they . . .*

I wave the smoke away. *They're saying I'm the most accomplished swimmer of my generation.*

She blows more my way, laughs a mean laugh. *They don't know a goddamn thing about you.*

Rehab takes time whether it works or not. Some people rehab over and over again like wheels rolling down hills. Mom flies Roxanne back to Glenwood to the local twelve-step inpatient program, run by psychiatrists who believe in the curing power of strong medication and manned by nursing nuns, a dire mistake. Then she goes to a tough-love rehab program in Minnesota that she describes as having some fat trucker with a crew cut trying to break her down to what he calls her *nitty-gritty,* which makes her want drugs bad enough to jump out a window and run away into the night with a fractured tibia. Then she goes to a rehab spa where she meets rich people to do drugs with and has international junkie love affairs that end badly in one of the New York boroughs. She eventually winds up in Montreal at a family-run, non-subsidized, one-on-one, real-life rehab. It's the one that clicks. She stops doing heavy drugs and becomes a highly functional recreational alcoholic/pot-smoking landscape artist as everyone sighs the sweet sigh of relief.

And I'm Hungry Like a Wolf

Sunny and I are sitting on a diving board massaging our calves with an oily organic concoction Babe's mom still sends the team on a regular basis. We're checking out some master swimmers at the end of the pool.

What about that one? I ask Sunny.

She shakes her head. *Married.*

I punch her in the arm. *You've got to be kidding me.*

She rubs her arm. *I'm serious. He's married.*

What kind of retard gets married young?

He's not that *young . . . We're not that young either, for that matter.*

I ignore her. *What about that cute guy?*

Come on! That's the Russian guy.

He doesn't look Russian; he looks Oklahoman.

Oh . . . him . . . I thought you were talking about the Russian guy.

I shift my eyes from a tall, skinny swimmer with the shoulder span of a tyrannosaurus to the other one: tall, dark, universally handsome, with one of those proud nasty faces. I'd seen him around. He's leaning over his gym bag, pulling out some goggles, his suit as low at it can go on his hip without revealing hair. Squint material. Not my type.

Not my type, I say.

The Russian guy notices me watching, stands up, puts on his goggles, salutes. I look behind me, no one. I stare at him with my mouth half open and before I have time to close it, he disappears under the water.

This is new. *What an A-hole,* I say. *He's Russian?*

Sort of. His parents are lawyers or scientists or doctors or something from Russia or Borealus or Boreaus, Borlulus. He was born there but moved here before he was two or five or something.

He's sprinting to the wall. *What's he like?*
He keeps to himself . . . On the arrogant side would be my guess.
And an ass. What was that salute about?
Sunny looks at me with her psych-major face.
What?

Every time I see him, he salutes or bows. I ignore him, but the energy it takes to avert my eyes makes them sting and the idea of him starts to infiltrate my swims anyway. He appears in my mind, dark and shifty, nodding or saluting, and I start to experience a tiredness felt only from a virus before it breaks out into something bad. Hot and heavy love scenes invade my mind; he's distant, interesting.

Supercoach E. Mankovitz has a series of succinct one-sided discussions with me. *We've got Pan Pacs in one month . . . that's four weeks from now. I'll be right over here if you need me.*

I flip him off in my head, plunge into the pool, but I run my fingers through my hair when I take my cap off, wear pink lip gloss instead of Carmex just in case. Once, I end up walking behind him, close enough to get details. I stare hard: his shoes are clean with clean laces, the bottom of his jeans *tatty,* his legs *long,* his canary yellow T-shirt *ironed,* his wide shoulders *set,* his neck *straight,* his head *shapely,* until he vanishes into the locker room and the air around me goes flat.

I make discoveries. The only thing that separates him from world-class times is that he doesn't care about anything; the only reason he swims is to compete in a triathlon in Hawaii in the spring, and apparently he's out to win. He's getting a master's in business, is smart. He wears a navy blue knit cap even though California is not cold, shaves both arms and legs. He makes no attempt to be liked so no one likes him. He quits, starts up, quits again. He has hissy fits where he throws his gym bag on the ground, kicks it, quits, slamming the gym doors behind him. He hates lifting weights, is apparently allergic to egg. Russia orders him to compete for them in the Olympics and legend has him saying *No way.* Women like him, but he is known as someone who dates then discards, thus the reputation of having a hard little heart, which he must have known is like dangling a dripping steak in front of a pack of ferocious animals.

I see him driving a car with different sorts of girls inside with long auburn, dark brown, or strawberry-flavored hair. He salutes if he sees me before I duck, adds a half marine salute with a queen of England twist to his repertoire.

We get close enough to talk.

I feel sick, hide it behind a neutral face and a new lip gloss I'm glad I'm wearing. *Quit saluting, will you. It's annoying.*

You love it, he says without breaking stride.

People don't treat you normally when you have gold medals, have broken world records, have a family of sponsors who star you in commercials where you have a new face painted on top of the other one, an agent who calls you up to inform you of your schedule, messengering your first-class tickets to your condo. They usually want a life like yours, but without the swimming. When people start treating me normally, I bring up a gold medal moment or the *Sports Illustrated* thing so they stop.

I steel myself with arguments: (1) I am more successful than he is; (2) I was born in America; (3) a lot of people I don't know know me; (4) nice swimmers can't get enough of me. But my head fills up with painful questions that repeat themselves over and over again. *How am I supposed to act? This isn't normal. What should I do with my face when he is around; should I arrange it to avoid him? How am I supposed to act? . . .* I start arranging my face all the time just in case he may be looking, even though the pool area is empty of Russian.

Sunny notices. *Is something troubling you?*

I'm fine.

What would a normal person do? I start dating a nice swimmer who could have been from Ohio. We go to barbecues and movies together, agree on most things.

After an impossible week sleepwalking through my swims like a lazy robot, Supercoach E. Mankovitz pulls his eyebrows up into his baseball cap and frowns: *Have you been eating sugar? You can tell me.*

Nothing but yams and I'm fine, I snap.

He takes off his cap and scratches the dent it leaves in his hair. *Perhaps . . . but you're taking your turns too late—rookie stuff.*

I look out into the water. *I'm fine. I'll watch it.*

After practice one day, the Russian guy is waiting for me. I see him, instantly prepare my body and face to walk by as though I am not pretending he's invisible, when he touches my arm and says: *I've been waiting for you.*

I immediately stop breathing and suffer the facial coloring consequences. He ignores it, says: *We should have dinner.*

I have to think quickly, don't, say: *I have a nice boyfriend.*

He studies me. *I don't think I've ever heard anyone say that before.*

This is bad. *A boyfriend, I meant to say.*

He's still studying me. *I have difficulty believing that.*

I have to think quickly, don't. *What do you mean?*

This is a source of amusement. *You know what I mean.*

I don't, am unprepared; all symptoms of nervousness reveal themselves as I scramble to disguise them. Something funny has happened to my blink. *I meant I have a boyfriend and he is a . . . What do you mean?*

A nice one? Well, maybe it's time you had a man friend.

It is such a stupid thing to say, I accidentally look at him and he laughs. His eyes are orchidy green, filled with swamp and an ocean of squint.

How Each and Every Thing Will Unfold

Peggy is bench-pressing her body weight, her face the color of a healthy Alaskan salmon. *We're being very quiet about Mr. Nasty, aren't we?*

He's not that nasty. I'm gripping the bar in an upright row.

For the last four months, all we've heard is how nasty this guy is, how emotionally disturbed and now . . . nothing.

He's not as bad as he seems, I say, suspending the motion.

At first everything seems practically normal, like scenes in a play with very good Method actors interpreting regular people with such enthusiasm it appears to be real. We eat sandwiches with avocado and watch the sea churn, have long talks to see who is smarter and in what way, eventually doing things in bed with an intensity I've never experienced before, which we never openly discuss. I pretend that it is as normal for me as it seems to be for him, a tactical error. I stop knowing exactly what I'm doing, suffer from unbearable surges of feeling, wanting to touch him when he is not around, conscious that self-obliteration is happening, that I risk danger, that this is dangerous.

I let him drive, look at him when he says things and keep on looking when he stops. There are his ears. My mind says things like *Well, he does have regular ears.* Everything feels so thundersome—my body, my arms, my sexual places—but I keep it to myself, even though the team is intrigued.

Bron and Leonard fly through my mind in a Model T Ford. Bron's driving, wearing a brown leather cap and thick aviator goggles. Leonard's wearing the same, but at an awkward angle as though he let her accessorize him like an obedient baby. He's studying the dashboard with no real interest, not a bat in sight. I need counseling, do not seek it, start showing a true kindness to some of the new swimmers I cannot stand, am all *toodle doo, that's okay.*

On the rare occasions he doesn't stay the night, I sleep as lightly as a nun on Christmas Eve. I stop going to the swimming BBQs because he thinks most swimmers are A-holes. He refuses to go to the costume parties even though I beg: *It'll be fun.* My condo becomes a cave on a tropical island.

Peggy says: *You're no fun.*

Slowness creeps up on swimmers slowly like panther until one day it is upon them. I watch it creep up on Sunny, watch her struggle, watch her plunge, watch pain no longer translate into speed, her times winding down a vortex of drain. She starts playing perky Dolly Parton tunes on her guitar, has embroiled therapy sessions with a man she calls Chuck.

She retires one month before Worlds, says: *It's time I move on.*

I beg her: *Don't go.*

She laughs. *I'm not going anywhere.*

I beg her again: *Please don't go, Sunny. Don't do this.*

I'm just moving on, Pip. I'm not dying.

I go to the Worlds in Peru and spectacularly beat my younger self with two new world records. People are amazed. On the plane home I don't sleep, but am not tired. I look out the porthole, am exuberant, exhilarated, inexhaustible, but quiet, as if the loud me has died and another me I am vaguely familiar with has been excavated. I say: *Burn, fucker, burn* at takeoff and landing, but my heart is not in it. At the airport, my eyes rip through hordes of people until they find him, then they rest.

At first he remains the slightly nasty guy who confuses me with his past-life foreignness, then he changes. I wonder if the not-nasty is a plot to throw me off, but at the end of the day, I can get him to do almost anything I want. I test him, casually say: *Would you mind picking up those things and putting them over there?* and he says: *Okay.*

I meet his parents, a very jolly father and a mother who studies me over her fork as we eat plates of cold things soaked in vinegar. Their accents are sweet, with the slight slowness of the mentally disabled. I'm made to understand that the Russian guy is their only son and as their only son is destined to succeed in a very large and extraordinary way. They had a daughter, Alena, who died mysteriously when she was eight months old. Many other bad things concerning cabbage and straw happened. They are a people who have suffered in a way that I, born in the center of the United States of Similar, could not understand. His mother leans over and whispers one hideous story after another that involve bloody vaginas into my ear as the Russian guy and his dad play some board game I've never seen before that looks really easy but which they assure me is not. I discover that masculine men leave the women to the women in order to recharge their maleness amongst males. Sometimes, the mother looks over my head and says something to her husband like *Eeky muzzle ga ga on her*. And the father responds without looking up: *Eeky muzzle on her dah dah*.

His mother is one of those women who pull at your arm when she talks because she wants you to remain looking at her. I realize later that she does this because once she starts to speak, your eyes automatically start searching for an exit. I wonder if they went through interrogations back in Russia.

On the way home, I say: *Don't leave me alone with your mom.*

He drives with one hand on the wheel, one arm stretching out the open window. *You weren't alone.*

You and your dad were doing other stuff.

In the same room . . .

She kept grabbing my arm and wouldn't let me look away, not even for a second. She was telling me horrible stuff about some crazy Ivor guy that couldn't possibly be . . .

I know what Ivor did. He sighs. . . . *She trusts you . . .*

Trusts me? She just kept talking and talking and talking. She thought I was from Chicago, she doesn't even know what I swim . . .

Why do you care? He stops at a red light.

Why do I care? I repeat, looking out the window to buy time. The small car next to us is stuffed with a lady with a big goiter under her chin smoking a golden cigarette. I watch her inhale, then let it go.

Yes. Does it really matter? he says.

Is this a test? No, I lie.

There we go, then.

Well, don't leave me alone with her.

You weren't alone.

His first name is Alexandre, but I like the middle one—*Stepanovich*—better. I like to say it; *Okay, Stepanovich,* or *Just a sec, Stepanovich.* But behind his back I call him the Russian guy and after a while so does everyone else.

He's a profoundly tricky person, sets traps I get caught in, as surprised as an animal hanging upside down from a tree.

Where did you get those? he says, watching me from the bed as I dress for practice.

In a store. I'm wary when he gets that look on his face.

What kind of store?

A big one.

Kansas or California?

California.

Did you pick them out yourself?

Of course! What's wrong with you?

Mmmmm.

What mmmmm? I'm sliding my hair into a ponytail.

Nothing.

What? Do you think they're ugly?

Yes . . . yes, I do. I think that most sane people over the age of nine would.

Are you serious?

Look at them.

I look at them. *They're just regular. White. Simple,* I say, adjusting the waistband with a finger. *Lots of women wear them.*

He crosses his arms behind his head, watching me. *That's their problem. They came in a package, didn't they?*

Of three. I'm not looking at him.

Exactly alike. He's still looking at me.

Yeah . . .

So you have many, he says, still watching me.

Yes. I'm putting on socks.

All the same color? He sounds like a lawyer in one of those shows.

No, I say. A shaft of sun is cutting through the curtains and landing on his legs. *I have some pink ones, some light blue ones. What don't you like about them?*

I don't like anything about them, he says. *They're for girls . . . You're not a girl.*

I change topics. *What's eeky muzzle on her dah dah mean?*

Where did you hear that?

Your mother always says it, I say, pulling some sweats on. *That and eensy snoodenia.*

He sits up, swinging his legs to the ground. *You misunderstood.*

I'd always thought of underwear as breathable hygienic basically white cotton muff protectors. On a larger, more meaningful scale, I'd also always thought I was a feminine woman because I had a nice healthy vagina and two good boobs, but the Russian guy gives the strong subliminal message that having a nice healthy vagina and two good boobs is not enough, exactly, to make a woman. I start to feel the wave of air and the thump as doors hit walls when I open them in a hurry. I start to feel the separation in my rib cage when I laugh out loud and the way heads turn in restaurants when I walk by with gigantic strides. The air flinches when I shout and I accidentally hurt people when I punch them in the arm; they wince. The Russian guy tells me that my favorite shoes have the heels of garden implements, that my hair does the same thing every day, that I should train it to do something other than sit quietly in ponytails. I think eyeliner makes me mud-eyed, that mascara gives a fake spider effect, that lipstick turns my lips into mini-vaginas, but the Russian guy deeply admires these things. It is when I am naked and not talking and not doing anything, lounging on my bed after practice in a hypnotic trance, that I find myself to be a most feminine woman, but I can't tell people this after I've accidentally bruised their eardrums. I put eyeliner on Cleopatra style, lie down on the bed when I know he's coming over, naked with special hair I comb the shapes out of, but my sexy hypnotic trance usually transforms itself into a drooly sleep that ruins the effect.

Dot flies in on a three-day furlough from saving the sad children of Portland, finalizing a divorce that is doing its best to destroy her. We go shopping, she pushing the hangers on the racks so violently they screech like a field of bats, me watching the clothes whiz by in a whirl. My eyes are naturally drawn to polka dots, the small white ones on navy blue, the thick cream ones on black. I halt some of the hangers mid-screech.

What's wrong with you? says Dot. *That's for old ladies and that's just ugly.*

We go to the lingerie section, where I am fitted for a real bra by a short muscular lady with color red hands who says: *Are you a gymnast or something?*

I'm six-two.

Oh. That's big.

Too big to be a gymnast. You could have been a gymnast.

I had my first child at seventeen, she says, smiling a creaky yellow and gray smile.

The smile causes my soul to confide. *I got my first period at seventeen.*

That happens, she says, standing on a chair and fitting me for a bra that takes my breasts and turns them into oranges that sit under my chin. She takes my breasts in her hands and puts them where she thinks they should go.

I am surprised before, during, and after, say: *It looks like I have oranges under my chin.*

She studies me, eyes serious under spikes of purple mascara, cocks her head, says: *No. It does not; they look nice.*

I turn myself over to her. She comes back with arms full of underwear made out of strips of ripped veil and bras with their own balconies as Dot sits on a peach velvet settee drinking a bottle of purified water, lost in her own thoughts.

Sometimes I stop listening to him when he says things and wonder *Why?* He has a slight space between his two front teeth. I look at the space and think *Why?* There he is holding his fork in his left hand and commenting on something I have not been following. There he is asking me if I am listening to him. There I am nodding *Of course,* but not. There he is putting down his fork; *I'm not going to talk if you're not going to listen.*

Masculine men are easily hurt, way worse than girls. And they need drastic doses of attention. The masculine man needs the feminine woman to run around him light as wind covered in transparent fabric like a naughty angel. He explains to me in one of his unguarded moments that he has Russian blood, which means he has strong thoughts about everything that happens in the world, and that he feels it necessary, essential, to yell at people who do their jobs badly. Yet I am unprepared. He yells at waiters who serve lukewarm food, oysters that aren't perfectly fresh, undercooked bacon in soggy BLTs, opening the sandwich as I squirm in my seat. He says: *May I speak with the manager, please?* or *I'd like to have a word with your supervisor.* Sometimes the supervising manager is the person he is already talking to and he raises one eyebrow, suddenly becoming very quiet as if this new revelation were too stupid to be true. He speaks down to funny-looking girls with funny-looking hair if they add things up the wrong way. I say: *Leave the poor girl alone.* He says: *A job is a job.* He speaks down to really ugly people who are lousy at their horrible jobs. I say: *Stop it! It's not that guy's fault.* And he says: *That guy doesn't give a shit about you, baby, and he just fucked up our order.* He is indiscriminate with his critique; no one is safe. He sends back bottles of wine, saying, *It's corked, It's vinegar, It's way too warm* as the wine guy looks back with cool wine guy eyes. He breaks away from long lines at the movies if the stupid people are saying their stupid things too loudly and we end up doing something else, even though I wanted to see the film. The worst is when we run into someone of his own species and the air gets hot as the violence brews. This happens with a mechanic, a locksmith, an unscrupulous computer programmer, and an obese florist who tries to sell him something that had been dead for a very long time. She wrapped it up and tied it with a pretty bow, obviously inept at judging a potential situation.

When things calm down, he acts all normal as if the night/day/afternoon were not ruined, asking politely: *How's your fish?* as if everyone in the waitstaff/restaurant were not staring at us with unconcealed displeasure and I say: *Fine* even though my fish is a piece of leather sole that's been dipped in the lemon polish the nuns use for the pews.

Once, a car parks too close, closing him in, and it takes ten minutes of bumper pushing to pull out. He gets out of the car without saying one word and bends the antenna with his bare hands as I watch with what has to be a stupid look on my face.

You just bent that guy's antenna.
I know what I did.

I stare at him with an amazed face and no words, but the bent antenna rotates in my mind. I can see it now, a very sad antenna with a little metal head twirling aimlessly on the hood. Loyalty requires silence during these moments, and I've already learned that if I say something, he's one of those people who'll blow.

He wears sweet perfume, the sticky kind that makes both the leather in the car and me sweat.

I say: *You smell kind of like a girl.*

What?

You smell kind of like a girl. I don't know what it is, but it's . . . sweet.

I don't think so.

What . . . is it Russian or something?

No. It's for American men. American men wear it.

Yeah, well, you smell like an American woman.

When he's annoyed, he fights nonviolent, nonverbal, no-eye-contact fights that last days, the silence pounding the air between us. He stays on his own, calls not. It wears me down, the tension. I dive into the pool and it's still there, inside. I sleep poorly, eat not, swim sad thrashing sets until E. Mankovitz feels compelled to give drawn-out speeches on focus that involve heavy sighs, clipboard slappings, veiny neck movements, international name-dropping followed quickly by international time dropping. He says: *Let's keep our personal life out of the pool.*

But all in all, the Russian guy is a very loyal black-and-white sort of person who is highly suspicious that anyone else's loyalty can match his own or that shades of gray exist in this colorful world.

You were dating someone when we met, he says one evening, after he sends back his steak.

I brace myself, biting into a grilled mushroom the size of a small hat. *We weren't dating . . . We were seeing each other in a very friendly, light kind of way.*

So you can do that, see more than one at a time?

You *asked* me *out,* I say, chewing.

I was just checking.

I swallow. *Just checking. What was all that saluting and squinting and waving?*

He leans in. *You know what that was about.*

I lean back, cross my arms. *No. I don't.*

Come on! Miss Olympus. He laughs a mean laugh.

Miss Olympus. I'm upset, hide it. *I'm one hundred percent accessible; everyone says so.*

You're one hundred percent accessible if you know you'll be worshipped.

I suck my breath in. *That's so not true.*

Mmmmmm.

Quit it with the fucking mmmm. Why did you bother if I'm such a . . .

Curiosity.

He uses the voice he uses when he watches the stupid news or reads something crazy in the newspaper or hears someone say something that he finds particularly idiotic. It is a voice that separates him from all other human beings, as though he's forgotten we're all walking on two feet straight to old age, then on to death. It is the voice he uses when he tells people what's wrong with them: merciless, infinite, containing an inarguable Truth that leaves no room for discussion, worse than Sister Nestor's when she was in a mood.

He starts using it on me, occasionally, here then there. *Is that bra pink? Are you really watching that? Does that come from Kansas? Is that something a nun would say? How about we cool it with the yams?* There's something about the tone, his shoulder posture, the way his eyeballs sit steadily in his head, that for someone who does not believe in a god or anything even remotely godlike, he sounds exactly like a secular pope. It does something to my pituitary gland, my hormonal, spleen, spinal, chakra, energy balance; it tweaks the internal organs and the nerves that support them; it takes the sympathetic nervous system and twirls it, making speech impossible for me, but when I calm down, I forgive him because he's Russian and everyone knows that Russian people are crazy.

Gigantic Gargantuan Fantastic

I'm wearing a dark blue silk dress with a Grecian neckline that the Russian guy bought for me. I love the dress but I loved the box first. No one had ever given me a box like that. It transformed me; I became one of those women who receive things in rectangular chocolate brown boxes with thick, pale pink velvet ribbons. They untie the ribbons with a swoosh, say *Oh wow! I love it!* even before they know what it is. We are in New York sitting in a well-lit glass box of a hotel that overlooks the city. The world is shining up and out; a gazillion lights beaming through the darkness, a chorus of noise rising above it softly like bubbles.

The Russian guy is standing in front of the window. *I love this place.*

I'm *Sports Illustrated*'s female athlete of the year. It will be the only night in my life where I will dine almost entirely surrounded by people taller than myself.

The Russian guy is beside himself with happiness, complains about nothing, keeps filling up my glass, his cuffs white, white over his brown wrists, covering my hands with his hot dry calluses from four-hour bike rides in the canyons. He says: *Let's live a little.* I drink four glasses of champagne and some red stuff that isn't wine, end up not reading the speech I'd written on yellow paper with blue ink that started out with *First of all, about the absolute honor that has been bestowed upon me* but make a new one up about dogs and loving teammates and coaches with superpowers and the power of positive recollection and the frostiness of snow in Kansas, which has become *Oooo Kansas! My Kansas!* I also grind my voice down and accidentally try to motivate them with my climb-evr'y-mountain speech as the Russian guy and Peggy laugh their asses off. There is near silence followed by cushiony open-palmed applause from the best boxers, gymnasts, football players, basketball players, figure skaters, divers, tennis players, wrestlers, hockey players, baseball players, etc., in the country, thus the universe.

A group of us go to a jazz dive bomb bar and drink vodka with cranberry juice. There's a combo playing with one mighty woman singing with one mighty voice. I tell her she's mighty and she shakes her head *no, no* while her mouth says *Why, yes; yes, I am.* I love the negation of the positive, the two meanings contained in one. My eyes interpret her gestures as my ears interpret her words and my mind works it all out like a trick. She does it again when she sings about love, singing *yes yes yes* with her lips while rolling both her hands into tight fists. After midnight, people's faces give in to gravity and I make the Russian guy take me back to the hotel, where I become a darker woman who flings chocolate brown boxes on the floor, pushing surprisingly drunk Russian guys down with one hand.

But happiness throws me off; every time I notice it, my warning lights turn on and everyone knows that warning lights attract trouble. During the trip home, I lay my head on his chest, feeling the strong beat of his erratic heart as it thumps, do not look out the window, do not speak, but do get jumpy when an ambulance blaring sirens rides through my brain. The Russian guy says: *Why are we so quiet?* And I lie: *We're not* because I don't know.

When we get back, he wants to move to New York, where we will become gigantic gargantuans. I feel the great weight of premature grief press down on my vital organs, explain that one doesn't swim in New York, that one couldn't wear flip-flops year-round, that it is difficult to have a car, that without a car one couldn't listen to one's own music as one drove through the world, and other various *Where would you train? What about your bike?* arguments while he holds my hand across a dark dinner table.

I'm talking about New York, he says with conviction.

What's the big biggie about New York? I say, unconvinced.

It's the most incredible city on the planet. Everyone wants to live in New York, he says with conviction.

No one swims in New York, I say, unconvinced, the great weight of premature grief squeezing my heart. *There are too many people to have any count. There's no in-between; it's all about got and not-got. It makes people covet. It's a very covetous place.*

He sighs, drops my hand. *You're quoting the Bible again. I wish . . . We live in California, for God's sake, California's a million times more . . . whatever . . . Listen, Mena, you're not a slippy seal anymore. There's other stuff out there to do besides swimming. You need to start thinking . . .*

Dippin' Dolphin and I don't like New York enough, I say. *It's not as nice as I need it to be; all those sad people walking around make me nervous. Look what it did to Roxanne.*

People are sad everywhere and Roxanne did what she did to herself by herself.

People are sadder in New York. New York made her crazier. Ask her.

He taps my knuckles with his knuckles, an ancient Russian ritual. *You've obviously never been to Minsk.*

It Can't Be Done
XXV Olympiad
Barcelona, 1992

Nineteen ninety-two is the year of the eight. I haven't done anything to my hair, am discreet and scientific, focused, my mind in an eight. When journalists smile and ask for grandiose predictions I can hang myself with, I smile and say: *Thanks for the compliment, Sherm, but let's just say anything's possible in the best of all possible worlds.*

Sherm looks at me and laughs. *Pip's all grown up. Where's that quote from?*

It's French. An ancient Bouvier quote, I believe.

A Bouvier quote? Wh—

The Superior E. Mankovitz intervenes. *Time's up, ladies and gentlemen. We have a long week ahead of us.*

Mankovitz and I are going for the impossible by pretending it's just another item on the list. I've been concentrating on laser beams running from the center of my body to the end of my lane. The beam originates between my eyes, cutting through the water, creating a space I ease my body through. Mankovitz has been experimenting with innovative coaching tactics, says: *There's nothing more beautiful than watching a great swimmer swim.* I feel steady in the water, calm. I let my body's natural buoyancy hold me in its arms, stretching, rolling, no more fight. I'm less tired after practice, less tired when I race, and my times are going down. I catch the Mankovitz looking at me, his face in an eight. When he catches me catch him looking at me, he smiles and nods. The smile and the nod mean *eight.* I smile and nod back. *Yes, of course. It's inevitable.*

He has me take secret ballet classes with a bitch of a ballerina. I weep inside when she stands next to me at the bar, pulling my knee up to my chest and holding it with her stick devil arms. I want to rip out her little chignon with my teeth; she wants to knee me in the sternum. We secretly fight to see who's stronger.

This okay? she asks, slowly pulling my arm out of its socket.

Just fine, thank you, I say, imagining her body on the floor of a pool.

I meditate with a Zen master, sit on his floor staring at the inside of my eyelids so that nothing about my goals feels diluted, delusional, or nuts.

For the first time in many years, my archenemies are one hundred percent female; there are no obvious guy parts in sight except for the well-developed pec. There are some Australians, an immature French chick with shoulders like a baby ape who keeps trying to stare me down with her walnut eyes, a Dutch chick, and a newfangled unified German Democratic chick who bears no resemblance to the East German Berliners of yore—she is the possessor of delicate hands, a normal neck. No surprises.

The Russian guy knows about the eight. He's the only person other than E. Mankovitz I have discussed it with, but that does not prevent him from giving me the silent treatment ten days before I leave for training camp in Majorca. The anger comes from a secret place inside his head he does not choose to share with me, but his silent treatment drips with *You're treating me like a boring swimmer you don't care about* innuendo, and I wish I hadn't been so forthcoming about my checkered past. I'm too wound up with Olympic energy to soothe him, just say: *Relax, Alex; everything's good.* A tactical error. His bad mood culminates in a hissy fit at the airport where he turns around and leaves without saying good-bye when another Team USA member, the idiot Randy Urid, grabs my butt.

He grabs everyone's butt, I yell to his retreating back. *That's how he says hello; he's an idiot. It doesn't mean anything. Come on. I can't believe this.*

He lifts one hand in the air without turning around.

Mankovitz notices, says: *You can take care of that later. We've got other things to concentrate on.* Then he smiles and nods *eight.*

This is it. I put two roasted organic almonds in each of my jackets. I lie on my bed, massaging my toes, my mind mostly in an eight, but troublesome flashes of Russia flare red, then go out.

Peggy is standing in front of the mirror doing something to her hair. *Did you see that Dutch chick?*

I'm half listening. *Yeah.*

Now she's sucking her cheeks in and making her eyes bigger. *Did you take a good look at the Dutch chick?*

Yeah. Yes. I looked at her.

She's turning to the side, looking at her profile. *Did you notice anything?*

I sit up. *No.*

She looks at my reflection in the mirror. I'm massaging my neck, my mind almost in an eight. *She's . . . what, did you think she was naturally that tan with big gluey eyelashes and dark pink lips? . . . You like thought she was born from supernatural pastel parents?*

I look at her reflection looking at mine. *Why do you do this?*

She smiles, baring her teeth, the orthodontist's child still looking for flaw. *What?*

Talk about things like this before an important, essential race.

She turns around and faces me. *I don't know . . . it's interesting, and in this case,* sad. *I mean, makeup and water—what's she trying to prove?*

Maybe she's in love with a swimmer and she's afraid if he sees her real face, he'll leave.

Did you think this up on your own or is this Sunny talking?

My own. I put my head on my knees, stretching my back into wicker basket.

I've been working with a hypnotist who's taught me to develop a new feel for the water. It works so well, water feels more vital than air. I'm as focused and as sharp as an elite Japanese barbecue set. I know exactly what's going to happen; all I have to do is let it unfold. The first gold will be the easiest. It'll get progressively harder when the press gets hold of the eight and starts applying their retarded pressure. I close my eyes to the vast quarry pit that is my mind, lightning flashing in shades of blood. I bid myself *Rest!* but do not. I look over at Peggy; she's resting, both legs up on the wall, head angling over the edge of the bed. This is our last Olympics, but we don't know it. Three years from now, Peggy will be heavy with Barney Rubble's child and my mouth will be wired shut for my own good. I'm blissfully unaware, almost knee-deep in an eight. *This is who I am. This is what I do.*

There they are, my feet, both of them, clinging to the surface of the starting block. I'm crouched, it's one thousand degrees, the sun's burning my shoulders into wood chips, my mind is supposed to be silent but it keeps insisting *Hey. Where's that goddamn Russian guy?* It's my fifth final and I'm getting tired.

I wait, my eyes on the four-meter mark. The beep surges; I charge. The pool stands up like a mountain; I'm hanging off its ledge, water snaking up my arms, trying to pull me back, water pressing at my feet, trying to make them stop. I can feel my sockets strain at the seams, and underneath, a tiny splash of lactic acid fatigue. I ignore the fatigue, roll, twisting both shoulders, pushing as hard as I can off the wall with a deep inner grunt, gliding in on a five. When I touch, the crowd goes wild. I should feel something but won't. My eyes find the Mankovitz; he's chewing a tight wad of gum, tapping his thigh with a rolled-up hat one, two, three, four, five. He looks at me, nods: *That's five.* I nod back, warm down in the warm-down pool, letting the water swash over me like air. I wonder not at the wondrous achievement of hard work combined with crazy desire and a sick competitive streak, just wonder where in the hell that fucking Russian guy is. I'd scanned the stands earlier, found the Peggys in big blue hats with red stars floating on them. I scan the stands now, packed with anonymous people, their faces blank with heat. *Where is he?*

I pull my hood up over my head, preparing to pass the press; they've gotten a whiff of the eight and are scrambling for news. I wave, smiling calmly, say: *Yes, that's five.* Then I see him, freeze. He's standing behind the security fence watching me, one cool piece of metal. He looks tired, says: *You know I don't like it when anyone touches you like that.* I say: *You get so upset over nothing.* He says: *This swimming thing, it's too much. It takes over everything.* I say: *I'm just trying to do what I do as best as I can.* He says: *I know how hard it is. You're swimming beautifully,* then he smiles and his nasty face opens like a window. This is when I love him. I say: *I love you when you're not mean* and he says: *I love you too and I don't usually do that*. My heart lurches into an eight. I smile, take a deep slow breath, my lungs whipping in relief. He looks at me, says: *You can do this*. I look back: *I know*.

And I do know.

I wait, as relaxed as a powerful animal preparing to pounce.

I swim, feeling Russian eyes upon me from somewhere I can't see. *Six*.

The Mankovitz is deeply excited. He smiles a tight smile and squints *Almost there* as I suck the salt off some roasted organic almonds and put my hand over my heart.

I wait.

I swim, my body lasering a clean trail I slip through, feeling the body of the fastest chick in Italy thrash frantically by my side until I lose her at the turn. *Seven*. Another podium passes in a strange electric blur. I bend my neck to be guillotined in gold as the crowd explodes, and the American flag rises beautifully in the sun.

I go back to the village, dropping into a deep and powerful sleep, my mind humming *eight* as Peggy slips into the room, falls into bed, and dreams until morning.

I wake up early on the day of the eight, open the shades, and look out over the stone and the glass and the steel of the Olympic stadium below, international peoples wandering about aimlessly like wind-up toys. Peggy opens her eyes, says: *You tired?* And I turn: *No*.

I spend the morning not in a dream but not of the world either. Things are quiet at the breakfast buffet, Peggy making eyes at a back-stroker from Sweden who carefully ignores her. I feel eyes upon me but when I look up everyone is busy eating.

I wait. My competitors want to beat me so badly, the air is thick with it. *I have to be taken down*. They don't even care who does it, just that it be done.

We file out to the starting blocks, the stadium painfully, arrestingly quiet. The Mankovitz is standing with a pack of coaches, Kyd by his side. I take my mark, my eyes on the spot I'll slice through like a knife. The electronic beep resonates and I find myself flying through the air almost as an afterthought. I can feel them behind me in the water, but I know they know what I know. *Eight. It's inevitable.*

I feel a deep relief easing its way down my body when I climb my last Olympic podium. It's over. My list is complete; I can now put it away.

I give the best interviews of my life in Barcelona, sitting carefully in my chair. I am exhilarated yet drained of all tension, like a Buddha in a deep wakeful sleep. After all the meets, all the banquets with the slide shows, all the appreciation awards, all the golds, all the silvers, all the bronzes, all the cakes we baked for his birthday, all the Christmas gifts we took twenty minutes finding, all the times spent in his office weeping ourselves into convulsions or staring him down, I saw the Mankovitz cry. I saw them, the tears, two shiny gray ones pooling up from that pouch thing he has under his eyes. When I touched eight, he'd remained crouching at the end of the lane, his head in his hands. It's changed things. He let me see him feel a closeness he will never mention and I let him see me feel mine.

Eight Is a Power of Two

Eight gold medals. Eight! I just about lost it. I really did. And I don't give a shit about swimming. Eight.

Roxanne's lying in her underwear on the diving board, a half-empty bottle of Gallo by her side. She's smoking a small doobie I watched her roll with one hand. I'm floating on my back staring at the stars. Dot's pretending to sleep in the hammock. It's as hot as July, but the month is October and the Russian guy is making himself scarce since my sisters arrived.

And that one chick who came out of nowhere . . . She's holding the smoke in as she speaks.

Tia Woodward, I say, floating on my back.

What a bitch. She exhales.

She just wanted to win, I say, going under.

I almost thought she had you a couple of times, she says when I come back up.

She wouldn't have caught me. I laugh, but only because it's over.

How do you know? she says, taking a swig.

You just know, I say, feeling my hair float around my face.

What was she, like twelve? She's getting wasted.

Eighteen.

Fuck . . . at eighteen. Let's see . . . I was . . . I was . . . She is wasted.

I'd already been to L.A., I say.

You're shitting me . . . you were eighteen? She sits up sideways, dangling her legs off the board.

Yeah. The moon looks like an eyeball in a vertical wink.

Dot gets up from the deck chair. *That's when Mom lost it.*

Roxanne laughs a mean laugh. *She was nuts way before that.*

I'm not in the mood to talk about Mom. *Let's not talk about Mom,* I say.

Dot sits down by the edge of the pool, grabs the bottle of Gallo, takes a big swig. *She was probably nuts from the beginning but no one knew it.*

It doesn't work like that, I say.

How does it work, then? Pray tell, Dot says.

You're great at the beginning until something bad happens and you have to think. Once you start thinking, you're lost. I'm pretty sure about this.

Then we stop talking for a while until Roxanne says, *I'm starting to freak out,* and we help her to bed.

Things get whirly after an amazing Olympics. You have to do the razor commercial in New York, then fly to Hawaii to host a master swim clinic. You get interviewed by the funny guys, who ask you the stupid questions to make the people on the other side of the TV laugh. You fly into Disneyland, go on all the rides, smilingly swim with live dolphins, lunch with some executives and their swimming children, wave with Captain Hook, fly out again. If you are dating a Russian guy, you have to be careful, calling him in the evenings with a moderate voice, underestimating any fun you may have had. You look at yourself and wonder what the future is supposed to do now, crawl into a bed someone else has turned down for the night. The sheets will be cool and tight, the windows sheets of glass containing major slices of sky, and underneath, a city teeming with life.

I'll take planes home thinking of nothing else but to see him. He'll be at the airport standing behind the crowds; sometimes he has short hair; sometimes he's shaved almost bald. He says: *How were the razors, swimsuits, goggles? How were the insurance people? How's Speedo? How's Timex? How's Hank?* And I'll rub the stubble on his head, say: *Good, good, good, good, good* and it all winds down again until I find myself standing at the edge of an empty pool, the warmth of its vapors stealing into the cool morning air, my toes gripping the surface of the starting block, bracing to plunge.

From Here to There and Back Again

Skating drill. Shark drill. Turtle drill. Ancient dull dead men say: *One day is, the next isn't.* Breathing drill. Two-beat rocking drill. Rock body. Rotate shoulder. Shift. Ancient dull dead men say: *O courage. O sorrow.* Watching clock tick drill. Feeling water flow drill. Body spearing focal point, mind lasering forward. *Time whips everything we know into foam.* I turn sharply, mind in electric hum, hear the same sound in my head that I did when Leonard sliced the newspaper in half with his Japanese knife, a consistent, growling rip: *Tah dah.* My shoulder. The pain comes in shock waves, rogue waves, freak waves, killer waves, surging, spilling, rolling, plunging. My heart tightens, I stop moving, let the water hold me up.

E. Mankovitz has various teammates and one janitor carry me to a car and brings me speeding to the hospital as I look out the window at various and sundry people driving their cars, their faces pressed forward with a private frown they reserve for the loneliness of the road.

I lie on my back in an ugly blue cloak while three doctors discuss my situation. The ceiling is composed of squares of thin white plaster surrounded by tubes of fluorescent light.

You most probably have a torn labrum; either we operate or you suffer forever is the subliminal message they are sending.

I'm cautious, a cautious heart thumping in my chest, say: *It doesn't hurt so bad,* refusing the kiss of death, although I feel its cool lips against my skin.

The Supercoach is quiet, his face in deep crease. *We're going to have to think very, very seriously about this, look at all our options.*

A famous surgeon with shriveled eyebrows is called in to discuss the possible benefits of surgery. He shows me what a surgeon can do, then starts reeling off statistics so I can't say I never knew. This is the thing I hate about medicine, the listing of what can go wrong. Knowing all the possible possibilities makes you stop all movement both voluntary and involuntary. If we knew anything about anything, sperm would freeze in their tracks. I picture my muscles shriveling into pieces of dry bacon. No swimming. Sitting around all day long. Time looming.

E. Mankovitz listens intently.

I stare him down. *I would be in a hospital, Ernie.*

No one stares E. Mankovitz down; he is anchored in bronze. *Under the best care.*

They'd tell me everything was okay. I'm starting to tremble.

Because everything would be okay, he says quite calmly.

But I wouldn't know it was okay until it was over.

No one knows it's okay until it's over.

But what if I find out it's not okay when the surgery's over, but they keep telling me it's okay? My teeth are chattering; I hold them down with one hand.

I'm losing you, he says. When I drive E. Mankovitz nuts, he shifts his attention to other things. He's studying his shoes now, white leather Adidas with simple dark blue stripes, says: *There's always rest and rehab.*

You heard what he said, all the things that could happen, I say, biting down hard on my knuckles.

He's the best, he says, walking through a black-and-white world. *It's part of his job to assess the risks.*

My brain's bleeding color. *There are so many sick people in hospitals . . . I could . . .*

Could . . .

I grab his hand. *I don't know. People die.*

He squeezes my hand, lowers his voice, and sticks to the truth. *People die because they're dying; the people who are healing, heal.*

A wad of chewed-up gravity lands on my chest.

I don't realize how panicked I've become until the Russian guy walks into the room and Mankovitz makes himself scarce. I grab Alex's arm, pulling and blabbering: *Alex. Alex. Help me. It hurts it fucking hurts my fucking shoulder is fucking killing me. I'm dead, dead, my body won't ever swim right again; it's all over. That surgeon with his fucking eyebrows—Did you see him?—he was warning me warning me warning me . . . Doctors have this thing that they do . . . everything, everything . . . this is it, this is it. Life is . . . it's . . .* My guts bubbling over like oil.

He holds me in his arms, keeping his perfectly symmetrical high-cheekboned Russian face very still, says: *Listen; we'll think this thing through.*

He takes me home, driving fast, both eyes on the road, thinking thoughts that will forever remain a mystery. He will present me with an option, one; all I have to do is to be a feminine woman and take it.

Weeks pass, he takes me out for dinner, doesn't complain about anything. The waiter says: *How is everything, sir?* and Sir says: *Just fine, thank you,* as I grow uneasy.

I've been thinking . . . things are coming together . . . I'm done here and now you have this shoulder situation . . . maybe it's time to move on. He's slicing a thick red steak.

Move on? My fork is hovering in the air.

Yes. Move on. I've got my degree. You've got your degree. Let's go to New York. He puts his knife down and looks at me.

Quit? I put my fork down.

Move on. He's sipping some water.

New York? The ripe hand of mature grief grabs my heart and squeezes.

Yes. He's uncomfortable, almost squirmy.

Now? The ripe hand of mature grief is wearing a black leather glove.

Soon. I'm setting some things up. He's slicing a thick red steak but not eating.

But I'm rehabilitating. Ernie says he knows this doctor who can do these amaz—

I want you to come. I want us to go. Start something new, you and I, together. You've spent enough time in the pool. Time to break out of prison. You can concentrate on the other things. He's getting exasperated, is starting to squint.

Other things . . .

Come on. There are so many . . . Commentary, for example. Speeches. You could be a consultant, run camps, coach. Lots of things. Television. Radio. Babies.

Television . . . radio . . . babies?
What's so shocking about that?
Babies are . . . I've never thought . . .

I stop mid-sentence, filled with a dose of terror so intense my palms start to weep. A baby floats into my mind. One: too small to be alive. Two: naked skin with visible veins and a throbbing spot on its head as its brain rushes underneath. Three: too soft to survive. What if you forget about it for a second and it rummages around in its bed until it buries itself in a blanket? What if you leave it on the bed and it rolls onto a knife?

I look at him with such abject horror that it strikes a chord deep in his ancient ballistic Russianness. He has given me the choice and I haven't automatically taken it.

He lets it go for eleven days, a ferocious smile sitting on the corner of his mouth like an upside-down comma. He lies down on the bed and sleeps on his back, closed-faced and inhuman, like Dracula. I smile back, non-ferocious but quiet also, pretending it will pass even though *danger danger danger* resonates along my spine. I sleep on my side, watch the light from a moon I can't see shift as the hours pass, say nothing. Tactical error.

I have long discussions with Sunny and Peggy about the future, reha-bilitation, what I am ready for, what I am not. We huddle together over Mexican salads served in taco bowls the size of cowboy hats that Mona would have frowned upon. Sunny says: *Babies don't die like that in the First World; it's rarer than rare.* She says this with her psychological *You need to see a professional* face.

My shoulder aches so badly I stop using it.

The Russian guy confronts me one night as I lie on the couch staring at the wall.

He touches my back with one of his hot hands. *So, what are you thinking?*

I brace myself, say: *Definitely not surgery.*

No?

I can't quit.

What? he says, his hand frozen in place. *What's your plan?*

I'm going to rehabilitate. Ernie says if we're lucky, maybe . . . then I'll concentrate on Atlanta. I'm just . . . not ready to retire. I'm too . . .

His eyes grow shiny with ice. He pulls the front door open violently, breathing slowly to calm himself down. I'm as still as a possum in the middle of a busy road. He turns, salutes, says: *If you're going to wait around and torture yourself until you start losing, go ahead, but if I leave now, I'm gone forever, baby. This is your last chance,* which makes me so nervous I accidentally laugh and he leaves forever.

I think of it as sick Russian torture, the not calling, the disappearance of personal items while I'm in physical therapy. I call, leave formal messages. *Come on, Alex. You know this is a difficult time . . . You're my . . . we can . . . you'll see . . . call me back. Don't be this way.* Tennis racquets disappear, the selection of bicycle shorts, the sweetie pie eau de cologne, books about the power of money, T-shirts, socks, shoes, a box of razor blades, and to my horror, a box of rubbers, until one day, on the counter, is his key. I get sharp pains in my chest, my left arm tingles, becomes numb, my heart thumping way too strongly. I panic, adrenaline coursing through veins, call the team doctor, wrenching with dread.

He listens to my heart, sighs. *We'll run some tests, but I'd say it's stress.*

Swimmers give me Russian guy sightings. Some enjoy it, others don't. They see him with one girl, then another, or maybe the first one changed her hair. Swimmers give me Russian guy news. He's quit swimming, is moving to New York, has gotten a job doing something gargantuan.

He contacts me before heading off to his shiny, strong, steel-reinforced, concrete, vertical life, speaking with a cool brittle voice, but I have already fashioned myself into a block of mortified wood, driving my Jeep up the high road of hell.

I say: *You left me alone at my darkest hour,* which is true.

He says: *Ahhh, the queen of me in the land of I,* and it's over.

Some people think of life in terms of meant to be and not meant to be. Some people say: *Well, maybe it just wasn't meant to be* and I say: *Oh fuck off,* practically spitting. I wake up at night to the bluish darkness of my well-lit condo as the radio swoons and the TV hums in unison. My motivational speeches start to become what the sponsors call *a little bit on the edgy side.* I stay exactly the same on the outside, pretending things are exactly the same on the inside, but you don't know what you've been relying upon until it has been removed, and you find yourself standing on a mountain of nothing.

Babe sends me handwritten instructions for optimum healing that involve meditation, visualization, sweating, the ingestion of living foods imported from Japan, stretching, clay cataplasms, and twenty-three different vitamins and minerals packed into organic ingestible bullets that look like compressed hay and cost $99.99 for a jar of thirty.

She tells me to be Indian to myself so I am Indian to myself. I hum, taking the time to speak quietly to my body: to all the bones and the muscles, to all the veins and the organs, both vital and secondary. I give praise to wise turtles, give praise to wise sky. I use gentle words for my muscles and organs. I use wise words for my heart and my mind. *I love you guys, you hold on, you let go, you take in some oxygen and breathe, you sweep the poison away and take the pain with it, you continue as is, you beat it, you get your fucking ass out of that slump, you fuck off and quit it, quit lying there slumping around feeling sorry for yourself letting everything around you shrivel up and die . . .*

One of my sponsors grows sorry, sends me the most expensive electronically enhanced exercise bike on the market. I ride it nowhere, making it go up hills as steep as mountains nowhere, making it speed back down as fast as I can, ignoring the pain because pain has forever been progress, unless you discount those times when pain is just something that hurts.

Nice swimmers want to take me to important barbecues. They call me up and ask me out, but the Russian guy has ruined them for me forever. I make brittle disastrous love with a good-looking one in his California king, sneaking home at four in the morning.

I lose, my heart a clenched fist.

I lose, pushed to the lame lanes.

Peggy dates Mr. Canadian Hockey, who looks at her like it's going to last forever. Peggy's Destiny wears Barney Rubble's face.

Isn't he cute? She is beside herself.

Be careful, I warn.

Don't be a jerk. She laughs.

Two months later she is sitting in Vancouver two months pregnant eating her mother-in-law's moist carrot cake.

Down the Uphill

I visualize. I close my eyes, watch my mind materialize. I hypnotize. I levitate. But when I slip into water, my left arm flails, my right arm overcompensates, my swim falls apart. A herd of brand-new swimmers with energetic ponytails and original musical tastes glide past me like rockets in outer space. I sense them, pull harder with every fiber of my winning mind, lose. They come up to me, towels around necks, shake my hand, tell me how they watched me swim when they were little. I say: *Thanks,* eyes hardening into the plastic snowflakes that kids stick to glass. Doubts about everything I've ever done wake me up at night, my light sleeps permeated by dreams I don't track. I'm slipping down and downer, don't have an ounce of horniness left in my entire body, my vagina as quiet as a cartoon clam. Dr. Sunny Lewis has a name for this that sounds really bad. The nuns pretended it was loneliness.

I watch the ceiling, say: *Quit watching the ceiling.*

Dot grows exasperated, tells me that I am suffering from an acute case of self-absorption and I know it to be so, but the answer answers not.

Supercoach E. Mankovitz informs me that true healing requires patience, his eyebrows entirely gray now in order to prepare him for the misery of death. I let him know I know he knows I know he is lying. Then I leave his office in a huff.

Father Tim blesses the air in front of the phone with his veiny right hand, sighs, says: *You'll get through this,* preoccupied with the unprecedented international priest crisis, Glenwood Sunday mass attendance at an all-time low.

Roxanne says: *Your brain's probably addicted to water; we're addicted people.*

I barely make it to Worlds, where everyone in the world beats me and a journalist from Japan asks if it upsets me personally when I let my country down. I don't get annoyed, my heart knee-deep in blank, say: *It will take a lot more than one of my crappy swims to bring down a great country like America.* But I let myself keep on sliding right down the ladder of success, down and downer I go. I plunge into pool, pull myself through chronic throbbing pain, climb out, stretch myself through chronic throbbing pain, go back home to empty apartment, sleep on couch in front of TV set in purple solar flare extra-deluxe mummy sleeping bag with hood.

Mom marries the chubby sheriff in a backyard gazebo ceremony that lasts three days. Glenwood opens her arms wide like an old familiar lady. I know everyone by heart. The world is changing as I watch the dancing golfer twist with the orthodontist's wife. Some classes at Holy Name are being taught by teachers in normal clothes with kids of their own. The world is changing as the Glenwood Brass Boogie Band gets down and Roxanne sits at a table of Encouraging Catholics, smoking a cigarette and staring into space.

Dot had all her negative energy removed in a sweat hut in Taos, New Mexico, is very calm. *Look how beautiful Mom looks,* she says, walking up and standing close to me, her hair in a complicated style that includes both braid and bun.

I look. She's surrounded by a flock of Dark Catholics, is hanging on to one of the gazebo poles with white hands as though she were a balloon caught between winds.

We're in our own backyard, Dot, I say. *The chubby sheriff hasn't been able to get her out.*

Quit calling him the chubby sheriff. His name is Ken, she says gently.

He likes it. I watch the chubby sheriff swing, his face flushed like a girl's.

No, he doesn't, she says less gently.

Yes, he does, I say.

No, he doesn't, Pip, she says, mean.

Yes, he does, Dorothy Rose, I say, mean.

No. He doesn't, Philomena Grace, she says, meaner.

Yes, he does, divorced Dorothy, I say, winning.

You're a real bitch, she says and leaves.

I wave *toodle do* to my mother; she wrenches one of her hands off the pole, waves *toodle doooo* back.

Lilly Cocoplat's life is drenched in disappointment.

My life sucks, she says. *I hate being married. I mean I really, really hate being married. And I'm living in Glenwood. Two miles from my parents. Why didn't you stop me? I should have been stopped.*

I think quick, say: *Look at poor old Tanya Slaughter with all those kids.*

She says: *I don't give a damn about Tanya Slaughter.*

I don't know what else to say so I say nothing.

She calms down, changes the subject. *Remember the vaginas?*

She looks the exact same as she did when we were little, but miserable, and my heart surges. I wrap my arms around her, say: *Only a cunt chip would forget the vaginas,* and she wraps her arms around me as our eyes sprout like water balloons with a million pinholes for all that is forever lost.

Press Off

Certain swimmers sense retirement before it hits them; others have to be beaten over the head with it. My brain says: *Atlanta, Atlanta; just wait until Atlanta.* My body says: *Fuck Atlanta. Who gives a shit about Atlanta? It's me or Atlanta.* When I trace the jinx back, it lands at the Russian guy's feet. I write him short, awful letters, then burn them in the sink.

Peggy comes to visit with her brand-new baby boy. She wears him strapped to her chest to try to hide the fact that she is now so fat she can no longer wear the symbols of love her husband gave her because her fingers are bursting out of her hands like bratwurst.

I open the door and my eyes say: *Puff Daddy.*

Her eyes respond with new non-Peggy wisdom: *Yes. I overdid it with the cake but do not want to discuss it at this time.*

My eyes say: *Wow. Your baby can hide you for a while, but one of these days you're going to have to put it down and what then?*

Her eyes say: *I know my own reality, Pip.*

My eyes say: *Fair enough.*

I organize a barbecue with the Seoul silver medalists. Babe flies in for the weekend, tan, blond hair streaked with brown. Sunny is wearing her hair in a serious bun so tight it widens her big mouth into trout. Everyone ignores Peggy's new butt, which is considerably larger than my lawn furniture. They offer me a panoply of sound unsolicited advice over chicken and glazed yams.

Time to retire, says Peggy.

Time to move on, says Sunny.

Time to do something else, says Babe.

Time's up, says Peggy.

Sunny insists that I hold the baby. *Hold the baby.*

I can't, Sunny. His neck . . . What if it snaps? . . . It kind of snapped with Peggy, I say.

It did not, says Peggy. *What's wrong with you?*

Did too, I say.

Did not, says Peggy.

She's trying to divert our attention, Sunny says to them. *Hold the baby,* she says to me.

My shoulder has been drastically weakened by consistent chronic pain, I say, pointing to my shoulder. *I could drop it.*

She's doing it again . . . Hold the baby, says Sunny.

Okay, okay, give me the baby, I say, holding out my arms.

See? says Sunny in a professional voice designed to soothe the savage heart. *You're holding a baby. You don't need to hold your breath. Nothing bad's going to happen.*

The baby is lying limp in my arms like a sack of potatoes left out in the sun.

You're turning red, says Peggy.

I'm fine, just fine, but I think you can take the baby back now. The baby is lying in my arms, long-lashed, wobbly-faced, puffy-lipped. *He seems . . .*

He's asleep, Sunny says. *He's fine. Keep holding the baby. And breathe. Breathe.*

When they leave, Dot comes. She sits in my recliner as though it were a straight-back, hard-wood, nun-punishment chair. She wants to take me away. I ignore her and her lady shoes. She thinks we should be together, help each other, bond. I ignore her and her lady heels, lie on the couch with a blanket over my head.

She speaks to my blanket. *So it's swimming or nothing?*

I speak into a light blue blend of cotton and wool, live to regret it. *Since when have I ever done nothing?*

She pounces. *You spent a lot of time doing nothing. Don't you remember? You watched reruns over and over again. You knew the lines. Don't you remember?*

I don't want to remember. *Some of the lines.*

She won't let it go. *You knew almost all of the lines.*

I don't think so.

She's obviously rehashed this in front of a paid professional. *You knew almost all of the lines,* she says. *And you ate those cherry pie things they took off the market.*

I hold the blanket up with my feet like a tent, feel my face turn a light shade of blue. *I'm not in the mood for this.*

You ate them for dinner, she says. *And you knew almost all of the lines to that stupid island show.* Dot will never learn when to stop.

I don't want to talk about this.

Of course you don't, she says. *Why would you?*

She beats me down, hammering the air with words until I find myself on a plane with her at my side. She's reading *Most Misunderstood Mammals* by Dr. Leonard Ash, thumps me on the arm. *Listen to this: "Fishing bats have an echolocation system so sophisticated they can detect a minnow's fin as fine as a human hair."*

I don't want to hear about bats at the moment, Dot.

You should read it. There's this part where he sat up all night waiting for a colony of snout-nosed bats to appear. He was on the Isle of Night with this guide named Tanguy who turned out to be the local drunk.

I don't want to hear about it, Dot.

We rent a house from a nasty lady on a small island in the middle of the shark-infested Caribbean Sea, where I float slowly next to the boat, afraid of the potential shark, thus afraid of everything. Life has proven that once bad things start happening, they're difficult to stop. *If a shark attacks, punch him in the snout.* Dot is wearing a huge floppy orange hat, sits staring at the horizon and commenting on the mysteries of life as I swim. I hear words, parts of words, the end of a dramatic sentence before dipping my head back into the water, eyes on the peel for a flash of gray, one hand balled into fist. I swim out into the open sea, its great depths opening below me. The depths layer downward, following the curve of the earth, silent creatures simmering with life below.

My shoulder hurts. I slowly swim back using only one arm, hanging on to the side of the boat just so I can breathe again. Confronted with my misery, Dot becomes calm and deeply expressive about loneliness, love's obliteration of self-reliance, the ebb and flow of human emptiness.

The shock of the heart is the original thunder, she says, taking off her hat and slipping into the water as the sky beyond her opens its mouth and yawns.

I like to snorkel, am not a diver, like to float on the surface and look at schools of fish spooling their way through Doric columns of light, shafts of sun, the fingers of God. That's what I think when the sun weaves its way down into a sunless water: *Ahhhh, the fingers of God.* Dot's in front of me, her flippers slowly flipping up, then down, her hair spread about her like reedy weeds. She's wearing a turquoise one-piece; her legs floating under her like two pieces of string cheese. She turns, her face cut in half with a snorkel mask, gestures *Look, look.* There are two sea turtles swimming in front of her, an old one and a new one, with green froggy faces, two marble eyes, a round snout. I feel my heart flood with love. I am at one with everything as my breath bubbles out my tube into the hot dry air.

When we get home, I fling myself on my bed and listen to the wind whistle through the wooden slats that cover the windows, watch thin lines of sun and wind drizzle through, dust alight in the air like diamonds.

The crazy lady calls at all hours in order to remind us that she had *meticulously counted the towels,* that the *towels have been professionally counted by a team of hired meticulous professionals.*

I'm not interested in your goddamn starchy towels, I finally say.

How dare you, she says, hanging up without an answer.

Dot sighs. *Someone who used to love her probably doesn't anymore.*

So what? I say. *She's an A-hole.*

I'm done. You want to read it? she says, changing the subject.

I look at the cover: a Mexican free-tailed bat caught in the midst of a high-altitude flight, the moon a tiny speck of gray, tropical trees etched green and black on sapphire sky.

Okay.

Progress, she says, pressing it into my hand.

A Man Without a Smiling Face
Must Not Open Shop

Back home I spend many hours lying on the couch watching TV in my purple solar flare extra-deluxe mummy sleeping bag with hood. My mother calls from the phone next to her pillow. *Why don't you do something else?*

I respond in kind. *Why don't* you *do something else?*

We're not talking about me, she says. *I've been through a lot.*

I get mad. *Who do you think was going through it with you, Mom?*

The Superior E. Mankovitz throws the healing net out into the vast ocean of sports therapists, healers, physicians, and reels it in, sending me to see a highly effective osteopath named Tara. She's wearing a white terry-cloth turban on her head that sticks with Velcro tabs. I ignore it. She explains that she is going to align my bones with my muscles, unblocking any chakra clogs with her magic Drano fingers. The energy is going to be released in my body in a blast like a roller coaster on its way around an uneven world. I might cry or vomit.

It takes a lot to make me cry. And I never vomit, I say, *not even when I'm sick.*

I close my eyes, my shoulder aching in rhythm with the construction work outside. She rubs something into her palms, then lifts them to her face and breathes in. She breathes deeply, says: *Neroli, I love neroli,* her hands gliding over me like warm oven mitts. I wonder if she's going to notice all the dead people.

Her hands hover, stop, hover, stop, hover, stop.

How long has this been going on? she whispers.

What? I whisper back.

This! These energies!!! Her turban slips.

Let me see . . . the energies . . . it's been a while now . . . twelve years. Can you see them?

I get flashes. It's hard to explain, but they need to be released.

I'm surprised. *Released?*

Yes. Her hands hover over my body, stopping underneath my forehead. *They need to do their own thing.*

I'm still surprised. *Do their own thing?* The neroli is invading all my senses; my mind is swelling with it.

She ignores me, taps my head with the tips of her fingers, taps a spot under my left eye, stirs the air in front of my throat with an invisible spoon, hands hovering quietly in front of my heart, whispering: *Open, open, open,* her arms opening wide in the international sign of open.

That works? I say, opening my eyes.

Well, you have to mean it, she says, getting down on her haunches looking for another oil.

She's starting to freak me out.

Relax, she says without turning. *No one is going to hurt you.*

I close my eyes. She rubs my shoulder with her mittens until I fall into a wakeful sleep. In my sleep, I see a clock, Leonard's old grandfather, pendulum swinging, wooden torso emitting the vague perfume of waxed lemon.

What are you doing? It's two o'clock in the morning. My mother is standing in our doorway, the light of the hallway twisting her into living shadow.

I'm sullen, exhausted. I've been swimming like a fool and Bron wants me to not sleep at night. *Nothing.*

Her voice is rising: *Why were you . . . yelling?*

I'm sullen, lie. *I wasn't.*

You were. I heard you. Her voice is advancing toward me.

Bron flips her back to the door when Mom walks into the room, deserting me. *Leave her alone, Mom; it's my fault, I woke her up,* she says without turning.

Are you upsetting her? How is she supposed to feel fully well again and . . . and . . . healed with you upsetting her? She should be asleep. Come here. Come here. Come here.

She's using her fangs to cut into my arm and pull me out into the bright hall.

I'm a sophomore now and have started to act like one. I squint under the light. *Leave me alone, Mom,* I say, my tired eyes adding: *Pig face!*

She's going to punch me, but doesn't know it yet. She's balled up one fist, her eyes squinched into slits, so mad she's shaking. When she punches me, her face is full of surprise at how much it hurts. She holds the fist that punched me gingerly with the hand that didn't. I take the punch in the jaw, hard. It snaps my neck back, but I don't fall. An epi-center of blackness blooms in my chest, pouring down my body like liq-uid lava. I remain standing, holding my smarting chin, feeling a new heart beat beneath it.

Pray. She's breathing hard. *Pray. Close your eyes and tell God with all your heart not to let anything bad happen, okay? Just tell Him. Ask Him.*

She pulls me into Leonard's study and we kneel on the ground in a mutual nervous breakdown. I put my head into my hands and pray. *Dear God don't let Bron die, dear God don't let Bron die, dear God don't let Bron die, dear dog don't let pigs fly dear dog don't let Roxy stray dear god listen to me pray everyday come what may.* But I see her dead and when I see her dead, I see me dead and when I see me dead, I am in the darkness and in the darkness, I am alone.

You asked too much of me, Mom. I was just a tall kid.

When I open my eyes, Tara's sitting by my side. *That one's still alive,* she says, *but she's got big problems.*

I feel like I'm going to heave. *I know,* I say, then I barf into a pale yel-low bucket as Tara rubs my temples with an oil that smells exactly like Manny. I watch the sun slap the window with its flat hand, eyes leaking irregular drops like rusty faucets. The construction guys are listening to loud radio. It's summer again. Old people are falling from their beds and breaking into pieces on the ground. Some kid was caught riding his tricycle on the highway. My shoulder feels as though a knife is being driven through it; my thoughts rush through my mind in a fast canoe. I lie down in the canoe and watch the sky fly by. Something inside me knows I'm not going to be swimming any faster, but I don't listen.

Destination Destiny

I train, lobbing up and down the lanes, not bothering to change in the locker room, driving home so slowly cars honk. *Man is not a reasonable creature.* I stand in front of the mirror, lopsided and moody, no equal sides, no equal angles. I sip a batch of record-losing grimlock, massage my feet with a mixture of rose oil and geranium, am Indian to myself for fifteen minutes, read a chapter of Bud Lancer's *Europa* I do not retain. The stars are out. I stare at their patterns begging like a leper, go inside to meet my destiny. *Man is but a deed undone.* I don't even look at it, stepping up with flexible toes, grabbing a nail file from the box I'd thrown on the shelf above the ever-reflecting mirror, slip, catch myself midair, slip again, falling as softly as a Manchurian crane in a dive bomb, until I hit my right shoulder blade on the edge of the bathtub, breaking it with a snap like a wing. This is what I see as I fall: a wide white world opening its jaws to swallow me.

My car takes me to the emergency room, pulling up quietly to the door. My feet take me inside, slapping the floor loosely like flippers. A squinty intern explains that ninety-nine percent of all accidents in General America happen in the home when Americans are doing something they assume requires no active thought. I try to explain that I am not general, but my words are absorbed by an ocean of drool-streaked blood and my teeth feel like they're dancing. At first they think my jaw has simply been dislocated, but then they realize it's broken and wire it shut for my own good.

I've felt this before. I'd sit in my pleated blue skirt and white blouse observing the kids with no dead people in their heads. I'd watch them eat pizza on pizza day, the entire cafeteria bathed in navy blue and white, mouths quietly chewing, minds blank. I was hungry to chew with blank pleasure-filled eyes while no one I knew was silently decomposing under the snow shoeless, in a sparkly sweater, a nice pair of jeans, a pair of my socks, without a good winter coat over her bones. The nuns are expert pizza chefs, use a blend of three cheeses that pull out in hot unbreakable strings you have to cut with your teeth. I wish I could see old Sister Belly throw one up now. I close my eyes, follow the flat Frisbee of dough as it wobbles up sideways like a spaceship, twirling flour as it falls in slow motion, gently, beautifully, back to earth and earth's waiting hands.

When I wake up, the Superior E. Mankovitz is standing at the window looking out at a nothing sky. My jaw is wired shut, my mind churning out fog. I pull him closer with one finger, say: *Where's Dr. Bob?*

He says: *I honestly don't know.*

His normal face has been replaced by an old one. *What did you do to your face?*

He pulls a hand through his ginger-gray hair, says: *Nothing.*

I grab his arm. *Where's Dr. Bob? Where did they go?*

He says: *I don't know.*

When I wake up again, he's still there, sleeping in a chair with a magazine over his face. I almost hit him when I throw my breakfast tray against the wall, causing great mortal pain to my shoulder. He doesn't even jump, just stands up and asks: *Who's this Dr. Bob?*

I get to thumping and convulsing: *He forgot everything he ever knew, then he died like a baby.*

He says: *It's time we talk.*

Time? I shriek.

Cosmic Drama

A droopy ponytail assembles itself at the nape of my neck; my shoulder wraps itself up in a clean white sling. The Superior E. Mankovitz stands directly behind me with steady, Supercoach eyes.

I thank the world through clenched teeth. *Thank you very much for everything.*

Then I retire, lying on a series of couches from Glenwood to California until my jaw heals. I'm twenty-eight. That's fourteen twice.

The Secret Glenwood Recovery Plan

Roxanne's standing behind me wearing a pair of black glasses with a broken rim she's repaired with tape. She's sucking hard on a Tootsie Roll. *I want a smoke.* My jaw's still wired and I'm on the cusp of a bad mood, a pair of wire cutters lying next to me on the couch just in case. I'm in a bad mood, speak between my teeth like Clint Eastwood before he kills. *You're supposed to be my fucking nurse, so don't fucking smoke because that means we'll have to deal with you fucking quitting again.*

She's in a bad mood, says: *I won't fucking smoke, but that doesn't mean I don't* want *to fucking smoke.* The telephone rings. We ignore it. Mom's upstairs under the cover of bed. The chubby sheriff is out bringing in the bad boys of Glenwood. It rings again. She looks at it. *You know that's Dot.* I don't look at it. *I'm not in the mood.* I'm busy watching the world do things inside the screen, anything: car races, shark attacks, tennis-playing tennis players who grunt like ogres every time they hit a ball, golf-putting old/slash/youngish guys who squint when they slice, midgets from Brazil chasing midgets from Spain across a long, grassy field. The more I watch, the less human I become. The legs that run the length of the couch are legs I do not know. The arms that sprout from my shoulders are arms I do not know. My brain is churning. I can feel it. *Was it not okay to look dead people in the face?*

My bad mood fizzles out. I look up at Roxanne. *All this isn't going to finish well.*

She says: *All what?*

All this, I say, pointing to the screen.

Roxanne has theories that come from marathons spent in front of the Nature Channel watching sea turtles hatch under miles and miles of burning sand and then try to reach the water before being demolished by an army of crabs. Roxanne's theories are reinforced by seas full of fluffy young penguin corpses smothered in inky oil, strangled fish found with strings of plastic in their mouths, the Bornean clouded leopard munching down on a gazelle. Roxanne finds absolute proof in kitten-devouring dingos, jackals with squirrel pulp between their molars, harrier hawks swooping down on a litter of baby field mice. A largemouth bass eats a trapped chipmunk, an elephant falls on its side and the earth gives, a monkey picks its teeth with bamboo, sea turtles sleep at the surface of the wild Sargasso Sea, killer whales plunge into dark arctic water, harbor seals bathe on warm craggy rock, fur seals wait for club, as Roxanne's eyes gather information about this horrible world.

Roxanne thinks: Plastic floating in ocean path; fish eat plastic until life finish. Heroin sitting on table; Roxanne shoot heroin until life finish. Door in bedroom; Mom shut until life finish. New self-help book sitting in self-help store; Dot buy self-help book until life finish. Water flowing through world; Pip dive in until life finish.

That's not a theory; that's a series of stupid thoughts. Life isn't about hatching sea turtles, I say.

She looks at me, annoyingly straight-faced the way some ex-almost-dead addicts can be, says: *Some don't even have a chance to hit the water. It's over before it begins.*

She's wearing blue overalls, has done something normal to her hair, which has done something normal to her face. I almost believe her.

Speak for yourself, I say, sipping frothy grimlock through a straw. *Dot and I saw old sea turtles, new sea turtles. They were swimming. Perfectly healthy. Graceful. You should quit watching the Nature Channel. It depresses you.*

I like the Nature Channel, she says. *It depresses* you.

You're not supposed to like the Nature Channel. Since my jaw's been wired shut, I'm easily excitable, spitting droplets of grimlock on my T-shirt. *It's depressing. Those fucking turtles. Those baby deer. The baby lions. It's fucking awful.*

She takes off the black glasses with the taped-up rim. *There are sweet moments. It's the way things are.*

No, it's not the way things are. I grab a blanket, wrapping it around me like a pastel muumuu. *It's some guy filming animals at their best and most sweetest possible moments, then when they are getting mashed into a bloody paste by animals we have seen in their best, most sweetest moments. Those nature guys want to freak us out; that's part of their job. There's no one to root for unless you prefer tree snakes over toads, panthers over zebras. That fucking octopus slipping through the crack in that disgusting aquarium and trying to run away . . . I thought I'd barf.*

You should see a psychiatrist. She looks normal again, but I know that she isn't. *You really should, you know.*

I've seen tons of psychiatrists, I say, lying back down. *They've given me a unanimous go-ahead. Thumbs-up. All systems go.*

You've got to be kidding, she says, putting her cracked glasses back on. *I wish I had a fucking smoke.*

Disappointing Atlanta

I fade quickly into a professional world-class elite motivator, someone so capable of motivating I waltz into a room, grind my voice down, look unsuspecting people in the forehead, and make them mine, no hopping necessary.

NBC grows sorry for me, wants me to comment on the action in Atlanta with my own microphone and an orange face. I want to want to do things so I say yes. For the first time in twelve years I watch the Olympics like the rest of the world, commenting with the celebrated Sherm Russel. He and his wife just had twin girls. She calls him every break, panicked. He says the same thing every time: *I'll be home this weekend, hon. Hold on, hon. Don't cry.* He reads the morning news with a frown slicing his face in half like a handsome priest concentrating on difficult passages in the Bible. I don't read the morning news but frown anyway as Jolie, the hair and makeup expert, sprays our faces with a silver pump that blows a beige film over our skin. I look like a biscuit, but later, when I look at the monitor, I look like all TV people, sane, healthy, relatively happy. When I sneeze, Jolie runs over and sprays parts of my face back on. Sherm says: *God fucking bless.*

Sherm comments. I comment back. Sherm comments again.

What would you say she is feeling at this very second, Pip? Sherm has a voice people listen to even if they don't want to.

Well, Sherm, I'd have to say by the way she's tossing her arms around the place that she's probably feeling a bit sickly, I say, tossing my arms a little bit to prove the point.

Sickly? He's raising his famous eyebrow.

Nervy. Look at Lindsey Lions; she wants everyone to think she's a tough guy by sneering and flipping that towel. Now look at South African Hayley Glennon, who is being very quiet, just pulling on her toes. . . . Toe pullers are by their very nature rather difficult to pin down and South Africans definitely have some things to prove. After looking at her stats, I'd say she has the best chance for the gold today. There's maybe even a world record in it for her. I know one hundred percent exactly what I mean.

Interesting, Pip . . . because she's pulling on some toes. You can see a world record in that? The eyebrow again, but this time he's smiling.

There are codes, Sherm, swimming codes that are invisible unless you crack them. . . . When I was rehabilitating, I spent about eleven months reviewing races, cracking the codes. . . . The truth is in the . . . You'd be amazed, Sherm, I say, my hands flying like birds.

I think we're all amazed, Pip, he says, then we take a break.

His wife calls and he says: *Don't worry, hon, hang in there* as I stare at my orange face in the mirror. I shouldn't have done this. There is nothing worse in the world for a tense world-class swimmer in the early throes of retirement than to watch other tense world-class swimmers swim without her. And tense world-class ex-swimmers should never be given an expensive set of binoculars to capture detailed action. I hold the binoculars to my eyes: Sonia Westerholm from Sweden sucks her thumb underneath her towel like a little baby. Hanna La Font, the Parisian chick, tries to psych out Californian Susie Jenks by making scissors out of her fingers and cutting her up. The devout Susie ignores her, praying as openly as a Dark Catholic. I watch them pull their suits out of their butts before standing up on the starting blocks, watch them thrust their bodies into the air, their inside faces finally free, teeth bared. They seem better than regular humans. Every single one of them. Even that nasty chick from Omaha who keeps telling me I'm her hero with a fake smile. There is no empty space where I should have been; all the spots have been filled. It hits hard, like sound physical punches to the solar plexus. I look in the mirror, still orange, still human, still tall, still loveless. *That's it, then.*

Because Sherm is a woman's man, he notices things. He leans over and whispers: *Try to take it down a notch, Pip, and enjoy; it's your sport at its best.*

I am enjoying it, Sherm, I whisper back. *Really. Very much. But it's as though I never . . . like does it . . .*

I wanted to be a baseball player, you have no idea . . . I get a twinge in my gut every time I cover the Series . . . He's still whispering. *But you, Pip, you were the baseball player. You were only seventeen years old when you knocked over poor Milt, who used to interrogate Ali, by the way—you should have seen them, anyway. You have eleven Olympic golds. A career that spanned three Olympics. Look what you did in Barcelona. Eight! I had tears in my eyes.*

Twelve Olympic golds, Sherm. And I didn't punch him exactly, I lie. *I pushed him. I swear that little guy was . . .*

He died last year. Cancer. He takes a sip of that vitamin water he likes. *We used to laugh about it . . . said he saw his life flash.*

I . . . he was . . . that was . . . I'm sorry. I don't like it when people die.

Don't be sorry. Sherm is chirpy again. *Highlight of his career. And he went fast. Anyway, you were the baseball player.*

Yeah, I was the baseball player.

It was great, wasn't it great? He's curious now.

It must have been great, I say, thinking. *But I was training hard and my mother, she was . . . she had this . . . dark people fed her grimlock through a straw because she was so . . . you wouldn't believe it . . . my sisters . . . and . . . Leonard. He had this favorite research bat, Rosy. Later they shipped her to . . . I . . . California seemed . . . I had this dog, Manny, the truest dog you ever could know, all dogs pale . . . like it went by . . . so no, yes . . . actually the only dog I ever had. June. June was. Sherm, it must have been great, but I was filling up time, playing it safe, you know, until something else happened, like, I probably won't know this is great until I'm dead or so old I can't . . . maybe . . .*

You look just fine now. He's smiling. *You can't even tell you broke your jaw.*

I only feel it when it rains.

Then take it easy; enjoy.

I change the subject. *I'm not the one with twins.*

He sighs. *It doesn't even run in my family. I'm the first.*

We Fall Because That's What We Do

My body changes; veins recede, muscles sink back into flesh, shoulders place themselves where shoulders should be, feet shrink, hands lose their power, eyes darken, hair darkens, knees rust.

Time passes. I try to get through Bud Lancer's *Destination Destiny*. Fail. Hank calls, encouraging. I try to get through Leonard Ash's *Most Misunderstood Mammals*. Fail. Take to wearing hats and hoods, like a thug. Hank calls, encouraging. His encouragement finally wears me down and I say yes to motivating Omaha. I pack a small suitcase, set the alarm clock on the table next to the couch, climb into my purple solar flare extra-deluxe mummy sleeping bag with hood.

It feels like it's going to rain in Omaha when I arrive. The moisture in the air creates an ache in my jaw, but the sky outside is blue and the ground remains dry. From the window of my cab, I watch clouds fraying the sky into strips of white cloth as I concentrate on my speech. The theme this morning is suffering. In the afternoon I'm going to focus on guts, stealing bits and pieces of Dr. S. Hammernose's celebrated theories that I've reworked as my own. I know my hotel room will smell like plastic violets, know my bed will be tightly starched, know that people will smile and nod, that I will smile and nod back, that the smiles and the nods will mean absolutely nothing. I'll stand behind my bodily surface like a holyghost, letting my outside explain outside things. They'll sit behind their bodily surfaces like holyghosts, their outsides listening to my outside things; thus, only outsides meet, which means absolutely nothing. I'm neither ready nor in the mood, but Hank's convinced I have to do something.

People don't like it when you look them in the eye; it makes them shy.

When I motivate, I usually aim for the forehead. I'll give the stronger-seeming ones an occasional flash of eye but follow it with a smile and a general forehead scan so they feel safe. My people like to be distracted. I move around, twirl my ankles, create movement my ponytail gets lost in. When I'm relaxed, they're relaxed. When I grind my voice down, they sit up and take notice. Sometimes I shake things up, coming at them from behind, get the ones slumping in the back.

I stand in a charcoal gray boardroom with a wall of glass overlooking shards of Omaha. I look out at the flat blue sky bathed in light and the thought comes. *Hey! What's wrong with you? What's all this holyghost stuff?* I stutter, pull myself back into a field of forehead, grind my voice down.

When your toes are gripping the surface of a starting block and there are twenty million people watching, there is only one place to go. Would my sturdy feet pull me through? Was that another world record or did the East German Berliners just pull ahead? Did Fredrinka Kurds overfluff her hair to compensate for the fact that there were masculine things happening inside her body or to draw all eyes away from that beard?

I mention not how my deep sleeps have disintegrated into no sleeps, how I awake to find myself staring at a black ceiling, how I buy a violet-tinged night-light that is supposed to do something I know it can't. Instead, I lower my voice, unleashing the East German Berliners, whom I paint using the dark palette of drama, giving them beards, moustaches, rubbery muscles, voices like tires on gravel, mean little hearts. I grind my voice down a notch: *I won't give up. I don't give up.*

A skinny man with gray and white hair raises one finger. He would like to know how to unleash his own not giving up, please. *That's a very good question,* I say. Then I pause, and in the pause my holyghost says: *Are you really going to be this full of shit forever?* The silence is so thick it stretches out over the unmotivated people of Omaha, out beyond the window across the plains of Nebraska to the four corners of this glorious earth, which causes everyone to squirm in their seats, except for me, who squirms standing. I scan the room—empty but for forty pairs of eyes eyeing me. I look down at my veiny hands; they're hanging off my solid wrists as usual, skin-colored. *Fine.* I look down at my feet sitting in my shoes. *Powerful.* I wiggle my toes, pressing them into the insides of my shoes, think, *Nothing's wrong,* but my heart does a flip, tripping over something it doesn't see, rumbling inside my chest like thunder. I use the rest of my energy conserving an aura of Olympic royalty; excuse myself for one moment by holding up one finger because my neck bones have collided into my collarbone, freezing my ability to form words. I go to the executive bathroom, fill up a sink with cold water, and stick my face in to instigate the dive response, slow my heart down. Either I've gone over the edge or these are the throes of dying.

The director of marketing, a curvy woman in navy blue patent leather stilettos, trots in like a quarter horse and stands next to the sink trying to fish me out. I speak to her feet.

I'm fine.

You don't seem so fine, she says. *You stopped breathing and your face tur—*

I'm really, really fine. All those doughnuts on the breakfast buffet this morning were . . . I couldn't identify those things they sprinkled . . . must have been sugar-based or worse, sugar-substituted, sometimes swimmers are . . . I'll be fine. I just can't believe it . . . Retirement's . . . Listen, I'll be back out in just one minute. Time me; I'm fast.

I look at the opposite of myself looking back in the mirror, say: *Remember the eight, cunt chip,* go back in to finish my speech.

When I walk into the room, I realize immediately that all my Olympic royalty has been replaced by common, eyes are drooping, mouth is drooping, the front of my shirt is drenched in water, revealing the black lace bra with the invisible straps the Russian guy gave me on my path to becoming real woman. My grindy voice lodges in my throat. I cough out words like a dog. I'm very annoyed at Russia, say: *We haven't heard the last of them yet.* I'm annoyed at dead people, say: *They could have tried.* My pearls have my neck in a strangulation hold so I rip them off. They unjoin in unison, rolling all over the room. An unmotivatable account executive gets on his hands and knees and finds them one by one. The room turns into Kansas winter, Kansas snowflakes floating out of the air conditioner like sad confetti, Kansas frost etching its way across glass.

I get cold. *Does anyone here have a blanket?*

This throws them off. *A blanket?* They look at each other. Silence struggles with discomfort. Discomfort wins. Some chick from development puts up a hand and politely inquires how to stay motivated. I sigh, my teeth chattering like teeth in a gag. *Do you know any dead people?* She sighs back. *Yes. Yes, I do.* I say: *And that doesn't motivate you?* My mind starts telling me that it is *definitely* time to go, so I go. But one of my pearls lodges in one of my shoes, and although my mind screams *Forget the fucking pearl, just go,* I kneel on one powerful knee and fish it out carefully with my finger as they watch, consumed by a silence as powerful as gravity. My mind says: *It's urgent you extract yourself from this situation.* I stand up, extract myself.

I call Hank later while I'm packing. I'm shaking and quivering as if someone had given me a specially designed pill. *I think I should stop the speeches for a while; I'm in no state to motiv—*

You're giving up a potentially easy situation, he says.

You do it, then, I say, stomach percolating.

He gets quiet, thinking. *I would*—he sighs—*believe me, but I don't have twelve gold medals and all those world records. . . . I don't know what to say to you exactly. Just . . . think. Think about it. Popularity ebbs. People stop caring. You have to work at it, stay out there.*

Out where? I ask, my voice rising.

You did things. Now talk about them until you start doing other things. Nothing just isn't a good idea for you right now. You're in transition. Transition is delicate.

We have to think of something else. People are starting . . . My speeches aren't what . . . I had a big problem today, Hank . . . I didn't . . . I don't know. I look into the mirror; things are bad.

Big problem? he asks.

I freaked out. I lost it.

Freaked out?

There'll be calls.

He's thinking again; the phone is quiet for one month. *You're tired, Mena. It's been a stressful year. Give yourself a break.*

I've been lying on couches in Glenwood, Kansas, Hank. Do you know where Glenwood, Kansas, is? My mother won't leave the house; did I ever tell you that? She's afraid something bad is going to happen. But all that happens is life.

No. No, you never mentioned it. That's—he's thinking again—*Well, what do you want to do; that's the issue here. What do you really want to do?*

I don't know. *I don't know,* I say. *I'm toying with maybe a world swim, one of those challenges . . . maybe a UNICEF thing.*

Fill me in, he says.

I could swim the English Channel for UNICEF or swim the Arctic Sea for UNICEF or maybe cross an ocean. There are people . . . I've been reading about these electric force field things that protect open-water swimmers from sharks or that one type of jellyfish or stingrays and . . . remember that guy everyone thought was crazy until he . . . well, he's not a good example but . . . I could swim around the world for world freedom or I could swim for . . . I don't know . . . or, or, on a smaller scale I could do free swim clinics in D.C. or I could swim for a cure or multiple cures for that matter or I could get a bunch of medaled athletes and we could go to Deception Island and hold a challenge that would—

Have we forgotten the shoulder? he says, his soft voice softer. *You'd end up dead. No one wants you dead. NBC's still looking for that kids' thing and . . .*

I told you I didn't want that kids' thing, Hank. I can't believe you're still going on and on and on and on and on and on and on and on . . .

Okay. Okay. We'll find something. I won't schedule any more speeches, but you're scheduled to swim with those autistic kids on Tuesday and we can't cancel now.

Fine.

Listen, we'll think of something. Let's just take our time to make sure the something's right.

When I get home, I can't look at myself in the mirror. I lean over the sink. *I'm sorry I'm sorry I'm sorry.*

Leonard appears, says: *We need to talk.* It is the beginning of the end of everything, a feeling so familiar, so pungent, I hold my breath.

Hank calls. *How's it going?*

My mother calls. *Glenwood will always be here waiting for you.*

Dot calls. *I'm sorry to say, but I think an I-told-you-so wouldn't be out of order here.*

Supercoach E. Mankovitz calls from his Florida fishing compound. *I spoke with Kyd yesterday and she strongly recommends you reconsider that coaching position. You'd be great.*

I'm lying on the couch in sweats with a hood I've tied underneath my chin. *I'm not so sure, Ernie.*

I hear the faint clamor of faraway bells. He raises his voice a notch, says: *What's your gut say?*

Fart and poop. *My gut's . . . It's . . .*

Take your time. There's no whistle; just listen to your gut. Call me when you know.

Roxanne calls and complains about her new boyfriend, the maestro. The maestro this and the maestro that. I say: *Leave the fucking maestro then* and she says: *What's up your butt all of a sudden?*

There is nothing up my butt; my butt is as empty as the sky when I look at it from my couch. When I accidentally run into the people I've been avoiding, they question me indirectly about my horrible face: *Bad flu going around . . . don't you think? Did you hear the wind howling last night?* While others take the direct route, looking at me earnestly, imploring: *What's wrong? What's wrong? What's wrong?* until I snap: *Nothing! Fuck off and quit asking me what's wrong.*

I watch old videos. Fredrinka Kurds twisting her fingers before a race, cracking each knuckle carefully like a dice-throwing card-sharp. She suffered from goggle paranoia, checking, fiddling, double-checking. I put the video on slo-mo; there she is making little circles finger by finger down to the thumb, there she is checking the lenses of her East Berliner goggles, holding them tightly to her eyes, hormones raging through her system, making her sick. Peggy growled, spit, shook, and huddled under her towel, flinging it off like Batman when they called her name. But she always dipped her left hand delicately into the water, christening the back of her neck like a priest. Babe had a series of little hops she did with a Mary Lou Retton/Princess Di wave, then she would shut her eyes with the same look on her face as Father Tim's when he was in the middle of a serious pray. I call her up. It is high noon on the reservation. Dr. Babe is taking a well-deserved nap.

Hey, Babe, I say in my tired voice.

Hey, Pip, she whispers in hers.

I consult one of the foremost sports physicians in the Western Hemisphere. I describe the cartwheeling heart, the shakes, the frozen body temperature, the negative thoughts I can't blast away with the positive thoughts, mentioning not the apparitions of the flying bearded skinny biodiversity scientist who happens to be my dead father. He listens intently, his old hands crossed on his lap, interrogates me for seven minutes. He slashes out a prescription for an anti-anxiety medication with a dash of antidepressant and hands it to me, his face as smooth as a Buddha.

I look at the prescription. *I have twelve Olympic gold medals.*

He looks at me. *Yes! But it's very light. Consider it a brain vitamin. You'll feel better.*

I look at his forehead. *I thought there was nothing physically wrong with me.*

He looks at me. *That's right.*

I look him in the eyes. *So. I'm not going to die . . . I'm not going crazy.*

He laughs. *Nooooo! That's just anxiety. Anxiety can't hurt you!*

I don't believe him, thus don't laugh. *So . . . I'm fine.*

He stops laughing, looks at his watch. *Technically, yes. Physically, yes.*

I don't look at his watch. *Healthy?*

He looks at me, smiles, rustles up some papers. *Absolutely.*

I ignore the rustling. *But . . . what . . . then . . . I don't understand . . . What . . . There's no other way? I mean . . .*

He stands up, shaking my hand with one of his dry old ones. *This will help calm your mind until you find the other way. You'll want to do things again soon. You'll sleep.*

I sit outside his office, the prescription sitting on the seat next to me, my Jeep idling into the air. I have to concentrate hard on my breathing; if I don't, it will stop. I watch the cars whizzing by in streaks of gray, gray trees standing solemnly offering gray fingers up to the sky, a gray lady with gray hair licking a frozen yogurt in a waffle cone the size of a rolled-up newspaper. I look up at the sky, but it's gone. All that's left is an empty plate.

It takes me a full two months to construct a formal letter of apology for the unmotivated citizens of Omaha. I discuss the fatigue of a busy schedule combined with the force of an overeager mind. I discuss the vagaries of retired life, the gap training has left in my life, how the lack of a good physical burn combined with a couple of powdered sugar doughnuts at the breakfast buffet turned a perfectly normal speech into an abnormal one. I write: *I've been to Russia. It's a very interesting country filled with fantastic people!* I write: *Olympic athletes are often sugar sensi-*

tive! I write: *I'm really, really sorry! I'm taking a sabbatical and will be out of the country for one year to get a much-needed rest, but the next time I'm in Omaha, I'd love to spend an afternoon with all of you!!!* I learned my lesson, though: If you try to talk about the true value of certain mysteries without any concrete thread of universal hope while rivers of mascara bleed down your white face, people will not like it, but if you choose only the attractive, tasty words, everything you say is a lie.

Every jumbo jet I've ever taken had a real reason waiting at the end of it. Every day I trained had another more important one waiting in the future. I'm descending. Heading toward purgatory, which hovers over the earth, which is covered with dirt, which is death. All around me people are experiencing the incredible reversibility of nature, yet continue to mouth words to songs they do not know. All around me people are walking toward their final demise, spending lots of money on expensive shoes they shall soon replace. I am surprised by one and all, breathing carefully, quietly conserving oxygen for when I'll need it most.

My mother calls: *I don't understand.*

Roxanne calls: *What the hell.*

Dot calls: *You can't escape from yourself.*

Supercoach E. Mankovitz calls: *Call me.*

Hank calls: *I'm not so sure about this.*

I vanish, sit in a metal box with unknown peoples of unknown origin looking out portholes zooming over wheat and corn and corn silos and pigs and pig huts and sheep and a mountain range and parts of the Mississippi. I fly into New York, which looks like a microchip, then get into another metal box with unknown peoples of unknown origin. I say: *Toodle do Russian fuckface* over Manhattan, falling asleep as we zoom over Greenland floating in the Atlantic like a fuzzy moth. In my sleep Dr. Leonard Ash wakes up; he's tan, skinny, talking to me earnestly with hat in hand. On my lap is one of the original first-edition copies of *Most Misunderstood Mammals,* dog-eared by Dot. When I wake up, I look out the porthole at the lights blinking red, wishing I could hold on to the feeling that I have in the air, where the only thing expected of me is exactly nothing, just sit and do what I am told until the plane lands and the bay doors pop open. What this means is that we are all the same. Crazy.

Just Tell Me What I Am
and I'll Be It

∽

O Eiffel Tower, Splendid Haze, O Falter

I'm standing in arrivals watching the metal door with the black rubber mouth spitting out the wrong suitcases one by one. A short, oily man pushes past me sucking hard on a cigarette, his smoke rising into the sullied airport atmosphere mixing jet fuel and spent breath with croissants and coffee. I wave my hands in front of my nose, move behind a blonde with a jet-induced putty face who lights one up and blows it in my ear. I elbow my way past her, grab my case as it swerves down the slide, pass two customs officials busy doing nothing. They don't even glance over as I walk by. Outside everyone is speaking a fast, liquidy French that's too annoying to follow, it's ugly, and one hundred and fifty people are waiting for a cab, one hundred and thirty-three of them puffing on a cigarette for dear life. I get in line, towering over them, cross my hands over my chest, stare at my gigantic feet as wisps of smoke curl their way up my nose.

I look out the window of the cab, watch the scenery careen from the unseemly to the wondrous as the ancient edifice of Paris etches itself slowly upon a sheet of gray sky. By the time we reach the inner portals of the city, my jet lag hits hard and my eyes turn to stone. I'm dropped off in front of my new address still deep in a daze, press the buzzer at length, explain who I am twice, am let in with a click. I drag myself up a creaky stairwell that winds its way tightly like the swirls in a shell. Madame Madame flings the door open before I have the time to knock, looks me down then up, yapping on and on about light, a blond cigarette fumigating her face. She takes the stairs like an invalid and I follow behind, watching as she wrestles with hundreds of keys tied together with a piece of red twine. She opens the door, walks into the apartment with one arm open like she's selling a car, says things I don't quite get, does some drastic Cleopatra things to her face, touching her big blond bun to make sure it's still there, says something else, then backs out, waving like a spastic.

I sit on my suitcase and do absolutely nothing, a universal sign of secular renunciation. On the phone, she didn't mention how the double bed is suspended above the dining room table on stilts, how you have to climb a ladder up and in, how the shower is perched in the kitchen next to a brown rickety oven, how the toilet is communal, sitting outside in the hallway behind a broken door, fuming like a dead smelly bear. She concentrated on the light, how the windows reveal a master skyscape that pulls in so much natural light, artificial light is simply unnecessary. A lie.

If one looks up, the windows hold broken rectangles of dark sky, but if one looks down, they reveal the depths of a concrete courtyard, empty but for one red bucket with a dirty mop standing in it like a tall, droopy, gray-haired, skinny guy who lost his job but does not care. I unpack my purple solar flare extra-deluxe mummy sleeping bag with hood, climb up the stilts, crawl into the bed, cracking my head so hard on a beam that my vision is replaced by a series of mangled yellow stars, and fall into the deep sleep of a crazy used-up person. When I awaken, it's night; the city's giving off a deep tangerine glow, proof that underneath many things are happening; electrical appliances are working full blast; a bunch of people I don't know are alive.

Press Mute

My third night here, there are fireworks. I stand on one of the small footbridges that crisscross the canal, watch them explode. Madame Madame nabs me in the hall, informs me they are celebrating the storming of the Bastille, the dismantling of a prison stone by stone accomplished in the best of humors that rebellion naturally instills in the French, and that normally Paris is a calm, civilized city filled with calm, civilized people with a good sense of museum etiquette. She lowers her voice, gets conspiratorial when she says *museum etiquette*. I make my face act like it knows exactly what she's talking about and she smiles. She was pretty before, has that deeply disappointed look ex–pretty people have. She's obviously dying of boredom, keeps touching her big blond helmet of hair as if she's afraid something bad's going to happen to it. I don't encourage her, wave *bye-bye* until she gets the hint and waves *bye-bye* back, then I climb up the stairs, open the door, place my chair next to the window, stare at the sky until it dissolves into my mother sighing.

This is what she does: she pulls the air into her chest where it rattles around for a minute, then she blows it out her nose like a bull. Her hair is folded into a knobby bun at the nape of her neck and she's wearing chalk-colored lipstick. She's standing at the automatic doors of Glenwood's Master Mall, her shifting weight confusing the sensors; the doors slide halfway open, get perplexed, slide halfway closed as she stares at me, both of her hands curled into tight fists. I look away, concentrate hard on the Christmas lights, blinking darkness, blinking light, blinking darkness, blinking light, and it hits me: *We were all crazy even then.*

I take showers in a ceramic box with a showerhead the size of a light-bulb swinging above, grow used to being naked in the kitchen, watching my yams bake as a lame stream of boiling water dribbles onto my head. I run out to the hallway, open the door to the smelly bear, hold my breath, and pee in streams I've been holding in for hours. There is not one good, ordinary, useful, or familiar thing in sight. During the day, the neighbors are gone and the depth of the buildings surrounding the courtyard absorbs the sounds of the city, but in the evening, they come back, open their windows, yell. Today the man downstairs told the woman downstairs that she was dumber than a broom and she told him that he was the hole in the middle of a great big ass. I shut the windows, say soothing things to myself in the quiet-again air like: *There, there. That's better.*

I don't speak. Weeks glide by in a world without words. I go to the grocery store when I'm hungry, lug stuff home in plastic bags. I sit at the table under my stilts and stare at the blank wall, the day stretching open before me like an empty hand. *No schedule, no coach, no dietician, no physical therapist, no race, no goal, no plan, no team,* destiny wrung out of me like water in sponge. I close my eyes, find Fredrinka masked in misery, muscles chained to bone. She's mumbling things I can't hear, her poor little beard the color of wood. Even her sidekick, that awful bitch, Dagmar, has changed; memory has pummeled her into something new. I'm wanting to wipe her out, old rage bleating in my heart: *She's going down,* but her raisin eyes fill with bitter East German Berliner tears she's too proud to let fall, her chin trembling like a tiny washing machine. She sits down on the starting block, staring blankly at goggles she's holding like flowers in Virginia ham hands and pity wields its magic sword. I pat Dagmar's veiny German ham, say: *There, there,* think: *No man, no love, no desire, no grip, no grasp, no first, no second, no third.*

Dawdle, Loiter, Stroll

I sleep during the day and wake at night and it's awful, but then my body adjusts and it's worse. I wake up alone on top of my stilts at dawn, one gray glare spreading across the gigantic gray face of the sky as it opens its eyes to weep. Sometimes the tears freeze to slush, slapping the roof like wet feathers. Sometimes the tears remain liquid, pounding as they fall. It doesn't seem to bother the Parisians any more than everything else they don't let bother them; they are in the exact same bad mood as the day I got here, carefully avoiding all unnecessary human contact and any kind of speech except the occasional *pardon*.

I stare at the white wall until I can't stand it anymore, lace my feet carefully into shoes, open door that leads to street, sweep myself into Paris like human dust.

The French have a verb for leaving your house for no apparent reason, walking around aimlessly with no identifiable goal: *flâner*. I flâne at home from hallway to bathroom to kitchen to window to suspended bed and back again. I flâne through museums, mindlessly following someone with interesting shoes, not in the least bit interested in the things on the wall. I flâne over canals, under bridges, down weaving cobbled streets. If Ernest K. Mankovitz were capable of world supervision like God Our Immortal Father, he would thrust one mighty red-knuckled hand and pick me up, pulling me safely out of excessive flânning's reach.

I flâne and flâne and when I flâne, light travels from my eyes, audible sound mutes into random hum, the future contracts, the past expands, Paris disappears, and Glenwood appears, bright and beautiful and dark and cold and snowy. I watch the snow. It removes itself flake by flake from a snowman I just made with my bare hands, floating softly up to the dark-starred sky. I walk backward and turn; Roxanne's walking backward with me, face open in a way I will soon forget. She's sticking her tongue in, letting flake after flake of snow re-form and rise. We pass through closing door as it opens, our coats grabbing on to those brass hooks Leonard hammered in one Sunday, and here I am, home. In-home silence mixed with in-home humming, in-home streaked windows and still, vacuumed air, the brightness splashing up from carpet out into night, disappearing instantly at the speed of light. I stop breathing it's so pretty.

I fall asleep at the first sign of night—*That's it, then*—wake up drooling in darkness to tinny zinc orchestras playing above my head as Leonard explains the elemental laws of the natural world, the pendulum swing theory, the genesis of time. When there is a storm, the windows do battle as though the walls have begun to breathe. When the windows do battle, it is impossible to sleep.

I call Roxanne at three in the morning. She sucks some kind of smoke into her lungs, says: *I liked you better when you were swimming* and *I told you not to go* when we both know perfectly well she couldn't stand me when I was swimming and that I was going to go anyway.

The higher the ratio of your own personal fuckups, the greater the potential for relief, she says.

What? I say.

Really fucked-up people can become even saner than regular people when they seek to find the greater relief that is inherently theirs.

How in the hell do you know?

Rehab, she says.

Which one?

Montreal, she says.

My mother calls from her headquarters in Glenwood, trying to sound like a person who leaves the house. *The past is the past, Philomena.* She sighs dramatically. *I don't know why . . .*

I sigh dramatically back. *The past is the past, Mom, and the future is the future, but inside, everything exists. What do you think of that?*

I think that one day you'll have a daughter, she says, *and the circle will be complete.*

I call Dot, lie. *It's fine,* I say. *Unusual and interesting. Everything's going really, really well.*

She gets annoyed. *Are you on drugs?*

Her annoyance is contagious. *Yes, Dorothy. I am.*

Why are you talking like that, then? You sound like you're addicted to something. She is talking to me like she talks to the disturbed, but without the professional kindness.

Like I'd be addicted, Dorothy darling. I've got a great view, although it has been raining quite a bit . . . I do get to thinking about poor old Fergus every once in a while, I say, feeling myself get pleasantly huffy.

She's taking a sip of that tea she loves, green with twigs and those special flowers that tranquilize naturally. *Thinking about Fergus? Have we been drinking, Pip?* She's blowing smoothly on her cup.

No, I'm doing very well, Dorothy. You said I'd . . . well, I haven't, I say, torturing the truth in triumph. *I'm relaxing and looking at the swimming stuff from another angle and—*

She interrupts, the tone of her voice echoing off my inner ear in an annoyingly familiar way: *People are killing each other every second, children are starving, kids graduate from high school and don't know how to read, the ocean's full of garbage, the world's off-kilter, heading toward certain ecological disaster, life's a big piece of shit, and all you think about is swimming. Swimming.*

I say: *Fuck you, Dot.*

She sucks in a wad of air, hangs up. *Click.*

Dead people with a healthy afterlife can listen, so I talk to them. It brings out the drama in me. I get down on my knees and say: *I'm sorry you're really dead. I am ashamed and I apologize. I was . . . an asshole. I didn't know.* Then I pull my hair out of its ponytail, crawl into bed on elbows and knees, avoid the beam, lie facedown on my pillow, weep.

They say: *That's okay. How could you possibly have known?*

I say: *Is it my turn soon? I feel like it's soon.*

They say: *Yes, as a matter of fact it is. How did you guess?*

The Wonders of the World Are Many,
But None So Much as Man

The rainy season starts; one night the sky opens and lets fall. I ignore it, not bothering to stand under the eaves as people run by with plastic bags protecting their hair, not bothering to move when they stab me with umbrellas the size of the parasols that surround the pool at the Glenwood Country Club. I keep on walking.

The point of flânning is to get lost but not care. All you have to do is keep flânning until you're found again or look up, and you'll see something famous: a tower, a church, a steeple, a bridge, a golden horseman, a golden angel, a dead poet, a boat howling by on the river, a great big store. I don't care, remain lost, watch Glenwood spring from Parisian streets neatly like an important image in a pop-up book. Glenwood is smattered with single-story homes, a vast nun compound fashioned in dark red rock, a driveway lined by coniferous trees emitting the tangy smell of real live pine. *Day? Tuesday. Year? One of them.*

The most staggering thing about Paris, other than the fact that it still exists, is how the buildings have been sewn together; old stone seamed to new stone, seamed to prewar brick, seamed to sheets of concrete, seamed to shards of metal, seamed to plates of glass. There are no visible spaces between the seams and no wood except for the doors and the trees standing around outside with their branches crossed. I pass them, staring.

I know that sugar is not a nourishing food, that it is pure chemical, extracted from beet, from cane, strangled from the leaves of exotic sugar trees. I know that it speeds up cellular death, that it contains no fiber, no minerals, no protein, no fat, no enzymes, that it is sticky, that when combined with fat it kills twice as fast, but life is moving toward death anyway and sugar tastes good so I order *chouquettes,* eating them one by one until the statues I pass look like propped-up dead people, night folds, and there is Fredrinka and I know she will never have a child.

A church appears in my line of vision, pulls me toward its heavy wooden door with strong, melancholic fingers. French churches sit in cool stony splendor with stained-glass eyes leaking in shattered blasts of jeweled light. They are filled with almost dead people and variations of the modern international nun. I find an empty pew and sit down. Most of the almost dead people are so old they have to hang on tight to the pew to prevent a bad fall. Jesus is hanging on his cross doing sad Jesus things. Mary is studying the tips of her own bare feet with sweet disinterest, random angels holding up the vaulted arches with vast muscular wings, the demons and the monsters seated below, on their haunches, narrow-eyed, shoulders to ears, hearts set in stone. I light a candle, watch the flame flick shadows across the beige and gray wall, kneel in deep genuflection.

I close my eyes; a variety of cakes are spinning on a fast-moving cakewalk, nuns quickly building a cupcake tower made entirely of coconut bugaloos. There is need and with the need there is yearning. Bron's got her eye on the Black Forest because she's always liked the mixture of chocolate and cherry. Her hair is long and thick and lustrous and wavy, her eyes shining like expensive buttons held up to the light. I watch her turn, watch cakes tremble.

Leonard says: *Observing bats, like observing all natural phenomena, demands as much luck as skill and as much skill as patience. Many species hide away so successfully by day as to elude all order of pursuit. Night after night, I have taken stand at the edge of an open space, the dark shore of a pond, the edge of a clearing in little-known forest, and I wait, facing the fading glow in the western sky. Most species start flying when it is not quite dark, but others do not appear until night has already fallen, and the only way to see them is to imagine.*

I open my eyes, heart pounding in an uncomfortable way, humid church air whacking me swiftly in the jaw. I do not flâne. I flee.

First to the Wall

I kick my shoes under the table, throw my coat on the floor, find a felt-tipped pen, draw a thin line from one wall to the other. I need to see the facts that memory has whipped up into thick gluey foam. One arrow flowing forward. One arrow flowing back. I start to fill in time. The uneven. The irregular. The vague. The exact. The past in black. The future, unknown.

Press Stop

I work all night, my pen gliding backwardly until I can't stand it anymore, put an emergency call in to the personal phone of psychologist to the troubled stars and their troubled children Dr. Sunny Lewis, who answers on the second ring with a qualified *Yes?*

I need to talk to you on a private, professional basis. I'm using my serious voice.

Okay. She is always serious.

I've got a problem . . . or maybe . . .

I'm here. What's up?

I've been visiting churches . . . and churches depress me, I say.

There's nothing wrong with visiting churches, Pip, she says.

I stare down statues. I stare down churchgoers. It's not even their fault. I think I won't do it again, but there's a church every fifty feet pulling me in like a magnet. I light a candle, stare down Mary until she turns into Barbie. . . . It's awful . . . and it's been raining practically every day since I got here. I asked my landlady about it and she said, "Oh that's not rain." But she's lying. It is *rain. When I go outside, I get wet. I'm living the same day every day, Sunny, worse than heavy training. I walk around the place, get pulled into a church, stare at Jesus until he turns into the Grinch, then I go home and hypnotize myself backward so that the things I've forgotten aren't . . . And now that's backfired. I've gone into fucking automatic hypnosis mode . . . things float upward. It doesn't feel good, Sunny. I don't feel well.*

Okay. Okay. Calm down. Don't worry. Let me think a minute . . . I'm going to see if I can get you a name. There's . . . I'll find someone in Paris. I'll call you right back. You'll be okay. It's nothing to worry about . . . everyone goes through a period of . . . doing things . . . they don't really . . .

I lower my voice into dim whisper. *I've been eating sugar again.*

This takes her aback. *A lot?*

Enough to make me . . . very, very ill, I say.

You'll pull through. I know you will, she says. *Remember Barcelona. They said it couldn't be done.*

Sunny calls back while I'm standing by my window cursing the nebulous future, the sky shooting a delightful array of gray bullets down randomly upon the world.

I found someone, she says. *She's supposed to be good.*

I crawl down my stilts, walk through sheets of sizzling gray drops until I find the door. I buzz from the street and my buzz is answered with a click. I walk up two flights of stairs and buzz again, and my buzz is answered with the door opening automatically to an empty waiting room. I hear murmuring behind a door and underneath it the sound of the street rumbling below. I sit down and make a list, as Sunny suggested, of the things I need to know. *What if your brain thinks up awful things and your body believes it? What if it makes you feel like you're sick, nuts, dying even though you're just fine? How come I'm only noticing things now? And if I accidentally hypnotize myself all day long, does that mean I'm crazy?*

When Esther sticks her head out the door, smiles, and says: *I'm Esther,* I immediately forget my list, leaving it crumpled up on the couch. A short man with a hook nose slumps out and away, avoiding me carefully with all of his senses. A bad sign. I follow her voice into the room and sit in the chair she indicates with her eyes. I open my mouth and words come out.

Hi. Recently I've taken to wearing blankets . . . well, not only, of course . . . I'll wear a blanket over clothes or . . . anyway I do feel better when I have a blanket . . . I wish I had a blanket now.

Are you cold? she asks, neutral.

Yes, I say, getting control of myself.

Good! Have a blanket! She seems genuinely pleased as she drapes it across my shoulders. It smells exactly like blanket. I relax.

Tell me about yourself, she says, settling back into her chair.

Which one? Wrong question. *I mean before or after?* Wrong question.

How about you tell me what brings you here? she asks, making things simple.

Where? To Paris? I ask, pointing out the window.

No, here. To me, she says, keeping her hands still in her lap.

Chopped Up, Universal, Strictly Personal

I don't know Esther's kindness is a screen so as not to frighten sad people away with her searing mind, so I tell the tales of these backward things and more. I gather my blanket about me and reveal how the space between my ears hurts, that sad nun melody vibrates along my spine, that art sucks on my essence like an invisible leech. I tell her that love is illiterate, incompatible with the heavy burden of life. I gather my blanket about me, give her my theories: that in-love people hammer new shapes into their objects, that life is a monster ache some people ride while others lie under it to be pressed dry like flowers. I tell her that the nuns knew this from the very beginning, that nuns have always known the impossibleness of everything, that this information has been catapulted into their minds by all the other lost nuns like a metaphysical boomerang, that every heart they'd ever shown us was crowned in thorns, bleeding a special blood that was darker than human blood, that every heart they'd ever shown us was whizzing downly, a stake driven through its epicenter. I gather my blanket tight about my shoulders, lower my voice, tell her that my mind keeps drawing me back to places I do not yearn to go, that nature's floating upstream in an unnatural way, that I am uncomfortable in the dark, that I do not want anyone or anything to erode, change, transform, or die. I tell her that everything is jumbled up in my head, that to get it straight, I have started writing it down on the wall underneath my bed, filing it backwardly year before year. I tell her that I know this to be crazy. I tell her I don't like it, the craziness.

She listens to the tales of the backward things and more, clears her throat and says: *I'm so sorry, but it really is time to go.* I look out the window and she's right. So much time has passed that night is here where there once was day.

Slippery When Wet

I fling myself through a fine city-mist; gray emissions from the gray cars make the mist taste like tin. People under orange umbrellas are orange-faced. People under red umbrellas are bloody. People under blue umbrellas are dead. People under no umbrellas are soggy. I hail them. They ignore me. I hail them again.

This is how I occupy my mind: *Left, right, left, right, left, right;* everything falls away, buildings dissolve, cars drive into gray rubble, people blur into one solid color—navy blue—and all that exists are my reliable feet until June appears, says: *Remember that awful sandwich I made out of pickles and Spam?*

I twirl down the up stairs, until I'm slouching outside by Father Tim.

Priests have to wait until they die to retire. Father Tim's soft brown hair is smattered with gray, sweet baby wrinkles crinkling his eyes, a small, nun-created cake-and-potato paunch sitting in the middle of his button-down like an extra pillow. He's leaning against his car, an ivory sedan with a brown pleather interior. He's come to see me now that my jaw has been freed.

His voice turns grave. *I'm going to have to tell you something you won't like to hear.*

I look at him. *Please don't.*

He ignores me. *There's not enough interest in swimming this year . . . The girls want soccer.*

So that's it, then. I sigh.

Yes, that's it.

The world's a wart, I say.

You might want to consider reconciling with God one of these days, he says.

I don't talk to God for real, Father Tim, I say.

The opposite of doubt is trust, he says.

Some of the meanest people I know are Catholic, I say.

The opposite of worry is faith, he says.

God works in a fear-inspiring way, I say.

That's the trouble with a human interpretation of the Holy Scripture, he says.

I'm an English major, Father Tim. I know metaphor.

I go inside, open the refrigerator, look in. There's a gallon of milk, three pots of jam, mole butter with mold on top, mustard, ketchup, Worcestershire sauce, pesto, a barrel of potatoes, butter, sliced turkey, the chubby sheriff's cold Budweiser. I look at the jar of mustard and say: *I am retired.* Nothing bad happens. Nothing good happens. Nothing happens at all.

I rummage around boxes, forage in closets, open drawers in desks that are not my own. I find things. A list of gifts from the famous Christmas raffle circa 1983: *One half ham, One half ham, Hand knit Santa set, Hand knit tea cozy, Embroidered Holy Pillow, Selected lots: Rum Fudge!* I find a small suede pouch containing Lilly Cocoplat's baby teeth, a blind and tattered Sweet Bonny, a copy of *Bats! Bats! Bats!*, pictures of me with bat ears drawn on in indelible ink, one of Bron's lists. She wrote:

No to Mary.

No to Joseph.

No to Jesus.

No to Pontius Pilate.

No to the Sacraments.

No to the Trinity.

No to absolution.

Death will be fine. Death will be fine. Death will be fine.

She died in the middle of the night, alone, December twenty-third. It was snowing. I didn't sleep, watched the snow falling, watched her bed pretending it did not look like a coffin. A good person would have done something else. I write it down on the wall:

A good person would have done something else.

Stop! I Bid Thee

When I get back to Esther's, I sit in my chair, gather my blanket about me, stare.

She looks at me.

I look at her.

She looks at me.

I look at her.

I break down first. *I can't remember one thing straight. Not one thing. The good stuff seems unbelievable and the bad stuff's fucking awful. How do people take it?*

Take what?

This. This. This. This. I say, jabbing the chair, the ceiling, the window, my feet, indicating the earth, the sky, mortality, the world.

In any old way they can, she says, and when I keep staring at her: *More often than not, badly.*

Sing Noël Sing We Joyously

I forget about Christmas until it starts showing up. A flash of red, a glimpse of beard, a bottle of wine wrapped in shiny green foil, the sweet creaky voice of a child echoing out into the courtyard yearning for Papa Noël and all that he brings. Someone flips a switch and a million lights begin to blink from beneath the arms of cold winter trees, along arches of brick, upon steeples of steel, illuminating the dark world as ancient mechanical puppets adjust their wigs, dust off their shoes, jump out of their boxes, and begin to dance. Temporary ice-skating rinks emerge, supervised by trees swathed in silver pearls, corks pop, and the whole universe is soaking deeply in Christmas, mists freezing and falling, people hidden under layer upon layer of colorful cloth, eyes dreaming and wishing and hoping and praying, and I know the only way it'll ever stop is when it's done.

I go to many sad French movies. During the movies, I keep my face pressed forward with a headache behind each eye because the characters' mouths are moving like motors. At the end, I should know how everyone dissolves into themselves, but I never do. When I leave the cinema, rain pelts me in the face, and the sidewalk becomes as reflective as mirror. The nuns make you think that everything happens up above, but all I see are clouds in heavy preparation, the crystallization of snow before it falls, the formation of wind, the pull of the moon, the occasional flick from a finger of sun.

My brain churns, singing: *Juuuunnnnne! It's Ja———son!* I'm standing next to the window looking down into the drive. You can see the glow of his cigarette through the windshield of his car. June pulls me back. *Leave it alone.* He sits there for hours; it becomes oddly erotic checking the window. Roxy and I get giddy, jump around and dance. Dot is worried. June's pretending to watch some TV show as she folds clothes, gnawing at her cuticles with her teeth.

Go tell him to fuck off, she says, pushing me out the door. *Just say: Hey, you! This is private property. Get off our land! June says fuck off or she'll call the cops!*

He is the first person I ever see lighting one cigarette off another. He knits his eyebrows together as though it takes thought.

Hey, he says, inhaling, *forgot my lighter.* I look at him, Glenwood's best-known bad man; he's cute in a rough, alcoholic sort of way.

Hey, I say. *June says it would be a good thing for you to probably fuck off and get off our property or she'll call the cops.*

Imperturbable. *Which one are you?*

I hate my name. *Philomena.*

The animal lover. . . . How tall are you anyway?

The swimmer. . . . Five-eleven. I lie.

Ahhh, the swimmer . . . tall order. He laughs an economical laugh that does not hit his face. *Tell June I'll be outside Gabe's at ten. You got that?*

Outside Gabe's at ten.

Tell her I'll be waiting. And tell her I'm sorry, okay? Tell her Jason says he's really sorry. Then he smiles, nods, starts the engine, listens to it purr for a second before reversing down the driveway as cool as a dark green cucumber.

I beg her: *Don't go, June.*

She sighs, runs her fingers through her hair, says: *I have to.*

When they are back in love again he calls, asking for *June bug.*

I stand in my kitchen waiting for dry spaghetti to absorb water so I can rinse the pan. My mind slips out the window and into the wind; everyone's in their own corner this Christmas. Dot's in Portland serving turkey to people who live in cardboard boxes, her heart a charred stump. Roxanne's in San Francisco pruning one of the maestro's expensive trees; it's unusually cold, so she's wearing fingerless gloves and an ugly hat. Mom's in Glenwood with a bunch of Dark Catholics preparing a feast. During the feast everyone will moan and cry in sadness, and in their sadness their hearts will lighten and blink in accordance with the Christmas lights strung upon the banister as the chubby sheriff watches TV in the TV room with an ice-cold beer.

I grab a pen, find a space on the wall, write:

French men are big sissies.

My skills off the wall are second to none.

This morning Esther sat in her chair all smiles and eardrums, a dark red poinsettia on the corner of her desk. I'd spent the morning in a tiny church staring at a detailed Jesus so hard he turned to bone. Outside it was raining minuscule flakes of wet snow, sad people were sitting on garbage bags they'd placed on the ground, a piece of cardboard engraved with their needs, ladies with layers of new face painted over the old passed me by in a scourge of nasty perfume, and Esther seemed so contained and dry, so even-fingered and calm-spirited that I couldn't help but be annoyed.

I looked at her and said: *What are you doing here anyway?*

Here? she asked.

Yes, I said, pointing aggressively to the room, her window, the door, my feet.

I live here. I work here. I'm raising my family here, she said.

There obviously must have been some sort of problem, I said, digging. *Some sort of reason you would flee your own country and install yourself here like a fugitive.*

Is that what you feel like? A fugitive? she asked, her jade earrings clinking faintly.

No, I said, sitting up straight. *I definitely do not feel like a fugitive.*

She was quiet then and I was quiet then too until the quiet strangled me and I couldn't stand it anymore. *What, do I look like a fugitive?*

And she asked: *What does a fugitive look like?*

How in the hell do I know what looks like what and who looks like who? I sighed, not mad anymore.

The spaghetti softens, so I slush it down the drain, pee in the shower, climb up into bed, smacking my head so hard on the beam that my eyes leak as my ears hum in pain. I suck on a French vanilla truffle in a dark chocolate shell. I do know what a fugitive looks like. She's a fifteen-year-old, six-foot-two secret girl. She has blue pebbles for eyes, sports uncomplicated ponytails, wears sweats to bed, has incredibly strong feet. She sucks on mint whips, chews on caramels, sits in planes daring them to drop.

Nature Is as Nature Does

French people are standing at a curb waiting for the light to change; there's an old lady with a blue plastic bag on her head pushing a half-dead poodle in an old baby carriage. The guy standing next to me lights his cigarette with one hand cupped to protect the flame. His cigarette flares with his nostrils as he sucks the smoke in. The red hand turns green. We cross the street filled with glued-together buildings dating from the seventeenth to the twentieth century. There's a window in front of me with tiered metal shelves housing delicious things I've never tasted. I pause, can see the outline of my reflection in the glass, the clouds zooming behind me, the earth twinkling and twirling, twittering like an idiot.

I have stopped looking at anything beautiful unless something unusual has happened to it. I notice: a statue covered in green tarp, a church with pockmarks, a stone face with a hacked-off nose, a gargoyle covered in dirt, a blackened mirror that can no longer reflect, a plant with brown flower, the dense quality of air, gray exhaust floating from diesel engines, a well-groomed dog squatting on a curb, a frayed golden sari lying in a heap underneath a filthy bridge, a handsome man with a machine gun at his hip. I squint at him; he ignores me. It takes four hours to cross the city on foot. When I get home my feet are puffy red boils. I soak them in a bucket with warm water as I watch the smaller droplets of rain smash into the window and slide sadly down until I'm sitting outside on a lawn chair underneath a tree, it's fall, and the leaves are spiraling down into a vast kaleidoscope across our unkempt yard. I'm watching Roxanne and Dot play Ping-Pong, Bron by my side. She looks at me and says: *My money's on Dot; she has hidden resources.*

Esther spends many dark and similar days quizzing me. Her quizzes are vast and glorious, spanning the length and breadth of self-inflicted human misery. I gather my blanket about me, struggle with the urge to sleep, learn that depression is not merely a moral sadness, that it does not have to be associated with the color blue. That feeling stumped is a simple pause in dynamics, that broken sleeps are not irrevocable like glass, that life is a series of breakdowns and regenerations, that being uncomfortable is often a clue. I learn that avoiding the beam in my bed only half of the time does not constitute a concentrated effort, that the athlete in me is not dead, that the person under the athlete in me is not dead either.

Esther says the toilet seat was my portal back into life. Esther says that if I fell through the portal into a new life, something, somewhere in my body probably knew it. Esther says that some people need slippery toilet seats in slippery porcelain crouching like tigers in their paths. Esther says: *We fall because that's what we do.* Esther says: *Even the noblest of trees have dark roots.* Esther says: *It takes a true champion to break some important bones and drive herself to the hospital.* Esther says: *It takes a special type of person to notice that you can bounce rain off a colorful surface and its color will always remain rain.* Esther says: *You're not doing so badly.*

I write things down. *I am not doing so badly.*

Nature is vast and glorious and generous and mean and small and shitty.

All creatures, even tadpoles, worms, cockroaches, and fleas, have eyeballs that will eventually close one last time forever and ever amen.

Hearts are designed to stop thumping; some will explode into brilliant pots of marmalade stew. Some will splutter and cough; others will have to be shot at, burned, stabbed, stomped on, crushed by unnatural force, or clogged with mixtures of sugar and lard, etc.

Green bananas turn yellow.

Yellow bananas turn brown.

Brown bananas are good for cake, but when you're hungry, everything tastes good.

Russian people are as fucked up as Kansans.

We're designed to survive.

When people don't know anything, they make things up.

Madame Madame nabs me in the hall, asks: *Is it true that American women believe if they don't have wrinkles, they won't ever die?*

I'm not in the mood, say: *Yes. American men too.*

O Father, O Father, Resurrection

Esther has expressive eyes. Her eyes say: *Perhaps you suck on your own head like a leech because you do not feel as though it is your role to partake in the creative life. Perhaps you demonstrate your strong love for your family with your strong love for your team.* Her eyes say: *Nuns are funny doughnut eaters who don't have sex.* Her eyes say: *Russian guys are probably as human as humans.*

But sometimes she gives her eyes a rest and speaks. *Let's talk about your sister.*

I say: *Which one?*

She says: *The one you don't discuss much.*

She died.

Yes. How old was she exactly?

Almost eighteen.

So you had the time to know her.

Yes.

What was that like?

I think about it. *She liked to scare me so much when I was a kid, I thought my name was Boo.*

When I mention Leonard, she says: *Are you referring to your father?*

And I say: *Yes.*

Why do you call him Leonard? she asks.

Because he wouldn't have liked it, I say.

After that, she calls him *your father,* says: *You sound angry. Are you?*

I'm surprised, lie: *Of course not. He's dead.*

I start to call him *my father* until one day I say *Dad* and nothing happens.

Bronwyn skates into my mind, says: *See? I was more complex than you ever imagined, not your average under-the-weather young adult.*

My father looks up from his book, surprised. *You thought I flew into the ground? Why in the world would you think I'd fly into the ground? My engines died before I did.*

Esther has an expressive face. Her face is all face. Her face of all says: *Retirement is not a fat pig with purple breath.* I write it in on my wall under the blank future: *Retirement is not a fat pig with purple breath.* Retirement is also not a tunnel with a cement wall or a wobbly popcorn manufacturing meaningless piece of shit expendable end finality conjecture that pulls one from cradle to grave. Her face says: *Russian men are like all subhuman earthlings, scrounging for happiness and peace in any old way that they can.*

I'm swimming again. Just to see what it does. I wake up in the morning, go straight to the pool, where slower humans scatter as I plunge. I'm better. My arms move in clean, whipping lines, my feet churn out power. Within five minutes I've bullied all of them out of my lane, am gliding in space. *An excess of goodness is just another dread of being oneself.*

In the locker room, a woman comes up to me and says: *Is it true that in America you can go to war and die for your country, but you can't drink a beer?*

I'm not in the mood, lie: *No.*

The nuns said *flute* instead of *fuck*. That's what Aloysius said every time I beat her at checkers: *Oh flute!* Roxanne played the flute for a while. She'd sit in the middle of her room and play it like a sad pothead *nah nah nah nah* . . . Her notes were death callers, rain makers, ear strainers *nah nah nah nah.* I'd bid her *stop!* as she sat on the ground Shawnee style, her breath flowing into metal, her fingers covering, uncovering, letting forlorn notes weep. I hear them again, the notes, as my ears break the surface of the water and listen to the hard dry world.

Float

The rains cease, the wall beside me full of scribbles I have to lean in to read. The sky shifts, revealing an ocean of black, revealing an ocean of star, revealing an ocean of moon, the world so quiet its silence wakens. I move a chair to the window and look up. A world of marvels. Star pods twirling into star flowers. Energy molecules. Black holes. White holes. Glowing dully. The universe expanding so we can fill it up with more and more shit. My mind bids: *Count! Twenty billion, nineteen billion nine hundred and ninety-nine million nine hundred and ninety-nine thousand, nine hundred and ninety-nine* ... until I find myself standing in front of a shiny dark green door sitting in the middle of a pale gray house, lacy ferns exploding out of a cracked terra-cotta pot. There's a chair by the door nobody sits in with a box of rusty nails on top, millions of them, in all shapes and sizes, morphing into dust. The floor of the porch has been painted white, but has not remained white; there is a line of gray marking the passage of shoe. The screen smells lightly of dust. I press the bell.

June told me there was no earthly reason for her sister to be named Chan because there was nothing Chan to her; she was soft and blond, with the wide high forehead of the mentally slow. I'd met her once before in the parking lot of a 7-Eleven. She was smoking a cigarette, chewing gum, holding a Slurpee in one hand, talking to a truckload of guys with a truckload of dogs behind them. I remember the cutoffs she wore—you could see her V.

Chan? I'm a friend of June's.

I know who you are. She's turned into a dough girl with muted doughy features. There are streamers hanging behind her and a dragon kite with a red tail.

June was . . . We lost track. I just had the wires removed from my jaw, am still lisping out of solidarity with my past.

She sighs. *She started drinking again.* Friendly dough features sink.

I sigh back. *A lot?*

She shifts a little from left to right. *Yes.*

All the time? I say, looking down at her tiny feet.

Like an alcoholic, she says with a hard laugh.

Do you know where she is? I ask.

No, she says, and a little boy with a little boy bowl cut runs up to her, grabs her legs, pulls. *I told her that if she left with that crazy . . . man . . . in a wheelchair not to call me ever again. She hasn't called.*

Jason? I say, staring down at the boy staring up at me, index finger deep in his nose.

Yes, she says. *He had a forklift on the side of his van. She left. That same day.*

A forklift? I say dumbly.

Yes, she says, and her son runs away.

Do you know where in Florida? I ask, leaning into the doorway.

Somewhere near West Palm was the last I heard, but she's mad at me, she says, taking a step back.

How long has she been . . . mad? I ask, looking into the box of nails.

Six years, she says, starting to get antsy.

Six years. I say. *That seems like a lot. She's not . . . dead, is she?*

Noooo. This surprises her. *Why would she be dead?*

Six years, I say, watching the poor dragon fly nowhere. *I don't know.*

When June's drinking . . . she's—she looks at me, shrugs—*you know June.*

She never comes back? I ask, but I know the answer.

She'd rather die, says Chan, crossing doughy Chan arms.

When you see her, tell her I haven't forgotten or anything. And tell her I said thanks. I stop leaning, start walking backward.

I will, she says, then shuts the door.

O Everlasting Death, You Bastard, Vile Yucker

My father visits me, standing taller and thinner than his own black shadow. He's cut his hair, is neatly shaved, wearing a soft gray flannel suit and very nice shoes. *Night bats are generally duller in tone, although a darker shade does not exclude a colorful life. The less-tutored mind tends to see a mystic connection. These are but a few of the great many marvels and mysteries to ponder.*

I say: *Thanks, Dad.* We hug and he pats me on the head.

When I wake up, his pat is still there. I touch it, look out my window at a thick layer of Kansas snow gathering on the sill. It's snowing downward, the slow snow that feels good to stand under and look up at. A million whirling flakes, insulation gathering on the arms of trees, on the legs of the rusty wrought-iron summer chairs, zooming down, spiraling in spirals, zipping, zagging, softly landing on my face melting into me and snow becomes me and I become snow. I'm waiting for Leonard, who is never late, my hair freezing into strings of ice as I watch the snow fall, the halo of white gold around the lights in the parking lot, the halo of electricity around the homes with single stories pictured in one big window multiplied by one block, then repeated throughout Glenwood. I am alone; the other Dolphins left a while ago. His car pulls up. He's wearing his Boris Yeltsin hat and a sad-lipped smile, says: *Sorry I'm late,* and pats me on the head, the night hacking his face roughly out of shadow. I say: *That's okay, Dad.* I sink into the passenger seat, not looking at what is coming along on the road, not having to. I am surrounded in safe, my father, his hat, this soft, cold world with tender, delicate foliage. Leonard is in a quiet mood, does not discuss erosion, corrosion, pollution, despair. The heaters are blowing full blast onto my face, turning the car into a hot, liquidy sauna. I close my eyes, look downer, vast and twirling, a myriad of island in the midst of some stream. I'm wearing a red swimsuit with GCC written in white swirly letters and it's suddenly summer. I perk up; summer does this to me.

I'm sitting on the tall lifeguard chair at the Glenwood Country Club. It's fucking hot; old people without air-conditioning are dying like flies, a new one every day. I layer zinc on my lips and the wings of my nose. Lifeguards get free lunch and anything they want to drink all day long, but other than that, I'm deeply disappointed. I saunter over to the concessions stand with my hot-pink visor shading the world a pleasant swash of psychedelic color. I order a couple of bottles of Gatorade. I thought I'd sit up there like every lifeguard I've ever seen, hard and cool, with evenly spaced brown toes sticking out of sandals with good grip, but the guy I'm shadowing is an A number one squint named Brent who spends his time checking out the chickees and letting me guard the lives. This is what he said to me the first day, he said: *If you need me, I'll be down at the deep end checkin' out the chickees.*

The Cocoplat is doing an internship at the Beaver Park Pool. She's shadowing an ex-Dolphin who drives a navy blue convertible with a creamy leather interior. On her first day, she'd given her a whistle in a special fun ceremony with the other lifeguards, three of whom were hot. They clean out lockers and skinny-dip after hours. They whiz by me hooting up a storm as I ride uphill on my bike, my legs steeping in lactic acid hell. Bron woke me up last night, said she was afraid. I stared at the darkness until her dark form emerged, and the fear enveloped us both in tight arms. I said: *Don't be afraid. I'm here.* And I was; I could feel myself being.

Glenwood Country Club kids have sick notions of fun. They lie on the floor of the pool with their eyes open, no bubbles of air leaving their mouths, and this for as long as they can stand it, or until I pull them out, blowing my whistle like a maniac. They float on their stomachs with their arms limp at their sides, secretly breathing through the web of their hair. I pull some out using standard Red Cross technique, gently, by the back of their necks, and not their hair as is later claimed. I get yelled at by the mothers, who then complain to Geo, the head lifeguard and Lord of All. The Glenwood Country Club kids catch on, devise new techniques, swimming fast, then yowling with cramp, waving spastically at me from the water as Brent checks out the oiled chickees and their mothers. I whistle like a maniac, pull them out using standard Red Cross procedure. They yell, shrieking as though I'm trying to kill them. Mothers get together in a huddle, whispering, stopping only to point up at me sitting in my chair, staring at the pink world below me with an amazingly neutral face. Geo calls me into his office, which is really the toolshed off the men's locker room, and gives me the *We can't all be lifeguards* speech, demoting me cruelly to the concessions stand, where I learn to develop the perfect batch of popcorn. It is crunchy, lightly salted, no strands of oil or butter derivatives, light as air, as filling and as perfect as Styrofoam.

Geo saunters by with a fake *sorry* sitting in the middle of his devil-wolf eyes. I laser him from under my visor: *Your real name is George and everyone knows it.*

At the end of the two weeks, I sit down with Brent, Geo, and Coach Stan for my evaluation. Geo and Brent speak in chime like church bells requesting input from God Our Immortal Father.

Overuse of whistle.

Overuse of shout.

Dangerous use of safety procedure.

Brent says: *She could have hurt someone, Coach. She caused considerable stress amongst our mothers . . . the mothers.*

Geo says: *Honestly, Stan. I've never seen anything like it.*

I am ashamed, slouch into chair. Stan looks at them for a thousand years without saying anything. The silence rolls heavily like an avalanche of rock. He says: *Are you kidding me? Is this a joke? She'll make a damn fine lifeguard. I'd like to look into the training methods you used. I won't accept this; I'll appeal. There'll be inquiries. If you'd like to take this conversation to the pool, my money's on her. It's up to you now, gentlemen.*

Geo is leaning his chair back on two legs, chomping on a piece of green gum. At the word *gentlemen,* he pauses in surprise.

Stan looks at him, box-jawed.

Geo leans forward, putting his chair back on all fours with a slam.

I feel a rush of joy, the hair on my arm rising in excitement, the deep inner workings of my brain twirling in the archaic dance of surprise joy.

I cross my arms and squint: *No more free Gatorade.* The room hangs with the perfume of stubborn balls, suntan oil, zinc oxide, Fanta, Old Spice, smelly feet, steaming shoe, tennis racquet, bleach, a lingering sausage burp. I can hear clocks ticking and golf men rumbling in that low golf murmur.

It doesn't take long. Geo swallows, his gum moves, life moves forward. *Okay. She passes.*

Stan drives me home. We stop for ice cream on the way, leaning on the hood of his hot car, trying to lick before it drips.

Stan likes to state the obvious, says: *Boy, this is cold!*

I am still amazed. *How did you know Geo's real name was George?*

He's not amazed. *That wasn't about Geo; that was about you.*

At the dinner table that night, Bron says: *How's the popcorn stand going, Buffy?*

Leonard looks over: *What popcorn stand? Who's Buffy?*

I look at her. She looks back and smiles, her eyes crinkling at the corners. *Oh nothing.*

My heart fills with an infinite, eternal love of all of life's great surprises and all of life's other things. She could do that sometimes.

I only see Sister Fergus one more time after the L.A. Olympics and that is when she's in her coffin. She is all folded up, her face as smooth as statue, her long heavy wooden cross with the worn wooden beads woven lightly through her waxy hands. I feel bad about this at least once a week, more around Christmas. She has white eyebrows and kitten whiskers. I close my eyes, the church bells clamor, the nuns raise their eyes to the blinding hot sun.

I avoid the cemetery, never go, not with flowers, not with candles, not with hand-painted stones or sturdy plants. I do not fall down upon her body buried deep under earth. I do not implore the Dark Catholics for inside information. I do not beg God for a real glimpse of heaven. I stay at home and have fights with myself:

Go to the cemetery.

I will.

No, really. Go to the cemetery.

I will, soon.

I walk the streets of Paris, accidentally skimming over what matters because I am afraid it will kill me and if it kills me, I shall die. I pluck the thought out, put it in the shower, turn the water on full blast, watch it glide down the drain, but at night I become a different person. The Russian guy understood these things, would look at me and say: *Everything is going to be okay; don't be nuts* and I believed him.

Small and Smaller
Until One Day You're Gone

I take to walking at night just to see what's out there. Hundreds of unsuspecting people march under volt upon volt of artificial light; five kids kick balls in a dark sculpted park; a skinny blonde cries into her phone; couples grope each other down by the water, cute cops with machine guns wander around in packs of three, buildings are glowing, windows are glowing, the flowers on the balconies are glowing, people are eating, elbows pressed into their sides, sliced *pain* sitting in a small wicker basket, candles flickering, lighters flicking, water flowing, church admonishing, gargoyles laughing, saints protecting, a golden Joan of Arc leaning into herself, a golden shadow of God shining in her eyes, crêpes flipping, butter melting, drunk guy pissing, man in tuxedo running, mean-faced lady in impossible shoes hobbling, taxis blurring, night convecting a dull rubbery heat. I keep walking. The Eiffel Tower sends out search beams that capture nothing but renegade cloud. I sit on a bench and concentrate on all the things I can do.

I can get up at ten.

I can sled recklessly down hills toward oncoming traffic.

I can ride in bumper cars all day long, be the weird chick at the fair.

I can hammer things into a pulp, put boots on, go outside, and saw down a tree.

I can snowboard off an icy mountain ledge into thin mountain air.

I can brag and swear at strangers.

I can sleep with non-swimmers, find one that I like. We can have nine babies together; none of the babies will die. I will teach them things, fill the world up, be very busy.

I can go back to school, learn something I'll remember.

I can take a shower in the morning and not get wet the rest of the day.

I can take cough syrup when I cough, aspirin when my head hurts.

I can cultivate tubes of lard around my middle, have myself another chin.

No need to smile ever again.

I can scare kids into swimming well. I'll have my own stopwatch I'll click when I feel like it. I'll yell at them until they cry, then make them get back in the water.

I can wind my way around cities, no destination in mind.

I can do zero percent nothing until I can't stand it anymore.

I close my eyes, put roller skates on, speed backward as fast as I can. Mom's so pregnant, her poor head looks fat; she's got both hands on her belly, both eyes to the sky. I wave, twirl, wave again, my ponytail flying in the wind. Leonard says: *I'll tell you a story of a bat whose lifeline was shorter than his wingspan, but boy could he fly.* I pass Bron, who's still fixing that ten-speed; she's banging on the spokes with what looks like nun shoe. I do some dangerously fancy turns, swooshing around her like a spastic fly. I know I won't fall.

O Joy, O Sunshine

Lilly Cocoplat and I are standing on a dark stage waiting for the lights to come up. It's taking a very long time; I'm starting to get antsy. Lilly senses it, grabs my hot dry hand with her sticky wet one. She's wearing a starched yellow dress with a shirred front and a row of tiny green buttons, green and yellow daisies embroidered across the chest. I'm wearing something purple that's pulling tight. The lights shine on us in a burst. The crowd claps. I squint. I'm wearing my ponytail on the side of my head, my mother's idea. It's pulling my eyes into a slight Oriental slant. I don't care; I'm busy going over the words in my head. There are a series of complicated modern dance moves too, but I'll cross that bridge when the music starts. It all seems impossible, very complicated.

The Cocoplat starts. *No one is happier than I. The God above, the clear blue sky.* Leonard has polished my shoes into a high-mirrored gleam. I look down at my face shining up through the laces: *Thanks, Dad.* He's easy to find, an enormously tall molten smudge hovering above the little ones. I smile, move a couple of fingers in a mini-wave. I do not yet know a dead person, have no idea where Russia is, enjoy swimming as an extracurricular activity. I start, have an awful voice: *No one is luckier than I. The sun above, the clear blue sky.* I'm wearing a thin gold cross; when I jump, its edges stab into my skin. I do not like boys, they're idiots. When one gets near us by accident, we pull faces, make farting sounds with our armpits, hold our noses tight in a pinch. Sister Joy's banging away on the keys; she's an emotional nun who plays the piano with her whole body. *I can be so happy.* The Cocoplat turns a perfect turn. I twirl, my ponytail whips me in the eyes; I hadn't anticipated this.

I believe in God; He's Old and Strong, but Gentle with Love, burning sinners into charred butterflies when He feels like it with a bolt that whizzes suddenly from His Hand. I know the seven deadly sins by heart, can recite them in order: *superbia, avaritia, luxuria, invidia, gula, ira, adcedia* but secretly avoid Jesus, still not sure about those thorns. I skid a little, catch myself in time. *I can be so happy.* We twirl together. We lock hands, turn, the Cocoplat slips, she's as light as a pillow, I'm dragging her a bit, adjust. We look at each other. Her eyes tell me everything is better than fine. My eyes tell her everything is better than great. *And when He takes me in his arms, Oooooo gentle lambs, from gentle farms.* We haven't learned the joy of changing the lyrics of songs into something terrible yet, but it's in our cards. *No one is luckier than I, the sun above, the clear blue sky.* We kneel down, sway like flowers, twirl, put our heads down into our arms, lie back in a doze. The lights come up; the crowd goes wild. It's my first major applause; my heart fills with love of life and all of life's things. Joy stands, then bows, bringing both arms up, pointing to the stage. The Cocoplat bows, we hold hands. Everyone's clapping. The Cocoplat twirls. I twirl with her. I do not know vaginas grow hair and bleed, that nuns are any different from other people except for the uniform. We start to dance. This is unplanned. The unplannedness is exciting. We're jumping with exciting twirling, my cross stabbing, my ponytail slapping me in the mouth. Fergus calls to us from backstage. *Come, girls! Come now, girls! Come!* We'd forgotten about her. We don't know death, but we know something bad's out there hovering. *Come! Come!* This is the first time I am formally hypnotized; I follow her hands with two round eyes. Lilly's immune, gives one more twirl a go, then a bow. Fergus pulls me gently with one hand, pushing one of the sixth graders out into the light with the other. He shoves Lilly back into the dark and we hug. It's over for us, but the clap is still churning.

I watch fat white clouds wrestle their way across a jet-black sky, ragged edges of Paris glowing brightly beneath. She must be divorced by now, surrounded by flocks of comforting Cocoplats. I call her up. *Lilly, you okay?*

She says: *Yeah, I'm better.*

I know things. I know that we are born to float, that we are gasping things, natural air captivators, breathing to the tick of the nanosecond, the microsecond, the backward, and the forward. I explain these known things to Lilly and we discuss them and she says: *Yes, this is true. But men suck.*

I talk nun, say: *Perhaps, my friend, but death should not be more of a problem than birth, although both being equally real, but for the apparent motion of the sun across sky, the phases of a finicky moon, the beat of the human heart. We can thus just forget about most of it and buy colorful sodas.*

She talks nun back: *Yes, but lo and behold I must cut my hair, for it is vast and unruly.*

And I say: *O verily. But one must not loseth oneself in the vast dilly-dally.*

And then we laugh.

Now, Now

I'm listening to the radio talk about the rain, looking at a map, humming. *I'm going to live each day as though there are amazingly many.* The sky's spitting bullets across central Europe. Berlin is covered in a canopy of cloud coming in from the density of Schwerin, across the Baltic Sea and the Atlantic, past Greenland, and into New York State, where it slides down across the Mississippi Valley. The sun's shining hard across Southern California, but certain parts of the Florida coast have been eaten by walls of wave; some people have their lives packed up in their cars; others carry what they have on their backs. My mother is reading a high-caliber book on asymptomatic agoraphobic cognitive behavioral response systems the chubby sheriff ordered for her. She's lying in bed, a fresh package of M&M's by her side. She's going to give outside life a second go. There's a new GP in town who explained that thoughts couldn't kill, which was a form of synchronitic strangeness because Esther's been trying to hammer the same thing into my own head. The GP explained that feelings couldn't kill either, no matter how badly they make one feel. Mom fell to her knees with relief, wept, almost had a nervous breakdown for old times' sake.

I looked at Esther and said: *It doesn't feel like it.* And she said, *It's a fact: human beings cannot kill themselves with thoughts and feelings. Can you imagine; we'd be dropping like flies.*

Mom said: *I wanted to kiss his feet.*

I said: *You didn't, though.*

Mom said: *Noooo.*

Esther said: *You thought you could kill yourself with sugar?*

I lied: *Not really.*

Esther said: *You thought because you felt you were dying, that you were dying?*

I didn't lie: *Yes, that is how it feels. Like it's over, all of it.*

Esther said: *Do you understand now? It's just feeling.*

I said: *Yes, I understand, Esther. Feeling. But that's how I won. That's how I did everything.*

Mom drives home from her doctor's appointment through the mottled green streets of Glenwood with both windows open, the wind whipping her hair in three directions; up, down, and out. I congratulate her, say: *That's great, Mom. I'm so happy for you.* She says: *Thanks.*

I walk home from Esther's office, watching shafts of gray light penetrate the green of the leaves. *I'm going to live each day as though there are amazingly few.* I feel flashes of bad endings and death—*feelings*—let them swim past me like dark fish. I pass a bakery specializing in Oriental delicacies: mashed almond, sugar, oil, covered in golden brown honey. One of them would probably make me sick for seventeen hours, give me major visions. I walk by; what's the point?

Father Tim is standing on a soccer field with an extra-large baseball cap on his head. He had a funny-looking mole removed from the tip of his ear that has left a hole kids make fun of and now he's careful. The Russian guy is a smudge standing in a navy blue suit looking out a shiny window reflecting a million shiny windows and a small rectangle of orange-flared sky. He is alone. Fredrinka Kurds is taking a short nap; she's sleeping on her side, her knuckles underneath her chin. Sister Fergus is invisibly whirling; all her radiators, lemon drops, donated tires, Virginia hams, Lawrence Welk shows, have morphed into flight, floating behind her like a tail of magic dust. Bron's still sitting on a curb next to her ten-speed, idly braiding her hair down her back; it's gotten blonder and she's pleased. She stops letting herself grow old, says: *I guess I don't have to do that anymore.* Leonard gets a crew cut and decides to be dead. He looks at me with that look he gets on his face when he's reading serious news: *I'm going to go now, Sugarplum.* He lets go of gravity, flying backward like an astronaut, waving. *Aim for the impossibilities; they keep one positively occupied.* I wave: *Thanks, Dad, I will. Bye, Dad, bye for now. I love you, I love you, I love you.* June's sitting in a car drinking something that no longer burns on its way down; she's decided to remember the things that she wants, letting the rest wait until her last day on earth. Roxanne's pregnant; she's sitting next to her maestro, crying her body into thumping convulsions. *How can someone like me be a mother? How can someone like me be a mother? How can someone like me be a mom?* The maestro's sitting next to her, so happy he's uncomfortable. Dot's cruising through downtown Seattle; she leans her head back into her seat, her eyes squinting against waves of watery sun. She's dating an Andrew, tells me she doesn't have to fix him because he's already better than normal. Peggy's standing in her kitchen trying to figure out what to mix; yesterday she steamed and puréed potato, pumpkin, twenty grams of fish both babies spat up over their white velvet jumpers. She's wearing dress sweats she's loosened under her belly and a hockey T-shirt. The Cocoplat's getting her eyes checked for glasses; she already knows what she wants—the thick ones with the heavy rims that change your face. She's moving to Minneapolis and wants to look smart.

I've never made a single decision in my life; the only thing I know is that I like to swim. *I'm going to live each day as though it contains meaning.* Madame Madame strongly suggested I repaint the wall so I do. Over the medals. Over the neck cords of the nuns as they slurp their Slurpees in the Kmart parking lot, over Ahmet Noorani's yellow cigarette smoking in the snow, over a school of eleven-year-old autistic kids floating quietly on their backs in a heated, dark pool as their mothers watch. I teach them the Dolphin kick and they know joy. I paint over the sky as it opens up and spits wet bullets across the plains of Kansas, over Ernest K. Mankovitz fishing by himself, a small tin soldier in a tattered tin boat, all alone on a wide-open sea. He's baiting the hook with thumb and forefinger. The light turns the worm translucent. They say they don't feel a thing, but how the hell do they know? There is not one cloud in the sky. I paint over his boat as it rolls with the sea. I paint over the sea as it builds into a wall of living wave that roars in to shore. I paint over the shores, inland, up into the plains. I paint and I paint until it is perfectly white. I know I will never motivate another human being as long as I live, but other than that, nada, nothing, zip. This is a world where time is measured in accomplishment; this is a world where time is simply motion done.

My suitcase is sitting next to the door with its straps shut. Madame Madame is standing behind the door preparing to knock. She will smell of cold smoke and soapy roses. I have a thought: *The beginning of the end.* I pluck it out, whip it around, have another: *The end of the beginning.* I'll hand her the keys, kiss both her cheeks, then this part will be over. I feel a feeling, a weep stuck in my gullet, but save it for later like a pelican. I don't know how anything else will unfold. I can't tell. People think a flip turn is a somersault; it's not. It's a roll. You twist your shoulders, you bend your knees, you touch the wall firmly with both of your feet, you push as hard as you can, you glide.

Acknowledgments

A poem for you Mr. Bill Clegg. Oooo how smart are thee, shiny brilliant almond guy? Oooo how wide and expansive is thy mind? How I shudder to contemplate the darkness of a life without thee *(here I fall on the ground in convulsions of sadness, unable to go on)* . . . Listen Bill: I hereby most formally declare my eternal gratitude, my love, my undying loyalty. I'll never forget how hard you worked, how generous you were with your mind, how whiney and flabby you made me feel at the end, how whiney and flabby I actually was. It is what it is because your thinking made it so, my darling. When I crushed every single bone in your hand in that car—I meant every single word that I said. So forever it is then.

It has been a sincere privilege working from afar with editor Jordan Pavlin, who makes remarkable things happen. If we were really old Chinese ladies, I'd put my hair up in a poofy hairstyle, stab a fancy golden umbrella in it, slap on some rice powder, wear a dress I have difficulty walking in, and bow before you until you get really irritated and have me removed. I would also like to thank all the other incredibly talented, seriously creative minds at Knopf: Maria Montclaire de Montonnaire Massey, Carol Devine Carson *(Jesus in goggles!)*, and all the smart, dedicated, wonderful copy editors I will never know, but whose presence made everything a zillion times better. Thank you, thank you, thank you for taking such magnificent care of the novel and infusing it with all of your energy. The honor is mine. And as for you, Miss Leslie Louise Amandine Levine—look! many middle names.

Mr. Matt Hudson. I hope you know I know how great you are and would like you to incorporate this knowing of your greatness into your being forever please. Thank you for all of your support and your patience and your faith and wishing you and Ms. Hannah Josephine love, love, and more love.

Thanks to Carol Gewirtz. From thought to realization to manifestation: I shan't ever forget it as long as I live.

Acknowledgments

Thanks to my darling Chad Kia. *OOOO who put the muck in the clay that molds us.*

Thanks to Alice Notley, whose amazing mind helped open mine.

Thanks to Marie Houzelle and Amanda Bay, who worked with me through thin and thinner.

Thanks to Mr. Hugh O'Neill for deconfusing my confusion until I accidentally reconfused it again. Also for all of your kindnesses and your smartnesses and your generosities and your messy desk and your mustache and your great family and your boat and P.S. I know that lasagna I made was awful and am ashamed of it still.

Thanks to my family for all of the material they so unwittingly provide. My beautiful sisters: Hayley, Joeanna, Tara; my squinty brothers: James, Emmett, Andrew, and Geo. Special thanks to Dr. James Keegan, his gentle mind, his bats. In memory of my beloved Grandmother May, my broomdancingly fantastic Grandfather Daniel, and the wonderful Margaret Morse Youngman, whose elegance and warm heart have remained somehow somewhere within mine.

You cannot write a novel without being a weird and lonesome freak. I thank you my darling Margaux, Sasha, and Roman for your vitality, your patience, your love, your humor. Nothing makes sense without you my darlings, and that is a fact.

And thank you firstly, lastly, most foreverfully to my husband, Philippe. This novel would not exist without you.

A Note About the Author

Nicola Keegan divides her time between Ireland and France with her husband and three children.